Queens of Romance

A collection of bestselling novels by
the world's leading romance writers

**Two classic summer novels from
international bestselling author**

BETTY NEELS

PRAISE FOR BETTY NEELS:

"Betty Neels works her magic to bring us a touching
love story that comes softly but beautifully."
—*Romantic Times* on *Dearest Love*

"*Making Sure of Sarah* is Betty Neels at her best
with a wonderful romance, compelling characters
and a delightful premise."
—*Romantic Times*

"Ms Neels uses animated dialogue and vivacious
characters to warm reader hearts."
—*Romantic Times* on *Marrying Mary*

MILLS & BOON
100
YEARS
of pure reading pleasure

100 Reasons to Celebrate

We invite you to join us in celebrating
Mills & Boon's centenary. Gerald Mills and
Charles Boon founded Mills & Boon Limited
in 1908 and opened offices in London's Covent
Garden. Since then, Mills & Boon has become
a hallmark for romantic fiction, recognised
around the world.

We're proud of our 100 years of publishing
excellence, which wouldn't have been achieved
without the loyalty and enthusiasm of our
authors and readers.

Thank you!

Each month throughout the year there will
be something new and exciting to mark the
centenary, so watch for your favourite authors,
captivating new stories, special limited
edition collections…and more!

BETTY NEELS

Summer Engagements

Containing

**Uncertain Summer
& Small Slice of Summer**

*M&B™ and M&B™ with the Rose Device
are trademarks of the publisher.
Harlequin Mills & Boon Limited, Eton House,
18-24 Paradise Road,
Richmond, Surrey TW9 1SR*

Summer Engagements © by Harlequin Books S.A. 2008

Uncertain Summer and *Small Slice of Summer* were
first published in Great Britain by Harlequin Mills & Boon
Limited in separate, single volumes.

Uncertain Summer © Betty Neels 1972
Small Slice of Summer © Betty Neels 1975

ISBN: 978 0 263 86685 8

025-0808

*Printed and bound in Spain
by Litografía Rosés S.A., Barcelona*

Uncertain Summer

BETTY NEELS

The
Queens of Romance
Collection

Betty Neels was a very special, warm and charming writer and individual; after retiring from nursing, she became one of Mills & Boon's best-loved authors with a phenomenal publishing record. No collection of romances celebrating our centenary would be complete without Betty, so we have specially selected two delightful summer romances to entertain you.

Betty Neels spent her childhood and youth in Devonshire before training as a nurse and midwife. She was an army nursing sister during the war, married a Dutchman, and subsequently lived in Holland for fourteen years. She later lived with her husband in Dorset, and had a daughter and grandson. Her hobbies were reading, animals, old buildings and writing. Betty started to write on retirement, incited by a lady in a library bemoaning the lack of romantic novels.

Over her thirty-year publishing career Betty wrote more than one hundred and thirty-four novels, was published in many different languages and over one hundred international markets. She sold over thirty-five million copies of her books. She continued to write into her ninetieth year, still pleasing her readers with her charming characters and heart-warming stories.

CHAPTER ONE

THE April sun was bright and warm even at the early
hour of half past seven in the morning; it shone through
the window of Serena Potts' bedroom in the Nurses'
Home, on to her bright head of dark hair which she
was crowning somewhat impatiently with her cap. The
cap was a pretty trifle, spotted muslin and frilled and
worn with strings, but she had tied these in a hurry, so
that the bow beneath her pretty chin was a trifle rakish.
She gave it an angry tweak, anchored the cap more
firmly and raced from the room, along the long bare
corridor and down two flights of stairs, into the covered
way leading to the hospital, to arrive a minute or so
later, out of breath, at the breakfast table.

Her arrival was greeted by cries of surprise by the
young women already seated there, but she took no
notice of these until she had poured her tea, shaken
cornflakes into a bowl and sat herself down.

'No need to carry on so, just because I'm early,' she
pointed out equably. 'Staff's away and there's only the
first-year students and Harris on, and you know what
Hippy's like if anything comes in a second after seven-
thirty.' She raised her dark, thickly lashed eyes piously
and intoned primly:

'You are aware, are you not, Sister Potts, that I will
accept no responsibility for any cases brought into the
Accident Room after half past seven precisely?'

She began to bolt down the cornflakes. 'I bet the
floors will be strewn with diabetic comas and over-

doses by the time I get there, and Harris will be arguing with everyone within sight.'

She buttered toast rapidly, weighed it down with marmalade and bit into it, and everyone at the table murmured sympathetically—at one time or another they had all had Nurse Harris to work for them—a scholarly girl, with no sense of humour and a tendency to stand and argue over a patient when what was really needed was urgent resuscitation. Serena found it difficult to bear with her, just as she found Sister Hipkins difficult. Hippy was getting on for fifty and one of the team of Night Sisters at Queen's, and while she was adequate enough on the medical side, she was hopeless in Casualty and the Accident Room; besides, accidents had a nasty habit of arriving just as she was about to go off duty, and she was a great one for going off punctually.

Serena wolfed the rest of her toast, swallowed tea in great unladylike gulps, said 'bye-bye' a little indistinctly and went off briskly to the Accident Room.

It, and Casualty, occupied the whole of the ground floor of one wing of the hospital. Each had its own Sister in charge, but as the two young ladies in question took their days off on alternate week-ends, it meant that today being Monday, Serena would be in charge of both departments until Betsy Woods, who had Cas, returned at one o'clock. She swung into the waiting-room now, casting a practised but kindly eye over the few people already seated on the benches. She recognized several of them; workers from one of the nearby factories, apparently accident-prone, with cuts and grazes clutching their tetanus cards in their hands as proof positive that they were up-to-date with their anti-tetanus injections and thus free from what they invariably referred to as the needle.

Serena wished them a cheerful good morning, stopped with no sign of impatience when she was begged to stop by an old woman who wished her to look at an injured eye, and having done this, offered sympathy and the mendacious information that the doctor would be along in a few minutes, and sped on her way again. Bill Travers, the Casualty Officer, had been up most of the night, Staff Nurse Watts had whispered to her as she met her at the door, and the chance of him appearing much before nine o'clock was so unlikely as to be laughable, but the old woman had needed comfort. She crossed the vast waiting-room to the Accident Room entrance and met Sister Hipkins coming out of it.

'And high time too, Sister Potts,' said Hippy nastily. 'No staff nurse and an RTA in! I'm sure I don't know what you young women are coming to—in my young days I wouldn't have dared to be late.'

'I'm not late,' said Serena with resigned calm. 'It's not quite ten to eight, I'm due on at eight o'clock, and you are off duty at the same time—I don't know where you get the idea that you're off duty at half past seven, Sister Hipkins.'

She didn't wait for an answer, but went on past Hippy, oblivious of her furious look, intent on getting to the case before Nurse Harris had a chance to do her worst.

The Accident Room was semi-circular, with screened-off bays and a vast central area to allow for the rapid manoeuvrings of trolleys and stretchers and the easy passage of the doctors and nurses. The curtains had been drawn across the furthest bay and she started towards it, her eyes searching the department as she went, to make sure that everything was in its proper place.

Nurse Harris was standing by the patient, looking important, and while doing nothing herself, issuing orders to the other two more junior nurses with her. Serena promised herself ten minutes with Nurse Harris later on, said calmly, 'Good morning, everybody,' and went to look at the patient—a man, young, and unconscious, presumably from the head wound visible through his blond hair. Serena took his pulse and pupil reaction and told the more senior of the two nurses to start cleaning the wound.

'His leg,' breathed Harris importantly, 'it's broken.'

Serena drew back the blanket covering the young man and saw the splints the ambulance men had put on. As she did so she asked:

'Did Sister Hipkins tell you to ring anyone?'

'No, Sister.'

'Then ring Mr Thompson'—he was the RSO—'ask him to come down here, please, and tell him it's an RTA. Head wound, probable fracture of left leg—badly shocked, unconscious.' And when Harris didn't move, she added with a patience she didn't feel, 'Will you hurry, Nurse, and then come back to me here.'

She was cutting the outside seam of the torn trousers covering the injured leg by the time Harris got back. She was doing it very carefully because if it was properly done, the trousers could be repaired. Experience had taught her that not everyone had the money to buy new trousers, although this man looked prosperous enough; she had noted the gold wrist watch and cuff links, the silk shirt and the fine tweed of his suit, and his shoes were expensive.

'Make out an X-ray form, Nurse,' she told Harris, 'and one for the Path Lab too—I daresay they'll want to do a crossmatch. What about relatives?'

Harris looked blank, and Serena, holding back impatience, asked:

'His address—you've got that? Was he conscious when they got to him?'

'Yes, Sister. But Sister Hipkins said we weren't to disturb him when he was brought in, and the ambulance men didn't know, because he was only conscious for a few minutes when they reached him.'

Serena counted silently to ten, because when she was a little girl, her father had taught her to do that, so that her temper, which was, and still was, hot at times, could cool. It was a silly childish trick, but it worked. She said with no trace of ill-humour: 'Go and make sure the trolleys are ready, Nurse, will you? then bring in the stitch trolley.'

Later, she promised herself, she would go and see the Number Seven, Miss Stokes, and see if something could be done to get Harris off the department. Her eyes flickered to the clock. Two part-time staff nurses would be on at nine o'clock, and thank heaven for them, she thought fervently. She had the splint off now with the most junior of the nurses helping her, and turned to wish Mr Thompson a friendly good morning as he came in.

He was a thin young man with a permanently worried expression on his pleasant face, but he was good at his job. 'I thought you might want to take a look at this head before the orthopaedic man gets here,' explained Serena. 'Sorry to get you down so early, Tom.'

He smiled nicely at her and set to work to examine

the patient. 'Nice-looking bloke,' he commented as he explored the scalp wound. 'Do we know who he is?'

'Not yet...'

'Unconscious when they found him?'

'No—not all the time, and he was conscious for a very short time when he got here.'

He gave her an understanding look. 'Hippy on last night?'

Serena nodded. 'I'll go through his pockets as soon as you've been over him.'

'Um,' agreed Mr Thompson. 'Where's this leg?'

She whisked back the blanket and pointed with a deceptively useless-looking little hand. There was a discoloured bump just above the ankle and a sizeable bruise. 'Pott's,' she said succinctly. 'Now you're here I'll get this shoe off.'

Mr Thompson obligingly held the leg steady while she eased it off and after he had taken a closer look said: 'You're right—X-ray, and we'd better see to that head too. I'll do it now, shall I? It only needs a couple of stitches, so if everything's ready I'll get down to it, then Orthopaedics can take over when he's been X-rayed.'

Serena waved a hand at the small trolley Harris had wheeled in. 'Help yourself. Do you want a local? He might come to.'

She looked down at the man on the examination table and encountered bright blue eyes staring at her. He smiled as he spoke, but she was unable to understand a word. She smiled back at him and said to no one in particular: 'Foreign—I wonder what he said?'

Her query was answered by the patient. 'I will translate. I said: "What a beautiful little gipsy girl."' His English was almost without accent. He smiled again

and watched admiringly while Serena's dark beauty became even more striking by reason of the colour which
crept slowly over her cheeks. It was Mr Thompson's
chuckle, turned too late into a cough, which prompted
her to say coolly, despite her discomfiture: 'We should
like your name and address, please, so that we can let
your family know. Could you manage to tell us?'

He closed his eyes and for a moment she thought he
had drifted off into unconsciousness again, but he
opened them again.

'Van Amstel, Zierikzee, Holland,' he said. 'Anyone
will know…' He turned his eyes on Mr Thompson.
'What's wrong?' he asked. 'I'm a doctor, so presumably I may be told.'

Mr Thompson told him. 'I'm going to stitch that
scalp wound,' he went on, 'then you'll have an X-ray.
We'll have to see about the leg too.'

'I must stay here?'

'I'm afraid so—for the moment at least.'

The young man looked at Serena again. 'I find nothing to be afraid of myself,' he said. 'On the contrary.'
He stared at Serena, who returned his look with a bright
professional smile which successfully hid her interest;
he really was remarkably good-looking, and although
she was a kind-hearted girl, and felt genuine sympathy
for the patients who passed through her capable hands
on their way to hospital beds, just for once she found
herself feeling pleased that Doctor van Amstel should
be forced to stay in hospital. She reflected with satisfaction that she was on excellent terms with the Surgical Floor Sister; she would be able to find out more
about him. Her hands, as busy as her thoughts, passed
Mr Thompson the local anaesthetic, all ready drawn up
as she told one of the nurses to get the porters. 'X-ray,

Nurse, and please go with the patient. He'll be coming back here to see the Orthopaedic side afterwards.'

She was spraying the wound with nebucutane when the patient spoke again. 'Sister, will you telephone my cousin? Ask for Zierikzee—the exchange will know— it's a small place, there'll be no difficulty.'

'Has your cousin the same name?'

'Yes, he's a doctor too.'

Serena nodded. 'Very well, I'll do it while you're in X-ray. Am I to say anything special?'

He frowned a little. 'No—just tell him.' He closed his eyes again and as he was wheeled away Mr Thompson said: 'Nasty crack on the head. Was it his fault?'

Serena led the way to her office and found the note the ambulance men had thoughtfully left for her. She found a policeman too, who wanted to see the patient and take a statement. She left Mr Thompson to talk to him while she got the exchange. She was connected with Zierikzee very quickly, and it was only when someone said Hullo that she realized that she didn't know if the cousin understood English. Obedient to her patient's instructions, however, she asked for Doctor van Amstel's house, adding that it was urgent. Apparently the operator understood her, for after a few moments a deep voice said in her ear: 'Doctor van Amstel.'

'Oh,' said Serena foolishly, because she hadn't expected it to be as easy as all that. 'I'm telephoning from London.' She added in a little rush, 'You understand English?'

'I get by,' the voice assured her.

'Well, we have a Doctor van Amstel in our hospital—Queen's. He's had an accident...'

'An RTA?' inquired the voice surprisingly.

'Yes.' She hadn't known that Road Traffic Accident was a term used in other countries. 'His car hit a bus.'

'His fault?'

Heartless man, thought Serena, worrying about a mere car when his cousin was injured. 'I've no idea,' she said coldly, and was taken aback when he chuckled.

'All right, Nurse—or is it Sister? Let me know the worst.'

She told him a little tartly and he said: 'Tut-tut, the same leg as last time, but at least it's not an arm this time.'

She asked faintly and against her will: 'Does—does he do this often?'

'Yes. I'll keep in touch, and thank you, Sister—er—?'

'Potts.'

'Incredible...goodbye.'

She put down the receiver slowly, wondering why he had said 'incredible' like that. Perhaps his knowledge of English wasn't as good as he would have her believe. A nice voice, though, although he had sounded as though he had been laughing. She dismissed him from her thoughts and turned to the work awaiting her.

There was no skull fracture, said the radiologist, just a nasty crack on the head and a clean break of the tib and fib, but the orthopaedic registrar, pursing his lips over the discoloured swelling, decided to call in Sir William Sandhurst, his consultant, not because he didn't feel more than capable of reducing the fracture and applying the plaster himself, but because the patient was a doctor and rated private patient treatment. For the same reason, Serena was asked to arrange for him to have one of the private rooms on the surgical floor, and thither, after the necessary treatment, the Dutch doctor was borne. Serena was busy by then, dealing with the wide variety of accidents which poured in non-stop during the day, but he had still contrived to ask her if she would go and see him later in the day and she had agreed. Moreover, when she had a moment to herself she had to admit to herself too that she was looking forward to seeing him again.

The morning slipped into the afternoon with the shortest of pauses for dinner because a bad scald came in and she didn't want to leave it; she went with the pathetic, mercifully unconscious child to the Children's Ward and returned to find a policeman bringing in two youths who had been fighting, using broken bottles. Teatime came and went before they were fit to be handed over to the ward. She heaved a sigh of relief as they were wheeled away and the junior nurse, just back from tea, said:

'I'll clear up, Sister. Agnes—' Agnes was the department maid who, between bouts of swabbing floors and washing paint, mothered them all—'has made you some tea, she's taken it into the office.'

Bill Travers had been doing the stitching; he caught Serena by the arm remarking: 'I hope I'm included in the tea party,' and when she declared that of course he was, walked her briskly to the office where the admirable Agnes had not only produced an enormous pot of tea but a plate of buttered toast as well.

As Serena poured out, Bill asked, 'Off at five? Are you going out?'

Serena was annoyed to feel her cheeks getting warm. 'Not just…that is, perhaps—later on.'

Her companion eyed her narrowly. 'What's this I hear from Thompson about the handsome young

Dutchman brought in this morning? Called you a beautiful little gipsy, didn't he?'

She looked suitably reproving. 'You are a lot!' she declared wrathfully. 'Nothing but gossip from morning to night!' she snorted delicately. 'He didn't know what he was saying.'

'Come off it, Serena, don't tell me you don't know by now that you *are* a beautiful little gipsy—at least you look like one. He must have been instantly smitten.'

Serena tossed her rather untidy head. 'Nonsense!' She caught her companion's eye and giggled engagingly. 'As a matter of fact, he was rather interesting.'

'And you're going to see him on your way off duty, I suppose? just to make sure Joan Walters isn't pulling a fast one on you? He's on Surgical, I take it.'

'Don't be beastly! Joan's my best friend. I'm only going to see if there's anything I can do—after all, he is a foreigner.'

'That's not going to stop the police asking awkward questions—it was his fault, driving an E-type Jag up a one-way street.'

Serena refilled their cups. 'No? Did he really? Lucky it wasn't a lot worse for him.'

'And that the bus he collided with was a bus and not some defenceless Mini.'

Serena got up. 'Look,' she said reasonably, 'you drive a Mini, and anything less defenceless I've yet to meet—it's nothing but a battering ram once you're in the driver's seat.' She smiled. 'I must get back, Staff White's on in ten minutes and I want to be cleared up before she gets here. There's nothing worse than other people's leftovers when you come on duty.'

She nodded airily and hurried back to make sure that

the department was clear once more. She had had a
busy day, but she didn't look in the least tired, only
untidy, but she was such a pretty girl that a shining
nose and a few stray curling ends did nothing to detract
from her appearance. She was a slim small girl and
this, combined with her outstanding good looks, made
it hard for people who didn't know what work she did
to believe that she was a nurse. She rolled up her
sleeves now as she went, looked at the clock, said: 'Off
you go,' to the student nurse who was due off duty,
and took the laundry bag from her as she spoke, so that
the other nurse could finish filling it with the used
linen. They were still hard at it when Staff Nurse White
reported for duty.

Serena went off herself ten minutes later, and quite
unmindful of her untidy pile of hair and shining nose,
went straight to the surgical floor. It was on the other
side of the hospital, three stories up, and as she had to
cross the main entrance hall to reach it, she took the
opportunity of posting some letters in the box by the
big glass doors. This done, she paused to look outside;
the day was still fine and the busy city street was
thronged with traffic and people hurrying home from
work. As she watched, a dilapidated Mini drew up, was
wedged expertly into the space between two other cars
and its driver got out and mounted the few shallow
steps before the door without haste. He paused within
a foot of her, and she was conscious of his eyes resting
upon her for the briefest of moments before he walked,
still without haste, across to the porter's lodge. She was
left with the impression of size and height and unhurried calm, but by the time she turned round to take
another discreet look, there was no sign of him.

She was half-way up the stone staircase to the first

floor when she met Miss Stokes coming down. Miss Stokes, who by virtue of the Salmon Scheme had turned from Office Sister Stokes to a Number Seven in the hierarchy of the nursing profession, smiled and stopped. She had been at Queen's for a very long time, long before Serena had arrived there to do her training, six years earlier. She was a pleasant, good-natured body, in whom young nurses willingly confided and with whom the older, more experienced ones conferred.

'Busy day, Sister Potts?' she wanted to know, and sounded as though she were really interested.

'Very, Miss Stokes, and if you can spare a second, when is it convenient to have a word with you?'

'Now,' said Miss Stokes, who was an opportunist by nature.

'Nurse Harris—' began Serena, and her superior nodded understandingly. 'Could she be moved, do you think? She's quite unsuited to Cas work, she—she isn't quite quick enough.'

'I know—I don't know where to put that girl. She's theoretically brilliant and she hasn't even mastered the art of making a patient comfortable. I had hoped that in the Accident Room she would be able to apply her knowledge.'

'She does,' said Serena, 'but the patients can't always wait while she does.'

Miss Stokes allowed herself a smile. 'I can well imagine she's somewhat of a responsibility. I'll move her, Sister, don't worry.'

'Thank you, Miss Stokes.' The two ladies smiled a farewell to each other and went their separate ways; Miss Stokes to half an hour's peace and quiet in her office, Serena to run up another flight of stairs and go through the swing doors at the top to the surgical floor.

Half-way down the corridor she met one of the staff nurses and asked her if Sister was around, and was told that she was, with one of the consultants.

'I've come to see the patient we sent up this morning, Staff—Doctor van Amstel. Is it OK if I go in?'

Staff thought so. 'He's in number twenty-one, Sister,' she advised her, and darted off with the faintly harassed air of someone who had a lot to do and not enough time in which to do it.

Number twenty-one's door was closed, Serena tapped and went in and came to an abrupt halt just inside the door because the doctor had a visitor; the large man who had got out of the dilapidated Mini— he had draped his length into the only easy chair in the room and unfolded it now at the sight of her, to stand silent and faintly smiling. It was the patient who spoke first.

'I've been waiting for you,' he remarked cheerfully, 'to brighten up an otherwise very dull day.'

'Dull?' Serena was astonished; people who had car accidents and broke legs and what have you didn't usually refer to such happenings as dull.

'Oh, yes, only not any more—it's turned out to be a red letter day, I shouldn't have met you otherwise, should I?'

She went faintly pink because although she was used to admiration, it wasn't usually quite so direct. She said repressively: 'I hope you're feeling more comfortable, Doctor,' put a hand behind her and started to turn the door handle. 'I'll come back later—or tomorrow...'

'Don't go on my account,' said the large man with lazy good humour, and his voice was the voice of the man who had spoken to her on the telephone. 'When Laurens remembers I daresay he'll introduce us, although I believe there to be no need—Miss Potts, is it not? I'm the patient's cousin, Gijs van Amstel.'

He smiled gently and engulfed her hand in his large one.

'How do you do?' Serena wanted to know politely, and remembering, added: 'Why did you say incredible?'

'Ah, yes—so I did. You see, your voice isn't the kind of voice I would associate with someone called Miss Potts.'

'He's right,' said his cousin. 'What is your name? And you had better tell me or I shall call you my beautiful gipsy and cause gossip.'

Serena choked; very much on her dignity, she said: 'Potts is a good old English name,' and before any one could take her up on it, went on rapidly: 'I only came…I didn't know you had a visitor…I must be going.'

'All right, Gipsy Potts,' the young man in the bed was laughing at her, but very nicely, 'but I haven't got a visitor, only Gijs, and he doesn't count—he's come over to bail me out and get a solicitor and see about the car.'

For someone who didn't count it seemed quite a tall order; perhaps he was a poor relation or a junior partner. She took a lightning look at the man standing on the other side of the bed. He was good-looking, she admitted rather grudgingly, if one should fancy a high-bridged nose and a determined chin, and although his tweed suit was superbly cut and of good cloth, it was decidedly shabby. He looked—she wasn't sure of the right word, for lazy wasn't quite right, perhaps placid was the better word, although she had once or twice detected hidden amusement behind the placidity. She wasn't sure if she liked him—besides, he had been beastly about his poor injured cousin.

The poor injured cousin continued: 'I shan't be in bed long, you know. As soon as I can get a good stout stick in my hand, the stitches out of my head and this damned headache gone, we'll go out and live it up.' He looked beseechingly at her. 'You will, won't you? And don't look like that—do say you will.'

She found herself smiling at him because she wanted to see him again quite badly; besides, he had the kind of smile to charm any woman. She answered carefully. 'Well, we'll see how you go on, shall we, Doctor van Amstel?' and looked away to encounter the surprisingly sharp stare of his cousin. His placid expression hadn't altered at all; all the same, she had the strong impression that he had been waiting to hear what she would say.

'Call me Laurens,' commanded the younger Doctor van Amstel.

Serena looked down at his still pale face on the pillow. 'I'm going now,' she stated in her pleasant voice. 'I hope you have a good night.'

She went round the bed and shook the hand the older man was offering.

'I hope you don't have too much trouble getting things sorted out,' she remarked, and thanked him politely as he went to the door and opened it for her.

She met Joan outside in the corridor. Joan was tall and slim and blonde and they were firm friends. She grinned engagingly when she saw Serena and said with a chuckle: 'Stealing a march on me, ducky? I know you saw him first...'

'I only came up to see how he was—I didn't know he'd got someone with him—some cousin or other...'

'Yes, rather nice, I thought, though I've only said hullo so far. A bit sleepy, I thought.'

Serena nodded. 'Yes, I thought so too. He's come over to see to everything—I suppose he's a partner or something. I saw him downstairs, he's got the most awful old Mini,' she paused, feeling a little sorry for anyone forced to drive around in anything so battered. 'Perhaps he's not very successful.'

'Can't say the same for the patient,' said Joan. 'I hear it's an E-type Jag he was driving and it's a write-off.' She sighed. 'I don't suppose he'll be here long, though. It's a simple fracture, once he's got his walking iron on and his head's cleared, he'll be up and away.' She gave Serena a shrewd glance. 'You like him, Serena?'

'I don't know—I don't know him, do I? But he's so alive, isn't he?' she appealed to her friend, who nodded understandingly; they had both dealt with so many patients who were just the reverse.

Serena went over to the Nurses' Home and washed her smalls and then her hair, went to supper and so, presently, to bed, feeling that the evening had somehow been wasted. It would have been nice to have gone out with someone—someone like Doctor van Amstel, who would probably have been ridiculously and untruthfully flattering and made her feel like a million dollars. She went over to her mirror and stared into it; she was almost twenty-five, an old maid, she told herself, although she had probably had more proposals than any other girl in the hospital. But she had accepted none of them, for none of them had come from a man she could love. She sighed at the pretty face in the mirror and thought, a little forlornly, that perhaps she would never fall in love—really in love, especially as she wasn't quite sure what sort of a man she wanted to fall in love with. She amended that though; he might possibly look a little like the owner of the E-type Jag.

She wasn't on duty until one o'clock the next day; she got up early, made tea and toast in the little kitchen at the end of the corridor, and went out, to take a bus to Marks and Spencers in Oxford Street and browse around looking for a birthday present for her mother, who, even though she was fifty, liked pretty things. Serena settled on a pink quilted dressing gown and then loitered round the store until she barely had the time to get back to Queen's. She went on duty with seconds to spare and found the department, for once, empty, but not for long; within half an hour there was a multiple crash in, as well as an old lady who had had a coronary in the street and a small boy who had fallen off a wall on to his head. It was almost five o'clock before she could stop for a quick cup of tea in the office and it was while she was gulping it down that Joan telephoned.

'When are you off duty?' she asked. 'I've got this mad Dutchman wanting to know when you can come and see him.'

'I'm up to my eyes,' said Serena, crossly, 'and likely to be for hours yet. I'm not off until nine o'clock anyway and I doubt if I get to supper at the rate we're going.'

'Come on up when you're off, then—he needs cheering up. That cousin's been in and I don't know what he said, but Laurens is a bit down in the mouth.'

'Laurens already!' thought Serena as she said: 'Surely he wouldn't be so mean as to upset him after the accident...'

'Well, Laurens did tell me that he's done this sort

of thing several times, and I suppose it's a bit of a nuisance for his cousin having to leave the practice and sort things out.'

'Probably,' commented Serena, not much caring. 'I'll come if I can get away in time.' She rang off, aware that whether she was on time or not, she would go.

He was lying in bed doing nothing when she got to his room at last. He looked pale and there was a discontented droop to his mouth which she put down to the after-effects of his accident; probably he still had a bad headache. But he brightened when he saw her and began to talk in a most amusing way about himself and his day. Of his cousin he said not a word and Serena didn't ask, content to be amused at his talk.

She saw him again the next morning during her dinner time, for she went, as she sometimes did, to Joan's office for the cup of tea they had before the start of the afternoon's work. It was, of necessity, a brief visit and as she left his room she passed Doctor Gijs van Amstel in the corridor. She wished him a good day and gave him the briefest of glances, because she had the feeling that if she did more than that he might be disposed to stop and talk to her, and for some reason—too vague to put into words—she didn't want to do that.

The next few days began to form a pattern drawn around her visits to the surgical floor. She still went out in her off duty, for she had a great number of friends. She shopped too and went to the cinema with Bill Travers, but the only real moment of the days was when she tapped on the door of number twenty-one and heard Laurens's welcoming: 'Come in, Serena.'

She had seen no more of his cousin, and when she mentioned it to Joan it was to discover that he had returned to Holland and would be back again shortly. And Laurens never spoke of him, although he talked about everything else under the sun. Serena listened, hardly speaking herself, wrapped in a kind of enchantment because here, at last, was the man she had been waiting for and who, she was beginning to hope, had been waiting for her.

It surprised her that Joan, although she admitted to liking Laurens very much, could find anything wrong with him. 'He's a charmer all right,' she agreed, 'but ducky, be your age—can't you see that if he can chat you up so expertly, he's probably had a lot of practice and doesn't intend to stop at you?'

Which remark made Serena so indignant that she could hardly find the words to answer such heresy. 'He's not,' she insisted. 'He's cheerful and nice to everyone, and why shouldn't we be friends while he's here?'

Joan smiled. 'I daresay you're right, Serena, only don't get that heart of yours broken, will you, before you're sure it's worth risking it.'

She went home that evening, to spend her two days off at the large, old-fashioned rectory where her father and mother had lived for most of their married life.

She caught a later train than usual that evening, because she had gone to see Laurens first and it was quite dark by the time she got out at Dorchester to find her father waiting for her in the old-fashioned Rover he had had for such a long time. She kissed him with affection and got in beside him, suddenly glad at the prospect of the peace and quiet of home. They didn't talk much as they went through the town and out on to the road to Maiden Newton because she didn't want to distract her parent's attention. He was an unworldly man in many ways; he had never quite realized that traffic had increased since he had first taken to motoring; in consequence he drove with a carefree disregard for other cars which could be alarming unless, like his family, his companions knew him well.

Serena, who had iron nerves and was a passable driver herself, suffered the journey calmly enough; there wasn't a great deal of traffic on the road and once through Frampton they turned off into a winding lane which although narrow, held no terrors for either of them for they knew every yard of it.

The village, when they reached it at the bottom of a steep hill, was already in darkness; only the Rectory's old-fashioned wide windows sent splashes of brightness into the lane as they turned in the always open gate. They had barely stopped before the door was flung open, and Serena jumped out to meet her family.

CHAPTER TWO

THERE were quite a lot of people in the doorway—her mother, as small as Serena herself and almost as slim, Susan, who was seventeen and constantly in the throes of some affair of the heart, so that everyone else had the utmost difficulty in remembering the name of the current boyfriend, Margery, twenty, and married only a few months earlier to her father's curate, a situation which afforded great pleasure to the family and her mother, especially because she was the plain one of the children, and Serena's two young brothers, home from boarding school for the Easter holidays—Dan was twelve and George, the youngest, was ten. Their father hoped that they would follow in his footsteps and go into the Church, and probably they would, but in the meantime they got up to all the tricks boys of their age usually indulged in.

It was lovely to be home again; she was swept inside on a cheerful tide of greetings and family news, all of which would have to be repeated later on, but in the meantime the cheerful babble of talk was very pleasant. 'Where's John?' Serena tossed her hat on to the nearest chair and addressed Margery.

'He'll be here. He had to go and see old Mrs Spike, you know—down by Buller's Meadow, she's hurt her leg and can't get about.'

Serena took off her coat and sent it to join her hat. 'Being married suits you, Margery—you're all glowing.'

Her sister smiled. 'Well, that's how it makes you feel. How's the hospital?'

'Oh, up and down, you know...it's nice to get away.'

They smiled at each other as Serena flung an arm around her mother's shoulders and asked her how she was. The rest of the evening passed in a pleasurable exchange of news and the consuming of the supper Mrs Potts had prepared. They all sat around the too large mahogany table, talking and eating and laughing a great deal. The dining-room was faintly mid-Victorian and gloomy with it, but they were all so familiar with it that no one noticed its drawbacks. Presently, when there was no more to be eaten and they had talked themselves to a standstill, they washed up and went back to the sitting-room, to talk again until midnight and later, when they parted for the night and Serena went to her old room at the back of the house, to lie in her narrow bed and wonder what Laurens van Amstel was doing.

Breakfast was half over the next morning when the telephone rang; no one took any notice of it—no one, that was, but Susan, for the family had come to learn during the last few months that almost all the telephone calls were for her, and rather than waste time identifying the young man at the other end of the line, finding Susan and then returning to whatever it was they had been interrupted in doing, it was far better for all concerned if she answered all the calls herself. She tore away now, saying over her shoulder: 'That'll be Bert,' and Serena looked up from her plate to exclaim: 'But it was Gavin last time I was home—what happened to him?'

Her mother looked up from her letters. 'Gavin?' She looked vague. 'I believe he went to…'

She was interrupted by Susan. 'It's for you,' she told Serena. 'A man.'

Serena rose without haste, avoiding the eyes focused upon her. 'Some query at the hospital,' she suggested airily as she walked, not too fast, out of the room, aware that if that was all it was, she was going to be disappointed. There was no reason why Laurens should telephone—he didn't even know where she was; all the same she hoped that it was he.

She went into her father's study and picked up the receiver. Her voice didn't betray her excitement as she said: 'Hullo?'

It was Laurens; his voice came gaily over the wire. 'Serena!'

'How did you know where I was?' She sounded, despite her efforts, breathless.

He laughed softly. 'Your friend Joan—such a nice girl—after all, there's no reason why I shouldn't know where you live, is there? What are you doing?'

'Having breakfast. I'm not sure that I…'

'You're not sure about anything, are you, my dear gipsy? I miss you. When are you coming back?'

'On Monday. I come up on an early morning train.'

'Not this time—I'll send Gijs down to pick you up, he'll drive you.'

She shook her head, although he wasn't there to see her vehement refusal.

'No, thank you, I prefer to go by train—it's very kind…'

'Rubbish! Gijs won't mind, he does anything anyone asks of him—more fool he.' He spoke jokingly and she laughed with him.

'All the same, I'd rather come up by train.'

He sounded very persuasive. 'Not to please me? I hate to think of you travelling in a crowded train, and at least Gijs can give you lunch.'

She said in a panicky little voice: 'But that's impossible. I'm on duty at one o'clock.'

'My beautiful gipsy, how difficult you make everything! Gijs will pick you up about nine o'clock on Monday morning. What are you going to do today?'

'Nothing very interesting, just—just be at home.' How could she tell him that she was going to make the beds for her mother and probably get the lunch ready as well and spend the afternoon visiting the sexton's wife who had just had another baby, and the organist's wife, who'd just lost hers? She felt relief when he commented casually: 'It sounds nice. Come and see me on Monday, Serena.'

'Yes—at least, I will if I can get away. You know how it is.'

'Indeed I do—the quicker you leave it the better.'

'Leave it?' she repeated his words faintly.

'Of course—had you not thought of marrying me?'

Serena was bereft of words. 'I—I—' she began, and then: 'I must go,' she managed at last. 'Goodbye.'

'Goodbye, gipsy girl, I shall see you on Monday.'

She nodded foolishly without speaking and replaced the receiver gently. She hadn't heard aright, of course, and even if she had, he must have been joking—he joked a lot. She sat down in her father's chair behind his desk, quite forgetful of breakfast, trying to sort out her feelings. They slid silkily in and out of her head, evading her efforts to pin them down—the only thought which remained clearly and firmly in her mind was the one concerning Gijs van Amstel; she didn't want to go back to London with him. The idea of being in his company for several hours disquieted her, although she didn't know why; he had done nothing to offend or annoy her, indeed, he had exerted himself to be civil, and she had no interest in him, only the fact that he was Laurens's cousin was the common denominator of their acquaintance, so, she told herself vigorously, she was merely being foolish.

She went back to her interrupted breakfast then, and although no one asked her any questions at all she felt compelled to explain into the eloquent silence. When she had finished, omitting a great deal, her mother remarked: 'He sounds nice, dear, such a change from your usual patients—is his English good?'

Serena, grateful for her parent's tactful help, told her that yes, it was, very good.

'And this cousin—he's coming to fetch you on Monday morning?'

Serena drank her cold tea. 'Yes.'

'Where will he sleep?' her mother, a practical woman, wanted to know.

Serena's lovely eyes opened wide. She hadn't given a thought to the man who was coming to fetch her, and now, upon thinking about it, she really didn't care where he slept. Perhaps he would leave early in the morning. She suggested this lightheartedly and her mother mused: 'He must be a very nice man then, to spoil a night's sleep to come and collect someone he doesn't even know well.'

'Oh,' said Serena, her head full of Laurens, 'he seems to do exactly what Laurens tells him—I suppose he's a poor relation or a junior partner or something of that sort. He's got the most awful old car.'

'Oh?' it was her father this time. 'Is he a very young man, then?'

Serena dragged her thoughts away from Laurens and considered. 'Oh, no—he must be years older—he looks about thirty-five, I suppose. I haven't really noticed.'

Her mother gave her a swift, penetrating glance and said with deceptive casualness: 'Well, we can find out on Monday, can't we?' she smiled at her eldest child. 'And how old is this Laurence?'

'Laurens,' Serena corrected her gently. 'About twenty-six.'

'Good-looking?' asked Susan, who had been sitting silent all this time, not saying a word.

'Yes, very. Fair and tall.'

'What a rotten description,' Susan sounded faintly bored. 'If you've finished, shall we get washed up? There's such a lot to do and there's never time.'

Serena rose obediently from the table, understanding very well that what her younger sister meant was not enough time to do her hair a dozen ways before settling on the day's style, nor time enough to see to her nails, or try out a variety of lipsticks. She sighed unconsciously, remembering how nice it was to be seventeen and fall painlessly in and out of love and pore for hours over magazines—she felt suddenly rather old.

In the end she did the washing up herself because Susan had her telephone call and the two boys disappeared with the completeness and silence which only boys achieve. She stood at the old-fashioned kitchen sink and as she worked she thought about Laurens, trying to make herself think sensibly. No one in their right minds fell in love like this, to the exclusion of everything and everyone else. She was, she reminded herself over and over again, a sensible girl, no longer young and silly like little Susan; she saw also that, there was a lot more to marriage than falling in love. Besides, Laurens, even though he had told her so delightfully and surprisingly that she was going to marry him—for surely that was what he had meant—might be in the habit of falling in love with any girl who chanced to take his fancy. She began to dry the dishes, resolving that, whatever her feelings, she would not allow herself to be hurried into any situation, however wonderful it might seem. She had put the china and silver away and was on her way upstairs to make the beds when she remembered the strange intent look Gijs van Amstel had given her when Laurens had suggested she should go out with him. There had been no reason for it and it puzzled her that the small episode should stick so firmly in her memory. She shook it free from her thoughts and joined her mother, already busy in the boys' room.

The day passed pleasantly so that she forgot her impatience for Monday's arrival. When she had finished her chores she duly visited the sexton's wife, admired the baby—the sixth and surely the last?—presented the proud mother with a small gift for the tiny creature, and turned her attention to the sexton's other five children, who had arrived with an almost monotonous regularity every eighteen months or so. They all bore a marked resemblance to each other and, Serena had to admit, they all looked remarkably healthy. She asked tentatively: 'Do you find it a bit much—six, Mrs Snow?'

Her hostess smiled broadly. 'Lor' no, Miss Serena, they'm good as gold and proper little loves, we wouldn't be without 'em. You'll see, when you'm wed and 'as little 'uns to rear.'

Serena tried to imagine herself with six small children, and somehow the picture was blurred because deep in her bones something told her that Laurens wouldn't want to be bothered with a houseful of children to absorb her time—and his. He would want her for himself... The thought sent a small doubt niggling at the back of her mind, for she loved children; provided she had help she was quite sure she could cope with half a dozen, but only if their father did his share too, and Laurens, she was sure, even though she knew very little about him, wasn't that kind of man. Disconcertingly, a picture of his cousin, lolling against the bed in his well-worn tweeds, crossed her thoughts; she had no doubt that he would make an excellent father, even though he did strike her as being a thought too languid in his manner. And probably he was already a parent. He was, after all, older than Laurens and must have settled down by now. She dismissed him from her mind, bade the happy mother and her offspring goodbye, and departed to make her second visit—a more difficult one—the organist's wife had lost a small baby since Serena had been home last, it had been a puny little creature with a heart condition which everyone knew was never going to improve, but that hadn't made it any easier for the mother. Serena spent longer there than she had meant to do, trying to comfort the poor woman while she reflected how unfair life could be.

It was surprising how quickly the weekend flew by, and yet, looking back on it as she dressed on the Monday morning, Serena saw that it had been a tranquil, slow-moving period, with time to do everything at leisure. As she made up her pretty face she found herself wishing that she wasn't going back to Queen's, to the eternal bustle and rush of the Accident Room, the hurried meals and the off duty, when one was either too tired to do anything but fall into one's bed, or possessed of the feverish urge to rush out and enjoy oneself. But if she didn't go back she wouldn't see Laurens. She tucked back a stray wisp of hair and stood back to inspect her person; she was wearing a short-sleeved silk blouse which exactly matched the deep clotted cream of her pleated skirt, whose matching jacket she left on the bed with her gloves and handbag, for she still had the breakfast to get. She put on the kettle, skipped into the dining-room and tuned the radio in to the music programme and went back to the stove, trying out a few dance steps to the too-loud music as she cracked eggs into a bowl. She dropped the last one on to the floor when a voice behind her said almost apologetically: 'I must take the blame for that, but the front door was open and although I rang the bell the music—er—drowned it, I fancy.'

She had whirled round and trodden in the egg as she did so. She said:

'Damn!' and then: 'Good morning, Doctor van Amstel, you're early,' giving him the briefest of smiles.

If he was put out by his cool reception he allowed nothing of it to show but said mildly: 'Yes, I'm sorry for that, too, but Laurens was so anxious that I should be on time.' His unhurried gaze took in the apron she had tied untidily round her slim waist and moved on to take in the singing kettle and the bacon sizzling in the pan. 'I'll come back in half an hour, shall I?' He gave her a lazy grin and sauntered towards the door just as Mrs Potts trotted in. Showing no surprise at the sight of a very large strange man in her kitchen, she said briskly: 'Good morning. You'll be the cousin, I'm sure. How very early you must have got up this morning, you poor boy. You'll have breakfast with us, of course, it'll be ready in a minute.'

Serena dished up bacon and put another few slices in. She felt all at once exasperated; she had been rude and inhospitable and the poor man had presumably had no breakfast; after all, he was driving her back. She said contritely: 'I'm so sorry—I was surprised—I think I must have lost my wits. This is Doctor Gijs van Amstel, Mother—my mother, Doctor, and this is my father,' she added as her parent joined them. She left them to talk while she got on with the toast, peeping once or twice at the doctor. He dwarfed her father both in height and breadth, his massive head with its pale hair towering over them all. He appeared to be getting on very well with her mother and father and something about his manner made her wonder if her first impression of him had been wrong—perhaps he wasn't a junior partner at all. Her arched brows drew together in a frown as she pondered this; there was so much she didn't know about Laurens and this man standing beside her.

They left directly after breakfast, with the entire family waving goodbye from the door and an odd housewife or so from the nearby cottages waving too for good measure. The car bumped a little going up the lane and the doctor said easily: 'Sorry about the car— I really must do something about it.' He slowed a little as they turned into the wider road. 'But I must get Laurens settled first. His car's a write-off, I'm afraid.'

'Was it his fault?'

He didn't look at her. 'Yes, but I believe his solicitor may be able to prove mitigating circumstances.' Something in his voice caused Serena to keep silent, but when he went on: 'Laurens has already ordered a new car,' she exclaimed: 'Another E-type Jag?'

'Yes—a car with great pulling power, I have discovered—especially where girls are concerned.'

Serena's lovely face was washed with a rich pink. 'What an offensive remark!' she uttered in an arctic voice. 'Just because you've got an old Mini...' she stopped, aware that she was being even more offensive.

'With no pulling power at all?' he was laughing at her. 'Too true, Miss Potts,' and then to surprise her, 'I wonder why you dislike me?'

'Disl...' Serena, not usually flustered, was. 'I don't—that is, I don't know you—how could I possibly... I've no idea what you're talking about.'

'No? Have you read Samuel Butler?'

'No—not to remember. A poet, wasn't he—seventeenth century. Why?'

'''Quoth Hudibras, I smell a rat; Ralpho, thou dost prevaricate.''''

The pink, which had subsided nicely, returned. 'I'm not prevaricating—well, perhaps, a little.'

'That's better. I always feel that one can't be friends with anyone until one has achieved honesty.'

She asked, bewildered: 'Are we to be friends?'

'We're bound to see quite a lot of each other, are we not? I think we might make the effort—I'm quite harmless, you know.'

She wondered if he was; his manner was casual and he talked with an air of not minding very much about anything—on the other hand, he read an early English poet well enough to quote him. She inquired: 'Where did you learn to speak such good English?'

They were going slowly through Dorchester, caught

up in the early morning traffic. He shrugged. 'Oh, I don't know—school, and visits here, and university.'

'A Dutch university?'

'Yes.' And that was all he said, much to her annoyance; for all his casual air he was hardly forthcoming. Never one to give up, she tried again. 'Do you know this part of England well?'

'Moderately well. I came here when I was a boy.' His lips twitched with amusement, he added: 'Visiting, you know.'

She didn't know, which was so annoying, but she gave up after that and sat in silence while he urged the little car along the road to Puddletown and beyond to Wimborne. They were approaching that small town when he observed; 'You're very quiet.'

There were a number of tart replies she would have liked to make to that, but instead she said meekly: 'I thought perhaps you liked to drive without talking—some people do.'

'My dear good girl, did I give you that impression? You must forgive me—let us by all means talk.' Which he proceeded to do, very entertainingly, as he sent the Mini belting along towards the Winchester bypass. Going through Farnham he said: 'I haven't stopped for coffee—I thought that a little nearer London would serve our purpose better. You're on duty at one o'clock, I gather.'

She admitted that she was. 'It was kind of you to come,' she began. 'It's taken up a great deal of your day.'

'Well, I can't think of a better way of spending it,' he replied pleasantly. 'I don't much care for London—a day or so is all right, but it's hardly my cup of tea.'

'Oh? What's your cup of tea, Doctor?'

'A small town, I suppose, where I know everyone and everyone knows me, a good day's work and a shelf full of good books and German to keep me company.'

She was aware of an odd sensation which she didn't stop to pursue. 'Your wife?'

His bellow of laughter rocked the car. 'My dog—a dachshund and a bossy little beast. He goes everywhere with me.'

'He must miss you.'

'Yes, but Jaap and his wife, who live with me, take good care of him.'

She tried to envisage his home. Did he live in digs? It sounded like it, but surely he had a surgery—or did he share Laurens's? She longed to ask but decided against it. Instead she started to talk about the hospital, a topic which seemed safe ground and devoid of conversational pitfalls.

It was almost midday when he turned off the A30 and took the road to Hampton where he pulled up outside the Greyhound. 'Ten minutes?' he suggested. 'Just time for something quick—it will have to be sandwiches, I'm afraid, too bad we couldn't have made it lunch.'

Serena murmured a polite nothing because her mind was so full of seeing Laurens again that even ten minutes' stop was irksome. She drank the coffee he ordered and nibbled at a selection of sandwiches with concealed impatience.

She had exactly fifteen minutes to change when they reached Queen's. She thanked her companion hurriedly, said that she supposed that she would see him again, and fled to the Nurses' Home, to emerge ten minutes later as neat as a new pin and not a hair out of place. She was, in fact, one minute early on duty—

and a good thing too, she decided as she made her way
through the trolleys, ambulance men, nurses and patients and fetched up by Betsy, who said at once: 'Oh,
good! Thank heaven you're here. I'm fed up, I can
tell you—not a moment's peace the whole morning.
There's a cardiac arrest in the first cubicle, an overdose
in the second and an old lady who slipped on a banana
skin—she's got an impacted fracture of neck of femur—oh, and there's an RTA on the way in—two so
far, both conscious and a third I don't even know about
yet.'

'Charming,' declared Serena, 'and I suppose no
one's been to dinner.'

'Oh, yes, they have—Harris. Yes, I knew you'd be
pleased, ducky, but take heart, you've got your two
part-timers coming on in half an hour. Harris can't do
much harm in that time.'

'You must be joking, Betsy. Thanks for holding the
fort, anyway. See you later.' Serena was taking off her
cuffs and rolling up her sleeves ready for work. She
cast her eyes upwards, adding: 'If I survive.'

She paused at about four o'clock when the immediate emergencies had been dealt with and the part-time
staff nurses, back from their tea, took over. In the office
she accepted the tea Agnes had made for her and
started to sort out the papers on her desk. It was amazing that so much could accumulate in two days. She
was half way through a long-winded direction as to the
disposal of plastic syringes and their needles when the
telephone rang. It was Joan, wanting to know impatiently why she hadn't been up to see Laurens.

'You must be out of your tiny mind,' said Serena
crossly. 'I haven't sat down since I got back until this

very minute and if I get up there this evening, it'll be a miracle.'

She slammed down the receiver, feeling mean, and knowing that her ill-humour was partly because she hadn't been able to get up to Surgical, and saw no chance of doing so until she went off duty that evening. She would apologize to Joan when she saw her. She poured herself another cup of tea and went back to the disposable plastic syringes.

It was gone half past nine when Serena at last went off duty. The night staff nurse and her companion, a male nurse, because sometimes things got a bit rough at night, had come on punctually, but there had been clearing up to do and Serena had elected to send the day duty nurses off and stay to clear up the mess herself. She had missed supper and she thought longingly of a large pot of tea and a piled-high plate of toast as she wended her way through the hospital towards Surgical. One of the Night Sisters was already there because it had been theatre day and there were several post-op. cases needing a watchful eye. She said 'Hullo,' to Serena when she saw her and added: 'He's still awake, do go in.'

Serena, tapping on the door of number twenty-one, wondered if the whole hospital knew about her friendship with the Dutch doctor and dismissed the idea with a shrug. He was in bed, although he told her immediately in something like triumph that he was to have a walking iron fixed the following morning and that his concussion had cleared completely. 'Come here, my little gipsy,' he cajoled her. 'I've been so bored all day, I thought you were never coming.'

'I told Joan…' she began.

'Yes, I know—surely you could have left one of

your nurses in charge for just a moment or two? I was furious with Gijs getting back so late—if he'd moved a bit you would have had time to come and see me before you went on duty.'

'He did move,' said Serena soothingly. 'I've never seen anyone get so much out of a middle-aged Mini in all my life. He was very kind, too...'

'Oh, Gijs is always kind.' Laurens sounded a little sulky and she gave him a startled look which made him change the sulkiness for a smile of great charm. 'Sorry I'm so foul-tempered—it's a bit dull, you know. Come a little nearer, I shan't bite.'

She went and stood close to the bed and he reached up and pulled her down and kissed her swiftly. 'There,' he said with satisfaction, 'now everything's fine—no, don't go away.'

She smiled a little shyly and left her hand in his, studying his good looks—he really was remarkably handsome. It was strange that all unbidden, the face of his cousin should float before her eyes—he was handsome too, but with a difference which she didn't bother to discover just then, although it reminded her to ask: 'Your cousin—I hope he wasn't too tired?'

'Gijs? Tired? Lord no, he's never tired. He went back to Holland this evening.'

Serena felt a faint prick of disappointment; she hadn't thanked him properly and now she might never have the opportunity. She said so worriedly and Laurens laughed. 'Don't give it a thought, he wouldn't expect it. And now let's stop talking about Gijs and talk about us.'

'Us?'

He nodded. 'I'll be fit to get around in a couple of days—I shan't be able to drive or dance, but there's no reason why we shouldn't have dinner together, is there, Serena? When are you free in the evening?'

She told him and he went on. 'Good—I should get away from here by Thursday or Friday. We'll dine and make plans.'

Serena, conscious that her conversation, such as it was, had become repetitive, asked 'Plans?'

'Of course, my beauty—there's our glorious future to discuss.'

Serena forced herself to remain calm. All the same, he was going a bit fast for her; perhaps she should change the conversation. She asked sedately: 'When will you go back to Holland?' wisely not commenting upon the future.

He smiled a little as though he knew what she was thinking. 'We'll talk about that later. Quite soon, I expect—my mother is worrying about me. She's a splendid worrier, though Gijs will be home by the morning and can soothe her down—he's good at that. If ever you want a good cry, Serena, try his shoulder. He's splendid in the part—doesn't seem to mind a girl crying, though I can't say the same for myself. I've not much patience for women who burst into tears for no good reason.'

He grinned at her and she smiled back, thinking how absurd it was for anyone to want to cry about anything at all. 'I'm going,' she said softly. 'Night Sister will hate me if I stay a moment longer.' She withdrew her hand.

'Come tomorrow,' he urged her as she reached the door. She turned to look at him and even at that distance, in the light of the bedside lamp, she could see how blue his eyes were. 'Of course.'

On the way over to the home she found herself wondering what colour Gijs's eyes were. It was ridiculous, but she didn't know; blue too, she supposed, and now she came to think about it, he had a habit of drooping the lids which was probably why she didn't know. In any case, it was quite unimportant.

Laurens went on Thursday, but not before he had arranged to see Serena on Friday evening. 'I'll be at the Stafford, in St James' Place,' he had told her. 'I'll send a taxi for you—seven o'clock, if that's OK.'

She had agreed, enchanted that she was to see him again so soon. She had visited him every day and they had laughed a lot together, and he had been gay and charming and had made no secret of the fact that he was more than a little in love with her, and even though she still felt a little uncertain as to his true feelings she had allowed herself to dwell on a future which excited her.

For once, and to her great relief, she was off duty punctually so that she had time to bath and dress with care in a dress the colour of corn. It was very plain and she covered it with a matching wool coat; the only ornament she wore was an old-fashioned keeper ring her father had given her on her twenty-first birthday which had belonged to her great-grandmother.

The hotel was small as London hotels went, but entering its foyer, she suspected that it catered for people who enjoyed the comforts of life and were prepared to pay for them. She hadn't thought much about Laurens's state as regards money. He had an E-type Jaguar, certainly, but a great many young men had those, affording them at the expense of something else, but it seemed that he could afford his Jag and a good life too. She inquired for him with pleasant composure and was relieved of her coat and ushered into the hotel lounge.

He was waiting for her, looking very correct in his black tie, although she found his shirt over-fussy. Even as she smiled in greeting her eyes swept down to his leg and he laughed. 'Serena, forget your wretched plasters for an hour or two—it's quite safe inside my trouser. I got one of the fellows to cut the seam and pin it together again.'

She laughed then. 'How frightfully wasteful! Are you all right here—comfortable?'

A silly remark, she chided herself, but she hadn't been able to think of anything else to say in her delight at seeing him.

'Very comfortable,' he told her, 'and now you're here, perfectly all right.' He smiled at her. 'Will a Dubonnet suit you, or would you rather have a gin and lime?'

'Dubonnet, thank you. When are you going home?'

'On Saturday—Gijs will come over for me. I'll be back in a few weeks, though, to collect the new car.' His hand covered hers briefly where it lay on the table. 'Serena, will you come over to Holland—oh, not now—in a few weeks. I want you to meet my mother.'

She blinked her long lashes, her eyes enormous with surprise. 'But why—I haven't any holiday due.'

'Who spoke of holidays? You can resign or whatever it is you do, can't you?'

'But I shall want to go back...'

'Now that's something we're going to talk about.' He smiled as he spoke and her own mouth curved in response.

She ate her dinner in a happy daze, saying very little, not quite sure that it was really all happening, until he asked suddenly: 'Why do you wear that ring? It's a cheap thing. I'll give you a ring to suit your beautiful finger—diamonds, I think.'

Serena felt affronted and a little hurt, but all the same she explained without showing it that it was her great-grandmother's and that she treasured it. 'And I don't like diamonds,' she added quietly.

Her words had the effect of amusing him very much. 'My sweet gipsy, you can't mean that—all girls like diamonds.'

Serena took a mouthful of crême brulée and said, smiling a little, because it was impossible to be even faintly annoyed with him: 'Well, here's one girl who doesn't.'

'And that's something else we'll talk about later,' he said lightly. 'When are you free tomorrow?'

She told him happily. 'And Saturday?' She told him that too. 'I'm on at ten for the rest of the day.'

'Good lord, why?'

She explained about weekends and was gratifyingly flattered when he observed: 'Just my luck—if it had been last weekend, we could have spent it together.'

'Not very well,' Serena, being a parson's daughter, saw no hidden meanings in this remark, 'for you can't drive and I haven't got a car, you know, and the train journey would have tired you out.'

She spoke happily because it had made everything seem more real because he had taken it for granted that he would have spent the weekend at her home. She certainly didn't notice the hastily suppressed astonishment in his voice when he answered her.

They talked about other things then, and it was only when she was wishing him goodbye, with the promise to lunch with him on the next day, that he said:

'You're quite a girl, Serena—full of surprises, too.'

He kissed her lightly on the cheek and added: 'To-morrow.'

She went to bed in a haze of dreams, all of them with happy endings, and none of them, she realized when she woke in the morning, capable of standing up to a searching scrutiny. She decided rebelliously that she wasn't going to be searching anyway. She dressed with care in the white jacket and skirt and decided against a hat.

They had almost finished their early lunch when Laurens said: 'I shan't see you tomorrow then, my sweet. I shall miss you—will you miss me?'

Serena had never been encouraged to be anything but honest. 'Yes, of course,' she answered readily 'very much. But you're coming back—you said...'

He laughed a little. 'Oh, yes, I'm coming back, and next time when I go you're coming with me, remember?'

'Well, yes,' she stammered a little, 'but I wasn't sure if you meant it.'

He put his head on one side. 'Then you must be sure. I shall ring you up when I get back, then you will give in your notice to your so good Matron and pack your bags and come to my home and learn something of Holland.'

'Oh,' said Serena, her heart was pattering along at a great rate, 'are you—that is, is this...'

'It seems so. How else am I to get you, my beautiful gipsy?'

They said goodbye soon after that and when he kissed her she returned his kiss with a happy warmth even though she couldn't bear the thought of not seeing him for several weeks.

It was fortunate that when she got on duty there was

a dearth of patients; it hadn't been so quiet for weeks. Serena sat in her office, making out the off duty and requisition forms and holiday lists and all the while her head spun with a delightful dreamlike speed, littered with a host of ideas, all of which she was far too excited to go into. It was like dipping into a box of unexpected treasure, and some of her happiness showed on her face so that her friends, noticing it, exchanged meaningful glances amongst themselves.

She had thought that she wouldn't sleep that night, but she did, and dreamlessly too, and she was glad to have had a good night's rest when she went on duty in the morning, for the Accident Room was going at full pressure. About half past eleven there was a lull, however, so she went along to her office and drank her coffee and thought about Laurens; she had forgotten to ask him at what time he was going; perhaps he was already on his way... The wistful thought was interrupted by one of the nurses with the news that there was a flasher coming in.

Only one ambulance man came in, carrying a very small bundle in a blanket. As soon as he saw her he said, 'Glad you're on, Sister. I got a battered baby here. Proper knocked about, she is...'

Serena forget all about Laurens then. She whisked into the nearest cubicle, saying: 'Here, Jones, any idea what happened?' She was already unwrapping the blanket from the small stiff form and winced when she saw the little bruised body. Without pausing in her task she said: 'Nurse, telephone Mr Travers, please—he's on duty, isn't he? Ask him to come at once—tell him it's a battered baby.'

She had her scissors out now and was cutting the

odds and ends of grubby clothing from the baby's body. 'Well, Jones?'

'Neighbours,' he began. 'They heard a bit of a bust-up like, and went to fetch the police—the coppers took the baby's dad off with them, the mum too. There'll be a copper round to inquire. Hit her with a belt, they said.'

'With a buckle on the end of it, Jones. The brute—I'd like to get my hands on him!' Which, considering she was five foot three and small with it, was an absurd thing to say, although the ambulance man knew what she meant.

'Me, too,' he said soberly. 'Shall I give the particulars to nurse, Sister?'

'Yes, please.' She was sponging, with infinite care, the abrasions and cuts, hoping she would be able to complete the cleaning process before the baby became conscious again.

Bill was beside her and as she wiped the last of the superficial dirt away, bent over the baby. 'Alive, anyway,' he observed, and spoke to someone behind her—someone she hadn't known was there and who came round to the other side of the examination table as Bill spoke. Doctor Gijs van Amstel. 'You don't mind, Serena,' Bill was intent on the baby, 'if Doctor van Amstel has a look? He's by way of being an authority on this sort of thing and he happened to be here...'

Serena nodded, staring at the calm face of the man opposite her, and then went a bright pink because if he was here, surely Laurens would be with him. She dismissed the idea at once because it was hardly the time to let her thoughts stray. She watched the large, quiet man bend over the baby in his turn. His hands were very gentle despite their size, and although there was

no expression on his face she knew that he was angry.
He said nothing at all until he had finished his examination. Then: 'I find the same as you Bill—concussion, suspected ruptured spleen—you felt that? and I
wonder what fractures we shall see…this arm, I fancy,
and these fourth and fifth ribs, there could possibly be
a greenstick fracture of this left leg—you agree?'

Bill Travers nodded and Serena found herself admiring the Dutchman for fielding the diagnosis back to
the younger, less experienced man. She gave Bill the
X-ray form she had ready and then sent a nurse speed-
ing ahead with it, and when she prepared to take the
baby she found that both men were with her. The
Dutchman seemed to know the radiologist too—the
three men crowded into the dark room to study the still
wet films and when they came out it was the radiologist
who spoke. 'A couple of greenstick fractures of the left
humerus, a hairline fracture of the left femur, and a
crack in the temporal bone—and of course the spleen.
Quite shocking…have the police got the man who did
it?'

'Yes,' said Serena savagely, 'they have, and I hope
they put him in prison for life.' She signed to the nurse
who had come with her and they wheeled the trolley
back to the Accident Room and presently the men
joined her.

'I've telephoned the boss,' Bill told her—the boss
was Mr Sedgley, tall and thin and stooping and wonderful with children. 'She's to go straight to theatre.
OK, Serena?'

She was drawing a loose gown over the puny frame.
She nodded and arranged a small blanket over the
gown, then wrote out the baby's identity on the plastic
bracelet she slipped on its wrist. Which done, she sent

for the porters and leaving the nurse in charge, went
with the baby straight to theatre.

When she got back Bill was still there, so was Doctor van Amstel. There was a policeman with them too
and Serena lifted her eyebrows at one of the student
nurses, who disappeared, to appear with commendable
speed carrying a tray of tea. 'You too, Sister?' she
whispered. But Serena shook her head; she couldn't
drink tea until she had got the taste of the battered baby
out of her mouth. She left the nurses to do the clearing
up and went back to her office; the case would have to
be entered in the day book and she still had the list of
surgical requirements to tackle. She was half way
through this when there was a tap on the door and
Doctor van Amstel came in. He wasted no time. 'You
must be wondering why I am here and if Laurens is
with me. I called to settle some bills and so forth and
convey his thanks—he didn't feel like coming himself.
And I want to thank you for taking such good care of
him and for cheering him up while he was here. He
hates inaction, you know.'

She sat at her desk, looking at him and wishing he
would go away. The baby had upset her—she was used
to horrible and unpleasant sights, but this one had been
so pointless and so cruel, and now on top of that this
man had to come—why couldn't it have been Laurens?

She said woodenly: 'That's quite all right. It must
have been very dull for him, but he'll soon be fit again,
won't he?'

He nodded. 'A pity,' he observed slowly, 'that we
shan't meet again.' His voice was casual, but his eyes,
under their drooping lids, were not.

'Oh, but I daresay we shall,' Serena declared. 'Laurens has asked me over to stay with his mother—I ex-

pect we shall see each other then.' She glanced up at him as she spoke and was surprised to see, for a brief moment, fierce anger in his face; it had gone again so quickly that afterwards she decided that she had imagined it.

'Indeed?' his voice was placid. 'That will be pleasant—when do you plan to come?'

'I—don't know. Laurens is going to telephone or write.'

'Ah, yes, of course.' He held out a hand. 'I shall look forward to seeing you again, Miss Potts—or perhaps, since you are to—er—continue your friendship with Laurens, I may call you Serena, and you must learn to call me Gijs.'

He smiled and went to the door and then came back again to say in quite a different voice: 'I'm sorry about the baby. I'm angry too.'

She nodded wordlessly, knowing that he meant what he said. He closed the door very quietly behind him and she listened to his unhurried footsteps retreating across the vast expanse of the Accident Room and wondered why she felt so lonely.

CHAPTER THREE

THE days were incredibly dull; it wasn't so bad while she was on duty, for the Accident Room, whatever else it was, could hardly be called dull. But off duty was another matter, and for the first three days she heard nothing from Laurens either. It was on the fourth morning that she had a letter from him, a brief, cheerful missive which told her nothing of the things she wanted to know. She waited two days before answering it and then wrote a stilted page or so in reply, and the following day was sorry she had done so, for a reed basket full to the brim with roses arrived for her with a card inside saying: 'To my gipsy from Laurens.' She felt better after that and better still when he telephoned that evening. He sounded in tearing spirits and her own spirits soared, to erupt skyhigh when he asked:

'Will you give in your notice tomorrow, Serena?— I'll be coming over in a month's time to collect the car, and I want to bring you back with me.'

She gasped a little, then: 'You mean that, Laurens? You truly mean that?'

'My darling creature, don't be so timid. Will you do it? I don't approve of working wives, you know.'

It wasn't quite a proposal, but it was probably all she would ever get. She agreed breathlessly and was rewarded by his: 'Good girl, I'll tell you the date and so on next time I ring up. 'Bye for now.'

She replaced the receiver because he hadn't waited for her to wish him goodbye—perhaps, she thought, he felt as excited as she was. She went up to her room, and while her common sense lay buried under a mass of excited thoughts, she wrote out her resignation.

She hadn't realized that Matron was going to be so surprised and so openly critical. She had accepted the resignation, of course; there was nothing else she could do, but she had questioned Serena's wisdom while she did so.

'You're a sensible young woman,' she told a surprised Serena, 'and certainly old enough to know what you're doing. But do you think you have given the matter enough thought?' And when Serena had nodded emphatically, went on: 'At least I will say this, if things should not turn out as you expect them to, you may rest assured that there will always be some kind of a job for you here—perhaps not in this hospital, but in one of the annexes.'

Serena had thanked her nicely, knowing that Miss Shepherd had her welfare at heart, knowing too, that nothing would persuade her to work in one of the annexes—Geriatrics, Convalescent, the dental department, Rehabilitation; she could think of nothing she disliked more, and in any case there was no need for her to think about them at all, for the likelihood of her returning to hospital was a laughable impossibility. She even smiled kindly at Miss Shepherd because the poor dear was all of forty-five and there was no wonderful young man waiting for her to be his bride, then thanked her politely and went back to her department and in due course, to the dining-room for her dinner, where her appearance, hugely enhanced by excitement and happiness, drew so many comments from her friends that she felt compelled to tell them her news, so happy in the telling that she didn't notice the worried little

frown on Betsy's face nor the look she and Joan exchanged.

It was Joan who spoke after the first babble of con-
gratulations had died down. 'Serena,' she began, 'are
you sure? I mean, you don't know anything about his
home or his family and you might hate Holland.'

'Well, I've thought about that, and I don't see how
I'm to know unless I go there and see for myself.' She
pinkened faintly. 'I mean, we—I can always change
my mind.'

Joan agreed with her a little too hastily and Betsy
said: 'Your parents, I bet they're surprised.'

'I haven't told them yet. I told them about Laurens
coming in and—and how nice he was, and of course
they met his cousin.'

'Oh, yes, I forgot. Though they're not a bit alike,
are they?'

Serena spooned sugar into her post-prandial cup of
tea. 'Heavens, no,' she agreed, and just for a brief moment remembered the gentle touch of Gijs van Amstel's hands on the battered baby. She had never seen
Laurens working, of course, but he would be just as
kind—and he was a good deal more entertaining. She
smiled and someone said: 'Oh, lord, we'll have to give
you a wedding present.'

Serena put down her cup. 'No, oh no, you mustn't—
I don't know when—there's nothing settled.'

'Time to save up,' said someone else. 'Give us
plenty of warning, Serena.'

They all laughed and presently dispersed to their various duties, and Serena, caught up in the usual afternoon rush, had no time to think about herself. She got
off duty late too, so that the half-formed idea that she
would write home and tell her parents came to nothing.

Time enough, she argued as she got ready for bed, when she went home the following weekend.

She had two letters from Laurens within the next few days—gay, extravagantly worded trifles which she read a dozen times and put under her pillow, as though, in her sleep, she could still read them. His mother, he wrote, would be delighted to have her as a guest for as long as she liked to stay; he would give her details of the exact date later on, and he was hers for ever, Laurens.

She didn't say anything to her mother until the morning after her arrival at the rectory—somehow it had been impossible during the evening before, with all the odds and ends of family news to exchange and a great deal of time taken up by Susan, who wanted to describe her latest boy-friend. They were in the kitchen, she and her mother, getting the midday meal, when she seized the opportunity to say: 'Mother, you remember the Dutch doctor?'

Her mother didn't look up from her pastry-making. 'Yes, indeed I do. Such a charming young man and so large and quiet...'

'Oh, not him,' said Serena impatiently, 'I mean the other one, the patient—the one who had the accident.'

Mrs Potts turned her pastry on to the wooden table top and looked at her daughter. 'Yes, dear?'

'Well, he's gone home,' Serena was finding it very difficult and she didn't know why, 'and he's coming back again in three weeks' time—to pick up his car, you know. He wants me to—to go to Holland and stay with his mother. I think he wants to marry me.'

Her mother picked up the rolling pin and proceeded to roll her pastry. 'Yes, dear—how very quick young people are to make up their minds these days. And are you going to?'

'I don't know,' and then with a sudden rush of honesty, 'Yes, I do know, Mother. I am going to.' She went on rapidly, slightly on the defensive although her mother had said nothing to make her so: 'I'm sure he'll come down and see you and Father when he comes over; you'll like him—he's fun, and—and he's charming, and…'

'You love him, darling?'

'Oh, Mother, I'm sure I do—everything seems different.'

Mrs Potts transferred the rolled out pastry from the table to the pie dish and started a complicated pattern-work around its edge.

'Your father and I will be delighted to meet—what's his name—Laurens, when he comes, and I'm happy that you're so happy, Serena, just as your father will be. When do you plan to marry?'

'Well, we aren't engaged; I expect he wanted me to go to his home first and meet his mother, but he's asked me to resign from Queen's…'

'You've not done that?' Her mother's voice was a thought sharp.

Serena was too deep in her own excited thoughts to have noticed. 'Oh, yes,' she answered airily, 'I have. I—I don't think Laurens wants to wait. There's no need; I don't know for certain, but I think his practice is a good one.'

'His cousin is a partner?'

'Yes, but I should think that Laurens is the one who does most of the work.'

'Why do you say that, Serena?'

'Well, his cousin…' she stopped, for actually she

had no evidence that Gijs was lazy or not very clever at his work, rather to the contrary; only little joking remarks Laurens had made from time to time. And Gijs had been very good with the battered baby. 'I daresay I'm wrong,' she finished. 'It's just that he seems so leisurely, if you see what I mean.'

'A good man to have with you in a tight corner, all the same,' pronounced her mother, 'but I daresay Laurens is just as sound a man.' She put the pie in the oven. 'Let's go and tell your father.'

If the Reverend Mr Potts was surprised at his eldest child's news, he gave no sign; he said all that was expected of him, forbore from asking tedious questions, and added his assurance to his wife's that he would be delighted to welcome Laurens at the earliest opportunity. They had finished their conversation and had wandered out into the garden when he asked gently:

'What do you know of his family, my dear?'

'Not much,' replied Serena. 'They live in this town—Zierikzee—it's small and old. I don't know exactly where Laurens lives—whether the surgery is one he shares with his cousin in the town and he lives somewhere else; I never thought to ask.'

'And you've received an invitation from his mother?'

'No, not a written one, but surely she will write—I can't very well go without, can I?'

'There's no reason why you shouldn't, since it's your future husband who wishes you to visit his home. I daresay I'm a little old-fashioned, but...'

Serena squeezed his arm. 'No, you're not, darling, and I wouldn't dream of going unless I get a letter.'

She went back to hospital after her weekend with a great deal to think about, for naturally, both her mother and sisters were already discussing the wedding; was it to quiet, or, as her mother suggested a little wistfully, a nice country wedding like Margery's with all their friends and family and Laurens's family as well, then Serena could wear all a bride's trappings… Serena secretly hoped for that too, she spent the journey back to London thinking about it—organza, she decided happily, made up very simply, and a net veil. The train journey had never passed so swiftly.

She wrote to Laurens that evening, telling him that she had been home and told her parents about her visit to him, but she said no more than that. And when he didn't write for several days she wondered if perhaps she had been too hasty—perhaps she should have waited and told them when he came over to fetch her, but then that would have been secretive and there was nothing to be secretive about. Her doubts were put at rest by the sight of a letter with a Dutch postmark upon it the following morning, although she was unable to read it at once; she had to wait until it was coffee time and she had a few minutes to herself. She had just taken the letter from its envelope when Mr Thompson walked in, to stay, drinking coffee, discussing a nasty lacerations of foot they had just dealt with. He then went on to discuss the weather, the appalling food in the hospital canteen, the breakdown of the middle-aged car he ran, and finally asked if she had heard any more from the Dutchman whose leg he had seen.

Serena answered cautiously that yes, she had; he seemed to be going on very well, even with his plaster.

'Oh, well,' said Mr Thompson, 'it was only a Pott's, wasn't it? He'll be able to shed his plaster very soon now. Back to work, is he?'

'I don't know.'

'He's lucky to have that cousin of his to run the practice,' said Mr Thompson forthrightly, and stared at her hard, so that she felt compelled to say: 'Oh, all right, Tom, you're dying to ask me if the grapevine's true, aren't you? Well, it is. I'm leaving—and I'm going to Holland, just for a visit.'

'Then why are you leaving?' he pounced. 'Surely...' he stopped, looking uncomfortable. 'It's not my business. We shall all miss you, Serena.' He got up. 'All the best, though, in case I don't get the chance to say it in private before you go.'

He was sweet, but she barely wasted a second on him. She should really go back to the Accident Room, but she had to read Laurens's letter first. It was, as usual, brief and amusing and said nothing at all—at least, nothing of the things she wanted to know. Serena refolded it slowly and went back to her work and was fortunate enough to be so busy that she had no time to give her own affairs so much as a thought. Only that evening, when she went off duty, she went to her room instead of joining the others in the sitting-room and sat down on her bed to think. That she was very much in love with Laurens she had no doubt, and that he was in love with her she was almost as certain, but perhaps he didn't want to get married, at least for some time, despite what he had said. Perhaps she had been too transparent, too eager—men didn't like to be chased. She decided, upon reflection, that she hadn't been either and felt a little better. Perhaps he was a man to hide his deeper feelings under a lighthearted manner... She got off the bed and went to take a bath, to be stopped on the way by Joan tearing along at a great rate. 'There you are!' she exclaimed, a bit out of breath. 'There's someone on the phone for you—Holland, they said—here, give me those—it's the box at the bottom of the stairs.'

It was Laurens; all Serena's doubts and worries melted at the sound of his voice; they disappeared entirely when he told her that his mother had sent her an invitation to stay, 'And I'll be over on the first of May, so be ready for me, my gipsy girl,' he finished.

'Yes,' said Serena breathlessly, and added: 'But must we go straight away? I wondered if you would like to go down to my home and meet my mother and father.'

She hardly noticed his pause. 'Not this time, darling girl—we could visit them later on. They don't mind you coming?'

She said no, wondering as she said it what exactly her parents' feelings had been, trying to rid herself of the idea that they weren't quite…but then they hadn't met Laurens. When they did they would have no reservations at all. She told him that she would do exactly as he wished and was rewarded by the warmth of his voice. 'I'll be over some time in the evening. I shall fly, of course, pick up the car and fetch you the following morning. We shall be back here by tea time.'

'You're sure your mother wants…' began Serena, and was instantly hushed into security by his, 'Of course she does—you'll have her letter in the morning. Now I must go, darling girl, I've friends waiting. 'Bye.'

The days passed, some fast, some slow, according to how busy she was at her work. Laurens didn't telephone again, but he wrote, less often now, but as he explained to her, he was back at work and a busy man. His mother had written too, a stiff, short letter containing a formal invitation and nothing more. Serena thought that probably she found it difficult to express herself in another language. She answered it with a nice little letter of her own and telephoned her mother to tell her about it. Mrs Potts' voice very youthful-sounding over the wire, exclaimed: 'Oh, good—then you'll be coming home before you go, won't you, dear?—and Laurens.'

Serena explained about Laurens. 'But I'll be coming myself next weekend,' she declared, 'and he says we'll come down later.'

She had felt relief when her mother merely remarked cheerfully: 'That will be nice, darling,' and not mentioned it again.

There were still several days to go before she went home when she decided to do the last of her shopping one morning; she wasn't on until one o'clock and there were one or two things she needed to buy and it was a lovely morning to be out. She took a bus to Oxford Street and spent an hour there spending rather more money than she had intended and enjoying herself hugely, so that by the time she called a halt she discovered that it was a good deal later than she had thought. The Underground was the answer, for she was passing Marble Arch subway. Within a few minutes she was on a Central Line train—it would take her to Aldgate and from there it was only a few minutes' walk to Queen's.

They were between the Bank and Aldgate when the lights went out. The train came to a sudden halt and its occupants were thrown untidily against each other while a few unfortunates, standing near the doors waiting to get out, fell against less yielding objects. Serena, who had been sitting between a fat woman and a smartly dressed matron who had been shopping like herself, found herself on the floor with a good deal of the fat woman on top of her and the smart matron, rather surprisingly, indulging in instant hysterics.

It was amazing how hopeless it was to do anything in total darkness; she was still clutching her parcels and her bag, hanging from its shoulder strap. The noise, if anything, was worse now and the dark profound. Serena swallowed rising panic and wondered if anyone felt as terrified as she did. If only she had a lighter, but she didn't smoke—perhaps the fat woman could help. She bellowed her request in that lady's ear and rather surprisingly had success. There were matches in her coat pocket—'With me fags,' explained a breathy voice in her ear. 'Put yer 'and in, ducks, and get 'em out.'

Serena did so, thankful that her companion showed no signs of panic. The pocket held an assortment of nameless objects, but the matches were there all right. Serena struck one and held it aloft. Its tiny glimmer served to light only a small part of the chaos around her, but at least it encouraged other people to do the same; within seconds there were matches being struck, and lighters, rather more lasting, were held aloft, their combined feeble rays merely serving to make the chaotic conditions around her rather worse. It was at that precise moment that she became aware of three things—that there were moans coming from the far end of the coach, that there was a faint smell of burning, and that she had a splitting headache. They all needed looking into, but first things first. She turned her head, wincing, and spoke into the dark on her left.

'There's someone hurt,' she shouted at the fat woman. 'I think I'd better go and see if I can help— I'm a nurse.' She pushed her parcels and handbag into the capacious lap beside her. 'Will you mind these, please?'

'OK, ducks. Which 'ospital?' –

'Queen's. Look, stay where you are whatever happens, you'll be safe.' She turned her head the other way. 'And you be quiet,' she commanded fiercely to the sobbing and shrieking matron. 'Can't you see you're making it worse than it is already?'

She got up and started down the coach, a difficult business because although no one had anywhere to go, they seemed unable to keep still. She was perhaps half way there when someone ahead of her shouted urgently:

'Hi—someone, there's a man hurt!' and hard on that cry came another one—a woman's voice this time, raised in a thin scream. 'Fire—I smell fire!'

'Oh, shut up,' said Serena to the mass of people around her, her own panic quite drowned in the urgency to reach whoever it was who was moaning. It was a pity that the smell of burning had now become unmistakable. Her exquisite nose twitched and a shiver of fear ran down her spine, made worse by the concerted rush by almost everyone in the coach to go somewhere. That there was nowhere to go didn't for the moment matter, the general idea was to get out; it would of course have been much easier if the darkness hadn't made it impossible for anyone to find the doors, which wouldn't open anyway. Serena, pushing slowly forward, heard glass break and hoped that no one had been caught in the splinters or been foolish enough to get out on to the line, although surely by now someone, somehow, would have got a message to the station ahead of them and the current would be cut off—the driver must have reached Aldgate and given the alarm.

She made a final effort and found that the moans were coming from the floor directly in front of her feet, but it took a good deal of pushing and shoving to get down to that level because no one wanted to make room for her and the unfortunate on the floor had either been forgotten or considered past help. At last a man, holding his lighter above his head, realized what she was trying to do and cleared a tiny space for her.

The man on the floor was in a bad way, and she saw no chance of moving him. One leg was twisted under him and he had a nasty gash on his face, probably caused by someone's heel. She looked up at the man with the lighter and called urgently: 'We've got to move him...' but the man shook his head, although by now one or two people were trying to help—but it needed more than one or two people. She crouched over him, telling him that he would be all right and that help was on its way, although he couldn't hear a word of what she was saying. At that moment there was a vivid flash, a loud bang, and the sound of fire crackling, and the homely sound wasn't homely at all, but there, in the dark, quite terrifying.

Until that moment, although there had been a good deal of shouting and pushing and confusion, no one, with the exception of the smart matron, had given way to panic, but now Serena from her crouching position on the floor could sense the panic rising around her; she felt panicky herself. If only it wasn't so dark... As though in answer a great beam of light was shone through the broken windows of the coach and a cheerful voice called:

'We're opening the doors at this end. Come out slowly, there's plenty of time and help to get you to the station.'

It was a pity that someone, over-anxious to reach safety, began to push from the rear of the coach; the urge to escape suddenly became frantic and several people went down before it. It took longer to clear everyone out than it need have done and even then there were several people lying prone. Serena lifted her head cautiously and peered at the man she had been shielding. He seemed no worse, but he certainly couldn't have been any better. She was relieved to hear a voice—a nice cheerful voice, from the doors.

'Looks as though we'd better get the medicos down 'ere,' it said. 'Pass the word along, Bill.' The owner of the voice came inside the coach and Serena called: 'I don't know about the others, but this man's got a broken leg...'

She was interrupted by voices and a number of figures carrying powerful torches. There were women's voices too, she recognized Betsy's rather high penetrating tones and called thankfully:

'Betsy—there's a man here!'

It was nice to see Betsy, looking competent and beautifully normal. She dropped on her knees beside Serena, gave her a quick look and called over her shoulder: 'Can I have a doctor here, please?' then turned her attention to the man.

Serena became aware that someone else had joined them. Doctor Gijs van Amstel. Betsy's torchlight picked out his large feet as he came to a stop beside them, and although his face was in gloom, Serena had no doubt that he looked as placid as he usually did. There was nothing placid about his actions though; she felt herself scooped up and carried away even while she was protesting that she was fine and what about the man with the broken leg?

He took no notice of her at all, but as he passed the group of people bent over the victims scattered around the coach he said: 'Bill, there's a man at the other end needs help, fast. Betsy's there. I'll take Serena straight back.'

Serena heard Bill exclaim: 'Serena, good lord!' and twisted a little in the doctor's powerful arms. 'I won't go,' she mumbled, and then contradicted herself by saying: 'I've got such an appalling headache.'

'I'm not surprised,' remarked Doctor van Amstel, and started off down the track towards the station whose platform had been turned into a kind of first aid post; people were being treated, bandaged roughly and dispatched to Queen's, but Serena couldn't see much of what was going on, and anyway the ache over her eye was fast becoming the only thing that mattered. She heard the doctor say something briefly as he tramped down the platform and through the barrier, up the stairs into the street where he shouted at a waiting ambulance, bundled her inside, shut the door on her and disappeared.

There were several other people in the ambulance, but no one spoke, and the journey was a short one. She was helped into the Accident Room, feeling all of a sudden very shaky, and was received with cries of surprised horror by her part-time staff nurse, who exclaimed:

'Sister, your head! You ought to be lying down—for heaven's sake!'

'I've only got a headache,' Serena explained. 'If I could sit down for a little while—Do go and see to the others, you must be up to your eyes.'

'We are—but there's plenty of staff.' Serena found herself being helped to one of the curtained-off bays, stretched out on its examination table while one of the student nurses arranged a paper towel beneath her head. 'Why,' she inquired fretfully, 'are you making all this fuss?'

'Just a small cut,' said Staff soothingly. 'Nothing much. I'll get it cleaned up and someone will come and put a stitch in it.'

Serena put up her hand and felt a sticky tangle of hair, then remembered how often she had besought patients not to touch their injuries. She said: 'Sorry—I shouldn't have done that,' and was surprised to find that her hand was not only filthy dirty but covered in blood as well.

'All mine?' she wanted to know, and heard Staff laugh. 'I'm afraid so, it looks awful, but it's not too bad—here's Doctor van Amstel.'

'Why?' asked Serena, her eyes closed against the headache but dying of curiosity.

'I was here with Tom.' He was standing beside her while her head was being cleaned up. 'It seemed sensible to go along with him as a couple of men in the emergency team were in theatre. You'll need a stitch or two—you must have had a crack on the head...'

'My bag,' said Serena urgently, suddenly remembering and taking no notice of him at all. 'The fat woman had it—and my parcels...'

'We'll see about them presently. Now keep still while I give you a local.'

He was gentle and unhesitating, but it seemed a long time. 'How many stitches?' she wanted to know, and made to sit up with a jerk when he told her quietly: 'Eight—you had a nasty cut from your eyebrow to your malar bone.'

Serena muttered 'Oh,' then was very sick, and Doctor van Amstel dealt with that with the same gentle deliberation that he had displayed while he had been stitching her. 'You'll feel better now,' he observed calmly. 'Staff's gone to get you an anti-tetanus injection and you'd better have a shot of penicillin—Tom will write it up, I daresay. I don't think I should.'

Staff came back then, and Miss Stokes with her, and Serena muttered crossly: 'I'm on duty at one o'clock,' and heard him say:

'It's not for me to suggest, but I'm sure her MO will want her in bed for a couple of days and then a few days' rest before she comes back to duty. I believe Mr Thompson is arranging for an X-ray.'

'I don't want an X-ray,' Serena interrupted abruptly. 'I'm perfectly OK. I didn't lose consciousness.' It was Miss Stokes who answered her.

'The doctor's gone, Sister Potts, but I'm sure he's right—I'll get Doctor Forsythe down as soon as I can and someone will help you to bed just as soon as you've been X-rayed.'

The next hour was a little blurred; X-ray, and being taken over to the Home and helped to bed and swallowing tablets, then told to go to sleep… She did, most thankfully, and wakened to find Mr Forsythe in the room. When he saw that she was awake he said briskly: 'Ah, good. What it is to be young and tough! No fracture, and that cut will heal in a few days; it's been stitched very nicely by our colleague from Holland. Two days in bed, young lady, and then a few days at home—stitches out after the fifth day and you'll be back at work again, none the worse.'

She listened to this heartening speech while something worrying niggled at the back of her mind. Mr Forsythe had been gone for some few minutes when she discovered what it was; if she had sick leave now, she wouldn't be able to leave at the end of the month. Her trip to Holland would have to be postponed, for she would have to make up the days she would be off sick before she could leave. She would have to let Laurens know as soon as possible. She lay awake worrying herself into another headache again, so that when Home Sister came presently to see how she was, she had to swallow some more tablets.

She felt better in the morning, partly because she was sure that Gijs van Amstel would come and see her or at least send a message. But he didn't come, and when Betsy poked her head round the door half way through the morning and Serena asked her if she would give him a message it was to be told that he had gone back to Holland the night before.

Serena was still wondering about Laurens. Of course Gijs would tell him as soon as he got back to Holland, she hadn't thought of that. She smiled, feeling relieved and said quite cheerfully: 'Oh. Now I must have a look…'

'Oh, time enough,' Betsy spoke rather too quickly. 'You're to stay in bed, remember?'

But when she had gone, Serena got out of bed and pottered over to the mirror, wondering why she hadn't done so sooner; perhaps she hadn't felt sufficiently interested. Her reflection was hardly a reassuring one— the cut was hideous although it had been most carefully stitched, but it would leave a scar. It didn't worry her too much, but she couldn't help but wonder if Laurens would feel the same way, for she imagined that to him beauty had to be perfect, and her face was no longer perfect.

It was two days later and she had packed her bag

ready to go home for a few days when the Home maid came in with a message to ask her to go downstairs as there was a gentleman to see her. Serena, to whom the last two days had been like two years because she had had no news from Laurens, went a delicious pink and squashing a desire to tie a scarf over her stitches, tore downstairs. It would be Laurens; she flung the door of the visitors' room open, her face radiant and stopped short. 'Oh, it's you,' she said, and went even pinker because she had been rude. 'I'm sorry,' she stammered, 'I thought it was…'

Gijs van Amstel smiled faintly. 'He couldn't manage it,' he told her cheerfully, 'so he asked if I'd slip over and see how things were. He's—er—very sorry. He asked me to give you these…' He waved towards an extravagant cellophane-wrapped sheaf of flowers. 'He also asked me to drive you home.'

She eyed the flowers with pleasure and answered somewhat absent-mindedly: 'Oh, that's quite unnecessary, I'm quite all right, except for this.' She put a hand up to her cheek and then dropped it again hurriedly in case he might think that she was fishing for sympathy. She need not have worried, for he said merely: 'I'm sure you are, but Laurens particularly asked me.'

'Yes, did he?' She smiled warmly, not at him, but at the idea of Laurens cherishing her. 'Then I'd better do as he asks, hadn't I?' She looked at him directly. 'Why are you over here so often?'

He answered without hesitation. 'Laurens isn't really fit to travel yet and he can't drive for another week or so. There's a certain amount of coming and going necessary to get his accident settled and the new car…' he was a little vague about the car, but she hadn't noticed, she was thinking that with so much time on his hands he must be a very unimportant member of the partnership.

'Shall we go?' His quiet inquiry disturbed her train of thought and she nodded at once. 'I'll get my things and come out to the car, shall I?'

She didn't wait for his reply but slipped back to her room, still thinking about Laurens.

She found Gijs waiting for her just outside the door. He took her bag saying, 'I left the car over here,' nodded vaguely to his left and started off with her following him through the parked cars, and when he stopped beside a dark blue Bentley, she said in a friendly voice because she had been rather cavalier in her treatment of him: 'What a gorgeous car! Don't you wish you were driving it?' She looked round her. 'I can't see the Mini…'

He put down her bag and produced some keys from a pocket; he sounded diffident when he spoke. 'Well, no—it's not here, we're going in this car.'

She goggled at him, then, anxious not to hurt his feelings because he really was the kindest of men, she said: 'Oh, has the Mini come to grief? Did you borrow this one? She's super, don't you find a lot of difference in driving it?'

He put her bag in the boot and closed it. 'No, not really—I've driven a Bentley before.' He opened the door for her and she got in. He must have some good friends if they lent him a Bentley, or perhaps Laurens had told him to hire it. She didn't like to ask and it was obvious that he wasn't going to tell her any more. She settled down in the comfortable seat as he got in beside her. Even in a car of that size, there seemed to be a great deal of him.

The car slid smoothly through the hospital forecourt

and out into the busy street and Gijs asked: 'How many days have you?'

'Five—far too many, for I have to make them up, you know. That means I can't get away until a week later than we had planned.'

'Very disappointing,' he spoke casually, 'and I'm sure Laurens is just as disappointed. He'll be over to fetch you, though. I was to tell you that and to explain why he hadn't written—the practice is a busy one—babies and so forth,' he added.

Serena smiled to herself, conjuring up a picture of Laurens hard at work despite his leg. 'I'm sure it is,' she agreed. 'Does he have any helpers—other than you,' she added hastily.

'Oh, yes. A secretary and a surgery nurse and a couple of receptionists.'

She sat silent, watching her companion pilot the car through the city traffic. It must be a big practice; she would have liked to have asked about it, but perhaps it would be better to wait until she was there and could see it for herself. Her musings were checked by her companion remarking: 'I thought we might go over Salisbury and through Blandford. There's a good place there where we might have lunch—the Crown, I daresay you know it.'

She hastened to accept and discovered that she was enjoying herself; he hadn't once commented upon the hideous little scar with its shiny black stitches standing up like miniature barbed wire; indeed, he hadn't mentioned the accident, nor inquired after her health; but he was taking the trouble to drive her home. She felt, for the first time in several days, relaxed, and at the same time she found herself surprised that he was such good company. Why, she wondered, hadn't she noticed that when he had driven her up to London?

They ate their lunch in a most friendly atmosphere, talking trivialities which she suspected he was deliberately keeping to. They ate ham off the bone accompanied by a delicious salad and new potatoes, and followed it with apple pie and cream and drank sparingly of a dry white wine which Serena, ignorant of such things, nevertheless found exactly right. She said so, and Gijs twinkled nicely at her and thanked her for her approval. Her answering smile was a little crooked by reason of the scar which still hurt, and it was then that she noticed for the first time that his eyes weren't blue like Laurens's, but grey.

She asked suddenly: 'You're older than Laurens, aren't you?' and watched his lips twitch as he answered blandly: 'Quite a good deal older. I'm thirty-six. And you,' he added deliberately, 'are twenty-four.'

For some reason this made her feel uncomfortable; it was as though he implied that she was in quite another age group than his own and that she had been impertinent to ask him in the first place. Well, she had been a little rude, she told herself honestly, and he had every right to be snooty about it.

They arrived at the Rectory in time for tea and it wasn't until they were seated round the table enjoying the substantial meal her mother considered desirable that Serena remarked suddenly: 'You know, I really am awful—I never telephoned you, did I? Supposing someone had gone all the way to Dorchester to meet the train. I can't think how I forgot.'

It was her mother who answered. 'Never mind, darling, I'm sure you still feel rotten. Doctor van Amstel rang your father this morning, so we knew you were coming by car.' She caught the sparkle in her daughter's fine eyes and added swiftly: 'Very thoughtful of you, Doctor,' and because her daughter's eyes were still smouldering: 'Do have some more of this cake, Susan made it. Her young man—no, I have to say boyfriend, don't I?—likes a domesticated girl, so she does most of the cooking at the moment because Eric comes to supper most evenings.'

'Eric?' queried Serena, instantly diverted. 'I thought his name was Bert.'

Susan, from across the table, sitting beside their visitor, snorted and tossed her hair over her shoulder. 'Serena, he was ages ago—besides, he didn't like dogs.'

Serena took another slice of cake and said understandingly: 'Oh, well, in that case he wouldn't do at all.' The Rectory housed two dogs and several cats as well as an odd rabbit or two, a hedgehog and a barn owl who came and went when he liked.

'You have a dog of your own, Doctor van Amstel?' the rector inquired.

The big man smiled at his host. 'A dog—yes, a dachshund called, with a great lack of imagination, I'm afraid, German. There is a cat too, called Hemel, because that is what I said when I first saw him.'

'What does *hemel* mean?' demanded Susan, making play with her eyelashes.

'Heavens—he is actually a very earthy beast, though.' They all laughed, and Serena, looking round the table, sensed that they all liked the doctor, which was wonderful because it meant that they would like Laurens even better; was he not younger? She was going to add 'and more amusing', but all at once she wasn't quite sure about that.

He went soon after tea and they stood, clustered

round the porch, watching him get into the car, but before he did so he turned back and came to a halt before Serena. 'Dear me, I almost forgot—I shall be coming for you in five days' time. I might just as well, I have to come to England once more. The next time it will be Laurens.'

She had no time to reply, only wave with the others as the big car skimmed up the hill towards the main road. She wondered why he had reminded her that it would be Laurens who would be fetching her. Did he really suppose that she would forget?

The five days went quickly; there was always so much to do at home, she found, and time enough to do it in. She was nicely tanned by the time the last day came and the scar, its stitches ready to come out, didn't seem to matter at all, perhaps because no one ever mentioned it. She helped her mother about the house, and cooked a little and found the time to do some knitting and reading and take the dogs for long walks. When the last morning came she felt regret, but it was mixed with excitement because very soon she would be seeing Laurens again.

This time Gijs van Amstel wasn't early but exactly on time, moreover he had breakfasted on the way, so there was nothing for it but to get into the Bentley without delay, smiling with determined cheerfulness until the rectory and the little group at its front door were no longer to be seen.

They were almost in Dorchester when the doctor said: 'You look very well—presumably the stitches come out the moment you get back. Will you think it unpardonable of me if we don't stop for lunch? I have several things to do and I'm going back today.' He turned to smile at her. 'Coffee, though—I should think we might reach the Hog's Back round about eleven.'

Serena said how nice and felt disappointed; she had expected, or at least hoped, that he would take her out to lunch again. She had enjoyed the homeward trip, but then there had been no hurry; apparently today there was. She said, faintly waspish: 'You really shouldn't have come—it's such a waste of time for you and I could perfectly well have gone by train.'

'Ah, yes, I know that, but remember Laurens asked me.' A remark which made Serena fume silently, for it sounded as though her companion had made the journey merely to do a service for his cousin and not because he enjoyed her company. But why, she asked herself reasonably, should he enjoy her company? Had he not once asked her why she disliked him and had she ever given him any real answer? She said woodenly: 'It's very kind of you to put yourself out,' and was enraged afresh by his idle: 'Yes, isn't it, but I'm a kind man when it suits me.'

It was quite a relief when he drew up in front of the hospital, helped her out, fetched her bag from the boot and went to the entrance with her, where he bade her a rather abrupt goodbye with the kind of lazy courtesy she had come to expect from him. She went over to her room feeling strangely let down, and even the sight of her healed face when the stitches had been taken out did little to restore her cheerfulness. She unpacked and went down to a late dinner, assuring herself that she didn't wish to see too much of Gijs van Amstel while she was in Holland, for despite his casual air, he disturbed her strangely.

CHAPTER FOUR

SERENA had expected the time to drag; that the days would seem endless before she would leave Queen's and go to Holland, but it was nothing of the sort; the Accident Room had never been so busy, and Laurens, who had written so seldom at first, was now writing or telephoning every day. She packed, gave a farewell party to her friends and staff, paid a duty visit to the Matron's office and found herself, at last, dressed and ready and waiting for Laurens. He was to fetch her during the early afternoon, for they were to travel on the evening ferry. It would get them to Zeebrugge by half past ten or so and there was only the matter of an hour or so's drive after that.

The weather was still very warm and sunny and Serena was wearing a sleeveless blue dress with a little jacket in case it got chilly in the evening. Her scar still showed pinkly against the tan of her face, but it had healed well, thanks to Gijs' neat stitchery, with no pucker to mar its line—in a month or so it would be, if not invisible, almost so. It didn't worry her any more—nothing worried her, life was perfect and the future a delightful dream yet to be lived. She took a last look round her room with a small pang of regret, because she had been happy there, and went down to the hospital entrance, exactly at the time Laurens had asked her to be there. He was waiting; her heart gave a thud of happiness at the sight of him and quickened its beat as he got out of the car—the new Jag—and

77

came towards her. There were plenty of people about; nurses going to and fro, consultants arriving, housemen hanging around waiting for their chiefs, but none of them deterred Laurens from kissing her in a most satisfying, if brief, manner, only the moment marred just a little for her when he held her back from him to study her face intently.

'Not bad,' he decided. 'A pity it had to mar your lovely face, but Gijs has done a neat job, I must say,' and then as though he sensed her feelings, hurried on: 'and how are you after all this time, my beautiful gipsy? More beautiful than ever, I can see that, despite the scar—let's hope it fades quickly, and thank heaven it wasn't right on your cheek, at least it doesn't show too badly...'

Serena, still breathless from the kiss, felt a small prick of dismay; it seemed to her that the scar didn't matter at all. Surely if you loved someone, you loved them, not their looks? She dismissed the worrying thought and gave him a dazzling smile. 'It will have faded in another week or two,' she assured him. 'I've heaps of luggage.'

While he was stowing it she asked: 'How's your leg?'

'Almost a hundred per cent. Gijs wasn't too keen on me driving back, but it hardly bothers me at all. Besides, it's my business what I do.'

He looked so sulky that she hastened to say something. 'Are you working too hard?'

'I'm not working at all, my beauty—I shall start this week.'

She got in beside him, remembering with an unwelcome clarity that Gijs had told her that Laurens couldn't come to see her because he was working so hard. She pushed that thought away too, to join the one about the scar; probably she was being over-sensitive and she could easily have mistaken what Gijs had told her.

It was the clear dark of a summer night when they landed in Belgium, and there was still quite a lot of traffic about, although this didn't deter Laurens from tearing along the uneven cobbled roads as though he were on a race track, and when they had crossed the border into Holland, and the roads were smooth and fast except in the towns where they were brick, he went even faster. 'We'll be in by midnight,' he assured her confidently, and they were, because they had caught the ferry at Breskens by the skin of their teeth, saving themselves half an hour's wait.

Serena peered around her, but there wasn't a great deal to see. In the semi-dark the flat land and sky merged into each other so that there was no horizon; it seemed no time at all when Laurens said in a pleased voice:

'Here we are,' and shot down a left-hand turn off the main road. 'I live on the outside of the town,' Laurens told her. 'The house isn't so very old, late eighteenth century—some of the houses in the town go back a couple of hundred years more than that.'

He swung the car into a narrow road and then turned again down a short lane, wide enough to take a car and no more. There were gates at its end standing open; he shot through them rather too fast and stopped outside the porched doorway of a solid square house. 'Here we are,' he remarked, and looked at his watch, 'and in good time too.'

He got out and opened the door and they went through it together. 'In you go, my beauty,' he told her.

'I'll get the bags later. Mother will be in bed but Sieska will be about somewhere.'

He pushed her gently into the hall and closed the door. The hall was dimly lit, but she could see that it was square and lofty, with a staircase ascending up one side of it. There was a light coming from the half open door close to her and Laurens directed: 'In here, Serena, I'll go and see what Sieska's got for us.'

She went through the door ahead of him, feeling strangely let down at their lack of welcome, although her common sense told her that their arrival was so late that her hostess could be forgiven for going to bed. All the same…

It was obviously a sitting-room, large and lofty-ceilinged and furnished a little heavily and with solid comfort. After the shabby Rectory, Serena found it a little awe-inspiring and far less welcoming. There were a pair of table lamps shining a rather tepid greeting and Laurens, following her in, said: 'Gloomy, eh? I'm going to find some food and coffee.'

He came back presently with a tray of coffee and sandwiches which they consumed without much talk and when he said: 'Well, my gipsy, what about bed?' she was only too ready to comply; she would have a good sleep and in the morning everything would be all right. He fetched her luggage and they went quietly upstairs to a square landing, its walls pierced at regular intervals by doors, one of which Laurens opened and ushered her inside. The room was long, narrow, and again, high-ceilinged. It had a green carpet, furniture of satinwood which was almost as heavy as that in the sitting-room, and it smelled very clean, of polish and lavender and methylated spirit, it also smelled as though no one had slept in it for a very long time.

'Don't know why Mother gave you this room,' Laurens commented. 'No one sleeps here much, but I don't suppose that will make any difference to you.' He put down her cases and turned to her, smiling. At least, Serena consoled herself a few minutes later, whatever the shortcomings of her welcome, there had been nothing wrong with his goodnight kiss.

She wakened to broad daylight and a gentle tapping on the door and a cheerful-faced girl came in with tea, smiled and nodded and went away again. Serena looked at her watch; it was eight o'clock. She drank her tea, dragged on her dressing gown and crossed the landing to the bathroom Laurens had pointed out to her the night before. She bathed without haste, dressed in the pale green dress she had worn in London and went downstairs, feeling uncertain. She was standing in the hall when Laurens came in from the garden, kissed her and took her arm. 'Mother never comes down to breakfast,' he told her. 'We'll have it now, shall we?'

He led her to a small room where a round table was spread ready for them, sat her down at it, poured coffee for them both and took a chair opposite her. Serena sipped the coffee, took a roll from the basket he offered and asked: 'Do you have a morning surgery?'

He shook his head. 'Gijs is doing almost all the work at the moment. I go in for the evening surgeries—I sit most of the time.'

'Your leg bothers you? Isn't it a bit soon to…'

'Lord, no—it aches a bit, but I've done this before, you know—an arm once too.' He shrugged. 'I've a stick to help me along and I'm having physio.'

'But driving all that way?'

'Don't get so worried, little gipsy Potts.' He sounded a little impatient; she helped herself experimentally to a slice of cheese—the Dutch ate cheese for breakfast, so if she was to become an adopted member of the van Amstel family, she had better cultivate a taste for it. 'Your mother?' she inquired tentatively.

'Oh, she'll be down presently,' he answered carelessly. 'Have you almost finished? I've a great deal of post to attend to, I think I'll go and get on with it while you finish, then we can have a look round.'

He strolled off, whistling, and she, left alone, lost her appetite for cheese. She was ladling sugar into her cup when the door did open and Laurens's mother came in. At least, it had to be his mother, because she was exactly like the image Serena had built up in her mind; tall and a little stout, with well dressed greying hair and his good looks; moreover she had a regal manner which left Serena in no doubt as to who was mistress of the household. The lady advanced to the table and Serena stood up.

'Miss Potts?' Somehow the crisp voice made her name sound ridiculous. 'You must forgive me for not staying up to welcome you, but it was a little late.' She smiled without warmth. 'Laurens has told me so much about you—I do hope that you will enjoy your little holiday with us.' She extended a hand and Serena shook it, hearing her own voice making suitable replies while her mind wrestled with the puzzle her hostess's words had given her. If she was here for a little holiday where was she supposed to go afterwards, and how long did a little holiday last? She would have to talk to Laurens urgently. He came in just then, kissed his mother, said easily: 'Oh, hullo, you two have met. Good,' and smiled at them both. 'I'm going to take Serena on a little tour of inspection, Mama.'

His mother nodded briefly. 'Of course, dear. Lunch

will be at half past twelve. Remember that we have a few friends coming in this evening, won't you?' She turned to Serena. 'We live very quietly, although we do a little entertaining amongst ourselves. We must try and think up something to amuse you while you are with us, mustn't we?' She smiled at them both and went to the door. 'Don't be late for lunch,' she warned them, and closed the door quietly behind her.

Laurens flung an arm around Serena's shoulders. 'Fetch your bonnet and we'll go. A quick look at the town first, and further afield this afternoon.'

It hardly seemed the right moment to ask what his mother had meant. She fetched her handbag and joined him in the hall. She walked beside him round the house to what must have been the stables and was now the garage, then got into the Jag beside him and nodded happily when he said:

'We'll go round the outside of the town and through the Noordhavenpoort. You couldn't have seen much last night.'

The gate looked imposing by daylight. They drove slowly through its deep arch, with the funny little painted shuttered windows piercing the thickness of its walls, and into the Oude Haven, a wide cobbled street dissected by a canal. To the left of them was a white painted wooden bridge leading to the other side of the canal and yet another, smaller gate. The street was lined with houses, all different, some large, some small; all old. Serena was still studying them when Laurens drove slowly on to stop again where the canal, filled in, had become a grassed garden with a bandstand in its centre. Beyond it was a cobbled market square, thick with parked cars. 'Look across the canal to the other side,' Laurens advised her. 'There is Gijs's house.'

She followed his pointing hand—the houses were packed tightly, all shapes and sizes. There was a small one wedged between a larger gabled one and a very much bigger one with a great door, whose framework and that of the vast window above it was surrounded by intricate plaster work. She turned her attention to its small neighbour.

'The little one,' she stated.

'No—the one next to it.'

'Not the big one with the door?' She tried to keep surprise out of her voice and failed, because the house was so unlike her vague ideas of Gijs's home. 'Isn't it a little large?' she ventured.

'Vast, but it's been in his family for generations—besides, he hates to be cramped. He suffered agonies in that Mini.' Laurens laughed and she echoed him uncertainly. 'Oh? Isn't the Mini his?'

He laughed again. 'No—when you telephoned about me, he got on the first flight and borrowed the Mini—God knows who from. He's got friends in the most unlikely places—some chap near London Airport, I believe.'

'I see,' said Serena calmly, and fumed silently. Gijs had deliberately misled her, and why? She would find out when she saw him. 'Is the surgery in his house?'

'No—in the centre of the town. Gijs sees his private patients at his own house, of course.' He turned away, obviously a little bored with the whole subject, and she made haste to ask: 'What's that old building on the left?'

This time they drove down the other side of the canal and going past Gijs's house, Serena peered closely at its windows, hoping to get a glimpse of what might be inside, but although the windows were enormous they were discreetly veiled with pristine white net curtains, although the funny mumble of windows in the older wing of the house were open and uncurtained. She observed obliquely. 'It is a large house. Your cousin's wife must have quite a job...' because she knew he wasn't married, but Gijs might be engaged.

Laurens gave a shout of laughter. 'Gijs married, or even thinking of it? He's much too lazy, though I must say he's such a silent man when it comes to his own affairs.' He darted a quick look at her. 'In any case, I shouldn't tell on him.' Which remark caused her to redden painfully. Perhaps she had been too curious, but after all, if she was to marry Laurens surely it was natural for her to want to know about his family.

They were back in good time for lunch, which they had with Laurens's mother, who made polite and intelligent conversation on trivial matters in her excellent, rather stilted English. That she was very fond of her son was apparent and that he was able to twist her round his little finger was still more apparent. Serena ate without much appetite because she felt that something wasn't quite right and she didn't know what it was.

It wasn't until later that afternoon, as Laurens drove the Jag across the flat green island to Brouwershaven, that Serena found the opportunity to air her doubts. They had been talking about his return to work and she seized the chance to say: 'Talking of returning to work, Laurens, your mother—when we met this morning, you know—she spoke as though I had come just for a few days on a casual visit—as though I'm going back to Queen's. Does she know—about us, I mean?'

'Well, more or less. You see, it's been rather a surprise to her, darling. She needs to get used to the idea.'

'But she must have known when she wrote to me—doesn't she approve?'

'Oh, come now, I didn't say that.'

'No, I know you didn't, but she doesn't know we're going to get married, does she?' Serena turned to look at Laurens and saw his sulky expression, but when he pulled into the side of the road and stopped the car and turned to face her, she saw that he was smiling. 'Beautiful girl, aren't you being a little bit intense about it all? There's time enough to think about getting married—we hardly know each other.'

He flung an arm around her and she sat rigid under it. 'Are you telling me you've changed your mind?'

He laughed and bent to kiss her cheek. 'How ridiculous you are, and how lovely you look when you're cross—did you know? All I'm saying is, let's stay as we are for a week or two; when Mother gets to know you she'll be as crazy about you as I am.' He kissed her again and she, feeling foolish at her outburst, kissed him back; everything was perfectly all right after all. They had only known each other a very short time and there was no hurry. She smiled back at him and said contritely: 'I'm a fool, aren't I? Only I did want your mother to like me and I suppose I'm a bit nervous.'

She was rewarded by another kiss and for the rest of the afternoon he was cheerful and lighthearted and attentive to her every whim. They had tea in Haamstede, a pleasant little resort in the dunes on the other side of the island, and then went back to Zierikzee so that they would have time to change before the friends his mother had invited should arrive.

There was no one coming to dinner, Laurens had said, Serena went downstairs at seven o'clock, wearing a pink crêpe dress which fitted her slender person exactly and flared gently into a wide skirt. It had a chiffon frill at its deep V-neckline and because she hadn't any good jewellery she didn't wear any, only the keeper ring, but she had taken extra pains with her face and swept her well brushed hair into its usual simple top-knot because she knew that it suited her that way. She hoped that Laurens would approve, and still more important, his mother.

The sitting-room door was a little open and she quickened her steps. The others must be already down—she opened the door wider and went in. Neither Laurens nor his mother were there, but Gijs was, standing, massive and quiet, before the empty hearth. He looked different, and it took her a few seconds to discover why—he was dressed differently. Now he wore a well tailored and elegant suit, perhaps a little conservative in cut but of a fine grey cloth; his tie was exquisite too, and he looked—she sought for a word and came up with wealthy, but that wouldn't do at all; that smacked of the ostentatious and Gijs could never be that. She broke the silence he hadn't attempted to break and said: 'Hullo, Gijs, I didn't know—that is, Laurens said that no one...'

He smiled faintly, looking down on her with a benign expression which annoyed her. 'Oh, but I don't count—I'm family, you see. I believe my aunt thought that four at dinner would be better than three.' He moved away from the hearth and came to stand in front of her. 'Enjoying yourself, I hope?'

He sounded no more than politely casual, but when she looked at him it was to encounter grey eyes which bored into hers with such intentness that she blinked under their stare. 'Very much, thank you, though I haven't seen much yet.'

He said without smiling: 'You have seen nothing yet.'

Which was a perfectly ordinary remark, but for some reason she found herself searching for its real meaning. She was still puzzling over it when Laurens came in with a casual greeting for his cousin and a warmer one for herself.

'Hullo. Mother not down yet? Have a drink, Serena. Sherry?'

She thanked him a little absentmindedly, accepted the glass he fetched for her and watched him pour gin and tonic for Gijs and then help himself. They were chatting idly when Laurens's mother came in. She was without doubt a handsome woman, the grey dress she was wearing, so simple and so expensive, put Serena's own dress completely in the shade and made her feel positively dowdy, an opinion shared by her hostess, if the brief appraising glance she cast at her as she settled herself in her chair was anything to go by. But her manner towards Serena was charming and gracious and remained so throughout dinner, even though she allowed no one to take the conversation out of her hands during the meal.

They had their coffee at table and then crossed the hall to the double doors on its other side. The drawing-room, without a doubt, and a splendid one, with long wide windows hung richly with crimson brocade and a number of tables and chairs scattered about its carpeted floor. Serena found it a little stiff and formal, although the flowers in their vases on the wall tables were beautiful and most artistically arranged. There were a number of paintings on the walls too and she would have liked an opportunity to study them, but her hostess patted the sofa where she had seated herself and Serena felt impelled to go and sit beside her, a little envious of the men, who had gone to the further end of the room for some purpose of their own.

Her companion settled herself against the cushions. 'And now—Serena, is it not? Why do I have such difficulty in remembering your name, for I have had enough practice, I must admit, Laurens has so many girl-friends—' she laughed a little and Serena dutifully echoed her, because there was nothing else to do. 'Tell me about yourself. I know that you are a hospital Sister—a *Hoofd Zuster*, are you not?'

There seemed little point in telling her companion that she was no longer working in hospital. Serena replied: 'Yes,—I'm in charge of the Accident Room at Queen's—quite a big hospital in London, where Laurens went, as I'm sure you know. We're almost always busy, but it's work I like doing.'

'And your parents?'

'My father is a country rector. He and my mother live in a small village in Dorset.'

'Clergy,' mused her hostess *sotto voce*, and asked; 'Rector? Is that an important post in your church—a bishop, perhaps?'

'Heavens no, just an ordinary clergyman.'

'And your mother?'

Serena recognized that she was being vetted, and since she was going to be one of the family, she didn't resent it. 'She helps my father in the parish—she's always busy.' She smiled a little, thinking of that cheerful, practical lady with her never-ending enthusiasm for the day's tasks.

'The house is large, I expect?' The voice was gentle but persistent.

Serena fell neatly into the trap set for her. 'Oh, yes,

Victorian at its worst and quite non-labour-saving. The housework's unending.'

'But living in the country, as she does, I'm sure your mother is able to obtain servants easily.'

'She does almost everything herself,' answered Serena, falling a little deeper into the trap. 'Mrs Palmer from the village comes in twice a week for an hour or so, but servants cost the earth in England.'

'Indeed? As they do in Holland.' Her companion's voice was pleasant, but Serena was uneasily aware that she had been got at. It was a relief when the men joined them and, a few minutes later, the first of the evening's guests.

There were quite a number; Laurens introduced her to the first half dozen or so and then turned to his duties as host, and when the group she was with drifted away one by one, she found herself standing alone, wishing that he would spare even a few minutes for her, for her hostess, beyond telling her to enjoy herself and remarking that Laurens would make sure that she met everyone, had drifted away to the opposite end of the room and was standing with her back to her. Apparently she had forgotten that she was there. Serena looked round her, searching for Laurens; he had forgotten her too. He was standing very close to a tall blonde girl, distinctly eye-catching and beautifully dressed. They were, she noticed, rage throbbing painfully in her breast, standing hand in hand. She tore her eyes away and met Gijs's steady look from the other side of the room; she turned her head away at once so that he shouldn't see the hurt surprise on her face.

He must have moved like lightning; she had taken two steps when his large hand came down firmly on her arm. She was conscious of relief as he said mildly:

'Keep me company in the garden, Serena—I'm not over-fond of these gatherings—such an effort to talk.' He smiled down at her lazily and there was no trace of pity, only faintly amused good nature. He had been propelling her towards the open window as he spoke and opened it wider for her to step through. Now she found herself outside in the warm evening air, the garden before her, his hand still on her arm, guiding her without haste around its formal beds and paths.

'Fantastic,' he murmured conversationally. 'This garden hasn't a blade of grass out of place—you should see mine.'

'Have you a garden?' Serena wasn't in the least interested, she was still seeing, far too clearly, Laurens standing hand in hand with the blonde.

'Yes, behind the house—you saw that, I expect?— it's very sheltered with a high stone wall. I enjoy an hour or so's gardening in it occasionally.'

The idea of her companion exerting himself to so much as pluck a weed momentarily diverted her thoughts. 'Oh? It doesn't seem quite your—your…' she didn't finish the sentence, but instead began a new, more urgent one.

'Who is she?' she asked.

He answered at once with a complete lack of surprise in his deep voice. It was as level and pleasant as it always was and Serena wondered crossly if he ever made the effort to be angry or unpleasant or surprised. Probably not.

'Adriana van Hoijden. They've known each other for years—brother and sister, you might say.'

'Does she live here—in Zierikzee?' Serena was aware that she was being foolish to let him see how upset she was, but she didn't care any more.

'In Haamstede—just outside the...'

'We went there this afternoon,' she interrupted him ruthlessly. 'What does she do?'

'Er—nothing that I know of. Money, you know, and an only child—poor girl. I'm sorry for only children, aren't you?'

She swallowed the next question because he so obviously wasn't going to answer it. 'Yes, I think I am.'

'Ah, at last I have found something about myself in which you can show some interest—I am an only child.'

She said woodenly, not caring in the least: 'I'm sorry. Did you find it very lonely?'

'When I was a little boy, yes. One learns as one gets older, however.' He turned her round and started to retrace their steps. 'And what do you think of Laurens's home?'

'It's—I haven't seen much of it yet. I've only been here a day.' It seemed longer.

'Ah, yes, so you have. You'll probably go on a conducted tour before very long. Is your stay a short one? I seem to remember asking you that before.'

'I don't know...'

'Surely not unlimited leave from the hospital?'

'I've left—you must know that, or can't you remember that either?' She sounded peevish and felt it.

'So you have, forgive me. I see that the scar is almost invisible. I'm glad—and may I add that you look delightful in that colour.'

He was only being kind, but at least he had admired her dress. Laurens hadn't even noticed it. She sighed and said thank you in a rather small voice, then heard him say: 'Well, we shall see, shall we not?'

They were approaching the house again. 'See what?'

she wanted to know, but he didn't answer, which was
infuriating of him, but led her inside again and stayed
with her, collecting people around him with no apparent effort, until she was surrounded by a friendly little
circle of people who all spoke English and seemed
pleased to talk to her. When she looked round for Gijs
presently, he had disappeared.

The evening was pleasanter after that; the circle widened and dwindled but never quite melted away, and
presently Laurens joined it and remained until the
guests began to leave. When the last of them had gone,
Serena, standing with him at the still open window,
asked: 'That pretty fair girl you were with, who was
she? I didn't meet her.'

He took her arm. 'There weren't any pretty girls,' he
said with satisfying fervour, 'only you,' which remark
made it all the easier to say: 'Don't be ridiculous, Laurens. She was gorgeous. She had on a pale green dress
with blue and green embroidery round the hem and
down the front of the bodice...'

'You should have been a detective, darling. Now I
know who you mean. That was Adriana van Hoijden—
I've known her for years, haven't seen her for ages—
nice girl, if you like blondes.' He bent to kiss her.
'Personally, at this moment I have a strong preference
for gipsy types.'

So she went to bed happy, or almost so. After all, it
was all strange to her and she could hardly expect Laurens's mother to welcome her with open arms. She reminded herself that she was a foreigner.

They spent the next morning looking over the house
and sitting in the garden and after lunch Laurens took
himself off, declaring that he had been idle long
enough and there was plenty of work which wouldn't

interfere with his leg. Which left Serena sitting uncertainly in his mother's company until that lady rose gracefully, declaring her intention of calling upon an old friend. 'And you, my dear, will be glad to have an hour or so to yourself to write letters, I have no doubt.'

Serena agreed; she knew that the perfect guest always had letters to write. She fetched pen and paper and applied herself to a letter home, very colourful as to description but a little thin on news, because there really wasn't any. By the time she had finished, her hostess had gone out, driving herself, rather surprisingly, in a Mercedes, and the afternoon, barely half done, loomed emptily before her. She sat doing nothing for a little while, wishing that by some miracle, Laurens would return. But he didn't, so presently she got up and fetched her purse and set off in the direction of the town. She took the outside road because it was the only one she knew and turned into the cool dimness of the gateway's entrance, to pause there so that she could enjoy the sight of the busy little town before her. It was thronged with people and cars, which were parked on either side of the canal as well as in the street. She started to walk across the little white bridge and stopped half-way because she saw Laurens's car, parked only a few hundred yards away. And Laurens was standing beside it, and beside him was Adriana van Hoijden.

Serena stood still, trying to make her mind work. Should she turn round and go away? But that smacked of mistrusting Laurens. But if she went on and they saw her, would it look as though she was spying on them? As she stood trying to make up her mind, still staring at them, Laurens bent his head and kissed the girl standing so close to him, and at the same moment

Gijs's voice behind her said: 'What's that cousin of mine doing, kissing my girl?'

'Yours?' The relief was so great that Serena smile brilliantly at him. 'You didn't say—I didn't know...'

'I didn't realize that you were interested,' he observed laconically. 'I asked him to tell her that I should be a little late getting here, and look at him—a good thing I know him well enough, and Adriana—not to mind in the least.'

Serena put a hand on his sleeve. 'Oh, I am a fool, aren't I?' she exclaimed happily. 'I had such a silly idea—I actually—she's so very pretty.'

'Very—come and meet her.' He took her arm and strolled off the bridge and on to the cobbles on the other side, pausing several times to point out the more interesting of the architectural features of the houses around them. By the time she had reached Laurens and Adriana they were standing apart, waiting for them. Before either of them could speak, Gijs remarked placidly:

'I was just telling Serena that it was a good thing I know you so well, Laurens, or I might take exception to you kissing my girl.' He spoke deliberately and Laurens answered him a little too quickly.

'Hullo, there. Serena, how lovely to see you—if I'd known you wanted to come into town I would have come back for you instead of working. I've almost finished, though.' He didn't look at Gijs but smiled at her charmingly so that her doubts melted away. 'You two girls haven't met—Adriana—Serena,' he waved an introductory hand. 'You saw each other last night. I can't think how you missed meeting...'

Serena put out a small hand and shook the rather languid one offered her, and she smiled with real friendliness because this beautiful creature was Gijs's girl, not some romantic attachment of Laurens's. This must have been what Laurens meant when they were talking about Gijs on the previous afternoon. She said with pleasure: 'How nice to meet you—I've been wondering who you were.'

The girl stared at her and for a moment didn't answer, but Serena didn't notice. 'We mustn't keep you and Gijs—I hope you haven't had to wait too long.' She smiled at Laurens as she spoke and the girl said uncertainly:

'No, we didn't.'

Gijs interrupted her. 'The car's in front of the house,' he told her easily. 'We shall be late if we don't go at once.' He was staring at her very hard and Serena, seeing the look, decided that perhaps he was one of those men who hid their real feelings under a façade of laziness, because at the moment he looked curiously tense, almost anxious. But she turned away when Laurens said: 'What about tea? I've almost finished, I can do the rest later—we'll walk back through the town, if you like.'

They split up, and as she accompanied Laurens across the street at the head of the canal she turned round to look at the others. They hadn't moved; Adriana was talking animatedly, or so it appeared from that distance, and Gijs was standing quietly, listening. Something about his attitude gave her the absurd idea that he was in a towering rage. She smiled at the thought because it was so ridiculous.

She forgot all about it during the next two days, for Laurens devoted himself to her, and his mother, while not showing any warmth towards her, at least fulfilled her duties as hostess. Serena, thinking over her days as she prepared for bed, had to admit that she had no fault to find with the older woman's manner; indeed she was fast coming to the conclusion that she was cold by nature and her rather distant treatment of herself was quite natural to her. She hadn't seen Gijs at all, and when she mentioned him idly to Laurens she was told rather shortly that he was busy with the practice. 'He's doing the lion's share at present,' he went on. 'He likes work, though you wouldn't think it to see him, would you?'

She had been there just over a week when Laurens told her that he would have to be away all day, leaving in the morning and not getting back until the evening. 'Hospital,' he said vaguely. 'Lectures and so forth, to keep us up to date, you know.'

Serena nodded. She knew all about the courses the GPs went to—it was done in England too. 'What about your patients?' she asked.

'Oh, Gijs will keep an eye on them. What will you do?'

'I don't know, but don't worry about me—I think I'll spend a lazy day in the garden.' She missed his frown, but when she looked at him he smiled at her. 'Not worry about my gipsy girl? Don't be silly. I know! Pieter Willems—you remember meeting him the other day? he's going to Utrecht tomorrow. How about going with him? You can potter round and he'll bring you back in the evening. Mother will be out all day, it couldn't fit in better.'

'But I don't know him very well—I really don't mind…'

He brushed her objections aside. 'Rubbish—I insist. I'll go and telephone him now.'

So it was settled, if not to Serena's satisfaction, at

least to Laurens's. She would be picked up the next morning at nine o'clock and brought home again in plenty of time for dinner in the evening.

She was having a solitary breakfast the next morning when Sieska came to tell her that there was a telephone message for her and when she went to answer it, it was Pieter who spoke. The trip was off, he explained in his careful English. His sister, with whom he lived, had developed a temperature during the night—Gijs had been and diagnosed 'flu and he didn't like to leave her—and would Serena forgive him?

She finished her breakfast and wandered aimlessly up to her room. She would have to do something with her day, Laurens had been so insistent that she should spend the day out that possibly Sieska was to have a day off as well. She went and fetched her handbag, patted her already tidy hair and went slowly downstairs; she would tell Sieska that she would be out all day. It was still only half past nine; the day stretched endlessly before her.

Gijs was in the hall. He stood relaxed as always, with the sunlight streaming through the open door on to him, and Serena, pausing on the stairs, saw what a handsome man he was, and how elegant in his conventional grey suiting—it was funny that she hadn't noticed when they had first met, even though he had been wearing tweeds. He said without preamble:

'Hullo, you're at a loose end, I gather from Pieter. I wondered if you would like to come with me on my rounds and then have lunch? I've an hour or so to spare this afternoon, and I should like you to see my house.'

Serena advanced towards him. Just then, at that moment, she liked him very much, for in a few words he had filled the long day for her without fuss or hesitation.

'Oh, I'd like that,' she said happily. 'May I really come with you? I won't be in the way?'

'No—I daresay you will have to sit in the car for quite a time, but you can listen to the radio, or go for a stroll. I haven't many calls.'

She smiled up at him. 'I was just wondering what I was going to do with myself all day and you turned up—I'm so glad. I'm ready whenever you are.'

He turned on his heel and led her out to the Bentley and she got in beside him, feeling all at once perfectly at ease with him.

'Dreishor—you've not been there yet? Only a village, but it's built in a complete circle round a rather lovely old building which is Town Hall, school—everything, in fact. The church is interesting too. You could wander round while I see my patient.'

'There's no doctor in the village?'

'Oh, yes, but he's on holiday, so I am standing in for him.'

'But aren't you busy? Laurens isn't doing a full day's work yet, is he, and today he's had to go on this course.'

He didn't hurry with his answer and when he did it was really no answer.

'There's not much illness at this time of year,' he commented, 'there are always cases in the hospital though and a certain amount of work with the tourists. Here we are.'

The village was exactly as he had described it. She did as he had told her, strolling round the cobbled circle, viewing the church and the trees around it and the Town Hall standing in its circle of grass and flower beds. She passed the doctor's house too, and the village shops, pausing to look in their small windows, and sure enough when she reached the car again, Gijs was waiting for her.

'Coffee,' he said, and took her into the low-storied hotel which made up part of the circle of houses. It was cool and quiet inside and she would have liked to have sat over her coffee, just idly talking. Gijs—she admitted to herself that she had known it already—was an easy man to talk to. But he had other calls to make and she knew better than to hinder him. They got into the car once more and took the road to Brouwershaven and half-way there, across the flat green fields, he turned off into a lane leading to one of the farms standing well back from the road.

'I shan't be long,' he told her, and was back within five minutes. 'A post-hospital case,' he explained, 'an appendix, doing very nicely now.'

He turned the big car and went back to the road to repeat the process several times, for most of the farms stood isolated in their fields.

'Now,' he said, 'we'll go back to Zierikzee for lunch—there's a short cut—it will take only fifteen minutes or so.'

He was as good as his word, well within that time they were going through the town gate and a moment later he slid to a gentle halt in front of the Mondragon restaurant.

They had a table by the window, and Gijs, from the attention he got, was obviously a well-known client. They talked as they ate, pleasant effortless conversation which lasted throughout the meal—Serena, later on, couldn't remember a word of it, only that it had been pleasant and restful and somehow reassuring. She had followed the chicken in Madeira sauce by a fresh fruit salad and coffee, and it was more than an hour later when Gijs suggested that she might like to see his house.

They entered through its massive front door; the hall was long and narrow with double doors on the left of them and half a dozen wide, shallow stairs on one side which ended in a wide archway, hiding, Serena guessed, the rest of the staircase. At the back of the hall was another archway, leading no doubt, to the kitchen. The floor was carpeted with a crimson carpet of great richness, soft and thick, and the walls were panelled to the plastered ceiling. The whole effect was surprisingly warm and welcoming.

'In here,' directed Gijs, and led her through the double doors into a large, high-ceilinged room, whose wide windows were curtained with apricot velvet. The floor was of highly polished wood blocks with a many-coloured carpet upon it. The furniture was a pleasing mixture of the comfortable and the antique, for the chairs were large and deep and well cushioned, upholstered in various shades of brown and apricot and peacock blue, and two or three of them were covered in needlework in a mixture of all these colours. There was a cabinet between the windows, with a brecciated marble top, its doors covered with superb marquetry, there was a Delft bowl upon it, filled with roses. Against the opposite wall was a console table, strewn with magazines, and above the great chimneypiece was a landscape, pale and vague and restful.

'What a lovely room,' breathed Serena, and her gaze went to the ceiling. 'Isn't that called strap work?'

'Yes—there's a painted ceiling in the next room.' He led the way to a door beside the fireplace. 'This is what we call a *tussen kamer*, a between room, it leads to the sitting-room beyond. Normally it doesn't have windows, but you see we have a small one. I use this room for entertaining, for it's not too large. I seldom use the drawing-room.' He smiled at her. 'I expect that when I marry, it will be used more often.'

His words gave her a curiously lost sensation which she ignored.

Later, when they had tea in the garden, lolling on the grass in the most comfortable manner and talking about nothing in particular, she looked up to surprise an expression on his face which she had never seen before, so unlike his usual placid calm that she forgot what she was about to say and asked instead: 'Why do you look like that?'

'Like what?' The look had gone—the bleak sternness she had seen; he was smiling lazily at her, his drooping lids hiding his eyes.

She said hesitatingly, still uncertain and feeling shy again and how could she feel shy with Gijs, that most comfortable of companions?—'Well, I'm not sure—angry? Did I say something to annoy you?'

'Heavens, no! I must have had a twinge of gout.'

She had to laugh then, and German the dog came and joined them where they were lying under a walnut tree and her odd, insecure moment was lost in the gentle pleasures of the afternoon.

But the feeling of shyness persisted; she had never been so aware of Gijs and he had done nothing to make her so. It bothered her, so much so that they had barely finished their tea when she declared that she would like to go back to Laurens's home, a declaration which was strengthened by the fleeting look of annoyance on Gijs's face. For some reason he didn't want her to go, but all he said was: 'Oh, come now, you can't go yet. You haven't met Lien and Jaap—they have an hour or so off each afternoon, they'll be back presently and they'll never forgive me if I let you go without meeting them.'

She was momentarily diverted. 'Oh? Then who was it brought the tea?'

'That is Wil, she comes in for a few hours a day.' He added, still persisting: 'Laurens won't be back until six at least and Tante Emilie has gone to Rosendaal, hasn't she? Stay another hour or two.'

He smiled at her invitingly and she was conscious of a strong desire to remain, for she was enjoying herself; she thought a little guiltily that she hadn't meant to, not quite as much as she had done, anyway. Almost subconsciously she found herself comparing Gijs's undemanding company with Laurens, whose volatile moods she had learned to watch for and who liked a cheerful companion who was always ready to sparkle and laugh at everything. Gijs, she considered, would be a wonderful person to have around if one had a headache or felt low—a disloyal idea she doused at once, even while a voice at the back of her mind told her clearly that even if it was disloyal it was also true.

All the same, she got to her feet, and even the advent of Lien and Jaap, elderly and kindly and deeply devoted to Gijs, could not keep her for long, and when Gijs saw that she was quite determined, he said no more but took her outside to the car and shut her carefully in and went round to his own seat and got in beside her, all very slowly. He didn't hurry back to Laurens's home either, but the journey was so short it took barely five minutes. At the gates she said firmly: 'Please stop here, there's no need for you to come any further. Thank you for a simply gorgeous day.' She smiled at him, touched him fleetingly on the arm, and got out of the car.

The gates were open, so she walked through them towards the house, turning once to wave to Gijs, who, for some reason, had got out of the car and was standing, doing nothing, beside it. She was almost at the front door when she heard voices and crossed the sanded drive to peer through the thick screen of shrubbery which bordered the garden. Laurens was there, so was Adriana. They were standing together—more than together, Serena's shocked brain registered. Adriana was in Laurens's arms and he was kissing her, and somehow Serena knew that this wasn't a chance meeting for them. Without wanting to do so, she stood, her sandalled feet rooted to the ground. There seemed no end to the kiss. She drew a long, difficult breath and suddenly released from her intolerable immobility, turned and flew back the way she had come, back through the gate—if only Gijs would be there!

He was. She flung herself at him and burst into tears.

CHAPTER FIVE

His arms felt comforting, but she hardly noticed that. When she had her breath again she declared savagely: 'You knew—why did you let me come back?'

If he found her question unfair he didn't remark upon it. 'If you remember,' he reminded her evenly, 'you insisted upon coming—I tried my best to make you stay.'

She swallowed tears and snatched the handkerchief he had thoughtfully offered to mop her face. 'But you know—about Laurens and Adriana—they're—they're...' she refused to finish the sentence. 'How long?'

When he didn't answer she banged his chest with her small clenched fist and said loudly: 'You're glad, aren't you? You never wanted me to come to Holland.'

She felt his hands on her shoulders and she was made to face him.

'You're quite wrong,' he told her gently. 'I was delighted that you came, but for all the wrong reasons. Look, you're upset. You know what we're going to do? You're coming back with me; you shall wash your face and comb your hair and I shall give you a drink, and you will sit quietly while I take evening surgery, and when that's finished I'll take you back again. You'll feel better by then—this is perhaps what you call a flash in the pan—you must give Laurens a chance to explain. I'm not qualified to give advice, but if you could forget the whole thing—' His grey eyes searched

105

hers. 'If Laurens loves you,' he went on slowly, 'everything will be all right, for everyone.'

He was right, of course. She nodded and sniffed forlornly. 'I'm sorry I said that,' she managed. 'I don't think I really knew what I was saying—you would never have been so unkind,' and then gasped as he answered pleasantly: 'Oh, but I would—I am. I didn't know that they would be there, although I imagined there might be a possibility, but since they were and you have seen them together, so much the better. Nothing is so bad if it is brought into the open.' He smiled a little, almost as though he had made a joke. 'Come along,' he said, and took her arm.

She wondered what Lien and Jaap thought when they arrived back at his house five minutes later, but she didn't really care. Lien took her upstairs to one of the lovely bedrooms and left her alone, throwing open a door to disclose a bathroom before she went. Serena, left to herself, took down her hair and washed her face and resolutely made it up again; she wasn't going to cry any more. It would probably be just as Gijs had said—a flash in the pan. When she was ready she went out on to the landing and started down the stairs, and Gij's voice called from the sitting-room: 'In here, Serena—I've five minutes before surgery.'

He barely looked at her as she went in but handed her the drink and waved her to a chair. She perched on the edge of it and took a sip, then asked, for something to say: 'I thought the surgery was in the town.'

'So it is—a couple of minutes in the car, and it won't matter if I'm a few minutes late for once.' He smiled at her vaguely and got up to let German in from the garden. Serena, her numbed brain warmed by the sherry, asked him: 'The other afternoon on the bridge—I've just this minute remembered—you said Adriana was your girl...'

He stood up and set his glass on one of the tables. 'Lies, wicked lies,' he observed with calm. 'Couldn't think of anything else to say on the spur of the moment.' He was already at the door. 'I'll be back within the hour,' he told her, and was gone.

When Gijs returned he drove right up to the house and got out with her, and with a reassuring hand on her shoulder, propelled her into the house. In the ensuing greetings, explanations and exchange of the day's news Serena found it necessary to say very little; Gijs seemed to be doing it all with a casual tact she hadn't expected of him. He went away after half an hour, waving a careless hand at her but saying nothing, and she waved back, feeling utterly lost.

But that night, in bed, she realized that she had no need to feel that either, for Laurens, despite what had passed between himself and Adriana, hadn't changed in his manner towards her at all. True, he didn't know that she had seen them, but he was full of plans—vague ones, but still plans, and full, too, of pretty little compliments, the kind a girl would expect to receive from a man who loved her. Serena, her head in a complete muddle and exhausted with so much to worry about, finally went to sleep.

She saw a great deal of Laurens in the next day or so and nothing at all of Gijs. Perhaps he had been right after all and there was nothing to worry about. She wrote letters to her friends at Queen's, struggled with the headlines in the Dutch newspapers and made conversation with her hostess, and tried desperately to forget Laurens and Adriana kissing each other in the garden, and almost succeeded. It was her hostess who shattered her hard-won sense of security.

They had taken their coffee into the garden because it was such a lovely morning and Serena had painstakingly talked about all the suitable subjects she could call to mind, when her companion inquired in a gentle voice:

'And when do you leave us, Serena?'

A leading question, thought Serena, and sought for the right answer. Either her hostess was unaware that she was entertaining her future daughter-in-law, or she had set her face against her son marrying. 'Well,' began Serena, thinking hard and aware of panic beginning to knot her breath, 'I…'

'You see, my dear, although I have no wish to see you go, you must see for yourself that with Laurens's approaching marriage to Adriana—you did meet her, did you not?—it would hardly do for you to be here. I mean…'

'What exactly do you mean?' Serena's voice, by some gigantic effort on her part, was quite steady.

'Why, it would look strange, you understand? I know Laurens has been delighted to have you here—he was, and is still, so grateful for all your kindness to him in hospital, but he's a very impressionable young man,' she smiled at Serena as though they might share a little joke about this side of his character. 'But I'm sure you are a most sensible young woman.' She waited for Serena to agree and when she didn't, went on:

'You do not perhaps know that Laurens is from *adel*—Adriana also.'

'And what,' asked Serena woodenly, 'is *adel*?'

'The nobility—Laurens is a *jonkheer*. In Holland

adel marry *adel*.' The words were said with a satisfied finality as though an undisputed fact had been stated which clinched the matter. Indeed, the speaker seemed to think that the matter had been clinched, for she went on smoothly:

'The weather has been perfect for your visit. How fortunate you have been, Serena. This warmth is really quite exceptional.'

And Serena, sick with humiliation and misery and anger, agreed in a terse little voice. She even enlarged upon the varieties of weather they had had, were having, and might expect to have in the near future. She then excused herself on the plea of letters to write and went to her room. She still felt sick, but when she looked at herself in the mirror, she looked a little pale and that was all; she had expected to see a drawn, haggard face, crisscrossed with lines of unhappiness. She re-did her face with care, for it gave her something to do and time to think. Later, when Laurens came home, she would talk to him and find out if what his mother had said was true. There was the chance that she had merely wished to discourage her from marrying him, and if Laurens really loved her, despite Adriana, it would be his chance to put things right. She had been surprised by her hostess's remarks about the nobility, but in this modern age, she argued to herself, it was surely not as important as all that.

She stayed in her room until lunchtime and arrived downstairs just as Laurens came into the house.

Before he could say anything at all, she said quickly: 'I'd like to talk to you, Laurens—now; it's important. It won't take long—could we go somewhere?'

He looked a little taken aback and then said readily enough: 'In here,' and opened the sitting-room door and ushered her in. He closed it carefully behind him and walked towards her.

'Stay there,' said Serena sharply. 'I was told by your mother this morning that you and Adriana are going to be married. I just want to hear from you that it's true, that's all. You see, I thought you were going to marry me.' It pleased her very much that her voice sounded so quiet and steady. She looked at his face and knew what the answer was going to be, for he looked, for a brief moment, ashamed at himself, but only for a moment.

'Well, gipsy girl, it wouldn't have worked out—us, I mean. I know I hinted, and just for a little while...but I never asked you to marry me. I told you not to fuss about that, didn't I? If I've been thoughtless—I'm sorry, and I was going to tell you about Adriana...' He smiled at her, his old, charming smile, 'No hard feelings, eh? I suppose I should have explained, but we were having such a good time and I suppose I didn't think you were quite so serious—no harm done, though.'

Serena stared at him speechlessly. It seemed to her that quite a lot of harm had been done—a broken heart and broken pride and no job any more; she realized then that he could never have known how she felt about him; for him it had been a jolly little affair, with Adriana, secure in her future, waiting until he was ready to settle down. Serena closed her eyes against the shame welling up inside her and without a word went out of the room before Laurens could do anything about it. She went out of the house as well. She heard him calling after her as she ran through the gates. If he chose to come after her, he would have to get the car from the garage first, for it wasn't outside the door and she didn't think he would come after her. His leg prevented him, for one thing.

Zierikzee was very small and she had nowhere to go. She had slowed to a walk because people might wonder what was the matter to see her tearing down the quiet road as though the devil were after her, although there were few people about; they were all having their dinners. She had reached the Noordhavenpoort by now, and began to walk faster, because of course she had somewhere to go and someone to go to—Gijs.

Jaap let her in when she banged the brass knocker, took one look at her face and led her through the house and out into the garden. Gijs was round the corner, outside the old wing. He was sitting on an upturned bucket, in his shirtsleeves, sucking at a pipe. When he saw her, he said:

'Hullo, I rather expected you,' and then spoke to Jaap in Dutch, pulled out another bucket from the wall and added: 'Sit down, make yourself comfortable.'

She sat obediently and he followed suit, and so they remained for several minutes, with Serena fighting tears and Gijs apparently content to ponder about nothing at all with closed eyes.

'He's going to marry Adriana,' Serena told him at last in a small tight voice. 'I didn't believe his mother when she told me, but then he came home and I asked him.' Her voice wobbled alarmingly and rose a little. 'He—he—so I ran away.'

'Very sensible of you. Now take a deep breath, dear girl, and tell me exactly what has happened.'

She did so, leaving nothing out. 'I didn't know about Laurens being a *jonkheer*—is it important? His mother said...'

'Not important at all, at least not in this day and age, but my aunt belongs to another generation—she sets great store upon such things.'

'Then why didn't Laurens…?'

He answered her with kindly patience. 'Laurens has behaved very badly—he's not a bad man, Serena, but he has a marked predilection for pretty girls. Anyone else but you…' He paused. 'You made a mistake, Serena—not of your own fault, let us admit, but now you must face up to it and then forget it. It will hurt at first, but not for long, that I can promise you.'

She felt the hurt bite deep into her as he spoke and a tear spilled down her cheek. 'That's right,' said Gijs comfortably, 'have a good weep—we can't talk until you have.' He put out an arm and pulled her head down on to his shoulder.

It was a great comfort to be able to cry and know that he didn't mind in the least; she sniffed and gulped and wept until she had no more tears left, and when he saw that she had at last finished, he pushed her back gently on to her bucket and got up from his own, stretched enormously, and then sat down again as though the exercise had exhausted him.

'And what are you going to do?' he inquired in the mildest of voices.

'I don't know.' She made her voice calm.

'In that case, might I suggest that you marry me?'

Serena turned her blotched face to his and gaped at him, and when she had her outraged breath again, said furiously: 'How dare you!'

'Well, yes,' he agreed placidly, 'that is something I ask myself, but I can't see anything against it, can you?'

He turned calm grey eyes to her flashing ones while

she went on struggling for sufficient breath to answer him as he deserved. 'There are heaps of reasons,' she managed furiously. 'For one thing, we don't—don't...'

'Love each other?' he supplied with no trace of embarrassment. 'My dear Serena, how like a woman to see difficulties where there are none! We like each other—at least, I believe you have overcome your dislike of me. You need, how shall I put it? a safe anchorage, and I need someone to keep an eye on Lien and Jaap and German, and myself of course, and to help in the surgery in emergencies, listen patiently and with intelligence when I need to air my views on some knotty problem—and someone to share my table, but not, I hasten to add, my bed.'

Serena's face flamed. 'Not—not...' she spluttered.

'Certainly not. Oh, let me set your boggling mind at rest. I'm a perfectly normal man, but hardly an impulsive one. I should wish our marriage to be a friendly and businesslike arrangement, at least until such time as you—we—should have got to know each other really well. One might call it an engagement, only with the difference that we should be married. There would be one proviso, of course; that should you find a man you loved, you would tell me at once, so that the necessary steps could be taken.'

She opened her mouth to utter, but he lifted a languid hand. 'No, dear girl, wait until I have finished. I don't agree with easy divorce, marriage for me should be for always, but in our case I think it would hurt no one since our feelings would be untouched.'

Serena digested this in silence; presently she said slowly: 'Yes, but you—what about you? Would you tell me?'

She looked at him and saw, to her great annoyance,

that he had closed his eyes, apparently exhausted by so much conversation. She raised her voice and said loudly: 'Well?'

He opened one eye. 'Dear Serena, I sowed my wild oats some time since—I'm far too busy for girls.'

'But I'm a girl.' It was ridiculous how indignant she felt.

He started to fill his pipe. 'Ah, yes—so you are, but I hardly think of you in general terms.'

She watched him light his pipe and waited for him to go on speaking, but he didn't; it seemed he had said all he intended to say. He puffed gently, his eyes half shut, which vexed her because it meant she would have to say something. 'It's a ridiculous idea,' she stated flatly and a little too loudly. 'Besides, if I lived here I should see Laurens...'

'So you would,' he agreed quietly. 'You would also be my wife.' He got to his feet for the second time. 'Think it over—it's not as ridiculous as it sounds.'

'Ridiculous? It's crazy—how can I bear to meet him and see him with...?'

For a split second the calm face above her changed to a stark, grim mask and in the same brief time was calm again. 'It won't be as bad as all that. You would have quite a busy life, you know. When you meet there will be other people there; you'll not need to see Laurens alone, unless you wish.'

'I never want to see him again,' she declared with a woman's fine logic, and burst into tears again.

Gijs pulled her gently to her feet and held her close. 'Now, now,' he spoke with firm kindliness, 'that's enough of the watering pot. We're going to have lunch and then I shall telephone Laurens and ask him to see that someone packs your things and leaves them here.'

'But I can't stay here!' She was startled out of her tears.

'Certainly not,' he agreed promptly. 'I've my reputation to consider. I shall take you to my mother.'

Serena stared at him, her mouth lamentably open again. 'Your mother? I didn't know you had one.'

'It's usual,' he remarked. 'I have a father too. I'll drive you over to their house before evening surgery and fit in my visits on the way back.'

'But I can't stay there.'

'You'll like it,' he was quite certain about that, she saw, 'and as soon as I can fix things this end I'll take you back to your home and you can meditate quietly about marrying me.'

She didn't know whether to laugh or cry again. In the end she achieved a damp smile and he said instantly: 'That's better. Come into the house, I'll pour the drinks while you effect repairs.'

He took her arm and drew her into the sitting-room through its open door, then marched her across into the hall where he shouted for Lien. Serena, waiting quietly beside him for Lien to appear, asked doubtfully:

'Did you mean all the things you said?'

'Every blessed word,' he assured her.

They lunched in the dining-room, at the back of the house and which she hadn't seen before. It was a pleasant room with windows overlooking the garden and well-polished mahogany furniture. It was a pity that Serena had no appetite at all, but she did her best and was grateful to Gijs for saying nothing about herself; instead, he talked idly about the town and the weather and the sailing which he enjoyed when he had the time, interrupting himself to say: 'I should have added crewing to my—er—needs.' He smiled so kindly at her that she wanted to cry again; instead she asked: 'How am I to tell my mother and father?'

'Why, write to them—you can do it now, while I'm arranging for your things to be sent over, and if I may I will write too. It shouldn't be too much of a shock—they have met me.'

She choked a little. 'You talk as though we were going to...'

'But we are, my dear, surprising though it may seem to you. When you have had time to think it over, I believe you may find the idea not unpleasant.'

'I don't know you,' she muttered miserably.

'Did you know Laurens? And you were ready to marry him. Did he ever ask you to marry him, Serena?' and when she flushed painfully, 'I shouldn't have asked that, but you have been living in a dream world of your own for several weeks; the real world won't be quite so hard, you know.' He grinned suddenly. 'I shall be a very good husband, and I do need someone to help in the surgery—my nurse is getting married shortly.'

Serena found herself laughing. 'You're ridiculous! You'll be telling me next that that's why you asked me to marry you.'

'Well, that wouldn't be quite true—I've told you my reasons for wanting to marry you—most of them anyway. I dare say we shall discover even more as we go along.'

'You won't hurry me for an answer?'

'No, but don't come over coy and wait for me to ask you again because I'm not going to. You can tell me when you're ready.' He smiled at her, 'And now write that letter while I telephone.'

Sitting beside him in the car an hour or so later, she reflected on the ease with which Gijs had seen to everything; her bags had arrived very soon after he had telephoned and if there had been a message with them he hadn't given it to her, and she didn't want to hear it. She had written her letter too, wasting a great deal of notepaper in the composing of it, and he had stowed it in his pocket to post on his way back. And now they were on their way to Renesse, where, it seemed, his parents lived. She had driven through it with Laurens and all she could remember of it was an hotel called The Pub, which they had laughed about together. The thought of that laughter almost drove her to tears again, but she held them back and asked: 'Is your father a doctor too?'

'Yes—he's more or less retired, though; he's getting on for seventy. He married rather late in life—he waited until he found the right girl.' He shot her a quick glance. 'He gives the occasional anaesthetic at the hospital and takes over the practice for me when I go away.'

'Oh, I should have thought that Laurens…'

'It's a large practice,' he told her gently.

They went through the pleasant little town of Renesse and out the other side, where the country was wooded and the houses, standing apart from each other, were hidden from the road. Gijs turned up a narrow lane leading towards the sea and without looking at her said:

'Don't be nervous, they're expecting us. I've told Mother that we are thinking of getting married but that it's still in the air.'

Serena clenched her hands on her handbag. 'You're being so kind,' she began, and was stopped by his easy: 'It would hardly do to show unkindness towards my future wife, would it?'

An answer she felt she should dispute because she hadn't said yet that she would marry him, but somehow she couldn't be bothered to argue, and now there was no time, for he had turned into a gateway and was driving slowly between trees along a sanded drive which presently unwound itself into a wide space before a comfortably sized house, red-tiled and gabled and not very old, and as though Serena had voiced her thought, Gijs observed: 'Not old, you see. My great-grandfather rebuilt it on the tumbledown ruins of the first one. We rarely came here while my father was in practice, but now he prefers to live here.'

They were out of the car by this time and he tucked a hand under her arm and kept it there as they went through the open front door.

The hall was surprisingly roomy with a staircase at its back with a little half landing and wings branching off each side from it. It was furnished in great good taste with a Regency wall table, two comfortable chairs upholstered in mulberry velvet and a grandfather clock. There seemed to be a great many doors leading from it, several of them half open, which made the house seem to welcome whoever was entering it. One of these doors was thrown wide now and a small woman, no taller than Serena, darted out. She was elderly with a still pretty face and her hair, streaked with grey, was ebony black.

She began to talk before she had reached them, in a clear high voice and in English, which, while strongly accented, was readily understandable.

'Gijs, dear boy, you are here, and with the so pretty Serena—and how glad we are to welcome you to our home.' She paused and stood on tiptoe to kiss her son and then turned to Serena and kissed her cheek too.

'You do not mind if I do this? I hear of you from Gijs and I know you already,' she beamed at them both, 'and my English is not so good, but it will improve. Come inside, there is tea, and you will stop a little while, Gijs?'

'Half an hour, Mama—I can't spare more time. Where's Vader?'

'In the cellar to fetch the sherry he keeps for just such an occasion as this one.' She smiled at Serena and said with great kindness: 'It is not often that we have so lovely a visitor.'

She bustled over to the small fold-down table beside one of the easy chairs in the sitting-room, upon which a tea tray was ready, and Serena, pushed gently into a small chair covered with exquisite needlework, gave an unconscious sigh; it was all rather like being at home. The welcome had been warm and sincere, and the room, furnished with the same delicately balanced mixture of antique and comfortable as in Gijs's house, had just the same feeling of homeliness. She looked up and caught Gijs's eyes upon her and smiled at him just as the door opened and his father came into the room. It was Gijs, of course—Gijs in thirty years' time, just as tall and broad but a little heavier, with eyes just as grey and heavy-lidded, only his hair was white and his pace was slower. They even shared the same voice, she discovered, when the older man crossed the room to shake her hand and bid her welcome before going to sit with his son over their tea and enter at once into earnest conversation in their own language, leaving her to be entertained by his wife, who having poured the tea, sat down beside her, saying cheerfully: 'The men, when they are together, always it is their patients and medicine and surgery—I am married a long time, but never do I get used to this talk,' her eyes twinkled kindly. 'You are a lucky girl, Serena, that you have experience of these things so that you do not shock.'

Serena drank her tea from the fragile china cup her hostess had offered her and agreed, and her companion went on happily: 'How I shall enjoy your visit; I always wished for a daughter to talk women's talk, you know—I hope that you will stay with us for a long time.' She turned round in her chair, reminding Serena forcibly of a small brown wren because her movements were so quick and so unpredictable. 'Gijs, you do not take Serena to England at once?'

He got up and came over to her chair and put an affectionate hand on her shoulder. 'Not immediately, Mama, but in two or three days' time. I have been arranging things with Vader. And now I must go. I'll be back tomorrow, but I shall be at the hospital, so I may be delayed.'

She patted his hand. 'Come when you like, my dear. We shall take good care of Serena, of that you may be sure, only it is a pity you are not here to drink the sherry.'

He laughed softly. 'I'll have a glass tomorrow, dearest.' He bent and kissed her, smiled briefly at Serena and went away. She heard the Bentley's subdued purr as he drove away; the sound made her feel very alone.

A feeling immediately dispelled by her host and hostess who at once engaged her in conversation, plied her with more tea and then took her upstairs to a small, pretty bedroom where Doctor van Amstel put her bags down and left his wife sitting in the chair by the window, talking to Serena while she unpacked. Presently she got up, saying that dinner would be in an hour and

would Serena come down when she was ready, and
went away too, and Serena was alone.

Several times during that afternoon she had longed
to be by herself. Now she was, and rather to her own
surprise instead of brooding over Laurens she found
her head full of the astonishing events of that same
afternoon. She still hadn't got over the surprise of
Gijs's proposal, but it now no longer seemed quite as
preposterous or so absurd. She wasn't sure how it had
come about, but he had been quite right when he had
told her that she didn't dislike him any more—indeed,
upon reflection she had to admit that she liked him
quite a lot, and what was more, was quite at ease with
him, just as she felt quite at ease with his parents,
which considering that she had just met them, seemed
extraordinary.

She changed her dress and did her hair and face, then
went downstairs rather thoughtfully, to meet her host's
kindly talk and her hostess's motherly preoccupation
with her comfort. They drank the sherry and dined,
waited upon by an elderly woman, very thin and tall,
who was introduced as Maagda, and who smiled at her
with great sweetness.

The rest of the evening was so like an evening in
Serena's own home that she could not help but feel the
comfort and security around her. There was a little conversation, the news to be watched on TV, and explained for her benefit and then discussed, the decision
to give her breakfast in bed, and finally, the gentle urging to go to bed, something she had been dreading.

In her room she undressed and bathed and finally
got into bed, and because she was afraid to lie in the
dark and think, she sat up against the square pillows,
turning the pages of a magazine someone had thought-

fully provided. She had been doing this for some ten minutes when there was a tap on the door and Gijs's mother came in.

'Not asleep,' she said with satisfaction. 'I think to myself, first Serena must talk and I shall listen and if she wishes, say nothing, and when she is empty of words, she will sleep.' She perched in a chair, folded her still pretty hands in her lap and went on, 'I think that Gijs wishes to marry you and I hope that you will marry him, but even if this is not so, if you want to tell me what happens today I will listen as a friend, you understand. That is what Gijs would wish.'

Serena had listened silently to her hostess. No wonder Gijs was such a dear with a mother like that; she was reminded forcibly of her own mother who would have offered the same brisk comfort and genuine sympathy. She had told it all to Gijs, but his mother was right, to tell it all again would be such a relief. She began without preamble, right from the very beginning.

When she had finished she asked rather forlornly: 'Does it matter so much that Laurens is—what is the word? *adel*?—or was it just an excuse?'

The little lady in the chair allowed herself a smile. 'It is important to my sister-in-law, you understand. She is, how do you say—too proud, therefore we are not such good friends. It was always the custom in Holland for those families from *adel* to marry amongst themselves, and still is, perhaps, but it is no longer so important—for me, it is of not the least importance.' She broke off to smile at Serena, 'Gijs is also *jonkheer*, as is his father.'

Serena sighed. 'Oh, dear—I didn't know. Well, that settles it. I could never marry him, it would look as though…'

She was halted by her hostess who fixed her with a compelling eye and declared: 'We are proud to welcome so lovely a girl into the family and with a good man of the church for a father. There could be no wife more suitable for my son.'

Serena jumped out of bed and knelt beside her hostess. It was, she felt, absolutely necessary to be honest with her, she was far too nice to pretend to. Besides, she was Gijs's mother he was nice too. 'I don't love Gijs,' she stated baldly.

To her astonishment, his mother agreed with her. 'Of course you don't—how would that be possible when you love Laurens? But love does not last unless it is cared for; it will die and you will have a whole heart again to give to Gijs.'

'But he said—he doesn't want...'

His mother bent forward and kissed her lightly. 'Men talk nonsense, my dear. It is for us women to know what they want. Now you will go to sleep, yes? and tomorrow is another day, Serena.'

So Serena got back into bed and her hostess bade her good night and darted away, closing the door silently behind her. Serena, lying in the dark, listened to her feet pattering down the stairs and was asleep almost before they had died away in the hall below.

She was given no opportunity to brood in the morning; her breakfast was brought to her and she had barely finished it when Maagda came to tell her that there was a telephone call for her.

Laurens, she thought immediately—he would apologize, he would... All the way down to the sitting-room she rehearsed what she would say, but when she picked up the receiver, Gijs said at once: 'No, it's not, Serena. Did you sleep?'

She swallowed bitter disappointment and at the same time was happy to hear his voice. 'Yes—yes, very well, thank you. How did you know…?'

'Perhaps because I know you better than you know yourself.'

She murmured, 'Oh,' rather at a loss, and asked if he was busy.

'Yes. Will you tell Mother that I'll be out for dinner this evening? Enjoy your day.'

He rang off, leaving her with the feeling that she had been done out of a pleasant chat, but of course he was busy, he had said so. She went back to her room and dressed, then went downstairs again to find her host and hostess in the garden. Doctor van Amstel was grooming an elderly Alsatian, his wife was cutting roses. They stopped these occupations as she crossed the lawn to reach them and Jongvrouw van Amstel, putting down her trug, said: 'There, here is Serena, and feeling rested, I hope. We will do the flowers together and then I will show you our home and perhaps you would like to take a little walk with the doctor after the coffee, of course.'

It was nice to have her morning planned for her, Serena helped with the roses in a dim, faintly damp room at the back of the house and carried them into the sitting-room and then, after a leisurely tour of the house, sat by the open window and drank her coffee while the doctor discoursed on politics, the weather and the state of the garden. Presently he declared that he was ready to take her and Biscuit, the Alsatian, for a walk, and they set off.

Their way led through a gate at the end of the garden and along a path across the wooded land behind the dunes. They had walked in silence for a few minutes when Doctor van Amstel told her: 'Laurens telephoned this morning—he wanted to see you. I told him that I would tell you and that you would decide if you wished to see him. I hope I did right, Serena.'

She had stopped walking and stood staring at nothing. In the quiet around her she could almost hear her heart beating with painful rapidity. 'Thank you,' she managed, 'I think I'd rather not see Laurens, at least not yet.' She had a sudden splendid vision of herself, cool and gracious, and Gijs's wife, greeting Laurens with friendly charm at some party or other, and wondered if it would really be like that. But she hadn't decided yet if she would marry Gijs. She started to walk again and the doctor fell in beside her. 'A wise decision,' he commented, and following her own train of thought she said: 'You don't know me.'

'I know my son, my dear. If we turn left here there is an excellent view.'

The day passed quietly, through its hours, and Serena, fighting hurt and unhappiness, struggled through them as best she might, undoubtedly helped by her companions, who took care not to leave her alone to mope. Indeed, it wasn't until she was in her room changing her cotton dress for something a little more formal for the evening that she realized that that was the first time she had been alone, and although she longed to give way to her overwrought feelings, she was bound to admit that their strategy had worked. There was no point in crying for crying's sake; the quicker she put a cheerful face on the future, the better. She was sitting before her dressing table mirror, ready to go downstairs, when there was a tap on the door, and Gijs came in. He said Hullo in a perfectly ordinary voice and sat himself down on the window seat. 'I've arranged for us to go to England the day after tomorrow—sorry I couldn't manage sooner.'

Serena turned to face him. 'It doesn't matter at all,' she assured him earnestly. 'You've been so kind, and it's such a bother. I could go alone.'

'So you could. Would you rather do that?'

His reply had been so unexpected that she blinked her beautiful, still puffy eyes in surprise. 'I—I—no—that is, unless it's difficult for you? I feel very mean, flinging myself at you like this and just letting you arrange everything.'

He shrugged his shoulders. 'There was nothing to arrange. Have you heard from Laurens?' His tone was so matter-of-fact that she found herself answering him in the same vein.

'He telephoned this morning—your father answered him. He wanted to see me, but I didn't want to, Gijs.' She raised her eyes to his. 'Later perhaps, if you're there.'

His face didn't lose its usual placid expression, but she had the peculiar feeling that something had exploded behind its calm, although his voice sounded much the same as usual. 'Just as you like. I think that would be sensible of you. Coming down? Father has that sherry waiting.'

The evening was tranquil and undemanding. Gijs stayed until almost midnight and never once did the conversation stray from the impersonal. When he eventually got up to go, Serena felt a pang of regret that she wouldn't be seeing him until he came to fetch her for their journey to England. Not wanting him to go, she asked: 'Did you write to Mother?'

'Yes, and I almost forgot, but it seemed to me as we can't leave early in the day, that we might spend the night in London—Richmond, I should say. I have an old friend living there, married to an English girl. They will be delighted to put us up.'

He didn't wait for her comments but patted her in a brotherly fashion on the shoulder, wished her the most casual of goodnights, and went out to his car.

It was inevitable that the next day the reaction should set in. The day had begun well enough, but during the morning, spent walking with her host, and the afternoon, in the garden with her hostess, the conviction that she was making an appalling mistake became firmly rooted in her mind. She should have seen Laurens at least, and given him the chance to explain. She should never have run away in such a ridiculous fashion, and certainly she should never have allowed Gijs to arrange her life for her. Perhaps even now Laurens was eating his heart out for her, too proud to see her or telephone. There was only one thing to do—she would telephone him at once. She smiled vaguely at her hostess as she got to her feet. 'May I use your telephone?' she asked in a voice which had suddenly become wobbly, and hurried into the house, oblivious of the anxious look which followed her. She actually had her hand on the receiver when Gijs said from the door: 'No, dear girl, don't do it—if you want to see Laurens, I'll take you to him.'

She jumped like a startled hare and dropped the receiver clumsily on to the table. 'Gijs—you made me jump! I didn't know you were coming...'

She trailed off, surprised at her feeling of guilt, and was still more surprised when he remarked blandly: 'I finished earlier than I expected at the hospital. Come along, we'll go now.'

'No, I don't think...' She was all at once perverse.

'Yes.'

He hadn't raised his voice, nor had he sounded angry, but she followed him silently from the room and out of the house to where the Bentley stood at the front door.

He drove silently and very fast, it seemed only a matter of moments before he was parking the car in front of the Mondragon. It was as she was getting out that she saw, too late, the Jag.

'I won't!' she said fiercely. 'You can't make me.'

He didn't bother to answer her but tucked a hand under her elbow and steered her across the cobbles and into the restaurant. He paused in the doorway and looked round the room; it was only half full and at one of the tables near the windows were Laurens and Adriana. Serena could have killed him when he raised a hand in a casual wave and murmured lazily:

'Well, well, see who's here!' So she waved and smiled too, her eyes glittering with rage and her colour high so that she looked truly magnificent.

'I hate you!' she whispered, and smiled once more as they were led to a table on the other side of the restaurant. When they were seated, she with her back to Laurens and Adriana, she repeated: 'Did you hear me? I hate you!'

'And very naturally. A healthy sign, too, dear girl. What would you like to drink? Something cooling, perhaps—Dubonnet with ice?'

He gave the order and sat back in his chair with such a relaxed air that Serena thought that he was about to go to sleep. 'I see,' he murmured, 'that I am to be cast in the role of enemy.' He cocked an inquiring eyebrow at her. 'Dear enemy, I hope?'

Despite his lazy air his eyes were very alert. She was

suddenly full of remorse. 'What a beast I am!' she burst
out. 'Gijs, I'm sorry. Why do you bother with me? I've
made such a fool of myself...' she faltered. 'I don't
think—that is, are you sure?'

'You asked me that before, dear girl. I can but repeat
myself. Yes.'

'But supposing I don't—and you take me home and
I...?'

'What you want to know is do I intend to blackmail
you into marrying me by taking you back to England,
thus making it necessary for you to be grateful. Tut-
tut, Serena, that is bird-witted of you—don't you recognize a friend when you meet one?'

It was fortunate that the Dubonnet arrived at that
moment, for she was on the verge of tears, and this
time they weren't tears for herself, but for Gijs because
she had been so beastly to him; good-natured, easy-
going Gijs who was proving a tower of strength. She
smiled mistily at him and said: 'Gijs, you are a dear,'
and then, when a sudden memory came unbidden into
her head: 'When you fetched me from hospital and
took me home, was it Laurens? It was you, wasn't it?
And the second time too—and the flowers.' She closed
her eyes for a moment because otherwise she would
have burst into tears; all this time she had thought it
was Laurens thinking of her and it had been Gijs being
kind and thoughtful. She opened them and said
steadily: 'You were so kind.'

'Dear girl, let us not exaggerate my good intentions.
Drink up, you'll need a little of our famous courage, I
think. They're coming over.'

They came. Serena, a little white and wooden as to
voice, smiled and nodded and murmured nothings
while Gijs, by some miracle, contrived things so well

that after the first greeting, she didn't have to speak to Laurens at all. They went at last and Gijs said at once: 'Now we'll have dinner, shall we? I'll just ring Mother not to expect us for a couple of hours.'

He strolled off, leaving Serena cold and empty of feeling except for a childish terror that Laurens would come back while Gijs was away. When he came back after what seemed an aeon of time, the sight of him warmed the cold inside her, it was like coming out of a cold mist into the sunshine. She would have liked to have told him that, but she felt sure that he would only laugh at such sentimental nonsense.

She thanked him warmly when they got back to Renesse. 'I want to talk to you,' she told him. 'There's such a lot I want to say.'

'All the time in the world to talk. Go to bed now; I'll be here at three o'clock tomorrow—and mind you're ready. I'm not allowing much time.'

She said good night a little shyly, was wished *wel te rusten* by his parents, and went upstairs to bed, where she fell asleep almost immediately, before she had had time to think anything at all.

CHAPTER SIX

THEY left the following afternoon, speeded on their way by a warm farewell from the doctor and his wife, with Maagda and the odd job man fulfilling the office of Greek chorus. Gijs's mother had kissed Serena when she had said goodbye. 'Come back soon,' she had said. 'There will be a welcome for you, my dear—and take care of Gijs.'

This remark had stuck persistently in Serena's mind ever since, popping out from time to time throughout their journey. The idea of Gijs needing anyone to look after him had never entered her head; he had seemed self-sufficient enough and perfectly able to cope with any situation which night arise, a theory largely due to his size and calm air, she had no doubt. Perhaps his mother was nervous of his driving, but although he drove fast he was a good driver and rarely put out; even in the Mini he had shown no signs of impatience. She remembered how she had sat beside him, wishing they could go faster so that she could be back at Queen's and see Laurens again…it seemed a long time ago.

'If I say a penny for them, I should only be teasing you and myself as well,' observed Gijs, breaking the long silence between them. 'We're up to time, with luck we shall be in Richmond by midnight.'

He was right; the journey was uneventful and Serena enjoyed it. Gijs was good company; he had given her a meal on board and accompanied her to the ship's shop to purchase whisky for her father and perfume for her mother, and then, because she had refused his offer of a cabin in which to rest, they had gone on deck and walked around and Gijs talked just sufficiently to keep her mind off her own thoughts.

They had got away quickly from the ferry, too, out of the quiet town and on to the A20 and the motorway, the big car moving without effort through the not quite dark of the summer's night. Presently he switched on to the A205, to circle the south of London and then turned off again for Richmond.

'You've been here before,' Serena hazarded.

'Yes, I stayed here when I came over to see Laurens—and at other times before then. Hugo's older than I, but we both went to the same medical school.' He turned his head to look at her in the gloom. 'Nervous?'

'Yes.' She felt his hand clasp hers momentarily. 'Don't be, they're nice.'

'Do they know about—about me?'

'If you mean about Laurens, no. They know that you have been staying with my people and that I'm driving you home—they also know that you're someone special.'

Serena felt her heart jerk at his words. 'But I haven't...'

He sounded very matter-of-fact. 'That makes no difference, Serena, you'll always be someone special, whether you marry me or not.'

'Why?' She tried to see his face and couldn't, but she saw him shrug.

'Oh—I suppose I like you more than most people I know.' He sounded off-hand and she was aware that her feelings were hurt, which, seeing that she had no feelings for anyone else but Laurens, was absurd. She opened her mouth, determined to pursue the subject, when Gijs said laconically:

'Here we are.'

He turned the car into a short private road close to the river, where there were several Georgian bow-fronted houses, as remote from the busy streets around them as they must have been when they were first built.

Gijs stopped at its end in front of a house with an oblique view of the river and got out. He didn't speak as he opened the door and helped Serena out, but she was grateful for the hand he tucked under her elbow; he had said that they were nice people, but they might ask questions and to answer them would be painful. But he gave her no time to hesitate and as they reached the door it was opened. The man standing there was as tall and broad as Gijs, but his hair was grey above a handsome face; it was a kind face too, and when Gijs said: 'Hullo, Hugo, this is Serena,' he took her hand and said: 'We're delighted that you have come, Serena—come in. Sarah is in the kitchen making the coffee.'

The house was as gracious inside as she had expected it would be. Serena had only a moment to look around her before the doctor's wife came in. She was a beautiful young woman with burnished hair and enormous eyes. 'I knew that the moment I went to the kitchen you would arrive,' she remarked serenely, and went straight to Serena. 'I'm Sarah, and it's lovely to have you.' She smiled with great sweetness, kissed Gijs and said, 'Hullo, Gijs,' then still smiling, but this time at her husband: 'Hugo dear, will you fetch the tray— it's all ready.' Her husband disappeared kitchenwards and his wife urged Serena to sit down and then sat down beside her. 'Did you have a good trip?' she wanted to know. 'We're going over in a month or six weeks.'

'With the twins?' asked Gijs.

'Of course. They'll be one, you know, and we thought it would be rather super if they had their first birthday in Holland.' She turned to Serena. 'One of each,' she explained happily, 'such a good start, don't you think? I'm almost thirty, you see.'

'Twins must be fun,' said Serena, and meant it. 'What do you call them?'

'The boy's Hugo, of course, the girl's called Rosemary.' She looked at her husband as she spoke and he put down the tray he was carrying and said smilingly: 'For a very special reason, but the next daughter will be called Sarah.'

'Ah, yes—Rosemary for remembrance,' said Gijs softly, 'I can't say that parenthood has taken its toll of either of you—you both look as though you've just left church, covered in confetti. How's the practice, Hugo?'

Sarah glanced at Serena and laughed. 'Here we go,' she said, 'bones and bodies!' She paused to pour the coffee. 'What do you think of Holland?'

'Well, what I saw of it I liked very much. I—we didn't go anywhere very much, but I thought Zierikzee was delightful. I should like to be there in the winter.'

Sarah gave her a considered look but didn't make any comment. 'Hugo's family live in the Veluwe—we go over fairly often. My people live near Salisbury—you're from Dorset, aren't you?'

They talked together happily until Gijs got to his feet saying that he had better put the car away and Hugo elected to go with him.

'Then I'll show Serena her room,' said his wife, 'and

you two can lock up—and don't stay up talking too late, darling.'

Her husband gave her an amused, fond glance. 'No, my love. Good night, Serena, sleep well.'

She wished him good night and Gijs too, and was instantly vexed at his casual 'Sleep well.'

He could at least have—have what? she asked herself. Why should he treat her in any way but the most casual? He didn't know if she was going to say yes or no, did he? She followed her hostess upstairs into a charming room with a little iron balcony overlooking the back garden.

Sarah sat down on the bed. 'This used to be my room—it's nice, isn't it?' and went on, as if in answer to Serena's look of inquiry: 'When I married Hugo I was in love with someone else, or at least, I thought I was.' She smiled. 'It didn't take me long to discover that it was Hugo all the time—so silly.' She got up and wandered across the room. 'The bathroom's through there. Gijs's room is on the other side of the landing and we're in the front.'

'Where are the twins?' Serena was peering into the bathroom with admiring interest.

Their mother beamed at her. 'Would you like to see them? We're both so crazy about them that we're apt to forget that some people aren't too keen on babies.'

She led the way across the landing and through a large baize-lined door.

'We've a marvellous nanny—a niece of Hugo's nanny, actually—she looks after the babies and us too.' She grinned disarmingly and led the way into the nursery where Serena and she spent several minutes peering at the small creatures in their cots.

'Hugo's very like Hugo,' commented Serena.

Sarah nodded. 'I couldn't have borne it if he wasn't.'

Serena glanced at her companion. The van Elvens must love each other very much. 'I expect Hugo thinks the same about the little girl,' she suggested, and felt a pang of envy.

She was awakened in the morning by a variety of sounds, small voices, mingling with the doctor's deep one and Sarah's gentle laugh: there were dogs barking too and once, a cat's miaouw. She wondered about getting up and was on the point of doing so when there was a tap on the door and an elderly woman came in with tea. She put the tray down on the bedside table and said cheerfully: 'Good morning, Miss Potts. I'm Alice, the housekeeper. Mrs van Elven asked me to tell you that breakfast is in half an hour, but if you like to have it in bed, you've only got to say so.'

Serena sat up. 'Oh, no, I'd like to come down.'

Alice smiled nicely and went away, and Serena sipped her tea, then dressed rapidly and went downstairs. There was no one in the sitting-room and she didn't know where the dining-room was. She was about to try one of the other doors in the hall when Gijs came in from the garden.

'Hullo,' he said cheerfully. 'Come into the garden. Hugo and Sarah won't be long. They always have a walk together before breakfast, nothing stops that. Did you sleep?'

'Yes, thanks. Gijs, you were right, they're very nice people.'

A moment later Sarah and Hugo appeared.

'Breakfast with the children, if you can bear it,' Sarah explained gaily, 'otherwise Hugo doesn't see enough of them. They're pretty awful feeders, I'm afraid, but Gijs doesn't mind—I hope you won't either.'

The meal was a cheerful affair; the twins chumped their way through egg and fingers of bread and butter and great draughts of milk and then, their faces wiped clean, went to sit on their father's knees while he finished, quite unpreturbed, his own breakfast. Serena sighed without knowing it and looked across the table at Gijs to find that for once his eyes were wide open, staring at her.

They left soon after breakfast, after the doctor had gone and after another cup of coffee and a gossip with Sarah and a final look at the twins. And when they went, Sarah said 'We shall see you again, Serena—this visit was far too short,' but to Gijs she expressed the hope that he wouldn't be late for dinner that evening as she kissed him good-bye. 'Hugo's got some interesting theory about something or other for one of his patients, I can't remember exactly what it is, but I'm sure you'll be wildly interested.' She grinned at him cheerfully.

They were barely out of sight of the house when Serena unable to restrain her tongue for a moment longer, demanded: 'You're coming back here tonight?'

Gijs slid the car into the stream of traffic. 'Yes.'

'But I thought—that is, I expected that you would stay the night at home.'

'You didn't invite me, dear girl.' He answered her without rancour.

'Gijs, I never meant not to, I just didn't think. What beast I am! Will you stay?' It suddenly became most important that he should. 'You could ring up Sarah.'

'I have to get back—the practice, you know.'

She knew it was an excuse; his father was taking the

practice for him, another day wouldn't have mattered, but she had deserved it. She agreed with him with an unexpected meekness and he began immediately to talk about something else.

They had coffee in Winchester, in the Close with the cathedral close by, and Gijs discussed architecture and gave her no opportunity to ask any more questions of a personal nature, but later, when they were streaking along the A31 towards Dorchester, she asked: 'Gijs, have you ever been in love?'

If he was surprised there was no sign of it on his face. He answered on a laugh. 'Oh, dozens of times, though I can't remember them all—there was one glorious redhead...'

Serena found herself taking immediate exception to the redhead. 'I'm not interested in what they looked like,' she snapped tartly. She didn't look at him, so that she missed the gleam in his eyes.

He was suddenly smooth. 'Why should you, dear girl? I wonder why you asked?'

Although he had asked the question he didn't sound in the least interested in getting an answer, which made it difficult for her to say: 'Well, I thought we ought to know more about each other.'

'A moot point and one upon you may rest assured. What did you think of the twins?'

Such a change of topic was impossible to ignore, so she answered coldly, feeling deflated; he had so obviously not wanted to talk about themselves.

It was just after one o'clock when they arrived at the Rectory, and this time there was no one at the open door, only her mother calling to them from the kitchen that they were to go straight in. Serena ran down the hall and across the uneven brick floor to where her mother stood at the stove. It was lovely to see her again; she embraced her warmly and her mother said: 'Darling, how lovely to see you—dinner's just ready. Run up the garden and tell your father, he's picking peas.'

Gijs had come in too, and Mrs Potts held out two rather floury hands. 'Gijs, we can never thank you enough.'

He smiled a little. 'You had my letter, Mrs Potts?'

'Yes—we both read it.' Her eyes searched his placid face a little anxiously. 'You're sure?'

'Of myself? Yes. Of Serena? Sure enough to take a bet on it.' He took her two hands between his own, flour and all, and gave them a reassuring shake and she smiled a little uncertainly at him.

'I couldn't wish for anything else—I never met Laurens, but I felt…' she paused. 'Serena has so much love to give and we were so afraid that she had given it to the wrong man. She's inclined to give with both hands.'

Gijs's nice firm mouth quivered ever so slightly. 'I know—will you trust me?' And when she nodded, 'I'll fetch Serena's luggage.'

He was at the door and Serena and her father were coming in from the garden when Mrs Potts said: 'Of course you're staying the night, Gijs.'

Serena stood very still, looking at him, hoping very much that he would say yes, but he refused, very nicely, and she said nothing while her mother voiced her protests, although she couldn't resist giving him an imploring look as he turned away—a look which he blandly ignored. She took care not to look at him again and although she chattered with brittle gaiety throughout their meal, she didn't address him once.

It wasn't until after dinner, when he was getting into the car for the return trip to Richmond, that the dream-like state she had been living in was swept away by the realization that he was actually going away—just like that—without a word as to when she would see him again. She wouldn't see him again; she ran across to the car and laid an urgent hand on the door, saying frantically: 'Gijs, you can't go!'

'You don't want me to go?'

'No—I've just thought, if you go now, I'll never see you again.'

'Quite right, dear girl.'

'Oh, Gijs, if you still want me, I'll marry you. I don't love you, you know that, but I like you so much—more than anyone else I know—and I'm happy with you, if you think that's enough. I can't imagine you not being there.'

He switched off the engine then. 'A little talk, my dear? Somewhere quiet—the kitchen garden, perhaps.'

He got out of the car and they walked round the side of the house and through the narrow wooden gate leading to the walled garden where her father grew his vegetables and fruit. It was quiet there and completely shielded from the house. Half-way down the path bordering the neat rows of beans and onions and peas, he stopped.

Serena didn't know what she had expected him to say, so she was wholly surprised when he remarked: 'A white wedding, Serena, don't you agree? Here, naturally, and soon. All our relatives and friends—brides-maids...'

She gasped at him. 'But I thought that you would want a very quiet wedding.'

'Why?' She saw his mouth twitch with amusement.

'I thought—it's not quite…' She stopped, frowning, because it was almost impossible to put into words what she wanted to say and she had the impression that he knew quite well and didn't intend to help her.

'Wrong, Serena. A wedding should be a happy occasion, and we intend to be happy, do we not? Not perhaps in the sense that most newly married couples are happy, but happy nevertheless. Besides, you will look very lovely in a white dress and a veil and all the other bits and pieces brides wear.'

'Yes?' she asked faintly. Put that way it seemed so sensible. 'Well, if you would like that.' She smiled at him doubtfully and he bent and kissed her gently on her cheek which somehow reassured her, as did his: 'Trust me, Serena, you'll have your doubts and fears, but I promise you they will mean nothing.'

Of course she trusted him, and said so, quite surprised that he should ask such a thing of her, suddenly content to let him decide everything for her. It was all the more disappointing, therefore, when he looked at his watch. 'I must go.'

'Please stay, Gijs—couldn't you possibly?'

He smiled lazily at her. 'No, my dear, but do you suppose that I could have five minutes with your father before I leave? The banns and so forth. How about a month's time for the wedding—there is no reason why we should wait. I'll be over again very shortly. Don't worry about notices in the papers and so forth, I'll see to all that—just concentrate on being a beautiful bride.'

She nodded wordlessly and they walked back to the house together and found her mother and father sitting together. Serena said baldly: 'Mother, Father, Gijs and I are going to get married, and Gijs wants to talk to you, Father.'

It was later, long after Gijs had gone and she had unpacked and had supper and gone to bed after an excited family discussion about her future, that she remembered that her parents hadn't seemed in the least surprised at her announcement, nor had Laurens been mentioned. She would, she decided as she got into bed, talk to her mother in the morning and try to explain.

Her opportunity to do this came soon after breakfast, with Susan dispatched on some errand or other, her father closeted in his study and her mother embarked on bedmaking.

Serena mitred her corner with unnecessary care and began: 'Mother, about Laurens—I've been an awful fool.'

Her mother thumped a pillow. 'No, dear, you would have been a fool if you had gone on with it and tried to alter something which couldn't be altered, and married him. It hurts now, but it would have hurt much more if you had married.'

Serena finished her side of the bed and sat down on it. 'It hurts now, Mother, and I can't think straight. I don't even know why I'm going to marry Gijs—does that shock you? I like him more than anyone I know— I like him more than Laurens, isn't that strange? but I don't love him. How can I when I love Laurens? And Gijs is so sure that it will be all right—he doesn't love me, you know. He wants a—a companion, someone to run his home and help him sometimes in the surgery and listen to him—oh, Mother, is it wrong of us to marry, not loving each other?'

Her mother gave her a loving look which she didn't see, nor did Serena see the expression on her mother's face—that of a small child with a secret she longed to share and mustn't. She came and sat beside Serena.

'No, love. And if your father had thought that he would have said so, even though you are quite old enough to do what you like with your life.' She got up off the bed. 'If any man can make you happy, it's Gijs,' she said positively.

'I didn't like him very much when we met.'

Her mother paused on her way to the door. 'My dear child, I loathed your father for quite some time before I fell in love with him.'

Serena contemplated her parent with open-mouthed astonishment. 'Mother, darling...'

'Yes, and don't you tell your brothers and sisters. I'm only telling you so that you realize that yours is by no means an isolated case.'

A week went by, during which Serena received a copy of the *Telegraph* with the announcement of their engagement in it, and another copy of *Elseviers Week-blad* from Holland with the same announcement, in Dutch, of course, but there was no word from Gijs, although his mother and father wrote; warm letters expressing their delight at the prospect of having her for a daughter-in-law. There was a stiffly worded note from Laurens's mother, but there was nothing from Laurens, and her disappointment was almost equalled by the sense of relief that he hadn't written. Sarah and Hugo wrote too, a warm, friendly letter; so did her friends at Queen's, all anxious to know when the wedding was to be, something which she couldn't tell them because she didn't know herself.

It was on the Saturday morning, as Serena came in from the garden with a basket of flowers, that she found Gijs standing in the hall with her father, chatting with the air of someone who had just dropped in for a casual ten minutes. She went towards him, foolishly put out because he hadn't come into the garden to find her, and even now, when he saw her, his greeting was markedly matter-of-fact and his cheerful 'Hullo, Serena!' did nothing to arouse her feelings, nor did the quick conventional kiss on her cheek. Still, she told herself sensibly, she didn't want it otherwise, did she, and neither did he, so why was she allowing such a trifle to upset her?

'You're staying, of course,' stated Mrs Potts, who had come downstairs to join them.

'You're very kind. If I may—I must be back on Monday, but that will give Serena and me time to discuss several things. Besides, I have to hear these banns read.'

'Very right and proper,' observed Mr Potts. 'And now if you'll excuse me, I must finish my sermon.'

'Take Gijs into the garden,' commanded Mrs Potts, 'and I'll make coffee presently.' She nodded in a satisfied way and started back upstairs again.

'But, Mother—the beds.'

'Blow the beds,' declared Mrs Potts inelegantly, and disappeared on to the landing above.

Serena glanced at Gijs and found him faintly smiling. He took the basket from her, set it on the hall table, then suggested: 'The garden, then, since your mother suggests it.'

'I didn't know you were coming.' Serena knew that she sounded grumpy as she spoke, but she felt so; it was annoying that she should be wearing an elderly cotton frock of a rather well-washed blue because she had intended to do some gardening. She hadn't bothered with her hair either, and it hung down her back, tied back with a ribbon.

He took her arm. 'No time to write,' he explained, 'and I was afraid to telephone.'

She stopped to look up at him. 'Afraid? Whatever for?'

'You might have changed your mind.'

She was shocked. 'But I promised.'

He didn't answer her, only bent his head and kissed her gently on the mouth, then took her arm again and went on walking. 'How many bridesmaids?' he asked.

'Well, none so far.' Really, he was the most vexing man, and so unpredictable! 'How could I ask anyone when I don't even know when we're going to be married?'

'Don't brides choose their wedding day? Let us see, the earliest date would be three weeks from Sunday, that's tomorrow—the Monday?'

She found herself laughing. 'Yes, all right. There's hardly time to send out the invitations, though. And they're not even printed.'

'We'll go to Dorchester this afternoon and see about that, and you can let the bridesmaids know—and buy your wedding dress if you wish.'

'Gijs, I couldn't possibly, not just like that. I can see about the bridesmaids—Susan, of course, and I thought I'd ask Joan—from Queen's, remember? But I can't buy my dress today—I think I'll have it made...'

She gazed into nothing, momentarily diverted by a beautiful vision in white—her mother's veil, naturally, and would Susan look her best in pink—and Joan? She repeated firmly: 'I couldn't.'

Gijs had stopped again. 'I almost forgot,' he said, plunged his hand into a pocket and took out a little leather box and opened it. There was a ring inside, three rubies encircled with diamonds and set in an old-fashioned gold band. 'I hope it fits,' he said, and picked up her hand and slipped it on. 'It's my grandmother's betrothal ring—there are two in the family—Mother has one, this is the other.'

She held it up to the sunlight and watched the gems sparkling. 'It's very beautiful, Gijs, I've never had anything so lovely before. Are—are you sure you want me to have it?'

His nice mouth quirked a little at its corners. 'Quite sure, dear girl, and if you have any more doubts, shall we have them now and settle them once and for all?'

Serena stared up at him. 'Haven't you any?' she demanded, and when he shook his head, she went on: 'I've one or two, yes. Gijs, I didn't know that you were a *jonkheer*—I asked your mother about it and she said it didn't matter—not to her—but what about you? L-Laurens's mother minded very much, she seemed to think that—Father's middle class, you know,' and then added hastily in case he should misunderstand: 'Not that I'm ashamed of that.' She drew a little breath. 'He's...'

'A very learned man—and a good and wise one,' Gijs finished for her, 'and since we are letting down our metaphorical back hair, there is something else: I have a good deal of money, Serena, something which I find relatively unimportant in my life. I would hope that you will regard it in the same light.'

'Well, I'll try, though I think I may have to get used to it.'

'I'll be there to help you. Straight back to work after the wedding, Serena—will you mind?'

'No, I shan't mind. The quicker I get used to being a Dutch housewife the better.' They were standing at the end of the garden, facing each other, and she reached up and kissed his cheek. 'Thank you for my lovely ring, Gijs—I'll try and live up to it.'

'And that's another thing. We had better shop around for a wedding ring.'

'Yes—and one for you?'

The sleepy grey eyes were all at once bright and intent. 'You like the idea?'

'Yes, of course—don't you?'

'Yes. Isn't that your mother calling?'

The weekend was a dream in which Serena knew herself to be living, and like all dreams, nothing that she or anyone else said or did seemed in the least strange, which was probably why, when Gijs left to return to Holland on Sunday evening, she kissed him goodbye with a fervour which, while entirely to be expected in a loving bride-to-be, was hardly called for in her case.

She hadn't a minute to call her own during the next weeks, still less time to think deeply about anything. Even a small country wedding, it seemed, needed a terrific amount of planning and organizing. She wrote invitations, shopped for clothes, spending her savings lavishly, and had her wedding dress fitted, and because Gijs couldn't spare the time to come to England again before the wedding, she wrote to him regularly. Not that he answered her letters, she hadn't expected him to, but he did telephone her almost every day. She looked forward to his calls more than anything else, and on the rare occasions when he did not do so, she moped round the house and went early to bed, a little cross.

It seemed hardly possible that she should wake one morning and know that the very next day was her wedding day and that Gijs would be with her within a few hours. He was travelling alone, ahead of his family, all of whom would stay in Dorchester and drive over for the wedding, but Gijs with Hugo van Elven, who was to be his best man, and of course, Sarah, were putting up at Cerne Abbas and he would be coming over to the Rectory that evening. To Serena the day seemed endless, with last-minute arrangements to make, the flowers to do in the church, lengthy discussions with Susan over the best hairstyle to adopt and Margery waylaying her as often as she could, in order to tell her, over and over again, how marvellous being married would be. They had just sat down to tea when Gijs came in with a casual, 'Hullo, everyone,' and a light kiss for her as he joined them. As he sat down beside her, Serena said: 'I didn't expect you just yet—did you get an earlier boat?'

'No—a Hoverlloyd—very quick, a bit further to drive on the other side, but that's no problem.' He gave her a bright glance and then dropped his lids. 'Are you ready?'

She passed him his tea and offered him the scones she had had time to make earlier in the day. 'I think so—there's been so much to do, but I don't think we've forgotten anything.'

For the rest of the evening Serena wasn't alone with him at all, and his brief goodnight was cool and friendly. She went upstairs to bed, a prey to a hotch-potch of thoughts while admitting to herself that it was a little late to try and sort them out.

The morning was brilliant. The wedding was to be at the early hour of ten o'clock, for Gijs planned to leave at half past one in order to catch the evening ferry, and even then he was cutting it a little fine. Serena indulged with the time honoured custom of breakfast in bed, entertained a constant stream of visitors to her room.

Alone at last, she began the business of bathing and dressing; she had finally decided on a dress of cream silk with long tight sleeves and a high round neck; its simple lines suited her slim figure and showed off her dark beauty to its greatest advantage. She had done her hair in its usual simple bun on top of her head. Now with Susan's doubtful help and Joan and Margery as audience, she arranged the veil, its wreath of orange blossom encircling the bun, its soft folds framing her face and shoulders. She looked quite nice, she admitted to herself as she stood before the mirror, although she was perhaps a little too pale—she turned to face her mother as she came into the room.

Being married, she told herself as she walked down the aisle on Uncle William's arm, with her father waiting for her at the other end, and only Gijs's broad back to pin her gaze to, was like a dream; she knew she was the bride, but it didn't seem quite real; she couldn't believe that in ten minutes she and Gijs would be man and wife. She would have liked to look around her as they made their slow way, but brides didn't look around them, not as they came into the church. She could do that presently, as they came out again, only then she would be holding a different arm.

It seemed no time at all before they were walking out of the church again. She hardly remembered the service or the kiss they had exchanged in the vestry; she had certainly heard no word of her father's little homily to them both. Now, her hand on his arm, she did look around her, smiling a little shyly at Gijs's family and friends, looking quickly past Laurens and over to the other side of the aisle where her own family were. They paused in the porch for the photographs, then walked across to the Rectory, where the sexton's wife and the postman's daughter were waiting in their best dresses to hand round the tit-bits her mother had ordered from Dorchester. The postman was there too, to serve the drinks and open bottles under the rector's mild direction; they smiled their good wishes as Serena and Gijs crossed the hall and went into the drawing-room, seldom used because it was too large and draughty, but on such an occasion as this one, a blessing in disguise, for it could hold fifty people with ease, and to make even more space the doors on to the garden had been flung open. Through them Serena could see the guests breaking up into small groups and start to make their way towards the house.

She hadn't been aware that she had been holding Gijs's hand, but now that he took it away, she was, and she put out her own hand again in mute appeal.

'Just a moment, my dear,' his voice was quiet as she felt his fingers at her neck. 'My wedding present, Serena,' he said, and kissed her before turning to smile at her parents and his own mother and father who had come to join them.

Serena put up a quick hand and felt. Pearls— they felt soft as silk between her fingers. She whispered, 'Thank you, Gijs,' and slipped her hand back in his, feeling his reassuring squeeze as the first of the guests came through the door.

She remembered reading once some novel or other in which the dim-witted heroine had declared on the last page that the hero was like a calm harbour after the stormy seas through which she had been struggling. Serena had thought at the time that the metaphor had been a singularly clumsy one—no man would care to be likened to a harbour; now she wasn't so sure, for she herself felt exactly as the tiresome girl in the novel had felt and Gijs, although not in the least like a harbour, had all its qualities. And now deep within her, she felt a faint warm glow in place of the stony misery she had been carrying around with her since the day she had gone to Gijs for help. She hardly recognized it, only, standing there beside him, she felt the beginnings of happiness.

CHAPTER SEVEN

THE glow was still there as she waved goodbye to everyone from the Bentley as Gijs drove away from the Rectory an hour or so later. Her head was filled with a kaleidoscope of sound and colour, people and voices, church music and wedding cake and, not least of all, Gijs putting the ring on her finger and promising to cherish her for the rest of his life. She twiddled the wedding ring on her finger and, anxious to appear at ease, asked: 'I hope you enjoyed the wedding, Gijs?' and saw the corner of his mouth lift in a smile.

'Indeed I did, my dear—I had no idea that being married was so enjoyable a process.' He shot her a quick sidelong glance. 'And the bride more than fulfilled my expectations—you were beautiful, Serena.'

'Oh—was I? I'm glad you liked me. I thought you looked pretty trendy yourself.' She put a hand up to the pearls at her throat. 'I haven't thanked you properly for these yet—they're fabulous.'

He pulled into the side of the road and stopped the car. 'Do thank me properly,' he begged, and turned to her, a wicked gleam in his eyes.

Serena was conscious of her heart racing and then a sense of disappointment when he added, 'Between friends, of course.' She leaned up and kissed him, telling herself that to feel disappointment was absurd; it wasn't as if they were in love—was she not in love with Laurens? And Gijs? He, apparently, wasn't in love

152

with anyone, so why should she suddenly remember Adriana?

'Not bad—not bad at all for a wifely kiss. I daresay you will get more experienced as the years roll by.'

She drew back a little so that she might see his face. She said indignantly: 'Well, really, you talk as though I'm the one who's going to do all—all the kissing!'

'Ah, but I don't need any practice.' She felt his arm pull her close as he kissed her; an entirely different affair from the short, light salute she had accorded him; indeed, he kissed her several times so that she became a little breathless and her cheeks pinkened delightfully, and when he at last loosed her anything she had intended to say had flown out of her head.

Then he glanced at his watch and with a casual remark to the effect that they had no more time to waste, sent the car ahead at a great rate, leaving her to brood over the fact that he had considered the little interlude a waste of time.

They had a late tea on board, although the restaurant was on the point of serving evening grills. Serena, watching a steward clearing a table and re-laying it for them, wondered how big a tip Gijs had given him. It would be strange not to have to worry about such things any more; she supposed that she would get used to it.

They were the first off at Zeebrugge and quickly took the lead from the other cars, for Gijs was racing to catch the ferry at Breskens. Once clear of that and on the other side of the river, he didn't slacken speed but tore on along the main road towards Goes and then over the three-mile-long bridge connecting the islands, and finally, Zierikzee.

They had made good time; it was still before midnight as he dawdled the big car carefully through the gateway and into the Oudehaven. It was almost in darkness. Across the canal the restaurant was still open and the street lamps cast their reflections in the water. Gijs's own house was lighted, the great square windows glowed as he drew up before the massive front door, thrown open at once to reveal Jaap and Lien, smiling broadly. Serena sat uncertainly until Gijs said: 'Home, Serena' in such a quiet voice she scarcely heard him as he helped her out.

Inside the house welcomed them; there were flowers everywhere, a delicious smell seeping from the kitchen, and Lien and Jaap both talking at once, shaking first her hand and then Gijs's. Presently Jaap went away to get the luggage and Gijs said something to Lien, who smiled and nodded and disappeared through the archway to the kitchen.

'I'll show you your room, dear girl—Lien's gone to put the supper on and Jaap will be up in a few minutes with your cases.' He took her arm and they went up the staircase together, to a passage with two doors in it, one of which he opened. He said matter-of-factly: 'The bathroom's through that door. I'm across the landing, first door on the left, if you should want anything. I'll be back in five minutes.'

He was as good as his word; they went downstairs together, to a cheerfully lighted dining-room, to eat the supper Lien had prepared for them and to drink the champagne Gijs opened, and when they had finished he said:

'You must be very tired, my dear. Go to bed and I'll tell Lien not to call you tomorrow. Ring when you wake and she will bring you your breakfast.'

It sounded super, but Serena, mindful that she was

now a housewife, protested: 'I'll get up, I'd much rather. Haven't you got your surgery in the morning? What time do you leave the house? Can't I have breakfast with you?'—she hesitated—'that's if you'd like me to.'

He had his head bent as he fondled German's ears. The little dog had given them an overwhelming welcome, and now he was standing on his short back legs, his head on his master's knee. 'I should like that very much. Breakfast is at half past seven, so why not come down in your dressing gown—you can dress afterwards. I shall be home for lunch about half past twelve, unless I get held up at the hospital. What will you do?'

'Do you mind if I go round the house again? I'm sure Lien will want me to see the cupboards and things and talk about food, and I hope she'll let me do the shopping when I've learnt more about it all.'

'Of course she will, but remember that later on, when you've found your feet, you're coming to give me a helping hand sometimes.'

The little glow inside spread; it was nice to be wanted. Her mouth curved into a smile. 'I shall like that.' She got up and he got up too and came round the table to her. 'Goodnight, Gijs.' She paused, considering how she should say what she was so anxious for him to know. 'I have a lot to thank you for, and I'm very grateful. I'll try and be a good wife—the sort of wife you want, I mean.'

'You're sure you know the kind of wife I want, dear girl?' he asked the question with a little smile.

'You said—that is, I think I know. I like you very much, Gijs—I'll be loyal to you, even in my thoughts.' She flushed brightly as she spoke because it hadn't been easy to say, and perhaps he knew that because he put his hands on her shoulders and bent and kissed her cheek, a calm, reassuring kiss, not at all the kind of kiss he had given her in the car.

'I know that, Serena, and never forget that I...like you too. Friendship is a very sound basis for marriage.'

He went to the foot of the stairs with her and stood watching her until she turned the corner under the arch. She turned and smiled at him there and then went on up to the top, to cross the landing to the room which was to be hers.

She was called in the morning by Lien with a cup of tea and when she looked at her watch it was to see that it was almost half past seven. It took her only a couple of minutes to wash her face and hands, comb her hair back and run downstairs to find Gijs, with German at his heels, coming in from the street.

'I'm late,' she declared, breathless and still a little sleepy.

'No—I walked German before breakfast so that we could have more time together over breakfast. Good morning, Serena.' He came towards her and she lifted her face for his kiss, but missed the gleam in his eyes.

'I could take German in the mornings, if you like, then you would have more time.'

'So I would, but you see, German walks me too. I don't see why we shouldn't go together and have breakfast a little later, do you?'

They went into the little sitting-room where breakfast was laid and Serena sat down and poured coffee for them both. 'I'd like that,' she said. 'Are you going to be busy today?'

She listened while he told her, and although she hadn't missed hospital since she had left Queen's, she found her interest quickening as he described some of his cases.

'Do you do any surgery?'

'Only in an emergency. I prefer general practice and paediatrics.'

'You don't look after the whole island?'

'Good lord, no, but the patients are scattered round it. You've been across the island, you've seen how isolated some of the farms are.'

He swallowed coffee and got to his feet. 'You shall come with me sometimes if you've nothing better to do, it will be a splendid way of getting to know the island. I must go.' He kissed her cheek and she felt the pressure of his hand on her shoulder and heard the door close quietly behind him.

She wandered upstairs presently and bathed and dressed, telephoned her mother because Gijs had reminded her to do so and then went downstairs to find Lien. It was easier going around the house than she had expected; Lien might not understand English, but she was sharp enough, and opening and shutting cupboards and drawers and pointing out their contents was just as effective as talking about them. Pleased with themselves and each other, they retired to the kitchen and with the aid of a dictionary, settled on the menus for lunch and dinner. It was almost eleven o'clock by then and Lien said firmly: '*Koffie, Jonkvrouw,*' and Serena, a little startled at being addressed so, went into the garden and drank the delicious brew Lien brought out to her, and because it was high summer and a lovely day and the garden was green and peaceful and she felt suddenly peaceful inside too, she went to sleep.

She awoke to find German's inquisitive, slightly anxious eyes within inches of her own and the sun blotted out by Gijs's shadow. She sat up at once, feeling foolish, exclaiming: 'I fell asleep, I never meant to—have you been waiting for me to wake up?'

'My dear girl, you were tired out—a long journey after the wedding and everything strange. How did the housekeeping go?' He grinned at her and she found herself smiling back at him, feeling lighthearted.

'Splendidly. Lien's such a dear. What a treasure she is!'

'Yes. I take care to surround myself with treasures. Come inside, I've something to show you before lunch.'

They went into the sitting-room in the old part of the house, its doors invitingly open on to the garden. Someone had filled it with flowers, and it smelled sweet, the sweetness tempered by the faint smell of beeswax. There was a hamper on one of the side tables. Gijs opened it and lifted out a very small Basset hound. 'For you,' he said.

Serena took the small creature in her arms and stroked its ears. She stared at Gijs, wanting, for some reason which she couldn't fathom, to burst into tears, perhaps because he had remembered her once saying she would like one, and had wanted to give her pleasure. She tucked the puppy firmly into the crook of her arm and put a hand on Gijs's arm. 'Thank you,' she spoke with fervour. 'How kind you are! I shall love him very much.' She kissed the puppy's nose. 'Will German like him?'

'I imagine so—they travelled together in the car for a good deal of the morning. What will you call him?'

'Oh, something short and easy, so that Lien and Jaap can say his name easily.' She closed her eyes the better to think. 'Gus,' she essayed, 'do you like that for a name?'

'Yes, it suits him, but you'd better try it on him first.'

The puppy approved, if by being licked by a small pink tongue was anything to go by. They went to the dining-room, German walking importantly in front of them, Gus still firmly in Serena's arms, and once they were there the problem of what to do with him during the meal was solved by German, who got into his basket as he always did and obligingly moved over to make room for Gus beside him.

The meal was a pleasant one, for there was Gijs's work to talk about, and when they were finished and were in the sitting-room drinking their coffee he asked her if she would like the idea of going on his afternoon rounds with him.

Serena looked up from the absorbing task of offering Gus milk in a saucer.

'Oh, may I? I should like that very much. When do you want to go?'

'In ten minutes or so—if I'm not held up too long we'll be able to get back in time for tea. I've a surgery this evening at half past five.'

'I suppose you wouldn't want me to come to the surgery too?' She was unconscious of the wistfulness of her voice.

'There's nothing I should like better. Father's still in England, as you know, and so is Laurens, and I'm single-handed. Rene's a great help, but we could use another pair of hands.'

She went to get ready for the afternoon's round then, feeling happy because she was going to be useful, even in a small way, and Gijs had sounded pleased because she had asked, and she wanted to please him.

There were quite a number of patients to visit—Gijs chose to do the country patients first—Dreischor, and then a farm on a lonely road in the centre of the island and then on to Brouwershaven, where he disappeared into a very small house in a narrow street which barely permitted the car's width. From there they went along the narrow brick roads with flat fields on either side, to Elkerzee, a very small village indeed, where, Gijs told her, there was an outbreak of measles amongst the children. He visited several houses and when he came back to the car, said: 'Well, one more, and then back to Zierikzee.'

It was almost five o'clock when at length Gijs stopped outside his own front door. There was another car parked there, a Mini—of a pleasing blue and very new. Gijs had parked behind it and when they got out took some keys from his pocket and put them in Serena's hand.

'Yours,' he said almost laconically. 'We'll go for a run this evening to make sure that you remember which side of the road to drive on.'

She gaped at him, clutching the keys. 'Mine? For me?'

He gave her a lazy smile. 'Why, yes, my dear. You may want to go shopping or visiting and certainly to see Mother and I shan't always be free to drive you. You'll need your own car.'

She was peering inside it. It was upholstered in dove grey and her name and address were engraved on a small oval disc on the dashboard. She said softly: 'Oh, Gijs—thank you! I can never thank you enough. I don't know what to say.'

He had opened the house door and she went past him into the cool hall.

'I'm glad you like it.' His placid face looked mildly pleased, no more. 'I expect tea will be in the sitting-room—shall we go through?'

She put Gus down and the little dog trotted off in German's wake. Gijs flung an arm round her shoulders as they went through the house and remarked: 'I should think we might leave Gus at home while we're in the surgery, don't you? He can have a nap in the kitchen, German will keep him company.'

The surgery, when they reached it half an hour later, was stuffed with people. It was in a cul-de-sac leading off Paternosterstraat, a flat-faced house the whole of whose ground floor was taken up by two consulting-rooms, a waiting-room and a little room squeezed in by the front door, where the patients gave their names and the notes were kept. Upstairs, Serena had time to notice, there were curtains at the windows and she wondered who lived there. She would ask Gijs, but not now, because it was already half past five and there were more than enough patients for him to see.

There was a young woman in the cubbyhole and Gijs greeted her cheerfully as they went in and said: 'Serena, this is Rene, she's leaving to get married at the end of the week. There's another girl coming soon, but in the meantime I'd be eternally grateful if you would give a hand—we've no nurse this evening either.'

Serena beamed at him, glad of an opportunity to help. She shook Rene's hand and squeezed herself into the cubby-hole, wondering how she could possibly be of use, for her Dutch, to say the least, was only fragmental. But Rene, she discovered after a few minutes, understood basic English at least and spoke a little too. Serena discovered too that it was a question of getting the patients' names right, for the filing system was exactly the same as it was in England and as far as she could see, the surgery was run on exactly the same lines as an English GP's. Under Rene's excellent tuition she began to make a little headway even though many of the names were quite unpronounceable, but there were easy ones and she was quick to learn and had a good memory. She began to enjoy herself.

The last patient went soon after half past six in an evening which was still very warm. Serena went out to the car with Gijs, shook hands with Rene who lived just down the street, and got in beside him. 'Nice work,' he praised her lightly as he edged the car back into Paternosterstraat. 'Do you think you could manage for a few days on your own until the new girl comes?'

Serena glowed. 'Oh, yes. I enjoyed it, though some of the names are very difficult.'

'Just at first,' he assured her comfortably. 'I don't know how you feel about it, but the headmaster of the MAVO school here is a splendid teacher and a brilliant scholar. I wondered if you would like him to give you lessons in Dutch.'

'It's funny you should say that, for I had only made up my mind half an hour ago that I would find someone to teach me—I was going to surprise you.'

She missed the sudden gleam in his eyes. 'How delightful. I promise not to ask how you're getting on and then you can still surprise me.'

They were back outside the house once more. 'Would you still like to try the Mini?'

'Please.' She was as excited as a small girl with a new doll; she could hardly wait for him to cram himself into the seat beside her before switching on the engine.

She acquitted herself very well. 'But keep to the island for a little while,' Gijs advised her, 'and make sure you know all the signs—you'll have to take a test, you know. I'll arrange that as soon as I can.'

She nodded happily. 'Where shall I put her? I don't even know if you've got a garage.'

'Lord yes, I'll show you where it is.'

It was in fact down a narrow *steeg* behind the house, built against the back wall of the garden and next to the cottage. Serena hadn't noticed the door in the wall by Lien's little home; it led into the back of a roomy garage which, a long time ago, must have been a house. Its exterior had been faithfully restored, even the garage doors were of massive oak with iron bolts and hinges. It was easy enough to reach by running the car up the narrow street beside the house and then turning sharply into the *steeg*. Serena, determined to deserve her present, drove the Mini round and parked it beside the Bentley.

'There's a key to the garage on that bunch,' Gijs explained as they went back through the garden door, 'and if you should happen to lose it Jaap has duplicates of every key I possess.' He sauntered across the grass, an arm on her shoulder. 'What time is dinner?' he wanted to know.

'The same time as always,' said Serena. 'Lien told me the times you liked your meals, and I'm not going to change anything for you.'

His arm felt a little heavier. 'No? We shall see!'

His voice had sounded strange and she didn't know how to answer him, instead she said: 'I think I'll go up and change my dress—it's been a lovely day.' She smiled at him and suffered faint chagrin when he agreed with a casual good humour that evinced no real interest.

The week went in a flash; she wondered at the end

of each full day how she could have imagined that she
would never have enough to do. And in two days' time,
when her parents-in-law returned from England, Gijs
had assured her that his mother would take her visiting
each day to meet their friends. 'And we shall have to
give a dinner party later on,' he warned her, 'but first
we shall get a great number of invitations. Mother will
give a reception for us very shortly so that all the people who would have come to our wedding if we had
been married here can come and wish us well and take
a look at the bride.'

'Oh,' uttered Serena, 'I shall be terrified!'

'No, you won't. We just stand together and shake
hands with everyone and I'll tell you what to say. I
daresay we shall dance afterwards.'

He dismissed the whole thing carelessly, but Serena
became thoughtful so that presently he said: 'Something worrying you, dear girl?'

'Clothes—what do I wear?'

'It will be black ties. Something pretty and bridelike.
Couldn't you wear your wedding dress?'

Serena eyed him with kindly pity. How like a man!
What woman would want to appear at her first important evening function wearing her wedding gown, just
as though she hadn't got anything else? 'Not really,'
she told him. 'You see, it's got a little train and it looks
like a wedding dress.'

His eyes twinkled. 'How stupid of me! Shall we go
and buy something? I could manage Saturday afternoon—we could try Amsterdam, or failing that, den
Haag.'

She shook her head. 'No, I don't think there's any
need. I've a rather pretty dress which I think might do.

Long, you know—cream gauze over silk with a pink velvet sash. I bought it because it was so beautiful...'

'What a good reason, it sounds just right. And that reminds me to tell you that I have opened an account for you at my bank—across the canal, next to the hotel.' He had given her a cheque book then and mentioned the sum he had paid in for her. 'Quarterly,' he added casually, and ignored her protest, 'and I don't expect you to pay for the Mini out of it—have anything you need for it put on my account.'

'But you're too generous. How can I possibly spend all that money?' she remonstrated, but all he did was laugh. 'Have a good try,' was all he said, and: 'Remember I told you not to let it become important, Serena.'

They went to dinner with Gijs's parents on the evening of their return, and Serena, who had been feeling a little nervous about it, was overwhelmed by their greeting. They sat round the dinner table, making a leisurely meal while they gave her messages from her family and then went on to tell her how lovely the wedding had been, and her mother-in-law interrupted herself to send her husband upstairs to fetch the wedding photos which Serena's mother had entrusted to her care. 'And now we must introduce you to everyone,' she went on enthusiastically. 'I shall, of course, give a reception for you both—we had better have a room at the Mondragon, and you must come with me when I go visiting, my dear, if you can bear with an old woman's company, and in that way you will get to know everyone very quickly. Has Gijs taken you anywhere?'

'He's had no time,' Serena smiled across the table at him. 'There's been the surgery to run single-handed,

you know. I've been going down each evening and
helping.'

Her mother-in-law gave a faint shriek. 'Gijs,' she
demanded, 'how could you ask of Serena that she
should work, and she a bride of only a few days.'

'But he didn't ask—' began Serena, but was interrupted gently by her husband.

'Dear Mama, did we never tell you that one of the
conditions of our marriage was that Serena should help
me from time to time?' He spoke seriously, but his eyes
danced with laughter and when he and Serena exchanged glances his mother declared: 'I don't believe
a word of it—you make the joke. There is no need for
Serena to work, there is enough for her to do with that
house to manage and presently the children.'

At which remark Serena blushed, a slow, painful
pinkening which spread over her lovely face until she
felt as though she was on fire and which was fanned
to an even more maddening brilliance by Gijs's bland:
'Just so, Mama,' and his wicked look directed at herself. She sat, fuming silently that she was fool enough
to blush in such a gauche and stupid fashion, and
thanked heaven silently when Gijs drew the conversation on to himself, giving her time to regain her normal
complexion. Presently her father-in-law went to fetch
some wedding presents they had offered to bring with
them, and these kept everyone agreeably occupied until
she and Gijs left, half an hour later. She talked about
them, at length and quite unnecessarily, for the entire
journey home.

She began her Dutch lessons the following day. It
had been arranged that she would have them each afternoon from half past four until just after five, which
allowed her to give Gijs tea at four o'clock if he were

home, and left her free for the surgery in the evenings. The new girl was there now, but the secretary never came in the evening, and the nurse was on holiday. The new girl was nice but a little slow, and although now that he was back, Gijs's father came in to help, Laurens hadn't returned yet. Serena would have liked to ask why, but Gijs had told her nothing and he might find it rather strange of her to inquire—as if she were still interested in Laurens.

By some magic on the part of Jonkvrouw van Amstel, the reception she had declared obligatory to give on their behalf had been arranged for the Saturday evening after her return. How she had managed to do this in such a short space of time was something Serena couldn't guess at. Presumably she had spent a day at the telephone, inviting everyone on the formidable list she had shown Serena. And Serena, not to be outdone by her mother-in-law's organizing powers, invited her and her father-in-law to dinner on the evening of the reception, for it would be the easiest thing in the world to go the few hundred yards to the restaurant in time to receive the guests, and besides, she had a nagging, unspoken wish to show them how well she had settled down as a good wife to Gijs.

She spent a great deal of time and thought over the dinner, and what with her natural anxiety to prove herself a good hostess and an equally natural desire to shine at the evening's entertainment, she was a bundle of nerves by the time the evening arrived. Indeed, her temper, already frayed round the edges, was quite uncertain by the time Gijs—unaccountably late—got home. He found her wandering around the dining-room table, clad in her dressing gown, her hair in an untidy plait, frowning at its exquisite silver and china, and when he inquired cheerfully if she shouldn't leave everything to Jaap, she said snappishly that she certainly would and what did it matter anyway, they might just as well have something out of a tin. She then burst into tears and made for the stairs where he overtook her easily enough and catching her by the shoulders, turned her round to face him. 'What's gone wrong, my pretty?' he wanted to know.

Serena sniffed, feeling slightly better already because he had called her his pretty.

'Nothing,' she managed, and sniffed again, and then as Gijs still waited, wisely aware that the nothing was a mere figure of speech, she went on. 'At least nothing much. I—I made a Charlotte Russe and it b-broke when I turned it out. Lien put it together again, but…and Gus made a puddle on the sitting-room carpet, and I know my hair's going to look awful!'

She ended on a faint wail and peered up at his kind face.

The hands on her shoulders gathered her close as he kissed her reassuringly.

'My poor little wife—but none of these things seem fatal to our evening. I presume Gus's accident has been dealt with, and no one need know about the Charlotte Russe. I shan't tell and I'm sure Lien won't—as for your hair, I find it very pretty as it is.'

Which remark she found so amusing that she giggled and Gijs said bracingly: 'That's better. Come along and have a drink, we've plenty of time. Are my things put out, by the way?'

She nodded, looking quite beautiful despite her red eyes and tangled hair. 'Yes—I did them after tea. I hope they're what you want.'

'Bound to be,' he sounded comfortably certain about it. 'What are we going to eat, or is it a secret?'

She told him. 'Well, Gurkas Norge for starters—you know, the Galloping Gourmet...'

'I don't know, but I daresay I'll catch up with you as you go along—a recipe book, perhaps?' he hazarded.

'A man—a cook. Cucumber and anchovies and cream cheese and sour cream and some caviare—they're rather expensive, I'm afraid.'

'But absolutely necessary for our first dinner party. What's next?'

She giggled and then said solemnly. 'Potts' Point Fish Pot,' and joined in his bellow of laughter. 'It's flounders and lobster and mushrooms and white wine—oh, and brandy...'

'Dear girl, you've excelled yourself. Don't tell me any more or I shall feel compelled to go to the kitchen and eat the lot. Quite obviously it will be the inspiration of the evening.'

'You think so?' They started to walk towards the sittingroom. 'There's the Charlotte Russe for afters, and coffee, of course. Only I don't know about the drinks.'

'I'll see to those,' he gave her a Dubonnet. 'Drink this up and then go and put on your party dress.'

A few minutes later she was on her way upstairs, to be arrested half way by his quiet voice, reminding her:

'Remember what I told you, Serena? You're going to meet Laurens, but as my wife. I know you saw him at our wedding, but weddings aren't quite real, are they, and this is.'

She looked down at him standing below her, his hands in his pockets, half smiling, quite unworried. She

could think of nothing to say in answer; she nodded
briefly and went on up to her room. It was while she
was dressing that she realized why he had said it; he
was afraid that meeting Laurens again would be un-
bearably painful for her, that she would need all her
pride and courage to speak to him. It was strange that
now she probed her feelings further, she didn't think
she was going to feel any of these things. Laurens, in
some mysterious way, had faded. She stared at her reflection and wondered why. She might have gone on
wondering for quite some time if Gijs hadn't knocked
on the door and come in. He was quite ready and wore
the air of a man who had spent at least an hour and
that a leisurely one, in dressing himself. She wondered
how he did it and wondered too how she had ever
thought him slow-moving, as obedient to his request
she stood up for his inspection.

The dress had been a happy choice, she knew; its
deep clotted cream showed up her tan and made her
dark hair even darker and her eyes more brilliant. She
had put on the pearls and had been fiddling with some
earrings; now she laid them down on the dressing-table,
spread her skirts and asked childishly, 'Will I do?'

He came and stood close to her, looking not at her
dress, but at her face.

'Oh, you'll do, my dear. You've never looked love-
lier, excepting on our wedding day.' He put a hand in
his pocket and took out something. 'You told me your
sash was pink. I hope these will match well enough.'

A pair of earrings lay in his palm, bright ruby stars
outlined with diamonds and with a single pearl drop.
Serena stared at them for a long minute before she
looked at him. 'For me?' She repeated his words and
touched them gently. 'But they're magnificent!'

'Great-grandmother's this time, and this goes with them.' He added a bracelet to the earrings; it lay there, winking and twinkling in the light, a lovely ornate band of rubies and diamonds and pearls, held together by gold links.

Serena goggled a little. 'Gijs, I—they're so lovely. Do you really want me to have them?'

'Indeed, yes. And there's this besides.' A brooch this time, of the same splendour as the bracelet, its pearl drops hanging down in a milky fringe.

She said, breathless: 'I'll put them on,' and hooked the earrings into her ears and held out an arm so that he might fasten the bracelet and then asked. 'The brooch—shall I wear it in the centre or a little to one side?'

He gave her a considered look. 'The centre, I think. They become you very well, Serena.'

She fastened the brooch carefully and turned to inspect her person in the mirror. The jewels were most becoming to her, as was the dress. She smiled at his reflected face and turned to kiss him. 'Thank you, Gijs. You give me so much, and I do so little.'

He said a little harshly: 'But I ask for nothing, Serena,' and then seeing her eyes widen went on in his usual mild voice: 'I see the hair went up without any difficulties after all. Shall we go down? Father and Mother should be here very soon.'

Much later that night, lying in her great bed, Serena looked back over the evening and knew it to have been a success, and fun too. Dinner had been all it should be and had been eaten with gratifying appetite by her guests, Gus had behaved with circumspection and she had sat at table, happily aware that she looked her best, that her mother and father-in-law liked her and that

Gijs was proud of her. She had arrived at the hotel, knowing that these factors had given her poise and confidence; when she paused at the entrance to the room where the reception was to be held and caught Gijs's eyes, no longer half hidden beneath sleepy lids, but gleaming with admiration, she had coloured faintly under his stare and smiled a little, and he had crossed to her side and taken her arm and murmured: 'Enchanting Serena,' and smiled with such warmth that she felt emboldened to say: 'Oh, Gijs, it's all right, isn't it? Us—our marriage—is it how you wanted it?'

She gave him an anxious, intent look, dimly conscious that if he was content, she was not. And she should have been; she had a good-looking husband who was goodness itself and kind too, and they were great friends, which was more than one could say of some husbands and wives. She had a lovely home too and more money than she knew what to do with—and Gus, and the rubies...

His voice had reassured her: 'Dear girl, you are exactly what I wanted. Now come over here and stand with Mother and Father—that's right, between Father and me. You don't need to speak unless you're spoken to in English, just smile.'

So she had smiled and shaken hands and allowed herself to be stared at, albeit in the kindest possible manner, and forgotten almost all the names Gijs was at pains to tell her; she had never seen so many strange faces, which made Laurens's familiar good looks all the more of a shock when he appeared suddenly before her. She met his blue intent gaze with dignity and a smile which, try as she would, trembled a little at the edges, because she had been dreading this meeting and now it was upon her.

She tried now to remember what she had said; something light and casual while the memory of Gijs's words that evening lifted her chin a fraction of an inch higher and steadied her smile. Gijs had helped too, as she had known he would, slipping an arm into hers and talking easily to his cousin, asking about his leg and his probable return to the practice, drawing her into the conversation without any apparent effort. Laurens moved away presently and Gijs said pleasantly, in a voice loud enough for those around to hear: 'How well Laurens looks, darling.'

He had never called her darling before, she reminded herself, lying wide awake in the lovely room; she would think about that presently. At the time she had no chance to do more than feel surprised; she was far too taken up with the necessity of telling Gijs something. She managed to whisper: 'I didn't really see him, Gijs—it didn't matter—it wasn't the same.'

It was three days later when Gijs asked her if she would go to the surgery with him that evening because Ina, the new receptionist, had tonsillitis and couldn't work.

She walked to the surgery because Gijs had rung her up during the afternoon and told her that he couldn't get home for tea and would she meet him there. The little town was quiet, the shops were closed for the day and almost everyone, even the tourists, was indoors getting ready for their evening meal. The weather was quiet too—the unnatural quiet of a pending storm. Serena, who hated thunder, looked at the sky and was glad to see that the clouds were still only a vague menace on the horizon.

The surgery was already full although there was quite ten minutes before it would open. She dived into the little room by the door and began the laborious job getting out the patients' notes.

Gijs arrived five minutes later, unhurried and quiet, but when he paused briefly to speak to her, she saw that he was tired. He had told her that Laurens would be coming and, she thought, a good thing too, for Gijs was doing too much. Laurens turned up twenty minutes later. She saw, with faint amusement, his look of amazement at seeing her there; the look was swept away, replaced by the gay smile she had found so irresistible and which now, surprisingly, left her unmoved.

'Hullo,' he said lightly, 'earning your keep already? Don't tell me old Gijs has sacked the new girl and given you the job of unpaid assistant?'

He had sounded spiteful and she didn't allow him to finish. She didn't raise her voice, but it held her contempt, as did her pretty face, scarlet with the strength of her feelings.

'How dare you speak of Gijs like that!—He's worth a hundred of you, he works twice as hard and he's the most generous man alive...' She paused for breath, as astonished as he was at her outburst.

'Well, well, what a nasty temper! I never knew before that you couldn't stand a tease.' He turned on his heel and she said quietly: 'You weren't teasing, Laurens.'

She was kept busy after that—too busy, so that she muddled up the cards of the two Mevrouw Anne Smits who had, by a strange coincidence, presented themselves at the same surgery at the same time, and sent them to the wrong doctor.

Laurens's door opened first to disgorge the wrong Mevrouw Smit, and following hard on her heels, Laurens. 'Good God, Serena,' he began impatiently, 'surely you can do something as simple as sending me my own patients?'

Serena, struggling to find a missing card, looked up briefly, determined not to lose her cool but a little pink all the same.

'I'm sorry. There are two Anne Smits here and I've got them muddled. You had the wrong one.'

'Of course I got the wrong one. Send in my patient and for heaven's sake don't keep me hanging about.'

'I don't really think you mean to speak to my wife in that fashion, do you, Laurens?' Gijs's voice was almost a drawl and he was smiling faintly, but something in his look caused his cousin to say hastily: '*Hemel*, no—sorry, Serena.' He smiled at her briefly and went back into his surgery, sweeping the right Mrs Smit with him.

Gijs said nothing more, only asked her about some tests she had managed to fit in somehow or other, and presently went back to his own consulting-room and closed the door.

The two men finished more or less together, but Serena, bogged down in strange outlandish names, was still opening and shutting drawers, tidying things away and filing letters for future reference. The telephone rang again and she put out a hand to take the receiver, but Gijs took it from her. 'You've enough to do, dear girl.' He eyed the neat lists of names and addresses she had compiled from the calls which had come in during surgery hours. 'I'll take it.'

He had dealt with it when Laurens came out of his room, his bag in his hand. 'I'm off,' he told them. 'I've a date and a couple of visits to do first.' He waved airily and Serena, finished at last, shutting doors and fastening windows, heard the Jag roar down the narrow street. She looked at Gijs. 'Have you any calls?' she asked.

'Yes, I must go to the hospital and see how that man I sent in this morning is doing, and I've a couple of patients to see in the centre of the island—shall I drop you off first?'

'May I come with you? Gus and German will be OK, I took them for a walk after my lesson.'

For answer he opened the door of the car, shut it after her and got in himself. 'Nice,' he remarked. 'The day has seemed very long; lunch was a rush, wasn't it, and I missed tea at home.'

'Would you like to stop now and I'll get you some. It won't take a minute.'

His hand brushed her knee lightly. 'My thoughtful wife—but I'd better get on, I think. There's a baby case due and I like to be free for those.'

'Yes, of course. Is the hospital going to take long?'

He shook his head. 'Ten minutes. Would you like to come in?'

She would have loved that—to see where he worked and meet the people he worked with, but it might delay him.

They were still out in the flat countryside, with Zierikzee visible on the horizon, when the thunder clouds suddenly bundled together to assume an awe-inspiring blackness. The wind came first, tearing at the Bentley, then the rain and lastly lightning, cracking through the sky in what must have been a magnificent sight to anyone who liked such spectacles of Nature. Serena sat rigid, trying not to hear the thunder bellowing around them; searching frantically for a spot in the wide sky which the lightning hadn't yet found. In the end she closed her eyes, but opened them instantly when Gijs said: 'Come closer. I didn't know you disliked storms—they're rather extravagant here at times. We're nearly home.'

She crept near to him. He felt solid and safe and he hadn't laughed at her for being afraid.

They played backgammon after dinner and she wondered if it was to keep her occupied because of the storm still raging outside. But presently it rolled away and Serena said goodnight and went upstairs, yawning realistically but longing to stay with him until the last rumble had faded and the last faint lightning had flickered itself out. But she knew Gijs had his letters to read as well as the pile of medical journals which arrived each week. She got ready for bed rapidly and got into bed. If the storm got worse she could always go downstairs and sit with him.

She wakened to lightning flickering round the room and the distant rumble of thunder once more, and because it was too hot to pull the sheet over her head she switched on the bedside lights, which, while not attempting to compete with the electricity outside, afforded some measure of comfort. She had been uneasily awake for ten minutes or more when she became aware of vague noises downstairs, and very faintly, Gus barking. It was half past two, Gijs would have been in bed hours ago and if he was going out on a case the dogs, used to his footfall in the house, wouldn't have barked. Lien and Jaap were in their own little cottage—the obvious answer was that someone was downstairs—someone who shouldn't be there. She lay worrying about it for a moment or two and when she could bear it no longer, got out of bed, put on her dressing gown, thrust her feet into slippers and opened the door.

The hall was quiet and dim and smelled faintly of flowers which she had arranged earlier in the day. She went through the arch towards the kitchen, going quickly before she had time to be afraid and as she drew level with the study door, it opened and Gijs came out, his bag in his hand.

Serena stood still, her hand over her mouth like a frightened little girl and said in a voice squeaky with fright: 'Oh, you're going out on a case.'

'Yes, darling. Did I disturb you? Gus mistook me for an intruder, I think. I'm sorry. It's the baby—remember the second farm we went to this afternoon.' He passed her on the way to the door and then came back, kissed her on the mouth and went outside into the storm without a backward glance.

Serena stood where he had left her, staring at the shut door, wishing she was with him, storm or no storm. Presently she saw the lights from the car sweep past the house and when they had quite disappeared, she went to the kitchen, made some tea and sat down to drink it with Gus in her lap and German snoring companionably in his basket. It was pleasant there, the curtains had been drawn against the night, so that the lightning seemed less frightening, the scrubbed table smelt nicely of soap and the light over the sink shone cheerfully on the rows of pans which were Lien's pride. The storm grumbled its way round the sky and Gus, warm and secure, went to sleep, his head, swathed in its ridiculous ears, pushed under her arm. In a little while she went to sleep herself.

Gijs was in the room when she woke up, and the beginnings of a pale dawn were edging round the curtains. She jumped up, dislodging an indignant Gus. Serena hadn't meant to go to sleep. She tossed her hair out of her eyes, fighting a desire to close them again.

'I'll make you some tea—it must be morning. Was everything all right?'

She studied his face as she put on the kettle. He was tired, more than tired, bone weary, but he smiled at her with his usual good humour.

'Now this is what I call luxury—a wife waiting for me with tea! Yes, everything was fine—just the baby held us up for a bit—a breech.'

'A boy?'

'Yes—they're delighted; the other two are girls.' He put his case down on the table and sat himself down beside it. 'Have you been here all night?'

'Yes—after you had gone I came to see if Gus was all right, and it was so cosy. I made some tea and then Gus got on my lap—he and German were good company.'

She made the tea and fetched two mugs from the dresser. 'My poor girl,' he said, 'you've had a bad night, but the storm's over now. It will be a lovely day.'

She looked at the clock on the wall; it was almost five. 'Did you get to bed at all before you were called out?' she wanted to know.

'Yes—for a couple of hours.' He smiled a little. 'Don't worry about me, Serena, this happens quite frequently, you know.'

'Yes. Will you go to bed now? There are still two hours…'

He finished his tea and got up from the table. 'A good idea—and you?'

She was suddenly shy. 'I'll just clear up these

things.' For something to do she went to the window and drew the curtains aside, letting in the morning light. It fell upon Gijs's face, highlighting its lines and furrows and bristly chin. She stared at him as though she had never seen him before, knowing in that moment that it was the face of the man she loved. She might have gone on staring for ever if he hadn't asked: 'What's the matter? Why do you stare so?'

'You're tired out,' she managed in a matter-of-fact voice. 'Do go to bed.' She thought he hadn't heard her, for he didn't answer, but after a moment or two he went to the door, and with his hand on the handle asked her: 'Do you know how beautiful you are, Serena?'

He didn't wait for her to answer. She heard him going quietly up to his room and when the door shut gently, she took the mugs to the sink and started to wash them up. She did it very slowly, while her tired mind absorbed the fact that she had fallen in love with her husband, who, when they had agreed to marry, had made it abundantly plain, in the nicest possible way, that his feelings for her were no more than affectionate.

CHAPTER EIGHT

OF course she didn't sleep. She went upstairs, hardly knowing that she was crying, and lay down on the bed, thinking back to the day at Queen's when she had first met Gijs. He had never been anything but kind, she told herself tearfully, and she had been ungrateful and thoughtless of his feelings. In the darkness she squirmed at the memory of her cool reception of him when he had arrived at her home to drive her back to hospital; she had thought then how marvellous Laurens had been to think of her, while in actual fact it had cost him no effort at all, only to persuade his cousin to drive miles to collect a girl he had barely met. She wondered briefly why Gijs had done it. The doubt, still faint, crept into her head that perhaps he hadn't married her for the reasons he had given her—they had seemed so sensible and reasonable at the time—but out of pity; he liked her, she knew that, and they were friends; one did a lot for a friend in trouble, and she had been alone and very unhappy.

She rolled over and thumped the pillows, wondering miserably what she should do. It would be embarrassing for him if she were to tell him, without any warning, that she had discovered that she loved him, but if she didn't, he would never know, would he? Perhaps it would be better if he didn't.

She got up and started walking up and down and round and round, and her brain, soggy with her crying, refused to think calmly or sensibly any more. She went

and had a bath and when she got back into the bedroom
it was to find her early morning tea waiting for her.
She drank it thankfully and set about the task of dis-
guising her tear-stained face. She must have succeeded
very well because when she went down to breakfast a
little later, Gijs accorded her the briefest of glances and
went back to his post, and presently got up to go. 'A
heavy day,' he excused himself. 'Don't expect me
home for lunch, Serena—I'll telephone if I find I can't
get back for dinner, so don't wait for me if I'm late.'

Serena met his eyes briefly. 'You don't want me at
the surgery this evening?'

He shook his head. 'Ina will be back, I think. Have
a nice day.'

He went away without kissing her.

She spent that day, and the succeeding days, doing
a variety of things to make herself believe that she was
neither lonely nor unhappy. Gijs seemed to be busy;
beyond their brief walk and the briefer breakfast following it and a rather silent meal at night, she saw little
of him, and when they were together she sensed a reserve that she had never noticed before, a reserve
which she didn't attempt to break down for fear of
showing her own feelings.

It was two weeks after the storm, on a dull, rainy
afternoon, while Lien and Jaap were in their cottage
and she had the house to herself, that someone knocked
thunderously on the street door. Serena hurried to answer it; Gijs hadn't been home for lunch, perhaps it
was someone with an urgent message for him. The girl
at the door was quite young, in her teens, and quite
distraught, so that she was prevented from speaking
with any degree of coherence. Serena waited patiently
for her to calm down a little, and then, in her newly

acquired Dutch, asked what was the matter. The girl
began again, this time more slowly and certainly more
clearly. She had slipped out, she explained—adding a
little wildly that it had only been for a moment, leaving
the two children she looked after while their mother
was at work; little children, Serena gathered. They
had been playing together in the kitchen—the girl
shrugged, an old room with a rotten floor—and they
had been jumping up and down as children will, and
while they had been alone there had been an accident.
It was vital that the doctor came at once.

'He's not here,' said Serena, struggling with her
verbs. 'Can't you telephone the hospital?' She saw that
the girl didn't understand her very well and repeated
'Telephone?' and was met with such a look of fear that
she drew back in astonishment.

'Not my children,' said the girl at last. So that was
it! She had been trusted to mind the children and she
had broken her trust and didn't want the mother to find
out. She would have to be persuaded—but in the meantime the children might be in real need. Serena pointed
to herself and said 'Verpleegster,' a rather comical-
sounding word, she considered, but it did mean 'Nurse'
in Dutch and at least the girl understood what she had
said, because relief spread over her young, frightened
face. Perhaps the accident wasn't too bad if she thought
a nurse would do. Serena decided to go with her and
have a look, it would be quicker in the long run than
standing there arguing, and perhaps by then the girl
would have calmed down and fetch a doctor if he was
wanted. She could ring Gijs herself, of course, but he
had said that he was going to be busy and now he
would be out on his afternoon rounds, anyway, it might
not be necessary to have a doctor at all. She ushered

the girl out into the street and closed the door behind
them.

They crossed to the other side of the canal and
walked rapidly and silently past the Melkmarkt, then
plunged down a narrow alley which led them into a
cobbled street which Serena recognized at once because it had the peculiar name of Hem. Half-way down
its length the girl turned into another narrow alley,
lined with old and rather decrepit houses. Into one of
these she hurried, muttering to herself, Serena hard at
her heels. But despite her hurry, the girl stopped to shut
the door carefully behind her before leading the way
down a minuscule hallway to the kitchen at its end.
She had been right, the floor was rotten; it had given
way in one corner, the snapped-off boards standing up
in splinters. There was something else in the corner too,
a small arm trailing on the ground. Serena dropped on
her knees and felt the boards creak under her. The
owner of the arm was lying below her on the damp
stickiness of the rubble and stones beneath the floorboards, very still and quiet, and equally still, another
child, a mere toddler, lay close by. The toddler lay
pinned by a board across its chest, the other child, a
little boy of five or thereabouts, had a great bruise over
his closed eyes and a splinter of wood protruding
through the shoulder of his jacket.

Serena leaned down and gently felt the smallest
child's wrist. The pulse was beating quite strongly and
she heaved a sigh of relief. The board across its chest
didn't look heavy, so she tugged at it gently and felt a
little sick when she saw that one of the nails sticking
out of the board had penetrated the small chest. She
would have to draw it out—but what to use for a dressing? The house hardly seemed the sort of place where

she might find a first aid box set tidily on a kitchen
shelf. She turned her attention to the little boy and her
sickness returned, for he must have fallen on a jagged
splinter of wood, for a broken sliver of it had pierced
his shoulder from the back; several inches showed
when she gently pulled his jacket back to have a look.
She needed help, and quickly.

'Politie,' she said firmly to the girl hovering behind
her, who instantly burst into tears, looking so terrified
that Serena might have felt pity for her if she hadn't
felt a little frightened herself.

'All right,' she said loudly and in English, 'If you
won't go, I will.' The police station was in Meelstraat
which was fairly close by; she could run hard all the
way. She started to get up, but the girl ran to the door,
banging it behind her before Serena could draw breath.
Serena, creeping back into the narrow dark space under
the floorboards, hoped very much that the girl had understood her and gone for help. There was nothing to
do but wait and see, and meanwhile she would have to
do what she could. It was awkward working in such
confined space; she gritted her teeth and prised the
plank off the toddler's chest; the nail had made only
the smallest of puncture wounds, but she was only too
well aware of the dangers of small penetrating wounds
inflicted by small dirty nails. But at least, when help
did arrive, the child could go immediately to hospital.

The boy was a more difficult matter; it would need
two people, one to support the child and take the strain
while the other drew out the splinter. She shuddered as
she examined the discoloured shoulder—she didn't
think that the bone was broken, but there would be
extensive damage to the tissues and quite a lot of bleed-
ing. She took their pulses, both, thank goodness, quite

strong, and prayed a wordless little prayer that Gijs would come.

He did, within minutes. She heard the street door open and recognized his quiet tread and called in a steady voice, for it would never do to burst into tears and make him ashamed of her, 'Over here, Gijs, and do be careful, the floor's rotten,' and then, because she couldn't help herself, 'How did you know? I believe the girl went for the police.'

'She saw me driving down Hem and stopped me. I've sent her for more help. Make yourself small, my dear, I'm coming down too.'

His voice had sounded different—angry? She wasn't sure; a tiny piece of her mind registered the fact even while she was telling him quickly and clearly what she knew. 'I took the plank off the baby's chest,' she told him, 'you can see the puncture wound from the nail. She's got a fierce bump at the back of her head, too.' She sighed. 'They've both been unconscious all the time, thank heaven.'

He was crowded in beside her, feeling the little body carefully. 'The nail penetrated between the first and second rib,' he told her calmly, 'and there's a fractured clavicle—I can't find anything else at the moment, excepting for the bump on her head.'

He leaned across her and transferred his attention to the boy and in a minute said: 'Serena, I'm going to get behind him. When I say so, lift him up. We've got to get this damned great splinter out of him.' He glanced at her in the half dark. 'Close your eyes while I'm doing it,' he advised her.

She kept them open, though, and when he told her to lift, did so. It was awkward because they were in such a small space; it meant she had to stretch her arms at an impossible, aching angle and hold the small body rock steady, while Gijs probed and poked and prodded. It seemed an age before he finally said quietly: 'Now,' and pulled with steady strength.

It was an ugly wound and it began to bleed at once. At a word from Gijs, Serena scrambled out to get his bag, just as the door opened and two policemen came in. She stood on one side then while the children were lifted out and laid on the floor on the other side of the room, and when Gijs said:

'Pass me the dressings, Serena,' she did so, then found the syringes and the ATS and drew it up. When she handed it to him he glanced down at her hands and said, 'You're badly scratched and there's a graze on your arm.' She looked in a surprised way at her filthy hands because she hadn't felt any pain and said rather stupidly, 'I'm very dirty.'

They put pads and bandages on the two children then and one of the policemen picked up the toddler and carried her outside. Of the girl there was no sign and when Serena asked: 'The mother? Has anyone told her?' Gijs nodded towards the second policeman. 'He's just off to fetch her now. Get into the car, you're coming with me to the hospital.'

'There's no need…' she began.

He picked up the boy. 'Do as I ask, Serena,' he commanded softly.

She sat in the back of the Bentley with the boy in her lap, with the police car, with the toddler inside, in front of them, sounding its siren and flashing its blue lamp.

The hospital was low-storied and built in the form of a wide V, and inside it was very like any other hospital she had been in. The procession she was following halted in Casualty and Serena found a quiet corner away from the little group round the children, wishing she hadn't come, because although Gijs had told her to come, he had apparently forgotten all about her. But he hadn't. After a few moments a nurse detached herself from the group and came towards her, drew her into one of the cubicles and looked carefully at her scratched hands and the graze, then cleaned them equally carefully. She went away again then, to return in a few minutes with a syringe.

'ATS?' queried Serena, and hoped it was the same in Dutch. Apparently it was, for the nurse nodded and smiled and then stood aside when a doctor came in— the doctor she had seen with Gijs. He smiled nicely at her and said in English: 'Your husband asked me to give you penicillin, Jonkvrouw van Amstel,' and plunged the needle in without ado. 'He says also if you will now go home—the police will take you, he will return later.'

He walked to the door with her and they shook hands and Serena, looking at herself for the first time, declared: 'My goodness, I should think I should go home! I need a bath, don't I—and some clean clothes.' She said goodbye and walked to where the little white police car was waiting. At home, in the cool, fragrant hall, she met Jaap's horrified look. She explained as best she could, stumbling over the awkward Dutch words because it was difficult to do so with the limited vocabulary at her disposal, but he understood enough and called to Lien who came hurrying from the kitchen, to bustle Serena upstairs, where she took off the disgusting dress and dirty sandals and ran a bath, commanding, in a motherly tone, that her mistress should get into it at once. She had frowned and tut-tutted over the scratches and graze and gone away, talking to herself, to reappear as Serena emerged from the bathroom with a tea tray and strict instructions to sit down at once and drink her tea and eat some of the delicious little biscuits Lien had just that minute taken from the oven.

It was nice being cosseted, even though she didn't feel in the least ill, only hurt because Gijs had had no time for her, and even as she thought it, she knew it was unfair because the children had, quite rightly, absorbed all his attention. She told herself bracingly that she was becoming selfish and spoilt, and the quicker she changed her ways the better. She finished her tea, did up her newly washed hair, spent a good deal of time on her face, and put on a new dress—a patterned voile of a pleasing shade of blue. It was almost five o'clock. Gijs might come home before he went to the surgery.

He didn't—he wasn't back by dinner time either. Serena waited for an hour and then, urged by Lien, ate hers, with a book propped up before her and the dogs to keep her company. It was almost ten o'clock when he came in quietly with a placid: 'Hullo there—sorry I couldn't let you know.'

She got up from the chair in which she had been curled. 'It didn't matter—you've been busy. I'll see about your dinner. Tell me, how are the children?'

'The little girl's all right—the clavicle was a clean break, and we excised the puncture wound—luckily it hadn't penetrated deeply. She's concussed but not deeply. The boy's more serious. We had to do an extensive excision of wound and open up a good deal to clear it of splinters. By some miracle it missed the bone, but the tissues are badly damaged. Still, he's young and tough. He's badly concussed, though.'

'Did you suture the wound or leave it open?' she asked.

'Open—I packed it with petroleum jelly gauze and sulpha powder.'

She nodded. 'Do you suppose it will heal by first intention?'

'Yes, I should imagine so.' He was smiling now. 'I told you how much I needed someone to listen to me, didn't I?'

She was at the door. 'Actually,' she said, 'if I were a really good wife, I should be in the kitchen, fetching your dinner. I've put the whisky out.'

She sat at the table with him while he ate and when he asked, gave him a lighthearted version of her own part in the afternoon's happenings. When she had finished, he observed: 'It was most fortunate that you were home. The girl lost her head.'

'She disappeared. Did anyone find her?'

He nodded. 'Yes, half dead with fright. I think she was under the impression that she would be sent to prison.'

'The poor mother…'

'Yes—her husband has left her and she's been trying to manage; too proud to ask for help. I've put someone on to that, they'll see to everything.' He passed his cup for more coffee. 'Was there any post?'

She got up and went to his study and brought back the little pile of letters, saying: 'I suppose they can't wait? Could I help?'

He smiled. 'Open them for me, there's a good girl, would you? You can throw out the circulars and so on and I'll scribble notes on the rest and Juffrouw Kingsma can deal with them in the morning.' He picked up a letter as he spoke and became immersed in it, so Serena collected the dinner things on to a tray and carried it away to the kitchen, then went back to the dining-room to wish him good night. He wasn't there. As she stood in the doorway, she heard the Bentley whisper quietly away from the front door and her eyes filled with childish tears; he could have at least called out as he went or spared a second to come and find her. She went up to bed and lay awake until she heard the car turn the corner of the *steeg* and sigh its way gently into the garage. It was after half past one. After a few minutes she put on her dressing gown and slippers; she would go down and make him a hot drink; he would be tired. She was almost at the bedroom door when she heard him coming upstairs and go into his room. He closed the door very quietly after him and the house became silent again. Serena took off her dressing gown again and got back into bed—it had been a silly idea anyway, had he not said that he didn't like her getting up at night? It was almost day before she went to sleep.

At breakfast he was his own casual self. They had taken their usual walk together and he had talked about the children and asked her about her scratched hands and praised her for her part in their rescue. It was towards the end of the meal that he mentioned that Tante Emilie would like her to go and have coffee with her one morning soon.

Serena buttered a roll. 'Oh? Did she telephone? I didn't know...'

'No, I saw her last night—briefly. There was a note, delivered by hand, with the post you gave me. It was from Adriana. She is at Tante Emilie's house for a day or two; she wanted to see me urgently, and we are such old friends...' He paused and Serena waited for him to continue, but he didn't, only looked at her thoughtfully as though he were deciding whether to tell her something or not. Not, she concluded, and murmured, for something to say, 'How nice,' at the same time longing to scream at him that she was tingling all over with a poisonous mixture of rage and jealousy and curiosity. She choked back these ill-bred feelings with a mighty effort and asked instead:

'Will you be late this evening?' and when he shook his head, reminded him: 'We have to go to the van Oppens for dinner, you know.' Doctor van Oppen lived in Dreishoor and she liked his wife. They would sit and gossip after dinner and the two men would smoke their pipes and discuss their work until Mevrouw van Oppen suggested more coffee or a drink, and then they would bid each other good night and Gijs would drive her home, talking of nothing in particular—and that, she thought savagely, would be another day.

But not quite, for when they got home that evening, instead of wishing her good night and going to his study, Gijs said: 'There's something I want to tell you—if you're not too tired?'

Serena went before him into the study and sat down in the smaller of the two easy chairs drawn up to the empty hearth. She hadn't spoken because she was speechless with the dread that he was going to remind her of his words when he had offered to marry her; that they should tell each other if they fell in love with someone else. She had all of the long day in which to think about his sudden departure the night before and he had made no secret of whom he had met, although he had given her no reason...but then, she had argued to herself, why should he? She might be his wife, but had they not married on the understanding that they were to be good friends with no deeper feelings involved? She had added and discarded conjectures for hours and had always reached the same total, that whatever he had said, he was in love with Adriana even though she had chosen to marry Laurens, and she—Serena had used her imagination here to embroider the story—knowing Gijs's feelings for her, had summoned him and he had gone at once, without so much as a good night. Perhaps, Serena had thought rather wildly, Adriana had changed her mind again, and didn't want to marry Laurens after all and had sent for Gijs so that she could tell him this. She sat very still, her folded hands on the silken lap of her dress, very aware of Gijs sitting opposite her. He seemed in no hurry to speak, so in the end, edgy with nerves, she remarked:

'It was a pleasant evening, wasn't it? I like Mevrouw van Oppen—she asked me to call her Wil. She gave me the recipe for that Bavarian Cream, and...'

'Serena, you're babbling,' said her husband, and smiled at her with a faintly puzzled amusement. 'I was going to tell you why I went to see Adriana last night,' his grey eyes searched hers. 'Perhaps you already know.'

'She's ill?' asked Serena, hope dying hard.

He shook her head. 'No, her health is perfect. I thought you might have guessed, or heard...'

It was, she discovered, more than she could stand; she was so steeped in her own imagined version of their meeting that she answered quite sharply: 'Yes, of course I've guessed,' and jumped to her feet. 'Do you mind if we don't talk any more now? I—I've got such a bad headache.'

She made for the door, not looking at him at all; she

barely heard his quiet, 'Good night, Serena,' as she closed the door behind her.

In her room she took off her shoes and curled up in the centre of the bed, her head a whirlpool of forebodings and memories and ragged thoughts without beginning or ending. Horrid, vivid flashbacks unfolded themselves before her eyes and the most vivid of them of the occasion when she had asked him if Adriana was his girl and he had said 'Lies, all lies,' and she had actually believed him. It all fitted so well—it was Adriana he loved, this quiet man who never showed his feelings to her, and when Laurens had stolen a march on him, he hadn't really cared what happened, and because he was kind and had felt sorry for her and liked her, and his own future was wrecked, he had suggested that they could do worse than marry each other. After all, she told herself bitterly, it couldn't have mattered to him whom he married. Just as it hadn't mattered to her. She choked on a sob; she'd made a fine mess of things. In the morning, when she felt better, she would talk to him. It shouldn't be too difficult, for he didn't know that she loved him, and as long as he didn't find that out... She got off the bed and started to undress, walking around the room, dropping things and leaving them where they fell.

But once in bed, she couldn't sleep for thinking about the morning and what she would say, getting very muddled and more and more confused as the night wore on. She would, of course, return to England; she would have to use some of the money Gijs gave her so generously, but she didn't think he would mind. She would drive the Mini to Schipol and leave it there, then stay quietly out of his way until everything was nicely settled with as little fuss as possible. There was his good name to consider. On this high-minded resolution, she at last fell asleep.

She overslept; Gijs had gone by the time she got downstairs, to eat a solitary breakfast with only the dogs for company. Still resolved to carry out her good intentions, although she was, in broad daylight, a little vague as to what exactly she would do, she attended to her household chores, took the dogs for a long walk along the *gracht* which encircled the town and arrived home to find a message from Gijs to say that he wouldn't be home for lunch. So she had a second lonely meal, and was just debating what she should do to fill the time before Gijs came home, when the telephone rang. It was Tante Emilie—her voice, coming threadily over the wire, inviting her with more warmth than usual to go and have tea that afternoon. 'Laurens is away at The Hague,' she explained, 'and Adriana has gone home, poor girl, so I am a little lonely.'

Serena agreed readily enough. It would help to pass the afternoon; anything would be better than giving herself the leisure to think. She remembered then that they were to dine at Renesse that evening, unless Gijs came home early there would be no time to talk before they went. It would have to be when they returned. Rehearsing, for the hundredth time, what she would say to him, she went up to her room to tidy herself.

Tante Emilie was in the garden, sitting in the shade of the trees, away from the house. She welcomed Serena with slightly more warmth than the cold politeness she usually accorded her, and began to talk at once about the wedding, the guests, Serena's wedding dress and the unfortunate circumstances which prevented her and Gijs going on a honeymoon. She enlarged upon this theme for some minutes until the tea tray was brought out, a diversion which Serena welcomed with relief. They were sipping the beverage when Jonkvrouw van Amstel changed the subject with startling abruptness.

'You know that Laurens is going to America?'

Serena put down her cup. She was surprised, but that was all, she didn't care in the least where Laurens went. She said carefully: 'No, I didn't.'

'I am surprised. Gijs has known for some weeks, but of course, he would hardly have wished to discuss it with you.'

'Why ever not?' Serena wanted to know.

Her hostess's look was a mixture of curiosity, triumph and pure mischief.

'It is still painful for him to do so, I imagine. He and Adriana...' She left the sentence in the air, to exasperate Serena. 'She and Laurens are ideally suited, of course, and they will be happy,' she gave this opinion with a certain smugness, and turned a sharp eye upon Serena, 'though I have no doubt that Gijs could win her back without any difficulty at all, although of course he is now hindered from doing so, is he not, my dear?'

Serena said nothing because her tongue was doing that most unlikely of things, cleaving to the roof of her mouth, which gave her hostess the opportunity to say: 'Laurens has a very good post in Pittsburgh.'

Serena would have liked to drink some tea, anything to delay having to speak, but she felt sure that her cup and saucer would rattle in her trembling hands, she crossed her feet, admired her shoes, drew a deep breath and asked with commendable calm:

'What about the practice?'

Tante Emilie shrugged her shoulders. 'Gijs knows

plenty of men who would be delighted to step into Laurens's shoes.'

'Gijs—last night…'

'Came at once,' said her companion with satisfaction. 'Of course we left them alone—it was something she and Gijs had to decide together.'

Serena, controlling her hands, drank her tea. And what was to happen to her—to them both? Sooner or later she would have to know, and it might as well be now; it would be far better if she knew the whole story before she saw Gijs. She winced at the thought, and Tante Emilie, who had been watching her, said with faint malice: 'Gijs seems very fond of you, my dear.'

Serena caught the malice although it puzzled her. 'I should like to see Adriana,' she stated.

'The dear child is in Amsterdam—with her family, you know—she went early this morning. They have a large house in Amstelveen…' She enlarged upon the house, its garden and its furnishings at some length, but Serena, who was nothing if not tenacious, said: 'Then perhaps you will give me her address; I should like to go and see her.'

Her hostess paused. 'Why, yes, of course you shall have her address, my dear. You could drive up and see her.' And she wrote it down, giving precise directions and advice as to how to get to Amstelveen and which part of the town to avoid. Serena, listening to her meticulous instructions, felt ashamed of her ill-feeling towards her hostess. She took her leave, telling herself that she had misjudged the lady after all.

Gijs was late home. He barely had time to shower and change before setting out for Renesse, and once there the evening lengthened out to so late an hour that by the time they were home again, Serena knew that it

would be hopeless to try to talk to him. Tomorrow, she
promised herself as she wished him good night and
paused on the stairs when he told her:

'I'll be in Utrecht all day, Serena. Will you be all
right on your own? I shall leave very early—with any
luck I shall be back for dinner.'

So that would be another day gone by—he would be
tired after such a long day, it would hardly be fair to
expect him to discuss their future. She told him quietly
that she would be perfectly all right, and resolved then
and there to go to Amstelveen. It was a splendid opportunity to get to the bottom of Tante Emilie's hints.

She didn't enjoy the drive to Amstelveen; the road
was empty enough as far as Vlaardingen so that she
had plenty of opportunity to think, and her thoughts
weren't happy ones. She hadn't seen Gijs that morning,
although she had heard the Bentley steal from the garage just after six, and when she had gone downstairs
she had found an envelope on her breakfast plate with
a note inside, written in Gijs's small, immaculate
handwriting: 'Buy yourself something pretty.' It was
wrapped round a little wad of money. He was, she told
herself, the most kind and considerate of men; the
thought was followed by another one, one of which she
was instantly ashamed; he could have been easing his
conscience.

It was getting on for noon by the time she reached
Amstelveen for she had gone the wrong way twice and
had had to stop to look at the road signs besides. The
house was one in an avenue of pleasant villas, un-
imaginative as to build but decidedly prosperous-
looking. She parked the Mini neatly and walked up the
short front path and rang the door bell. She had to ring
again before anyone answered it and when the woman

at last came to the door Serena had the impression that
she had been expecting her, but she must have been
wrong in this; the woman had difficulty in understanding Serena's frugal Dutch and when she did at last
reply it was to shake her head and say: 'The Juffrouw
has left, this morning—early.'

'Where to?' asked Serena, ever dogged.

'Friesland, north of Leeuwarden—many kilometres.'

Serena, who had spent a long time poring over maps
and mileages when she had had the Mini, spent a few
minutes turning kilometres into miles—miles didn't
seem so far, but even when she had done that it was
still ninety miles away, and that was only to Leeuwarden. She could never get there and back again to Zierikzee before Gijs got back in the evening. In the Bentley with Gijs driving it would have been easy
enough—besides, she didn't know the road and the
woman, when she questioned her further, wasn't disposed to be helpful. She thanked her and went back to
the car, feeling deflated.

She got home again about three o'clock without having stopped for lunch.

'There's a tray ready for you in the kitchen, *Mevrouw*,' Jaap told her. 'If you like to go into the house
I'll fetch it along to you—unless you lunched on the
way?'

'No, Jaap. But don't stop your gardening. I'll take it
with me as I go.'

She carried it through the house and set it on the
dining-table. Its contents looked delicious, but she
wasn't hungry. She fed German and Gus with wafers
of *rookworst* and ham, feeling a little guilty about it,
drank the coffee in the thermos jug and then carried it
back to the kitchen and went up to her room. The dogs

went with her; the three of them got on to the bed and
presently went to sleep.

It was tea time when she wakened. Gijs didn't come
in until eight o'clock, when they ate a dinner which
Lien had miraculously managed to hold back for an
hour without ruining any of it, and over it, Gijs told
her about his day at some concourse or other; Serena
listened carefully, asking intelligent questions and pay-
ing attention to his answers and all the while longing
to say: 'Gijs, why can't we talk—really talk?' for he
seemed remote, and getting more remote all the time.
Over coffee she said:

'There's a great deal of post for you today, shall I
fetch it?' and when he said that no, he would read it
presently, she saw her last chance of saying something
sliding away until the next day, and who knew, he
might be away from home again. Rendered reckless by
frustration, she asked suddenly, her tongue saying the
words she really didn't wish to utter:

'Gijs, were you ever in love with Adriana?'

He leaned back in his chair and smiled a little and
said lazily: 'What man wouldn't be in love with such
a pretty creature at some time or other in his life?'

Which was no answer at all, so that she tried again,
her voice a little too high and loud. 'Are you still in
love with her?'

His expression didn't change. The smile was still
there, only his eyes were half closed so that she was
unable to read their expression.

'You're not serious, dear girl?'

And that wasn't an answer either. She nodded. 'How
can you bear to let her go?'

He was filling his pipe and didn't look at her. 'Who
told you that Adriana was going away?'

'Your aunt—Tante Emilie. I had tea with her two days ago. She hinted... Gijs, did Adriana ask you to go and see her?'

'Yes.' His voice was bland.

'You went to make her change her mind?'

'Yes.'

'Did you succeed?' Her voice wasn't loud any more, but a small dry whisper.

'Yes, dear girl.' He leaned back a little further in his chair, his eyes still half shut. 'Aren't you going to ask me what was the reason for my asking?'

'I know.' Serena was proud of her voice; in her ears it sounded unflurried and calm, so it was all the more infuriating therefore when he remarked placidly, 'Are you being just a little over-hasty?'

She eyed him across the table. He didn't look as though he cared a button for her opinion, over-hasty or otherwise. She had her mouth open to say so when there was a hammering on the front door knocker and Gijs went to open it, calling to Jaap to stay where he was in the kitchen, as he did so. Serena heard him talking to someone at the door and then he was back again, with Laurens.

He greeted her with a mixture of gay charm and apology which at any other time might have flattered her, but now his: 'Hullo, Serena, have you forgiven me for my bad behaviour at the surgery?' left her unmoved. She got to her feet and smiled with something of an effort. 'Yes, of course, I'd forgotten all about it. Will you have some coffee?'

'No, thanks—I'm only here for a few minutes. Adriana wants to see Gijs and nothing would do but that I should fetch him myself.'

Serena said slowly: 'I thought Adriana was in Friesland.'

Laurens had already turned away, ready to leave. He said over his shoulder:

'Friesland? You've been dreaming—she's still at Mother's house. She certainly wouldn't go all that way.' He laughed across to Gijs, standing by the door. 'I've had to stand down for Gijs, you know.'

The two men took their leave of her and she supposed that she had answered them sensibly because, beyond a casual good night, they said nothing. As the front door closed behind them she found herself wondering how it was that Laurens could be so cheerful at the thought of losing Adriana to Gijs, and that was another thing—why had Tante Emilie told her that Adriana was in Amstelveen and then, when she had got there, why had the woman who had answered the door told her that Adriana was in Friesland? She could think of no sensible answer and after roaming round the house doing nothing, she went and sat down with an open book on her lap; she would read quietly until Gijs came back and they would discuss everything with calm and sense. She read the same page several times, telling herself that he wouldn't be more than half an hour.

But he didn't come back in half an hour. Serena waited for another half an hour and then another and finally went up to bed. She lay awake a very long time, but Gijs still hadn't come.

He greeted her with his usual placid friendliness the next morning, and without giving her a chance to take the conversation into her own hands, talked about everything and anything but themselves. They were seated at breakfast and she was still trying to frame a sentence urgent enough to engage his attention, when he looked up briefly from his post to ask:

'How would you like to go to England?'

She got up to let Gus into the garden and kept her back to him as she answered steadily: 'Yes, I should like that. Could—could it be arranged easily, without anyone…' She was interrupted by the telephone. It was a long call. When Gijs came back Lien was in the room with some household query and Serena said with determined brightness: 'Will you be home to lunch, Gijs?'

He thought he might. At the door he turned to look at her. 'I want to talk to you, my dear,' he told her as he went out.

The morning went on leaden feet. Serena occupied it with unnecessary tasks, getting in Lien's way until that poor woman suggested that Serena might like to go to the butcher and order the meat and call in at the grocer for the particular brand of mustard Gijs preferred. Serena went willingly; it would distract her thoughts, which, having been given full rein since breakfast, were in such a state of muddled truth and fiction that she no longer knew which was which.

When she arrived home Gijs was already there. His bag was on the table in the hall and as she shut the door he came downstairs, not hurrying, although she was struck by the sense of urgency he conveyed, so strong was it that she began to apologize. 'I didn't know you would be home early. I went to the shops— I won't be a minute.'

She started for the kitchen, but he intercepted her with one leisurely stride, taking her packages and tossing them on to the table, and unleashing Gus, who, delighted to see German again, ran to meet him in the garden. She felt his arm on her shoulders as he led her through the door beneath the stairs, past his study, to the sitting-room at the back of the house. Gijs stopped in the open door leading to the garden and turned her round to face him. When he spoke his voice was casual; he could have been talking about the weather.

'My dear, it seems to me that things aren't turning out quite as I—we had hoped. We are friends, are we not? and yet we seem unable to understand each other...my fault, I know. I've been busy—too busy. Life must have been dull for you these last few weeks, but I promise you an end to that—there will be changes...' He looked all of a sudden withdrawn, and Serena, who had put her own interpretation on his words, said impulsively: 'How can you bear it? It's worse than you thought, isn't it? Is Adriana going with Laurens to America—I mean when he goes?'

He looked at her with faint surprise. 'I believe so. Serena...'

'They're going to be married...?' She stared at him as she spoke and saw that his face now had no expression upon it at all. Suddenly she couldn't go on; she didn't want to hear, to have to put into words, all her unhappy, hopeless thoughts. She would go away, she thought, quickly, without talking about it. She could leave a note for Gijs telling him that she didn't want to be married any more and he would be free for his Adriana, for it was obvious to her that Laurens would stand no chance at all if Gijs were free. Adriana had taken him as second choice and because Tante Emilie had set her heart on it. She didn't know about Laurens, whether he loved Adriana or not, and she didn't care.

'You're not listening,' she heard Gijs's quiet voice

cutting through her busy thoughts. 'Never mind. I've chosen the wrong moment, haven't I? But there's time enough for what I have to say. Let's have lunch. Isn't it this evening that we're having dinner with the Wisselaars?'

She followed his lead; lunch passed off surprisingly pleasantly, with no more awkward questions requiring answers. They kept to trivialities while behind Serena's bleak, lovely face, her brain seethed. Gijs had only left the house five minutes, and she was at the telephone, asking the exchange to get the number of Doctor van Elven, in Richmond.

Gijs was home for tea, although late. As he joined her in the garden he apologized for his delay. 'A telephone call, just as I was leaving the hospital,' he explained. She noticed how bright his eyes were as he spoke, even though his face wore its habitual calm expression. She passed him his tea, her imagination, rioting around inside her head, had already supplied the caller—Adriana, of course. She took an angry breath and choked over her tea, then was forced to suffer the humiliation of having him pat her on the back while she struggled to get her breath.

Serena dressed very carefully that evening; Mevrouw Wisselaar was the *Burgemeester*'s wife, a lady with an extensive wardrobe, the reason Serena gave herself for putting on a new and very expensive little dress she had bought at a boutique she had discovered in Veere when she had driven herself there one afternoon. It was a peach pink chiffon, pleated and cunningly cut with long full sleeves and little pearl buttons fastening the deep cuffs. She put on the ruby earrings and the kid sandals she had bought in England before she married, picked up the matching handbag and took a quick look at herself in the mirror. The whole effect, she was bound to admit, was most successful, only she must remember to smile.

Gijs was waiting for her in the sitting-room when she went in. He looked her over without haste and said finally: 'Delightful—I hope I'm the one you want to impress.'

Of course it was, but she had no intention of letting him know that. What good could it possibly do—and anyway, he was only being kind and polite as he unfailingly was. She said flippantly: 'Well, actually, no. It's for the *Burgemeester's* wife, she has smashing clothes, you know, and I felt like competing.'

He smiled. 'I imagine you'll win easily. Is there to be anyone else there?'

Serena told him as they went out to the car, and during the short drive she chatted, feverishly, about this and that, terrified that he would start to talk about her going to England. But he made no mention of it; it was as though he had forgotten his suggestion, and once at their host's house, she saw very little of him for the entire evening, for at dinner she sat between an important lawyer from The Hague and an elderly and charming *dominee* from Veere; both gentlemen seemed bent on improving her knowledge of their country and she rose from the table, her head reeling under the facts and figures and statistics they had fired at her.

To avoid a silence on the way home she told Gijs about the elderly gentlemen and had even managed to laugh with him about it and go on to talk about the evening in a quite gay manner. Parting from him in the hall of their home, it struck her forcibly that this would be the last time she would do that. Tomorrow she would be in England, at Sárah's house, and he…he would be with Adriana, perhaps. She wondered if he and Laurens would quarrel about Adriana, or would Gijs arrange everything quietly and competently, as he had arranged? She forced herself to stop thinking and lifted her face and presented a cheek for Gijs to kiss, then turned away to go upstairs; she was on the bottom step when she was arrested by his voice, very casual and drawling.

'I should have told you sooner, Serena. I have to leave very early tomorrow morning—another meeting—an important one to me. I shall be gone before you are up. What were your plans for tomorrow?'

'Plans? I—I...' she had been taken by surprise. 'I don't know. I expect I shall take the car. I hope your meeting will be a success.'

His quiet voice followed her up the stairs. 'It will be,' he said.

CHAPTER NINE

SERENA heard Gijs leave just after six. She had had a wretched night and several times she had been tempted to discard her plans; to go and talk to him, to see Adriana, Laurens even, anything rather than go away. There were so many small reasons why she should stay, too. They had begun to matter to her—his parents, of whom she had become very fond, Gus, whom she loved, the ever-increasing circle of friends and last but by no means least, the lovely old house and the bustling little town. Life without these things, and above all, without Gijs, did not bear thinking about. She wept a little and then dried her tears quickly, telling herself that giving way to self-pity would do no good at all. Dressed, and with her bag packed, she crept downstairs to the garage where she left her bag in the Mini, then went back to put the letter she had written to Gijs in his study, and then to the kitchen.

Lien was already up, and Serena, who had anticipated this, embarked on a long story about going to visit someone a long way away and it was such a nice day it seemed a good idea to go early.

Saying good-bye to Gus and German was hard. Serena hadn't realized how hard when she had laid her plans, nor had she envisaged the wrench she would experience as she said good-bye to Lien and Jaap with a cheerfulness which sat ill upon her poor white face. She went round to the garage, trying not to look back at the house and doing so despite all her resolution.

She got into the Mini, her throat thick with the tears she was determined not to shed, and backed it into the *steeg*, then drove slowly past the house, remembering to wave to Lien who was still standing in the doorway.

There was a fine rain falling when Serena's taxi drew up outside the van Elvens' house in Richmond. It spattered down gently on to the pink linen dress and jacket she was wearing and on to the small straw hat which matched them; an unsuitable outfit in which to run away, she had known that when she had put them on, but they looked gay and carefree, and she had the childish idea that they might cheer her spirits. They had done nothing of the sort; she watched the taxi drive off and then rang the bell in a state of near panic. Now that she was here she wondered what she should say to Sarah, for she hadn't told her a great deal over the telephone—perhaps she wouldn't ask. She had been a fool to come. She half turned from the door, but it was too late, Alice had opened it, to greet her smilingly and take her bag as she ushered her into the hall, and now it was certainly too late because Sarah was coming through a door, looking more beautiful than ever.

'Serena, how lovely to see you!' she kissed her warmly. 'Come in, my dear.'

She opened the sitting-room door as she spoke and Serena went past her into the room. She had forgotten how kind Sarah was, as kind as she was beautiful; she would tell her everything and ask her advice—there would only be the two of them; Hugo wouldn't be home until the evening or late afternoon.

She was wrong. Hugo van Elven was there, standing with his back to the empty fireplace, and beside him stood Gijs, his hands in his pockets, very much at his ease.

Serena lost her breath, caught it again and turned, intent on escape, but Sarah was behind her and had shut the door and was leaning against it. 'Presently,' thought Serena tiredly, 'I shall be able to sort this out,' and walked on strangely shaky legs a few steps forward as Hugo came across the room to meet her. He took her hand and smiled and said: 'Dear little Serena, we seem to have been waiting a long time.' He looked over her shoulder and exchanged a glance with his wife, who opened the door. Serena hardly noticed them go, although she heard the door shut behind them.

The impulse to rush across the room straight into Gijs's arms was very great, but she resisted it because she wasn't sure why he was there, nor, for that matter, if he would welcome such a demonstration. He could be in London for some reason connected with his work—she had to know. She swallowed from a dry mouth and asked flatly: 'Why are you here?' She was pulling and tugging at her quite expensive handbag with no thought as to the damage she was causing.

For someone so unhurried in his movements, Gijs moved with surprising speed. The misused handbag was taken from her grasp and her hands taken in his.

'Dearest heart, where else should I be but where you are?'

Her heart threatened to choke her. She stared at his tie, a nice grey silk one; a small piece of her stunned brain approved of it. She kept her eyes steadily upon it and asked: 'How did—how could you possibly know?'

'My darling, Sarah telephoned me yesterday evening.'

Her beautiful eyes left the tie and flew to his face.

She said on a surging breath: 'Well—well, how absolutely beastly of her! I left you a letter.'

'Yes? I thought perhaps you might. And don't think badly of Sarah. Do you remember that I told you once that one day I would tell you about her and Hugo? I think this is the moment.' He had released her hands and put his arms around her, holding her away a little so that he could see her face. 'When Hugo and Sarah married, she didn't love him—she had been—er—jilted and he caught her on the rebound. She ran away too, it took Hugo more than a week to find her. She is far too fond of you—and me—to let history repeat itself. So she telephoned me.'

Serena's eyes were back on his tie. 'She could have made an awful mistake. How did she know that I—how did she know anything?'

His voice was calmly reasonable. 'Well, my darling, she knew that I love you, just as your parents know.'

She looked at him then, the colour rushing into her pale face. 'Mother and Father—I don't understand—and Sarah...' She thought it over while her eyes searched his. She said at length: 'But you didn't tell me.'

'You didn't want to know, not at first, did you, my dearest dear? Your lovely head was still full of Laurens. You had to empty it of him before you could even notice me, and just when I was beginning to think that you had discovered that it was I and not Laurens you loved, you chose to stuff your head with a great deal of nonsense which, most unfortunately, made sense.'

It was like unravelling wool; she caught hold of the nearest conversational strand and pulled gently. 'I don't understand. Tante Emilie—she told me that day I went to tea that you and Adriana—that it was you, even though she and Laurens are going to get married, and when I asked you you said you'd been in love with her. You went to see her that evening and you didn't come home until half past one in the morning, and then Laurens came to fetch you.'

'And I tried to tell you, my adorable, pig-headed, addle-pated wife. Adriana is going to America with Laurens, you know that, but she may not go without being vaccinated. For some reason she had never been done as a child and she was terrified to the point of hysteria. She made such a fuss when Laurens attempted to vaccinate her that he gave up and she sent a note round asking me to do it. I persuaded her to have it done, but she didn't screw up the courage until the evening Laurens came for me. Do you not remember that he told you that he was having to stand aside for me?'

Serena gave a sniff because she wasn't sure if she was going to laugh or cry. She said pettishly, 'I thought he meant that you and Adriana—how ridiculous!' She sniffed again, wild laughter bubbling up inside her, warring with tears. She was still undecided which should win when Gijs solved the problem for her; he kissed her with such thoroughness and at such length that by the time he had finished she had forgotten everything else, or almost everything. Despite the kiss she persisted: 'But Tante Emilie—she told me that you and Adriana—that you loved her, and I thought that if I went away—I thought that perhaps you had married me because you couldn't marry her and I was out on a limb anyway, and it wouldn't have mattered,' she drew a breath which ended in a sob. 'If you read my letter, you would see what I mean,' she ended, aware that she hadn't made herself very clear.

Gijs kissed her again, taking his time about it. 'I very much doubt it, my darling.' He sounded as though he was laughing, but he must have understood at least some of the half-finished sentences, obscure references and pure conjecture, for he added: 'Dearest Serena, what a lot of mistaken thinking you have been doing.' He sounded very comforting, just as his arms, holding her tightly now, were comforting. Serena, her voice muffled by his shoulder and still intent on getting everything quite clear, tried again. 'Tante Emilie told me...'

'Tante Emilie seems to have had a lot to say and none of it to a good purpose. She is old-fashioned, prejudiced and a doting mother, but above all she is obsessed by the family. A very long time ago, when I was a young man and Adriana was an even younger woman, I fell in love with her—I fell out of love within six weeks or so as one does at that age, but Tante Emilie decided that it would be a splendid thing if we were to marry. It was a bitter disappointment to her when I showed no desire to do any such thing; you can imagine how pleased she was when Laurens, years later, decided that Adriana was the girl for him, but then he met you, my darling, and you are very beautiful, you know, and he is susceptible to beautiful girls. Poor Tante Emilie; you were the stumbling block to all her plans. I don't think she could quite forgive you, so she took a pretty revenge by allowing you to believe that Adriana and I were still in love with each other, a piece of nonsense Adriana will be the first to disclaim.'

Serena gave a weak chuckle. 'Oh, Gijs, darling Gijs, what a stupid creature I've been—vaccinating Adriana, and all the while I thought...I went to Amstelveen to see her.'

Her husband took this unexpected turn in the conversation in his stride.

'Tell me about it, dearest.' Which she did with a fair amount of coherence and then lifted her lovely, faintly tearstained face to his so that he was forced to remark: 'I can't blame Laurens in the least for falling for you—I did myself, the moment I set eyes on you.'

'In the front hall of Queen's,' added Serena happily. 'Did you really? I didn't fall in love with you, you know, although I knew you were there.'

'Yes? I made up my mind to marry you on the way up to Laurens's room. I knew that it would take time and patience, but I had plenty of both, and I have found that if one has patience enough one gets what one wants in the end.'

He smiled down at her and she wondered how she could ever have imagined that he was casual and easy-going, for just at that moment he looked very alert and his eyes, no longer hidden by their drooping lids, had a glint in them which set her heart tripping over itself in a most disturbing fashion.

'How nice,' he observed slowly, 'that we don't have to get married, and how equally nice that we can go home together.'

Serena snuggled her head a little deeper into his shoulder. 'In time for evening surgery?' she inquired flippantly.

She was crushed in a gentle hug. 'Father is taking over for this evening—he'll take over for a week while we have a honeymoon, too. Shall I tell you where we're going?'

She nodded. 'Though I don't mind if we don't have one.'

He ignored this remark. 'Scotland. Hugo has a tiny cottage in Wester Ross. We can go when we like.'

'It sounds lovely! When shall we go? Oh, Gijs, I'm so happy I think I'm going to cry. Laurens told me once that you were very good at letting girls cry on your shoulder.'

'Not girls, dearest—just you, and later on, our daughters.'

Serena said gently: 'No, little boys, all like you.'

'There is such a thing as compromise, my love,' said Gijs on a laugh. 'How about an equal number of each?'

She sniffed too late, a tear trickled down her cheek. 'Oh, Gijs, I do love you.'

'And I love you, my darling.' He kissed her again by way of proof. 'I believe that I shall tell you so very frequently for the rest of our lives. In the meantime, though, I think we might allow Hugo and Sarah to return, don't you? Hugo is waiting to open the champagne and Sarah and Alice have concocted a magnificent lunch—besides, we haven't a great deal of time in which to catch our plane.'

'What plane?' asked Serena, her thoughts already flying ahead, in Zierikzee.

'I've booked on the five o'clock flight, I thought it would be nice if we had dinner together in our own home.'

'Super!' uttered Serena, and turned a bright smiling face to Sarah and Hugo as they came in.

It was dark before they were back in Zierikzee. Gijs had driven fast from Schipol and they hadn't talked very much because there wasn't any need, only as they crossed the stretch of water between Oude Tonge and Zijpe, and saw Schouwen-Duivenland before them, Serena said: 'I can't see Zierikzee, but I know it's near. I'm so happy!'

Gijs' hand rested briefly on her knee. 'My dear heart, did you really think that I should allow anything else? You are my life, without you there would be nothing.'

They tore along the empty road across the island, to slow down at the towering gateway and pass beneath it and into the quiet of the Oudehaven. Gijs wasn't hurrying now. They passed the Mondragon, its lights cheerful in the darkened town, and turned across the head of the canal and so to the other side—the side where home was. As Gijs drew up, Serena could hear German's staccato bark and Gus's excited treble, and when he opened the door, the two dogs hurled themselves at them in an ecstatic welcome, and Lien and Jaap came hurrying from the kitchen. They were standing, all of them together, when the telephone rang, and Gijs, his arm in hers, crossed to answer it. She stood within the circle of his arm and heard him say:

'I have her here, Mama, safe with me,' and when he put down the receiver she said in a surprised voice: 'Your mother knew!'

'Yes, darling. I had to ask Father to take the surgery, you see, and Mama is good at putting two and two together.'

'She must think I've been an awful fool.'

Her husband's arms drew her close. 'No, she doesn't.'

'And you—what do you think?' inquired Serena.

'Come into the sitting-room and I'll tell you,' said Gijs. 'It may take some time.'

Small Slice
of Summer

BETTY NEELS

CHAPTER ONE

BIG BEN struck midday, and the sound, though muffled by the roar of London's traffic, struck clearly enough on Letitia Marsden's ear, causing her to put down the recovery tray she had been checking and look expectantly towards the doors separating theatre from the recovery room. Mr Snell had begun a Commando operation some three hours earlier; at any moment now the patient would be handed over to her care. The doors swung silently open at that very moment and she pressed the buzzer which would let the orderly know that she must come at once, and advanced to meet the theatre party and receive the still figure on the trolley from the hands of the scrub nurse.

'Hi, Tishy,' said that young lady in a cheerful whisper. 'Everything's OK, buzz if you want any help.' They cast a combined professional eye over the unconscious man between them. 'He's been a nasty colour once or twice, so keep your weather eye open.'

Letitia nodded. 'What's next? A cholecystectomy, isn't it?'

Her friend and colleague nodded. 'Yes—this one

should be fit to move before Sir gets through with it, though. The anaesthetist will be out presently— he's new by the way, filling in for Doctor van den Berg Effert.' She raised her brows in an exaggerated arch. 'Super, too.' she handed over the theatre slip, cast an eye on the clock, murmured: 'So long,' and slid back through the doors.

Letitia began her work, silent save for the mut- tered word now and then to the attendant orderly, one Mrs Mead, a middle-aged lady of great good sense, who had the added virtue of doing exactly what she was asked to do without arguing about it— her whole mind, save for one minute portion of it, concentrated upon her task, and that tiny portion concealed so deliberately beneath her calm cringed away from the grotesque appearance of the patient; the flap of skin already grafted, later to be used to cover the extensive operation on his throat, gave the man, lying so still, a quite unhuman appearance, and yet she was fully aware that later, given skilled nurs- ing, expert skin grafting and time, his appearance could be made perfectly acceptable even to the most sensitive. She noted his pulse, his pupil reactions and his breathing, charted her findings, and because his colour wasn't quite to her satisfaction, turned on the oxygen. She was adjusting it when the door opened and a gowned and masked figure came un- hurriedly in, to join her at the patient's side. A large man, very tall, and when he pulled down his mask, extremely handsome with it, with fair hair already flecked with grey, bright blue eyes and a long straight nose whose winged nostrils gave him a somewhat arrogant expression. But his mouth was kind when he smiled, and he was smiling at her now. She didn't smile back; since her unfortunate experience with the Medical Registrar she distrusted men—that was to say, all men under the age of fifty or so. She frowned at him, her eyes beneath their dark brows as bright a blue as his, her ordinary face, with its run-of-the-mill nose and large generous mouth, framed by the theatre mob cap which concealed the great quantity of dark brown hair she wore in a well-ordered coil on the top of her head.

'OK?' asked the giant mildly.

She handed him the chart with its quarter-hourly observations. 'His colour isn't quite as good as it was,' she stated, 'I've started the oxygen.'

He nodded and handed back the chart, looking at her now, instead of the patient. 'Call me if you want me,' he answered her, still very mild. 'The name's Mourik van Nie.' He turned on his heel and slid through the doors, making no sound, and moving, considering his size, very fast.

She got on with her work, saying what was necessary to Mrs Mead, her mind on her patient. It was only after an hour, when the giant had been back

once more, pronounced the patient fit to be transferred to the Intensive Care Unit and gone again,
that she allowed herself to speculate who he was.
Dutch, she supposed, like Doctor van den Berg Effert, one of the few men she liked and trusted and
wasn't shy of; but then he was married to Georgina,
her elder sister's close friend; they had trained together and now Margo was Sister on the Children's
Unit, and Georgina lived in the lap of luxury and a
state of married bliss in Doctor van den Berg Effert's lovely home in Essex. She and Margo had
been there to stay once or twice and Letitia, living
in a fool's paradise in which the Medical Registrar
was the only important being, had imagined herself
living like that too—only it hadn't turned out like
that at all; he had taken her out for a month or two,
talking vaguely about a future, which she, in her
besotted state, had already imagined into a fact
which wasn't fact at all, only daydreams, and then,
when she had refused to go away with him for the
weekend, had turned the daydream into a nightmare
with a jibing speech about old-fashioned girls who
should move with the times, and ending with the
remark that she wasn't even pretty... She had
known that, of course, but she had always thought
that when one fell in love, looks didn't matter so
very much, but she had been too hurt to say anything, and how did one begin to explain that being

the middle girl in a family of five daughters, strictly but kindly brought up by a mother with decidedly old-fashioned ideas and a father who was rector of a small parish in the depths of rural Devon was hardly conducive to being the life and soul of the swinging set.

She had said nothing at all, not because she was a meek girl, but because she was too choked with hurt pride and rage to make sense. She had thought of several telling speeches to make since that unhappy occasion, but since he worked on the Medical Wing and she spent her days in Theatre Unit, there was small chance of their meeting—and a good thing too, although her friends, meaning it kindly, kept her informed of his movements. He was currently wrapped up with Jean Mitchell, the blonde staff nurse on Orthopaedics, whom no one liked anyway; Letitia, in her more peevish moments, wished them well of each other.

The Commando case was transferred to the ICU.; she handed him over to the Sister-in-charge, repeated the instructions she had been given, put his charts into her superior's hands, and raced back to the recovery room. The cholecystectomy would be out at any moment now and she had to fetch the fresh recovery tray and see that Mrs Mead had cleared the other one away and tidied up. They were nicely ready when the doors swung silently open once more. It had been a straightforward case; she received her instructions, obeyed them implicitly, and when the anaesthetist loomed silently beside her, handed him the chart without speaking; there was no need to tell him the things he could see for himself: the patient was ready to go to the ward and she stood quietly waiting for him to tell her so, which he did with an unhurried: 'OK, Staff, wheel her away. There's an end-to-end coming out in a few minutes, old and frail; do what you can and let me know if you need me.'

And so the day wore on. Letitia was relieved for a late dinner and found the canteen almost empty, though the Main Theatre staff nurse was still there and a handful of nurses who had been delayed by various emergencies.

Letitia wandered along the counter with her tray, looking for something cheap and nourishing; she had bought a dress on her last days off and her pocket was now so light that buying her meals had become a major exercise in basic arithmetic. She chose soup, although it was a warm June day, a roll to go with it and a slab of treacle tart, because starch was filling and even though it was fattening too she was lucky enough not to have that problem, being possessed of a neat little figure which retained its slender curves whatever she ate. She paid for these dainties at the end of the counter and went to join her fellow staff nurse, Angela Collins, who cast a sympathetic eye at the contents of her tray, said fervently: 'Thank God it's only a week to pay-day,' and addressed herself to her own, similar meal.

Letitia nodded. 'Holidays in four weeks,' she observed cheerfully, and thought with sudden longing of the quiet Rectory. The raspberries would be ripe, she would go into the garden and walk up and down the canes, eating as many as she wanted. She sighed and asked: 'How's theatre? There's only that resection left, isn't there?'

Her friend snorted. 'There was—they popped two more on the list while Sister wasn't looking. She's fighting mad, but Mr Snell's doing his famous wheedling act and that new man has the charm turned full on—he's got her all girlish. I must say he's rather a dream; a pity he's only here while our Julius takes a holiday.'

'I thought you liked him.'

'Our Julius? Of course I do—we all dote on him, but he's married, isn't he? To your sister's best friend, too.'

Letitia nibbled at her roll, making it last. 'Yes, she's a sweetie, too.'

She wolfed down the treacle tart. 'I've still got some tea, shall we make a pot?'

They hurried over to the Nurses' Home and climbed to the top floor where the staff nurses had their rooms, and because there were several girls off duty, the tea was stretched to half a dozen mugs, sipped in comfort on Letitia's bed to the accompaniment of a buzz of conversation until she looked at her watch, discovered that she was almost late, and flew back through the hospital once more, walking sedately in those parts where she was likely to meet Authority, who frowned on running nurses, and tearing like mad along the long empty back corridors.

The afternoon went fast; it was half past four before the last case was wheeled away to the ward and Letitia, aided by the faithful Mrs Mead, began clearing up. Between them they had the place stripped, cleaned and put together again by the time Big Ben chimed five o'clock. Mrs Mead had gone and Letitia had taken off her theatre dress and mob cap and was standing in the middle of the room doing absolutely nothing when the giant walked in once more.

'Not got home yet?' he asked carelessly as he crossed to the outside door. 'Good afternoon to you.' He smiled vaguely in her direction and she heard him walking rapidly along the corridor which led to the wards. When she couldn't hear his footsteps any more she took one final look round the recovery room and went in her turn out of the door. As she passed the Surgical Wing she caught a glimpse of him, standing outside Sister's office, deep in conversation with Staff Nurse Bolt, another friend of hers. They were both laughing and it made her feel a little lonely: he could have stopped and talked to her, too.

She had to hear of him later that evening, when half a dozen of them were sitting round consuming the chips they had been down the road to buy—cheaper than the canteen and filling—besides, someone had come back from days off with a large fruit cake and, between them they had gathered tea and sugar and milk and made a giant pot of tea. They had cast off their frilly caps and their shoes and some of them were already in dressing gowns and the noise was considerable. It was Angela who brought up the subject of the newcomer. 'He's fab,' she uttered to anyone who cared to listen, 'huge and smashing to look at, and one of those lovely slow, deep voices.' She turned her head to look for Letitia, pouring tea. 'Hey, Tishy, you must have had time to take a good look—didn't you think he was absolutely super? Just about the most super man you've ever set eyes on?'

There was silence for a few seconds; every girl in the room knew about Tishy and the Medical Registrar, and because they all liked her they had done their best to help her by saying nothing about it and ignoring her pinched face and red eyes. It was a pity that Angela hadn't stopped to think. Several of them spoke at once to save Tishy from answering, but she spoke with her usual composure. 'I didn't really look at him—we were too busy. He knows his job, though.'

There was a chorus of relieved agreement before someone wanted to know if the rest of them had seen the trouser suits in Peter Robinson's, and the talk turned, as it so often did, to clothes.

Letitia was on duty at eight o'clock the next morning. The list was heavy enough to begin with, petering out after dinner time, so that by four o'clock she was clearing the recovery room in the pleasant anticipation of getting off duty punctually at half past four. As indeed she was. She wandered through the hospital on the way to her room; several of her friends were off duty too, they might have a few sets of tennis, it was a lovely day still. She stopped to look out of a window and saw Doctor Mourik van Nie getting into a car—a splendid BMW convertible. She studied its sleek lines and admired the discreet grey of its coachwork before she turned away, wondering where he was going.

Jason Mourik van Nie was going to Dalmers Place. An hour or so later he joined Julius van den Berg Effert and Georgina on the terrace behind the house. Polly, their very small daughter, was almost asleep on her father's knee and Georgina exclaimed in relief as he walked out of the french windows. 'There you are—Polly refuses to go to bed until you've kissed her good night.' She smiled at her husband's friend. 'If you'll do that right away. I'll whisk her off to bed and Julius shall get us all a drink.'

Jason smiled at her, kissed his small goddaughter, exchanged a brief *'Dag'* and sat down.

'Stay where you are, darling,' said Julius, 'I'll pop this young woman into her bed and bring the drinks as I come back.'

His wife gave him a warm smile. 'Tell Nanny I'll be up in ten minutes unless Ivo starts to cry.' Her smile widened and Julius grinned back at her; Ivo was just two months old, a tiny replica of his father, whereas little Polly was like her mother with a gentle prettiness and most of her charm. She wound a small arm round her father's neck now and smiled sleepily at him as he carried her into the house.

Jason watched them go. 'Julius is a lucky man,' he said quietly. 'You, and the enchanting Polly, and now Ivo.'

'I'm lucky too,' Georgina told him, 'I've got Julius.'

'I hope someone says that about me one day,' he observed. 'May I smoke my pipe?'

She nodded. 'Of course. Did you have a busy day?'

'So-so. One Commando to start with and a couple of abdominals, then we petered out with appendices.

Snell was operating again. Oh—Theatre Sister sent her love, I've forgotten what she said her name was and I couldn't identify her very well; she was gowned up and masked, the only face I've seen clearly in these last few days was in the recovery room—quite unremarkable, though—it belongs to someone called Tishy.'

Georgina smiled. 'Little Tishy. She's Margo's young sister—she must be twenty-three, I suppose, she qualified six months ago. You didn't like her?'

Jason stretched his long legs and studied his enormous, beautifully shod feet. 'I hadn't really thought about it,' he admitted carelessly. 'Mousey girls with heavy frowns aren't quite my line.'

'Oh, she doesn't frown all the time,' stated Georgina quickly, 'it's only because you're a man,' and as her companion's brows shot up: 'She was almost engaged to the Medical Registrar, but he switched his interest to a dashing blonde on Orthopaedics—I daresay she was more accommodating. I don't know what he said to poor little Tishy, but ever since then she's shied away from anything male under fifty.'

'Julius too?'

'Julius is thirty-seven,' his loving wife reminded him, 'but Margo is a friend of mine and of course I know Tishy too; she's been here once or twice, so she knows Julius quite well as well as working for him. He takes care to be casually friendly, bless him. She's a splendid nurse.'

She turned her head and her eyes lighted up as they always did when she saw her husband.

'Sorry I was so long,' he apologized as he set the tray of drinks down. 'Great-Uncle Ivo telephoned—wants to know when we're going over to Bergenstijn. I told him we'd be there before the summer's over. The theatre's closing at the end of July, we'll go then if you would like that, my love.'

Georgina agreed happily. 'Lovely, Julius—we can all go. Cor and Beatrix and Franz-Karel can drive them over. Dimphena will be with Jan, I suppose, but they could come over...'

Jason studied his glass. 'What a quiverful you took on when you married Julius,' he observed idly, 'four cousins of assorted ages.'

'Don't forget Polly and Ivo. But the others—they're not small any more; Karel's a post-graduate and almost finished with hospital, and Franz is sixteen, that only leaves Beatrix and Cor, and now Dimphena is married there's quite a gap.'

'Which we shall doubtless fill within the next few years,' commented her husband softly.

'I'm envious,' said Jason slowly, and Georgina threw him a quick glance.

'No need,' she told him kindly, 'you only have to

lift a finger for all the prettiest girls to come running.'

'That's all very well as well as being grossly exaggerated, but none of these same girls had ever
succeeded in convincing me that I can't live without
her.'

Georgina got up. 'One day there'll be a girl,' she
assured him, 'though probably she won't be pretty
or come running. I'm going to see to Ivo.'

She ran indoors and the two men sat in silence
for a few minutes, Presently Jason spoke. 'As I said
to Georgina just now, you're a lucky devil, Julius.'

'Yes, I know.' He added thoughtfully, 'I was
thirty-three when I first met Georgina.'

'A reminder that I'm thirty-five and still haven't
met my paragon?' They both laughed before plung-
ing into a discussion as to how the day had gone in
theatre, absorbed in their world of anaesthetics.

It was later that evening as Georgina sat before
her dressing table brushing her hair that she said
suddenly: 'Julius, can you think of a good reason
for having Tishy down here?'

Her husband's eyes met hers in the mirror.
'Tishy?' he queried mildly. 'Why Tishy, darling?'

'She could be exhausted,' went on Georgina, taking no notice, 'worn out with work and needing a
few days' rest...'

Julius had become adept at reading his wife's mind. 'She would have to work fast.'

Georgina gave him a doubtful look. 'That won't do, then,' she stated positively. 'I daresay she can't bear the sight of him, and he's hardly noticed her.'

'My love, is it wise to play providence? They're a most unlikely pair; just because Tishy is getting over hurt pride and Jason chooses to remain a carefree bachelor it doesn't mean that they'll fall into each other's arms.'

'No, I can see that, but it would be nice. If we just gave them the chance...'

But as it turned out there was no need of that.

Two days later, with the list almost over for the day, Letitia was starting on the clearing up, her mind happily occupied with plans for her days off, due to start in the morning. Two days, she mused, and almost no money so she wouldn't be able to go home, but she could go to Epping, where an elderly aunt lived—no telephone, unfortunately, but Aunt Maud never minded an unexpected visitor for a couple of days. She had a dear little house on the edge of the forest and it would be pleasant after the heat and rush of London and the hospital. If Margo had been there they could have gone together, but she was on holiday, up in Scotland with friends. Letitia nodded her head in satisfaction, glad that she had made up her mind, and looked impatiently at the theatre doors; the case should have been finished by now, it was hernia and shouldn't have to stay long in her care. She looked at the clock, calculating how soon she could get away that evening, then turned round to see who it was who had just come in from the outer door.

It was the very last person she wanted to see; Mike Brent, the Medical Registrar, lounging in, very sure of himself, his good-looking face wearing a smile which not so very long ago would have melted her heart and now, rather to her surprise, made no impression upon it at all.

'Hullo,' he said, 'how's little Tishy? Haven't seen you around for quite a few weeks—I was beginning to think you might have run away.'

She eyed him steadily. 'Why should you think that?'

He shrugged his shoulders. 'Oh, well—no hard feelings.'

She arranged a recovery tray just so before she answered him. 'I'm busy, there's a case...'

He interrupted her impatiently. 'Oh, come off it, Tishy. To tell you the truth I've been a bit worried; didn't like to think of you feeling jilted and all that, you know—after all, I couldn't help it if you took me seriously, could I? And you're a bit out of date, aren't you. I mean, the odd weekend doesn't mean a thing...'

'It does to me.' Neither of them heard the theatre door open, Doctor Mourik van Nie's voice startled them both. 'Perhaps if I might break into this most interesting discussion on your love life?' he suggested placidly, and turned to Letitia to study her furious face with gentle amusement.

'This next case coming in within a few minutes— she's not so good.' He ignored the other man completely and began to give her instructions; by the time he had finished Mike had gone.

She boiled with temper while she dealt competently with her patient, damping down her furious thoughts so that she might concentrate on the matter in hand. Only some half an hour later, the patient transferred to the ward, nicely on the road to recovery again, did she allow her mind to dwell on the unfortunate episode which had occurred. And funnily enough it was the Dutchman she was furious with; for coming in like that and overhearing Mike talking all that hot air. She paused, aware that his words, which at one time would have been quite shattering to her, were, in fact, just that. She had, let her face it, been a fool; she was well rid of him, even if her pride was still ragged at the edges. But that Doctor Mourik van Nie should have been a witness to such a nasty little scene—that was a different matter entirely; he must have found it amusing; he had stared at her as though he had never seen her before. She felt unreasonably annoyed about that, so that she clashed and banged her way around the recovery room before finally leaving it in a state of perfection. The quicker she got out of the hospital and into Aunt Maud's placid company, the better.

In her room she flung a few things into an overnight bag, changed into the tan jersey cardigan suit with the shell pink blouse she had bought instead of eating properly that month, coiled her long hair neatly on the top of her head and, nicely made up, dashed out to catch a bus.

The Underground was crowded; she didn't get a seat until the train had left Leytonstone, and it was a relief when she at last got out at Epping and went into the street. The crowds were a little less now, but the rush hour wasn't quite over; track was still heavy coming from London. She was standing on the kerb waiting to cross the street when a group of people passing her unthinkingly shoved her off the curb into the path of the oncoming cars. She had a momentary glimpse of a sleek grey bonnet and heard the squeal of brakes as the bumper tipped her off balance. She fell, hoping desperately that her new outfit wouldn't be ruined, aware as she fell that she had done so awkwardly and that her left ankle hurt most abominably. She had no chance to think after that, because Doctor Mourik van Nie was bending over her. 'Well, I'm damned,' he said, and then: 'Does anything hurt? The bumper caught you and you fell awkwardly.'

Letitia sat up, glad of his arm, comfortably firm, round her shoulders. 'I was trying to save my dress. It's my ankle, otherwise I'm fine.'

A small crowd had collected, but the doctor took no notice of it, merely scooped her neatly off the ground and carried her to the car, where he sat her carefully on the front seat. 'Let's have a look,' he suggested calmly, and slid her sandal off a decidedly swollen ankle. 'A sprain, I fancy. Stockings or tights?'

'Tights.'

He produced a pair of scissors from a pocket. 'Sorry about this—I'll get you another pair,' he promised as he made a neat slit and cut the nylon neatly way above the ankle. He was reaching for his bag in the back of the car when the policeman arrived. Letitia sat back, listening to the doctor's quiet answers to the officer's questions, the eager chorus of witnesses, anxious to allow no blame to rest upon him, and her own voice, a little wobbly, giving her name and address and where she was going and why. By the time things had been sorted out the ankle had been firmly bandaged and her head was beginning to ache. She didn't listen to what the doctor said to the policeman—indeed, she barely noticed when he got in beside her and started the car;

she was suddenly sleepy. The car was comfortable to the point of luxury; she closed her eyes.

They were almost at Dalmers Place when she woke up again; she recognized the road almost at once. 'I was going to my aunt in Epping,' she began worriedly. 'My days off, you know.'

'You went to sleep—the best thing for you. Does she expect you?'

'No.'

'Then there's nothing to worry about. I'm taking you to Dalmers Place. You're a friend of Georgina, aren't you—and Julius? They'll be delighted to put you up for the night.'

She turned to look at him, quite shocked. 'Oh, you can't do that—invite me there without them knowing, whatever will they say? If you'd stop... oh, dear, we've gone through Bishop's Stortford, haven't we? Could you go a little out of your way to Saffron Walden? There's a station there—I could get on a train back to Epping.'

'Hopping all the way? Don't be absurd. Besides, I feel responsible for you—I knocked you down.'

'But it wasn't your fault, and really I can't allow you...'

He interrupted her in a placid voice. 'Dear girl, what a mountain you are making out of this little molehill! And you know that you're dying to get to bed and nurse that painful ankle.'

She had to laugh a little then and he gave her a quick sideways glance and said: 'That's better,' and a moment later slowed the car to allow Mr Legg, who did the garden and lived in the lodge at Dalmers Place, to come out and open the gate for them, and then drove, still slowly, up the short, tree-lined drive to the house where he stopped before its door, told her to stay where she was, got out, and went round the side of the house.

Georgina looked up as he reached the terrace. 'Hullo,' she greeted him cheerfully. 'We were just beginning to wonder what had happened to you.'

'I've brought someone with me, I hope you won't mind—it's Tishy.'

He was quick to see the quick look his friends exchanged and went on smoothly, 'I could take her on...' to be cut short by Georgina's fervent: 'No, Jason—we're delighted, really, only Julius and I were talking about her—oh, quite casually,' she avoided her husband's twinkling eye, 'and it's funny, isn't it, how when you talk about someone they often turn up unexpectedly. Where have you left her?'

'In the car. She sprained her ankle—I knocked her down.'

Georgina was already leading the way. 'Oh, how unfortunate!' she exclaimed, meaning exactly the opposite. She glanced at Julius over her shoulder.

and when Jason wasn't looking, pulled a face at him. 'But we must thank Providence that it was you, if you see what I mean.'

CHAPTER TWO

LETITIA SAT in the car, feeling a fool. Her ankle throbbed, so did her head, and she had been pitch-forked into a situation which had been none of her doing. Probably Georgina would be furious at having an unexpected guest at less than a moment's notice. True, she had been to Dalmers Place before, but only in the company of her sister Margo—it was Margo who was Georgina's friend. She sought feverishly for a solution to her problem and came up with nothing practical, and when the three of them came round the house and crossed the grass towards the car, she found herself studying their faces for signs of annoyance. She could see none; Georgina was looking absolutely delighted and her husband was smiling, and as for Doctor Mourik van Nie, he wore the pleased look of one who had done his duty and could now wash his hands of the whole tiresome affair.

Georgina reached the car first. 'Tishy,' she exclaimed, 'you poor girl—does it hurt very much? You shall go straight to bed and the men shall take another look at it—you look as though you could do with a drink, too. Thank heaven it was Jason who knocked you down and not some stranger who wouldn't have known what to do.' She paused for breath and Letitia said quickly: 'I'm awfully sorry— I mean, coming suddenly like this and being so awkward.' Her eyes searched Georgina's face anxiously. 'You don't mind?'

'Of course not, it'll be fun once that ankle stops aching.' She stood aside while Julius said Hullo in a welcoming way and Jason said matter-of-factly: 'I'll carry you in.'

'I can hobble, I'm sure I can.'

He grinned. 'I shouldn't bet on that if I were you.' He had opened the car door and swept her carefully into his arms. 'Which room?' he asked Georgina.

'Turn left at the top of the stairs, down the little passage, the second door.'

Letitia wondered if the doctor found her heavy; apparently not, for he climbed the staircase at a good pace and with no huffing or puffing, found her room without difficulty and sat her down in a chair. 'Georgina will help you undress,' he told her with impersonal kindness, 'and we'll come back later and take another look at the ankle.' He had gone before she could frame her thanks.

Half an hour later she was sitting up in bed, nicely supported by pillows and with the bedclothes turned back to expose her foot; by now the ankle was badly swollen and discoloured. The men came in together with Georgina and Letitia wasn't sure whether to be pleased or not when neither gave her more than a cursory glance before bending over the offending joint, which they agreed was nothing more than a partial tear of the ligament and hardly justified an X-ray. 'We'll strap it,' they told her. 'You'll have to rest it for three or four days, then you can start active use—a couple of weeks and you'll be as good as new.'

'A couple of weeks? But I've only got two days off!' She was appalled at their verdict.

'Sick leave?' suggested Doctor Mourik van Nie. He sounded positively fatherly.

She stared at him; they were all being very kind, but she was spoiling their evening. She said quickly: 'If I could go back to St Athel's with you in the morning—there's a list at nine o'clock, isn't there?—I could see someone. That's if you wouldn't mind taking me.'

He gave her a long considered look and she felt her cheeks grow red.

'No, I won't take you, you silly girl. Georgina has already said that you're to stay here until Julius pronounces you fit to travel, and that won't be for a few days.'

'Of course you'll stay,' chimed in Georgina warmly. 'I shall love having you; these two are driving up to Edinburgh at the weekend, to some meeting or other, and I wasn't looking forward to being alone one bit. And now I'm going to see about your dinner, you must be famished.'

'And I'll telephone St Athel's,' Julius suggested, and left the room with his wife, leaving Doctor Mourik van Nie lounging on the side of the bed.

'That's settled,' he commented, and smiled at her, and for some reason she remembered that he had smiled that afternoon when he had come upon her and Mike.

'You're all very kind,' she said crossly, because her head still ached, 'but I don't like being a nuisance.'

He got to his feet so that she had to tilt her head to look up at him.

'My dear girl,' he said, and his voice was bland, 'the sooner you stop imagining that because one man said you were—er—old-fashioned, the rest of us are villains and you're a failure, the better. I'm surprised at you; you seem to me to be a sensible enough girl, and when you smile you're quite pretty.'

He strolled to the door. 'You'll feel better in the morning,' he assured her as he went out.

Letitia stared at the shut door; probably she would feel much better in the morning, at the moment she felt quite sick with surprise and temper—how dared

he talk to her like that?—it was possibly these strong
feelings which caused her to burst into tears.

She was wiping her eyes when Georgina came
back, and she, after one quick glance, made some
thoughtful remark about delayed shock and proffered the glass of sherry she had brought with her.
'Dinner in half an hour,' she said cheerfully, 'and
Julius says a good night's sleep is a must, so he's
coming along with a sleeping pill later on.'

Letitia sipped the sherry. 'I've never taken one in
my life,' she protested, and then remembering what
the Dutchman had said, added meekly: 'But I will
if he says so.'

She felt a lot better after her dinner and better still
after a long night's sleep. Indeed, she woke early
and lay watching the sun gathering strength for another warm day, and she heard the car drive away
too. That would be Doctor Mourik van Nie, she supposed, and she felt an unreasonable pique because
he hadn't come to inquire how she felt, but of course
she wasn't his patient, only an unfortunate incident
at the end of a long day.

She sat up in bed, wincing a little at the pain in
her ankle, and thought about him, willing to admit,
now that it was morning and she was feeling better,
that he had been quite right even if a little outspoken, the previous evening. She had been sorry for
herself, she admitted that now, although she hadn't

much liked being dubbed as sensible, but he had said that she was almost pretty when she smiled. She smiled now, remembering it, and turned a beaming face upon the maid who presently tapped on the door with her early morning tea.

The day rolled along on well-oiled wheels; the house came alive, breakfasted, and settled down to the morning. Julius came early, examined the ankle, pronounced it to be going along nicely and left Georgina to help her out of bed and into a chair by the window and presently they all had their coffee there, with Polly playing happily and baby Ivo asleep in his cot. It was when Julius got up to go to his study that Letitia asked a little diffidently if he had telephoned the hospital.

'Did I forget to tell you? You are to stay here until I consider it all right for you to travel, and it has been left to me to decide if you need a week off after that.'

She was unaware of how plainly her thoughts showed on her face. 'Home for a few days?' suggested Georgina, reading them correctly. 'One of the men can take you up to town and drop you off at the station...' She stopped and smiled, looking so pleased with herself that Letitia was on the point of asking why, but Julius spoke first, to say that he would be back very shortly and carry her down to the garden. 'Far too nice a day to stay indoors,' he

pointed out kindly, and when she thanked him, adding that she hoped she wasn't being a nuisance, he
went on: 'Of course not—we're treating you as one
of the family, Tishy, and Georgina's delighted to
have your company while we're away, and in any
case, just to prove how much we take you for
granted, I'm driving her to Saffron Walden very
shortly. Nanny will be here with the babies, of
course, and Stephens will bring you your lunch and
see that you're comfortable. You don't mind?'

He had struck the right note; she felt at ease now
because she wasn't spoiling their day after all. 'Of
course I don't mind—it will be super doing nothing.
You're both so kind.'

Julius went away and Georgina smiled and offered to get a rather fetching housecoat of a pleasing
shade of pink for her guest to wear. Letitia put it on,
admiring the fine lawn and tucks and lace. It had a
pie-frill collar and cuffed sleeves, and looking down
at her person, she had to admit that lovely clothes
did something for one… 'I can leave my hair, can't
I?' she asked. 'There's no one to see.'

Her kind hostess bent down to pick up a hairpin.
She said: 'No one, Tishy,' hoping that Providence,
already so kind, would continue to be so.

The day was glorious. Letitia, lying comfortably
on a luxurious day bed, leafed through the pile of
glossy magazines she had been provided with, ate a

delicious lunch Mrs Stephens had arranged so temptingly on the trays Stephens carried out to her, then closed her eyes. It was warm in the sun; she would have a crop of freckles in no time, but it really didn't matter. She had spent a lot of money she really couldn't afford on a jar of something or other to prevent them, because Mike had told her once that he thought they were childish. Thinking about it now, she began to wonder exactly what it was about her that he had liked. Whatever it had been, it hadn't lasted long. She remembered with faint sickness how he had told her that she wasn't pretty. 'Not even pretty,' he had said, as though there was nothing else about her that was attractive. She frowned at the thought and pondered the interesting question as to what Doctor Mourik van Nie would find attractive in a girl. Whatever it was, she felt very sure that she hadn't got it. She dozed off, frowning a little.

She woke up half an hour later, much refreshed, and saw him sitting in an outside garden chair, his large hands locked behind his head, his eyes shut. She looked at him for a few seconds, wondering if he were really asleep and why was he there anyway; her watch told her that it was barely half past two; theatre should have gone on until at least four o'clock. Perhaps, she thought childishly, he wasn't really there; he had been the last person she had thought about before she went to sleep—he could be the tail end of a dream. She shut her eyes and opened them again and found him still there, looking at her now. 'You've got freckles,' he observed, and unlike Mike, he sounded as though he rather liked them.

'Yes, I know—I hate them. I bought some frightfully expensive cream to get rid of them, but it didn't work.'

'They're charming, let them be.' His voice was impersonal and casually friendly and she found herself smiling. 'I thought theatre was working until four o'clock today.'

'It was, but at half past twelve precisely some workman outside in the street pickaxed his way through the hospital's water supply. Luckily we were on the tail end of an op, but we had to pack things up for the day. Do you mind if I go to sleep?'

She felt absurdly offended. 'Not in the least,' she told him in an icy little voice, and picked up a magazine. Unfortunately it was *Elle* and her French not being above average, looking at it was a complete waste of time; even the prices of the various wayout garments displayed in its pages meant nothing to her, because she couldn't remember how many francs went to a pound.

'You're a very touchy girl,' observed her companion, his eyes shut, and while she was still trying to find a suitable retort to this remark:

'Am I right in suspecting that this—what's his name—the Medical Registrar was the first man you ever thought you were in love with?'

She sat up and swung her legs over the side of the daybed. 'I won't stay here!' she exploded. 'You have no right…you don't even know me…ouch!'

She had put her injured foot to the ground and it had hurt. The doctor got out of his chair in a patient kind of way, lifted the stricken limb back on to the daybed, said: 'Lie still, do—and don't be so bird-witted,' and went back to his chair. His voice was astringent, but his hands had been very gentle. 'And don't be so damned sensitive; I'm not a young man on the look out for a girl, you know. I'm thirty-five and very set in my ways—ask Julius.' He closed his eyes again. 'I'm ever so safe, like an uncle.' There was a little pause, then he opened one eye. 'I like that pink thing and your hair hanging loose.'

Letitia had listened to him in amazement and a kind of relief because now she could think of him as she thought of Julius; kind and friendly and big brotherish. Two short months ago, if Mike had said that, she would have been in a flutter, now it didn't register at all—at least, she admitted to herself, it was nice that he liked her hair. She took a quick peep and was disappointed to see that his eyes were closed once more.

He wasn't asleep, though. 'Where is your home?' he asked presently.

She cast *Elle* aside with relief. 'Devonshire, near Chagford—that's a small town on Dartmoor. Father's the rector of a village a few miles on to the moor.'

'Mother? Brothers and sisters?' His voice was casually inquiring.

'Mother and four sisters.'

His eyes flew open. 'Are they all like you?'

She wasn't sure how to take that, but she answered soberly: 'No, they're all pretty. Hester—she's the second eldest—is married, so's Miriam, she comes after me, and Paula's the last.'

'And where do you come?'

'In the middle.'

'And your eldest sister—Margo, isn't it? She's George's friend?'

'Yes, they trained together. Margo's away on holiday. She's going to get engaged any day now.'

He opened an eye. 'I always thought,' he stated seriously, 'that the young lady about to be proposed to was suitably surprised.'

Letitia giggled, and just for a few moments, in her pink gown and her shining curtain of hair, looked, even with the freckles peppering her nose, quite pretty, so that the doctor opened the other eye as well.

'She and Jack have known each other ever since she was fifteen, but he went abroad—he's a bridge engineer, so Margo has gone on working while he got his feet on the ladder, as it were, and now he's got a marvellous job and they can buy a house and get married.'

'And you will be a bridesmaid at the wedding, no doubt?'

'Well, no—you see, we drew lots and Miriam and Paula won. It's a bit expensive to have four bridesmaids.'

The corners of his firm mouth twitched faintly. 'I daresay two are more than ample. I have often wondered why girls had them.'

She gazed at him earnestly as she explained: 'Well, they make everything look pretty—I mean, the bride wants to look nicer than anyone else, but bridesmaids make a background for her.'

'Ah, yes—stupid of me. Do you set great store on bridesmaids, Letitia?'

She was about to tell him that she hadn't even thought about it, but that would have been a colossal fib; when she had imagined herself to be in love with Mike, her head had been full of such things. 'I used to think it was frightfully important, but now I don't imagine it matters at all.'

'You know, I think you may be right.' He heaved himself out of the chair and stretched enormously. 'I'm going to get us a long cool drink and ask Stephens if we can have tea in half an hour. Can I do anything for you on my way?'

She shook her head and sat back, feeling the sun tracing more freckles and not caring. She wasn't sure what had happened, but she felt as though Jason Mourik van Nie had opened a door for her and she had escaped. It was a lovely feeling.

The drinks were long and iced and he had added straws to her glass. She supped the coolness with delight and exclaimed: 'Oh, isn't this just super?' then felt awkward because he might not find it super at all.

'Very.' He was lying back again, not looking at her. 'Do you suppose you could remember to call me Jason? I call you Tishy, you know, although on second thoughts I think I'll call you Letitia, I like it better.'

'Mother always calls me that, but they call me Tishy at the hospital, and sometimes my sisters do too when they want me to do something for them.'

They had their tea presently in complete harmony and she quite forgot to wonder where Georgina and Julius had got to, and when Nanny came out with Ivo in his pram and Polly got on to the doctor's knee, she lay back, listening to him entertaining the moppet with a series of rhymes in his own language, apparently quite comprehensible to her small ears. She watched him idly, thinking that it was pleasant doing nothing with someone you liked. She gave herself a mental shake; only a very short time ago she hadn't liked him, but when she tried to remember the exact moment when she had stopped disliking him and liking him instead, she was unable to do so. Her thoughts became a little tangled and she abandoned them when Jason broke in on her musings with the suggestion that she might like to recite a nursery rhyme or two and give him a rest. She had got through 'Hickory, Dickory, Dock' and was singing 'Three Blind Mice' in a high sweet, rather breathy voice when Georgina and Julius joined them and the little party became a cheerful gossiping group, with Ivo tucked in his mother's arms and Polly transferred to her father.

'Ungrateful brat,' remarked Jason pleasantly. 'Letitia and I are hoarse with our efforts to amuse her and now she has no eyes or ears for anyone but her papa.'

'You got back early?' Georgina asked, and smiled a little.

Jason repeated the tale of the workman and his pickaxe and everyone laughed, then the men fell to making plans for their trip on the following day until Jason said: 'I'll carry Letitia indoors, I think, she doesn't want to get chilled.' He got up in leisurely fashion. 'Where is she to go?'

'The sitting-room—we'll have drinks, shall we? No, better still, take her straight up to her room, will you, so she can pretty herself up, then you can bring her down again.' Georgina looked at Letitia. 'You're not tired, Tishy?'

'Not a bit—how could I be? I've been here all day doing absolutely nothing. It's been heavenly, but I feel an absolute fraud.'

'Until you try to stand on that foot,' remarked Jason, and picked her up. 'Back in ten minutes,' he told her as he lowered her into the chair before the dressing table in her room and went away at once. She barely had the time to pick up her hairbrush before Georgina came in. 'Don't try and dress,' she advised, 'or do anything to your hair,' and when Letitia eyed her doubtfully: 'You look quite all right as you are.'

She went away too, so Letitia brushed her hair and creamed her freckles and sat quietly, not thinking of anything very much until Jason came to carry her downstairs again.

The evening was one of the best she could remember, for she felt quite at ease with Georgina and Julius, and as for Jason, his easy friendliness made her oblivious of her appearance and she even forgot her freckles. She reminded herself that two months ago, out with Mike, she would have been fussing about her hair and wondering if her nose were shining and whether she had on the right dress. With Jason it didn't seem to matter; he hardly looked at her, and when he did it was in a detached way which didn't once remind her that her hair was loose and a little untidy, and her gown, though charming, was hardly suitable for a dinner party. He carried her up to bed presently and before he left her took a good look at her ankle.

'Quite OK,' he pronounced, and wished her goodbye, because he and Julius would be leaving very early the next morning.

The house, after they had gone, seemed large and empty, a fact to which Georgina agreed, giving it her opinion that it was because they were two such large men; all the same, the two girls contrived to spend a pleasant day together, with Stephens and the gardener to carry Letitia down to the garden and the two babies to play with. Julius telephoned twice, the first time shortly after they had arrived, and the second time a few hours later, just as the girls were going to bed. Letitia wondered what Jason was doing, but she didn't like to ask Georgina, who, for some reason, didn't mention him at all, but when Julius telephoned the next morning, she couldn't refrain from asking at what time the men might be expected back.

'Well, there's no telling,' explained Georgina. 'They both drive fast and awfully well and I daresay they'll take it in turns, which means that they'll do it in about six hours. They can do seventy on the motorway, you see, and that's almost all the way. They'll be here for tea.'

And she was right. Letitia was entertaining Polly with a demonstration of 'Here's the church, here's the steeple' when she heard men's voices and looked up to see them strolling towards them. Neither looked in the least tired, although they ate an enormous tea.

'No lunch?' asked Georgina.

'Well, my love, I had promised myself that we would be home for tea,' Julius smiled at his wife, 'and Jason liked the idea too.'

Letitia watching them, thought how wonderful it would be to be loved as much as that. She sighed, and Jason asked at once: 'Are you tired? Do you want to go indoors and rest?'

She shook her head. 'No, oh, no, thank you.'

His voice was kind. 'One more day and then I should think you might try some gentle exercise. How does the ankle feel?'

She hardly noticed when the others went indoors and Jason started to tell her about Edinburgh and their meeting. She was surprised when Julius came out to ask them if they wanted to go in for drinks before dinner. The day, though pleasant, had been long, now the evening was going far too quickly.

The next few days went quickly too, each one speedier than its predecessor, or so it seemed because she was enjoying herself so much. It was a week after her accident, when she had been hobbling very creditably for a couple of days, that Julius gave her his verdict that she was to all intents and purposes, cured. Jason wasn't back from hospital, she was sitting with Georgina and him, lingering over tea, watching Polly tumbling around on her short fat legs, and thinking how content she was. But it couldn't last, of course; she said at once: 'Oh, that's good. Do you think that I should go straight back to St Athel's?'

'Lord, no, Tishy. A week's leave—you can stay here if you care to—we love having you.'

She smiled at them both because they were so kind and they must have wished her out of the way on occasion. 'You're awfully kind,' she told them, 'but I'd love to go home. If I could have a lift up to town I could catch a train. Would you think me very ungrateful if I went tomorrow?'

'Yes, very,' said Julius promptly. 'Make it the day after.' He smiled as he spoke. 'Do you want to collect more clothes before you go?'

'No, thanks, I've some things at home—they're a

bit old, but I shan't be going anywhere, so it won't matter.'

So it was settled, and when Jason came home nobody thought of mentioning it to him and she didn't like to say anything herself, although presumably, as Julius was still on holiday, it would be Jason who would have to give her a lift. It wasn't until the next morning, after he had left the house, that Georgina remarked: 'Oh, by the way, Jason says he'll take you all the way, Tishy, if you don't mind leaving quite early in the morning.'

Letitia buttered a piece of toast and sat looking at it. 'I couldn't let him do that,' she said at length. 'I mean, it's miles away, even in that car of his.'

It was Julius who answered her. 'Well, he'll be home after tea, why don't you talk to him about it then? And if you'd really rather go by train, he can still give you a lift up to town.'

So she was forced to contain herself until the early evening, for Jason was late home. By the time he strolled in they were all in the drawing room with the children in bed and dinner but half an hour away. Julius got up to get him a drink. 'A bit of a rush?' he wanted to know.

'The Commando went wrong—he picked up eventually, but it lost us a couple of hours, we didn't finish until six o'clock.'

Georgina glanced at the carriage clock on its bracket. 'You made good time.'

He had taken a seat at the other end of the sofa where Letitia was sitting. 'The car went well.' He looked at Letitia. 'How far to Chagford, dear girl?'

She jumped because she hadn't expected his question. 'Well...yes, the thing is Georgina told me...it's very kind of you to offer me a lift, but I really can't...if you wouldn't mind dropping me off at Paddington...' She stopped, aware that she wasn't making much of a success of it.

'I think you've got it wrong,' explained Jason, at his most placid. 'I'm going down to Plymouth tomorrow—I have to. I might just as well take you as not—the car's empty and I'm not going more than a few miles out of my way. It's no sacrifice on my part, Letitia.'

She told herself that she was relieved to hear that even while a faint prick of annoyance shot through her; would it have been such a sacrifice if he had been asked to drive her down to Chagford? Probably; he had called her touchy, hadn't he? And damned sensitive, too—and he had wanted to go to sleep instead of talking to her. That still rankled a little. He must find her incredibly dull after the glamorous young ladies he was doubtless in the habit of escorting. She said in a wooden voice:

'Well, thank you, I'll be glad of a lift. When do you want to start tomorrow?'

'That brings us back to my question. How far to Chagford?'

'A hundred and eighty-seven miles from London.'

'A good road?'

She frowned in thought. 'Well, I don't know it very well. It's the M3 and then the A30 for the rest of the way, more or less.'

'Good enough. We'll go round the ring road and pick up the motorway on the other side of London. Leave at nine sharp? You'll be home for tea.'

'It's quite a few miles to Plymouth from my home,' she reminded him.

'That's all right, Letitia,' he told her pleasantly. 'I enjoy driving, it makes a nice change from theatre, you know.'

'That's settled, then,' said Georgina comfortably. 'Let's have dinner, Mrs Stephens has made a special effort by way of a farewell gesture to you, Tishy, so we mustn't spoil it.' She turned to Jason. 'You'll be back in a day or two, won't you? Spend a day or two here on your way home.'

'Thanks, George, but only an hour or so—I can't expect Bas to do my work and his for ever.'

'You do his when he goes on holiday, but I know what you mean. Still, we'll see you when we come over on holiday.'

'Of course. Julius and I might even get in some sailing.' A remark which triggered off a conversation about boats which lasted through dinner, and although the talk became general afterwards, Letitia, on her way up to bed an hour or so later, discovered that beyond casual remarks which she could count on the fingers of one hand, Jason hadn't talked to her at all. She went to bed a little worried, for it augured ill for their journey the next day. Would they travel in silence, she wondered, or should she attempt to entertain him with lighthearted remarks about this and that? It was a great pity that she knew nothing about sailing and not much about fast cars. And it would bore him to talk about his work. She was still worrying away at her problem like a dog at a bone when she at last fell asleep.

CHAPTER THREE

IT WAS A glorious morning and bade fair to be a hot day; the tan jersey suit was going to be far too warm before very long. Letitia wished she had something thinner to wear, until she saw that Jason intended travelling with the BMW's hood down. She prudently tied a scarf over her hair, assured him that she liked fresh air, bade her friends good-bye and got into the seat beside him, eyeing the restrained elegance of his cotton sweater and slacks; he was a man who looked elegant in anything he wore, she considered, blissfully unaware of the price he paid for such elegance.

'Warm enough?' he wanted to know, and when she said yes, nodded carelessly and with a last wave took the car down the drive, past the little lodge and into the lane. 'Nice day for a run,' he observed, then lapsed into silence. Now would be the time, thought Letitia, when she should embark on a sparkling conversation which would hold him enthralled, but there wasn't an idea in her head, and the harder she thought, the emptier it became.

'Ankle all right?' asked her companion, and she embarked with relief on its recovery, her gratitude to Julius and Georgina and himself, and how much she had enjoyed her stay at Dalmers Place. But even repeating herself once or twice couldn't spin her colloquy out for ever; she lapsed into silence once more, looking at the scenery with almost feverish interest in case Jason should imagine that he might be forced to entertain her.

They were slowing down to go through Epping when he said blandly: 'This erstwhile young man of yours—did he train you to speak only when spoken to?'

She was instantly affronted. 'What a perfectly beastly thing to say! Of course not. I—I can't think of anything to talk about, if you must know.'

'Dear girl, I'm in the mood to be entertained by the lightest of chat, and surely you're used to me by now—Big Brother Jason, and all that.'

She laughed then and he said at once: 'That's better. I thought we might stop for coffee before we get on to the motorway—Windsor, perhaps, with luck we should be able to lunch in Ilminster, unless there is anywhere else you would prefer?'

She shook her head. She didn't know of any restaurants as far-flung as that; when she had gone out with Mike he had taken her to unpretentious places where he always made a point of assuring her that the food was good however humble the establishment appeared to be. She suspected that his ideas of good food weren't quite in the same category as Jason's; certainly the hotel where he chose to stop for coffee was a four-star establishment, the kind of place Mike would have considered a great waste of money. She savoured the luxury of their pleasant surroundings and began to enjoy herself. Jason was a charming companion and amusing and not in the least anxious to impress her. They went on their way presently, nicely embarked on the kind of casual talk which demanded very little effort and allowed for the maximum of laughter. Letitia hardly noticed the miles as they slipped by under the BMW's wheels, and when they stopped in Ilminster, she said regretfully: 'How quickly the time has gone!'

The doctor smiled gently, remarking merely that he was hungry and hoped that she was too as he ushered her into the George Hotel. 'See you in five minutes in the bar,' he suggested, and left her to tidy her wildly untidy hair and re-do her face. The freckles were worse than ever, she noted with disquiet, and then decided to ignore them; Jason had said he liked them.

The hotel was a pleasant place. They had their drinks and then ate their lunch with healthy appetites; cold roast beef, cut paper-thin, with a salad so fresh that it looked as though it had just been picked from the garden, and a rhubarb pie which melted in the mouth to follow, accompanied by enough clotted cream to feed a family of six. They washed down this splendid meal with a red Bordeaux and rounded everything off with coffee before taking to the road once more, making short work of the miles to Exeter, and once through that city and out on to the Moretonhampstead road, with the hills of Dartmoor ahead of them, they slowed down so that they might miss nothing of the scenery around them.

Somehow it didn't surprise her to learn that the doctor had been that way before, she suspected that he was a man who got around quite a bit without boasting about it—all the same, she was able to point out some of the local sights as they went along, and when they had gone through Moretonhampstead and slowed down still more to go through Chagford, she told him about the Grey Wethers stone circle close by before directing him to turn off the road and take a winding lane leading off towards the heart of the moor.

'It's such a small village that it isn't on all the maps,' she explained, 'and the road isn't very good, although a few people use it when they want to see Yes Tor, but most of them go from the Okehampton road, it's easier.'

Her companion grunted and dropped to a crawl; the lane had become narrow and winding, sometimes passing through open wild country with enormous views, and then dipping into small, densely wooded valleys which defied anyone passing through them to see anything at all.

'We're almost there,' offered Letitia placatingly as Jason swung the car round a right-angled bend, 'and you won't need to come out this way; there's a good road over the moor that will get you on to the Tavistock road.' She pointed down into the valley running away to their left. 'There's the church.'

The lane became the village street with a scattering of cottages on either side before it widened into a circle with an old-fashioned drinking trough for horses in its centre. The church lay ahead with the rectory alongside, a wicket gate separating its garden from the churchyard, past which the road wandered off again, up the hill on the other side. Jason, still crawling, afforded Mrs Lovelace, who ran the village shop and post office, and was the natural fount of all local gossip, an excellent opportunity of taking a good look at both him and his beautiful motor-car as he turned into the rectory gateway, slid up its short drive and stopped soundlessly before its porch.

The garden had appeared to be empty, but all at once it was full of people; her father coming round the side of the house to meet them—a middle-aged, rather portly man, of medium height and with a cheerful face, and her mother, who rose, trowel in hand, from the middle of a clump of lupins ornamenting the herbaceous border, and four girls, all pretty, who came tearing out of the door to cluster round the car.

Letitia cast a lightning glance at her companion and found him to be as placid as usual, only his brows were raised a little and a smile tugged at the corner of his mouth.

The introductions took quite a few minutes and the doctor bore up under them with equanimity. They were out of the car by now and Letitia, having made Jason known to her parents, started on her sisters.

'Margo,' she began, 'back from Scotland, I daresay you've seen her at St Athel's, and Hester, she's married to a doctor in Chagford, and Miriam who's married to a vet in Moretonhampstead, and this is Paula, who's still at school.'

He shook their proffered hands and submitted to a battery of eyes without appearing to mind.

'A little overpowering,' murmured the Rector as Letitia was drawn, with a lot of talking and laughter, into the family circle. 'So many women—of course, I'm used to them, bless their hearts, but they might possibly strike terror into a stranger's heart.'

The doctor laughed: 'Hardly that.' He turned round to look at them, gathered in a charming bunch round Letitia. 'You must be delighted to have them all home together,' he observed to Mrs Marsden.

She smiled at him, a small, still pretty woman.

'Yes, it's wonderful, and it happens so seldom. How kind of you to bring Letitia home—such an unfortunate accident...'

'I was the cause of it, Mrs Marsden.'

She shook her head. 'But not to blame; Letitia wrote and told me exactly how it happened; it was hardly your fault that she was pushed into the road.' She looked with interest at the BMW. 'It's a beautiful car, Doctor...' she wrinkled her nose, 'I'm so sorry, I've forgotten your name.'

'Jason.'

She smiled at him. 'Such a nice name. You'll stay to tea?'

'I'd like to very much.'

'That will be delightful,' observed the Rector, who had joined them silently. 'You and I will be able to hold a rational conversation and let these featherheads gossip themselves to a standstill.' He beamed at his visitor. 'Do come inside—are you by any chance interested in porcelain? I have one or two pieces of which I'm very fond, they are in my study...'

'Tea first,' decreed his wife firmly. 'Perhaps afterwards, if Jason has time.' She turned to look at the doctor. 'You're more than welcome to stay the night, we have any number of empty rooms.'

'I should have liked that, but I have to be in Plymouth this evening, but perhaps I might call on my way back and be shown the porcelain?'

'Splendid—I shall look forward to it,' his host agreed. 'And now—tea.'

They had the meal round the large rectangular table in the dining room, because, as Mrs Marsden explained, they had never quite got used to the idea of just a cup of tea and a biscuit. 'When they were younger, the girls had long cycle rides to and from school and always came home famished, and the Rector usually finished his visits about half past four or five, and somehow, even though all the girls are away from home, excepting Paula, we keep to the old habit.'

If the doctor found a table spread with a starched white cloth, plates of bread and butter, scones, little dishes of jam and cream, a variety of small cakes and a large fruit cake only waiting to be cut, a little different from his own idea of tea, he said nothing—indeed, he made a hearty meal, equally happy discussing eighteenth-century soft paste figurines with the Rector and the pleasures of living in rural surroundings with his hostess, while goodnaturedly answering the questions the girls put to him—all but Letitia, who was a little silent; it had just struck her that she was unlikely to see him any more. He had only taken over Julius's work at St Athel's to oblige him, and Julius was due back—he would go back

to his own country and become, in time, a vague
someone she half remembered. Even while the
thought crossed her mind, she knew that wasn't true;
Jason wasn't someone easily forgotten. She longed
to ask him what he was going to do in Plymouth,
and when Paula, who had no inhibitions about asking personal questions when she wanted to know the
answers, asked just that, Letitia listened with both
ears, while at the same time gazing attentively at her
mother, deep in a tale about repairs to the organ.

'What are you going to do in Plymouth?' Paul
asked with shattering directness.

'I have to meet someone.' The doctor's voice was
mild.

'I bet it's a date—or are you married?'

He laughed at her, not in the least put out. 'You
might call it that, and no, I'm not yet married.'

The word yet worried Letitia. Did that mean that
he was about to get married? It seemed likely, and
she was a little surprised to find that the idea didn't
please her at all, which, for a girl who had recently
broken her heart over another man, seemed strange,
especially as she neither liked nor trusted men—
young men—any more, although he had assured her
in the most avuncular fashion that he had no interest
in her, hadn't he? which meant that she could like
him without changing her ideas... She frowned and
then smiled when he spoke to her. 'I'm coming back

this way in a couple of days, Letitia—just for an hour or so. Will you be here.'

'Oh, yes—I'm not going anywhere.'

He nodded. 'Good. If your ankle is up to it, you shall show me some of your beloved tors.'

'You could see them just as easily from Plymouth,' pronounced Paula. 'With that car of yours, it would only take you...' she paused, 'though perhaps it would be wasting your time—I mean, you can see a for any time you're this way, but if you've got a date...'

She was frowned and shushed into silence. 'Oh, all right, I won't ask any more questions and I'm sorry if I was rude—I was only trying to save your time; Tishy knows the country round here awfully well. She goes about looking in hedges and badgers' setts and birds' nests and things—she'll be better as a guide for you than anyone else I know, and if you're not stuck on her, you'll pay more attention to the tors, won't you?'

This outrageous speech brought a choked back laugh from the doctor, a surge of colour to her knowledgeable sister's cheeks and a chorus of protest from everyone else. When it had died down Mrs Marsden said apologetically: 'I'm sorry that Paula has been so rude. I don't think she meant to be impertinent; the trouble is that in these days the young are encouraged to speak their minds.'

Jason's face was calm and placid once more. 'Don't apologize, Mrs Marsden. I have a young sister myself and I'm quite accustomed to her expressing herself in much the same way.' He smiled at Paula, who grinned back, quite unrepentant. 'Have you any more brothers or sisters?' she wanted to know.

'Four other sisters,' he told her with a twinkle, and the rest of the girls, but not Letitia, chorused: 'Five of them—just like us.'

Letitia found four pairs of eyes turned on her 'Tishy, you didn't tell us.'

'I didn't know.'

'Oh, Tishy darling—' it was Paula again, 'why didn't you ask? I know you don't like men any more, but Jason's used to girls—I mean sisters, if you see what I mean.' She smiled in a kindly way at Letitia, who was fuming silently. 'I expect he thinks of you as a kind of sister—and sisters ask questions,' she shot a look at Jason. 'Don't they?'

She looked round the table triumphantly and her father remarked dryly: 'I think it must be very nice for Jason to have five sisters, but I wonder if they annoy him sometimes?'

'Oh, frequently. Luckily the four eldest are married so their husbands get the lion's share of them, and I don't see a great deal of Katrina, the youngest.'

The talk became general after that and not long after Jason declared that he would have to go. Everyone went outside to see him off with a great deal of waving and a host of instructions as to the best way to go, and a reminder that he was to call in on his way back. Letitia watched him drive away, her temper still doubtful, for he had said almost nothing to her other than the briefest of good-byes; she went back indoors with her sisters, feeling peevish.

But it was impossible to feel put out for long; she hadn't seen any of them, save Margo, for some time, and there was a great deal to talk about. The evening flew by, and when she went to bed she was so tired that she went to sleep as soon as her head touched the pillow. And in the morning she had no chance to be by herself, even if she had wanted it. Margo was going back to St Athel's after lunch, and before she went she wanted to hear all the latest news of Georgina and the hospital too, and now that Paula had gone off to school and Miriam and Hester had gone to their own homes, they had the time for a talk while they did the household chores together.

The house seemed very quiet after Margo had gone, Letitia left her father to work in his study and joined her mother in the garden. It was a gloriously hot day, and Letitia lay back on the grass, aware that the sun was playing havoc with the freckles again, while her mother's gentle flow of conversation eddied and flowed round her head; it was the kind of conversation which needed almost no answering, and Jason wasn't mentioned once.

She borrowed her father's car the following day and drove her mother into Chagford to have coffee with Hester, and then on to Moretonhampstead to have lunch with Miriam and admire the baby. It was almost tea time when they left, and that evening her mother had to attend the Women's Institute, which meant that Letitia got the supper ready while she was away, played a rather one-sided game of chess with her father, and took Shep, the old retriever, for his short evening amble. She thought she wasn't in the least tired when she went to bed, but she slept at once, to wake to yet another lovely morning. Her ankle felt fine again and there was nothing for her to do at home; a walk would be splendid and perhaps resolve the puzzling restlessness she seemed unable to shake off, so that when her mother suggested that she might like to go for a ramble up towards Yes Tor, she was more than ready to agree.

Half an hour or so later, the washing up done and the beds made, she set off, wearing old slacks because of the brambles, and a cotton shirt which had seen better days, and because there was no one to see, she had simply tied her hair in a ponytail.

Her path led her away from the road which ran

through the village, and presently it wasn't a path at all, but a well-worn track running over grass and heather. It plunged presently into a charming little wood which filled the whole of the valley between her and the tor. She would sit there, she promised herself, before climbing the hill on the other side. She meandered along, looking where she was going because of the ankle, and wondering at the back of her mind why Jason hadn't telephoned to say when he would be coming; perhaps he had thought better of it—perhaps the date Paula had asked about really was a date, after all. Had he imagined that she would stay at home every day in the hope that he would come, or didn't he mind if he never saw her again, despite his friendly suggestion about the tors? She was uncertain—that was Mike's doing; he had said one thing and meant another, and for all she knew Jason was like that, too.

She was half-way through the wood, looking for somewhere to sit, when she saw the boy. He was lying a few yards from the path, on his stomach, his head turned sideways away from her, resting on his arms. A gipsy, she guessed; they often spent a few days tucked cosily in the valley and nobody minded, for they were only a small party of two or three caravans and bothered no one. She said hullo as she passed him, slowing her steps in case he woke up and wanted to talk, but he didn't answer. She walked on and then stopped. Supposing he wasn't asleep? He could be ill—dead even. She went quietly through the bracken and bent over him. He wasn't asleep, but neither did he see her properly. His face was white and his eyes, half open, were clouded. She knelt down beside him and took a closer look. Here was a very sick boy, and in a high fever; she wondered how long he had been there and why no one had come to look for him, and when she took his pulse it was far too rapid and when she felt his skin it was hot and dry. She would have to get help; it would mean leaving him lying there, but there was little chance of anyone coming along the track—she might wait all day.

The gipsies usually camped down by the little stream which ran through the wood at the bottom of the valley, where it branched away towards the open country again; Letitia had passed the rough grass track between the trees only minutes before. If he had come from there, the chances were that they hadn't missed him yet. She took a last worried look at the boy and ran back along the path and down the track. It led steeply downhill, winding and un-even between the trees, until it resolved itself into a delightful small clearing, with the stream skipping and rushing over the grey stones of its bed, and the trees encircling it, so that everything was shaded and cool, and but for the birds, very quiet.

She had been right; the caravans were there—two of them, with a little tent pitched between them, the horses hobbled close by and a lurcher dog tied to a caravan wheel. It barked when it saw her, but the bark sounded appealing more than menacing, and when she called 'Hullo there!' no one answered at all. She stood still for a moment, wondering what to do, when she caught a faint sound from the caravan furthest from her. A little nervously she crossed the grass and knocked on the open door, and when she heard the sound again, went in. It was dark inside and very hot and smelly too, and amidst the furniture crowding its interior, an old man lay on a bunk bed against one wall. He was ill too; even in the half-dark she could see that. She said at once in her practical way: 'Hullo—you're not well, are you? What can I do to help?'

He muttered and mumbled at her and finally waved a feeble arm towards the door. 'The other caravan?' she asked, and he nodded.

It was as crowded as the first one, more so, because here were two people, a youngish man and a woman. The man appeared to be unconscious, but the woman, Letitia was relieved to see, looked as though she might be strong enough to talk.

'How long have you been like this?' Letitia asked her gently.

The woman stared at her, blinking uncertainly. 'A day—two, I don't know.'

'The boy—I found a boy. Is he yours?'

The dark eyes came alive for a moment. 'Yes— he's ill too? He went to find someone.'

'Listen,' said Letitia, 'I'm going for help—I shan't be long, can you hang on for a little longer? My father will get a doctor to come...'

'The parson?'

'That's right. I'll see to your son too. Don't worry.' She looked around her and found what she was searching for; water, cooled in the kettle—a great black kettle dumped on the floor under a table. She filled a mug and gave some to the woman, then wetted the man's lips before she crossed to the other caravan and gave the old man a drink too. Then she fetched a pan and filled it with water for the dog— the beast would be starved as well as thirsty, tied up like that. Her eyes lighted upon a hunk of cheese on the table; she snatched it up and offered it to the poor creature, who demolished it in a couple of gulps. The horses would need attention too, but they would have to wait a little longer. She started back up the track, going as fast as she could.

Where it joined the main path she paused. Perhaps she should get the boy to the caravans first and make him as comfortable as possible before she went for help, but with all the will in the world, she knew she couldn't do it; he was far too big for her to carry, and to drag him over the rough ground would be madness—besides, her ankle, though mended, might not stand up to such treatment. She turned to the right, in the direction of the village, barely a mile away.

The sight of Jason, coming along between the trees at a steady, unhurried pace, would have filled her with surprise, but all she was conscious of was relief. She said desperately: 'Oh, there you are—what a mercy!' She gulped deeply, being still short of breath from her haste. 'They're all ill—the gipsies—and there's a boy.' She waved an arm behind her. 'The dog's starving too, and there are two horses…'

She felt his hands, firm and reassuring, on her shoulders. He didn't waste time repeating her not very clear remarks, nor did he ask what she meant by them. He asked in a calming voice: 'Where are they? Take your time—it will be quicker in the long run.'

He was right; Letitia took several long, steadying breaths. 'Down that track—there's a small clearing at the bottom, there are two caravans there. The boy's along this path—I think he's unconscious.'

'Lying on the path?'

'No—to the left, a few yards from it, you can see him…'

She felt herself pressed gently down on to a fallen tree. 'Sit there. I'll get him first, then you can show me where the others are.'

Letitia sat, suddenly tired, wondering if she had dreamed it all. But not the boy, at any rate; within a very few minutes she saw Jason coming back, the boy in his arms. As he reached her, he said in an easy voice: 'Now, dear girl, lead the way,' and she started off down the track once more, but more slowly this time because though Jason was a giant of a man, the boy he was carrying must have been quite heavy.

They reached the clearing without mishap, and the dog, hopeful of more food, strained at its chain and barked its head off. The old man opened his eyes as Letitia went into the caravan and mumbled something as the doctor laid his burden down on the second bunk.

'The boy first,' said Jason, and took off his jacket and cast it through the door on to the grass outside. 'The others are in the caravan over there, I suppose?'

'Yes—do you want me here?'

'Not for the moment—see if you can get a kettle of water going, they need cleaning up, and perhaps you can cool some it for them to drink—boiled water can't do them any harm, whatever it is.'

She nodded wordlessly and crossed over to the

larger caravan, found another kettle, already half filled with water, and set it on a Primus stove. There were a great many dirty cups and plates about too; she collected them up and piled them into a tin bowl and carried them outside; presently she would wash them up. She found a bucket too and fetched water from the stream, then gave it rather awkwardly to the horses before beginning a hunt for something to give the dog. The cupboards were well enough stocked with food; she selected a packet of Rich Tea biscuits and a tin of corned beef, mixed them together on a plate and laid it before the dog, who polished it off with delight, washed it down with more water, and then allowed her to take him off his chain, tie a length of rope to his collar, and fasten him to a nearby tree, where he lay down at once and fell asleep.

The kettle was on the boil when she returned and as the woman was dozing still, she went to see what the doctor was about, for it seemed to her that he was being a very long time.

The caravan seemed hotter and gloomier than ever as she went in, and smaller too by reason of his size, but he had got both of his patients out of their outer garments. They lay in a smelly heap in one corner and he was bending over the boy.

'There you are!' he exclaimed, his tone implying that she had been somewhere or other enjoying herself. 'I wish I had my bag with me. We'll have to get help as quickly as possible, I fancy. Can I leave you to get these two reasonably clean and give them a drink? And throw out as many clothes as you can, will you? I'm going to have a look at the others.'

She did as he had bidden her, although to get the occupants of the caravan really clean was beyond her, but at least she bathed their faces and hands and unearthed fresh blankets before she tossed their discarded clothing out on to the grass. She was barely finished when Jason joined her. 'The woman's not too bad,' he told her. 'The man needs attention as soon as possible; he and the boy and the old man must have been ill for several days. The woman told me that there's another caravan expected this evening. I think the best thing we can do is to get this lot to hospital, get the place cleansed and wait for the arrivals. They might be able to take over the animals—they're friends of these people, I presume.'

It was a relief to have someone there, making decisions in a calm way. Letitia nodded. 'I'll go and wash the other two,' she told him. 'The old man has a rash on his chest, but you'll have seen that.'

She went to pass him, but he caught her by the arm and swung her round to face him. 'Yes, dear girl. Typhoid.'

'Ty...oh! Are they bad?'

'If you mean are they going to die, no, I don't think so—not if we can get them to hospital within a reasonable time.' His hand was still on her arm. 'Have you by any lucky chance had a TAB injection lately?'

'Yes, a month ago—we had a carrier on the surgical wards.'

'Splendid, so you're safe.' He took his hand away and gave her a little push. 'Off you go to your tasks. I'm going back to your home to ask your father to telephone the local doctor and arrange for someone to stop the other caravan when it comes. You'll be all right here?'

'Yes. Jason, no one's had typhoid...' Her eyes were a little worried, though her voice was as matter-of-fact as his.

He smiled reassuringly. 'I shall stand by the gate and bellow,' he told her, 'then I shall come straight back.' He turned away. '*Tot ziens.*'

She had no idea what that might mean, but it sounded cheerful. She called ''Bye,' and made her way over to the second caravan, and presently, armed with more warm water and soap, began her work. The woman, when her face had been bathed and her hair tidied and she had been got into a clean garment, looked hearteningly better, but the man hardly stirred. Letitia gave them both a drink and went to see how her other patients were faring. The old man was still muttering, but the boy looked a little better. She went outside again and added the clothes from the other two to the pile on the grass and went to put on another kettle, giggling a little as she did so; it reminded her of an old film, where invariably in an emergency hot water was called for, whether it was needed or not. Now there was no emergency any more, only a need for her to wash her hands. A cup of tea would have been welcome, but there was nothing safe to drink from. She was drying her hands on the seat of her slacks when Jason came back, and it wasn't until she saw him coming towards her that she realized just how glad she was to see him again.

CHAPTER FOUR

HE WAS CARRYING his bag under one arm and she recognized the family picnic basket in his hand. In the other he held a small suitcase. He put it and the picnic basket down under the trees and came towards her, moving with a calm air of purpose which she found reassuring. 'Hullo,' he greeted her. 'What pillars of strength your parents are. Your mother had the basket packed within five minutes—you've had no lunch, have you? Sit down now and eat something and drink the tea.'

'I'm quite all right,' she began.

'I know that, but do as I say, or you won't be of much use later on when there'll be work to do. Your father telephoned the local doctor; he's on his way. Once he's seen these poor souls, we can get them away.' He started towards the caravans. 'I'm going to take another look—go and eat your sandwiches, and save a cup of tea for me.'

She was glad of the food and still more of the tea, but she wasted no time on her scratch meal. Five minutes later she was beside Jason as he examined the boy once more. He looked round as she sidled past the table and chairs and cupboards. 'Your Doctor Robinson has asked for a couple of ambulances; it's going to be quite an exercise getting the four of them down to the road, but once they're away the third caravan can come in and take over the animals while the Health people get these places fumigated.' He nodded towards the pile of clothing outside. 'I'm afraid that lot will have to be destroyed.'

Letitia was giving the old man a drink. 'Father has a stock of clothes he keeps, he'll fit them out again. The jumble sales, you know.'

The doctor looked a little at sea, but it was hardly the time to go into the manifold blessings of the village jumble sale—besides, she could hear footsteps. They belonged to Doctor Robinson, who greeted her with the freedom of an old friend and edged past her to join Jason. Presently the two men went over to the second caravan, to join her after a few minutes.

'No doubt of it,' pronounced Doctor Robinson, 'it's typhoid all right. Luckily you happened to come this way, Tishy, and luckier still that you have had your TAB so recently. I've just been suggesting to our good friend here that you should both go to the Isolation Hospital and get cleaned up.' He eyed Letitia's person. 'Nothing smart you mind parting with, I daresay? All old stuff?'

She was on the point of replying when Jason said: 'I asked your mother to put a few things in a case for you—you can change in the hospital, and leave that stuff to be burnt.' His tone implied that it should have been burnt months ago, so that when she asked: 'And what about you?' her voice was tart. How dared he criticize her clothes; that her slacks were a bit shabby she was bound to admit and the cotton shirt had seen better days, and neither had been improved during the last few hours, but what could it matter to him anyway?

'Oh, I've a change of clothes,' he told her carelessly. 'Perhaps you would make sure that they're more or less ready to go?'

His voice was that of a consultant asking a nurse on his ward to carry out his instructions; kindly, distant and polite. Letitia found herself obeying. She was rather despairingly searching for some sort of nightwear for the boy when she heard voices and the tramp of purposeful feet, and peered round the door to see the clearing suddenly full of men—ambulance men, clad in protective clothing, bearing stretchers. They started about their business with cheerful competence, and one by one the patients were strapped to their stretchers and borne away, leaving the two doctors, the horses, the dog and herself.

'They'll be along to get this lot cleaned very shortly,' observed Doctor Robinson. 'They'll take you along in one of their cars, I daresay—can't offer you a lift myself, I'm afraid.'

'The animals,' said Letitia, not caring a great deal as to the arrangements suggested. 'I won't go until there's someone to look after them—I'll wait until there's someone...I daresay they'll be here before the caravans are sealed.'

To her surprise Jason agreed with her. 'That dog looks as though it could do with some exercise and I need to stretch my legs. I'll free the horses too and then get them tied where they can get at the grass.'

'The dog won't understand,' persisted Letitia, aware that she was being childish about the animal.

'Probably not, but I'll talk to these gipsies when they get here—and his boss won't be away all that time, you know. Typhoid isn't the long-drawn-out business it used to be now that we have Chloramphenicol.'

'Yes...I was just wondering if I could have him at home with me—I know I have to go back in a day or two, but Paula will look after him and Shep and Bossy won't mind. Do you suppose he would stay?'

'Probably. There's no harm in trying—the boy could collect him when he's better.'

Doctor Robinson closed his bag. 'Well, I'll be on my way—you two will be all right?' He shook hands with Jason, pinched Letitia's cheek and

started off along the track. Before he disappeared
from view he turned to call: 'I'll tell those men to
hurry themselves if I should meet them.'

He was barely out of sight when Jason declared
that he would see to the horses at once and then
attend to the dog. 'Well, I'll start getting the caravans ready for the men,' declared Letitia, ever practical. 'Empty cupboards and drawers and get the
canned stuff out of the way—the rest of the stuff
will have to be dealt with, I suppose?'

'I should imagine so. Do you want any help?' He
had picked up a bucket and was already walking
away from her. She said 'No,' because in the circumstances it would have been silly to have said
'Yes,' the question having been rhetorical. She
plunged into the nearest caravan and worked with
such a will that by the time the men arrived she had
almost cleared the second one as well. Of the doctor
there was no sign; presumably he had gone with the
dog. She went forward to meet the Health team, uncertain as to what she should do next; when he appeared silently from the thickly growing trees at the
side of the clearing, the dog at his heel. From then
on she had no need to do anything; he seemed to
know exactly what was needed, what had to be
done, and who was to do it, and while he made no
attempt to interfere in any way Letitia could see that
he was regarded as being in charge of the business.

It was late afternoon by now and she was hungry
again as well as longing for a cup of tea. The men
worked fast, though; presently they declared themselves satisfied with their work and prepared to go.

'And you go with them, dear girl,' Jason advised
her. 'Take your case with you—I'll wait until these
other folk arrive, arrange about the horses and see
about the dog.'

There was something in his voice which made her
say 'Yes, Jason,' in a meek voice of her own, pick
up the case and join the Health team. One of the
men took the case from her with a cheerful: 'Come
along, miss,' and she found herself walking away
beside him, the other men trailing behind her, while
their leader stopped to speak to Jason. She wondered, as she went, when she would see him again—
perhaps she wasn't going to. The thought stopped
her in her tracks; she wanted to see him again. Just
once more, she pleaded silently, even if he calls me
dear girl in that offhand voice and doesn't really
look at me—if only I were pretty, he might...

She followed the men up the track, feeling light-
headed—probably, her common sense told her, because she was so empty inside, but her heart gave
her another reason: she had fallen in love with Jason
Mourik van Nie, and although common sense
pointed out that she couldn't have done anything
sillier or more unsuitable, her heart would have none

of it. Common sense at times could be a dead bore, said her heart, and love was often silly and unsuitable and sometimes hopeless. As long as she remembered that and started, without waste of time, to forget him, not much harm would have been done. The thing was to be practical about it and use her good sense. Her father had always said that she was the only one in the family blessed with that commodity; now was the time to prove it. She plodded on, not feeling in the least sensible, longing to relieve her pent-up feelings with a good cry.

She saw him two hours later; he was waiting for her outside the hospital, leaning up against the BMW's sleek bonnet and talking to one of the doctors, but he saw her as she walked through the door and as the other man walked away called: 'Over here, dear girl—what an age you've been, though I must say the result seems worth it.'

She had wondered how she would feel if and when she saw him again, but she had imagined nothing like the wild rush of feeling which caught at her breath, but she snatched at the remnants of it and said sedately: 'I'm sorry if you've been waiting, I didn't know…'

He looked surprised. 'You didn't imagine that I should leave you stranded here, did you? I did what was necessary and managed a lift back to your home to fetch the car.' He smiled at her, his eyes crinkling into little wrinkles at their corners. 'I like the out-fit—and the hair's very smart, even though it does turn you into a young lady.'

What had he considered her to be before, for heaven's sake? she wondered crossly; she had only washed it and coiled it in its usual knot on top of her head, and as for the dress, there was no knowing why her mother had chosen to pack the flowered cotton shirtwaister which she had been keeping to go to church in—it was the only decent thing in her wardrobe at the rectory, except for the jacket and dress she had travelled in, but at least she felt clean once more.

Jason opened the door. 'Jump in,' he invited, and she jumped.

The BMW made short work of the journey to the rectory, and beyond a number of observations concerning the gipsies, and his assurance, in reply to her question, that the third caravan had arrived, had parked on the edge of the wood, had taken the horses into its owner's care, and had handed over the dog without demur for the time being, the doctor had little to say. And nor had Letitia; she had too much to think about.

They were accorded a welcome fit for heroes and led indoors into the dining room, where the lurcher, a little bewildered, sat in an old box, being sized up by Shep and Bossy the cat. 'I've a meal ready,' exclaimed Mrs Marsden. 'You must be famished, the pair of you. Sit down, do, and when you've finished you can tell us all about it—what excitement—those poor souls…' She departed kitchenwards, her voice becoming fainter and taking on strength as she returned with a tureen of stew, its fragrance filling the pleasant old-fashioned room. She bade her husband fetch the vegetables and began to ladle their supper into plates, an act which the lurcher found sufficiently encouraging for him to sidle forward, eyeing Shep and Bossy warily. 'Presently, my dear,' Mrs Marsden admonished him. She sounded absent-minded; she had just noticed the expression on Letitia's face and wondered what had happened to put it there.

'You'll stay the night, of course,' she bade the doctor in a motherly voice. 'Such a pity Paula is at Miriam's she would have loved to have seen you.'

'May I? I had intended to cross on the midnight ferry. I could drive through the night, of course…'

'Out of the question, Jason—you know you're tired, you need a good night's sleep. Leave as early as you like in the morning. We're early risers and in the summer it's no hardship to get up with the sun.'

'How kind you are.' Letitia, her eyes on her plate, was aware that he was looking at her. 'If I could leave before seven o'clock? I could go through Dover; it's a good deal nearer.'

'Which way do you usually go?' asked the Rector.

'Harwich, it's convenient for Dalmers Place.'

Letitia looked up. 'Are they expecting you? Shouldn't you telephone?'

He was making great inroads into his supper. 'I would be grateful if I might do so.'

'And arrangements about your crossing tomorrow?' the Rector wanted to know. 'I'll take my chance.' Jason smiled at his host. 'I shall have time to look at your porcelain after all, sir.' Which meant that after supper he disappeared into the Rector's study, the dogs in attendance, and Letitia saw nothing of him until bedtime, and that for a brief moment only, when he wished her good night and good-bye at the same time, with the observation that he would be gone before she was up in the morning, and that in a cheerfully casual tone which precluded her from saying more than that she hoped that he would have a good journey. She even smiled at him with false brightness and thanked him once more for doing so much to help her, but all the answer he gave was: 'Ah, but I didn't see the tors after all, did I?'

Letitia wakened very early and lay listening to the familiar little sounds the old house made in the quiet-hours; creaks and sighs and the occasional tip-

tap of small mouse feet behind the wainscoting. Neither she nor Bossy, who had chosen to sleep on the
end of her bed, took any notice of these faint noises;
they were too used to them, but they both sat up at
the sound of almost silent footsteps crossing the
landing and going downstairs. Jason, already up.

Presently Letitia heard his voice, very quiet, in
the garden, and when she peeped from her window
it was to see him going down the drive, the lurcher
on a makeshift lead, Shep trotting with them. She
could dress quickly, go downstairs and get his
breakfast—she was on the point of doing just that
when she remembered that he had evinced no strong
desire to see her again; indeed, he had taken it for
granted that she wouldn't be up so early and had
made no effort to persuade her to do otherwise; she
remembered, too vividly, his careless good-bye. It
would serve him right she decided pettishly, if her
mother overslept and he got no breakfast at all, but
this uncharitable wish was stymied; she heard her
mother go downstairs and soon after, the sound of
Jason's return. There was nothing for it but to go
back to bed.

Letitia sat up against the pillows, listening to their
distant voices, and sniffing at the delicious smell of
bacon coming from the kitchen. In a little while she
heard Jason in the garden again and then the click
of the BMW's door. He was going—she scrambled

from her bed and ran to the window, just in time to see the car's stylish back disappear through the rectory gate. The wish to throw wide the window and yell at him to come back was very great; there was so much she wanted to tell him—that he had helped her to recover from Mike, that she liked him, that she would miss him. She would be able to say none of these things now; that she wouldn't have said them in any case was a small point she chose to ignore. All that mattered was that he had gone.

'Don't be silly,' she told herself sharply, and because bed was impossible now, wandered downstairs in her nightie and barefooted, to perch on the kitchen table and drink tea with her mother. She wanted to talk about Jason, but didn't; instead she plunged into plans for going back to St Athel's with a fervour which deceived neither her mother nor herself. Though both ladies were well aware that that wasn't what she wanted to talk about, Jason wasn't mentioned once.

The day went slowly by, following the exact pattern of all the Sundays Letitia could remember at home. Church, breakfast, church, lunch, then help with Sunday School and Evensong to finish the day. Not that her father expected her to attend all the services; all he asked was that one member of the family should be there. She shared the day with her mother, because Paula wouldn't be home until after tea, and sat quietly through Matins, listening to her father's voice and the enthusiastic singing of the surprisingly large congregation, and admiring, as she always did, the carving on the rood screen, and all the while her thoughts were miles away, with Jason Mourik van Nie, driving his BMW back to his own country. And Holland to Letitia, who had never travelled outside the land of her birth, might just as well have been darkest Africa or Cape Horn, all equally unreachable.

She spent her last day at home picking raspberries, helping Paula to cut out a dress when she got back from school, and cleaning, with great care, her father's small collection of figurines. Jason had liked them, her parents told her happily; what was more, he had known what he was talking about. 'A knowledgeable young man,' went on the Rector as he watched his daughter at work. 'I should like to know him better—he's quite an expert on Coalport, you know.' He added wistfully: 'It's a pity he lives so far away.'

Indeed it was a pity, agreed Letitia silently, and said aloud: 'Yes, Father.'

'You won't be seeing him again?' he inquired of her.

'No, dear—he only came to St Athel's to take over from Julius while he took a holiday.' She made her voice light and disinterested, and beyond declaring that it was a great pity that such a promising acquaintance should come to an end, her father said no more. She applied herself to the cleaning of a much prized Shepherd Boy with Dog and allowed her thoughts without any effort at all, to return to Jason.

Back in hospital, she found the next few days difficult; for one thing the recovery room without the possibility of seeing Jason from time to time had become, for the moment at any rate, positively dull. She did her work with the high standard of efficiency demanded of her; she saw the patients safely into theatre and then, after the surgeons had dealt with them, received them back again and encouraged them to regain consciousness once more, aided by all the latest gadgets science could devise, and once they had opened their eyes she gave them something to ease their pain, waited for their blood pressure to become normal once more and then saw them safely back to their wards. It was a busy way to spend a day, and never two days alike. Each patient was different and needed different things done for them; she was kind and gentle and absolutely reliable, but behind her calm she felt terrible; it was as though part of herself had gone with Jason—the important part, leaving only the outside of her, the part that showed, to go on working and eating and talking and trying to sleep at night. It began to show in her face and her friends were forced to admit amongst themselves that Tishy had become decidedly plain just lately, and some of them thought she might still be pining for the Medical Registrar.

She was aware that her modest looks were suffering. She spent more time than she had ever done before on her make-up, but that didn't help much. It was Margo, meeting her on her way to dinner, who expressed sisterly concern for her appearance.

'You look as though you need a good holiday,' she remarked, 'even though you've been home. As it happens George wrote today asking me down for my days off and wondering if you could come with me. You always have Saturdays and Sundays, don't you? OK, I'll give myself a week-end and we'll go down to Dalmers Place next week-end. How's the ankle?'

'Fine,' said Letitia, trying to make up her mind if she wanted to go, and added, unable to prevent herself. 'Will there be anyone there?'

'Lord, yes. It's George's birthday—we'll have to get a present.' She frowned in thought, then went on: 'Cor and Beatrix and Franz and the older one, Karel, will be there too, but I don't think Dimphena can get over until next week, but that Jason Mourik van Nie is bringing his youngest sister over—it should be fun. Have you got anything to wear, Tishy?'

'No,' said Letitia instantly, seeing this as a sign from heaven that she wasn't to go and not sure if she were glad about that or not. Seeing Jason again would be wonderful, but it would be awful too. She wouldn't go. This worthy determination was knocked for six by her sister's next remark, though. 'Not to worry, I've some money tucked away and you can pay me back later. What do you need?'

'Nothing—that is, I don't think I'll go, Margo.'

Her sister gave her a considered look. 'George will be very hurt if you don't, and she'll be bound to find out, because Julius would tell her.'

'Well,' said Letitia reluctantly, 'in that case... I've got that tan thing and the blouse, I could go in that, couldn't I? I left that pretty shirtwaister at home—a pity. I haven't anything to wear in the evening, though there's that blue crêpe that Miriam couldn't get into because of the baby...'

'That thing?' Margo sounded scornful. 'We'll do better than that, love. Are you off at four?' and when Letitia nodded: 'Good, meet me in my room as soon after that as you can manage, we'll go shopping.'

They found what they wanted; a plainly cut silk voile with an elegant line to it, in a pretty pale green, and because it was a little more than Margo had intended to pay, they pooled what money they had and found a coffee and white striped cotton dress, a straight sheath into which Letitia's nice little figure fitted very well. 'No one needs to know where it comes from,' Margo pointed out as they hurried back to the hospital. 'It looks marvellous on you and they'll never guess that we got it at the British Home Stores, and you've got that lovely suede belt that will go with it exactly.' She gave a satisfied little nod. 'You'll look lovely, Tishy.'

Letitia thanked her eldest sister and said she hoped so, all the while knowing that her hope that Jason might find her lovely was just too silly for words. But the green dress was very pretty—he might at least look at her. She remembered the casual glances he had cast in her direction; perhaps this time he might look, really look at her.

They met the next morning and he hardly glanced at her on his way into theatre, striding through the recovery room with a casual 'Hullo, dear girl,' and not waiting a second for her to reply. Not that she had anything ready to say; she had been taken completely by surprise; she had had no idea that he was in England, let alone anaesthetizing that morning. She stood holding a recovery tray in much the same manner as a Grecian girl holding an urn, her mouth slightly open. Then she snapped it shut and almost dropped the tray as Julius strolled through in his turn. He stopped, however, wished her good morning as though he really meant it, and expressed pleasure at her impending visit. 'Nice to have a few friends from time to time,' he remarked. 'How's the ankle?'

She told him that it was fine, remembering that Jason hadn't bothered to ask, then flushed under his kindly eye. 'You look as though a couple of days off would do you good,' he commented as he went on his way.

It was to be a busy morning with a long list, being added to every now and again as emergencies came in, and Letitia was kept busy, but not so busy that she didn't see Jason each time he came into the recovery room, and each time she couldn't help but notice and he was going out of his way to be friendly, so that by the end of the morning she was on top of her small world again. To come plummeting down again at the end of a long, hot afternoon.

She had gone into the little cubbyhole where they washed the instruments and replenished the trays and trolleys. Mrs Mead had already gone, the room was quiet after the day's ordered bustle, she stood leaning against the sink, still filled with odds and ends which needed to be washed and dried and thought about Jason being so nice—he had been like that at Dalmers Place when he had told her he was like an uncle…she wished, upon reflection, that he hadn't said that, perhaps when he saw the new green dress…her thoughts were disturbed by the swing of the theatre door and the deliberate tread of feet.

She had thought that the men had all gone, but it was Julius's voice:

'Coming back for dinner, Jason?'

'Good of you, old man, but I've a date.'

'With Tishy?'

Jason's careless: 'Lord, no,' seared her like a hot iron. 'Wibecke van Kamp is over here, you know—we're dining together.'

'Good-looking girl—knows how to wear her clothes too.'

'Handsome, I should have said.' Jason's voice was dry, and in the little pause which followed Letitia summoned up the courage to walk out and let them know that she was there; eavesdropping was a rotten, low-down trick and none knew it better than she, being a parson's daughter, but she was halted by his voice. 'How's Tishy? She looked a bit down in the mouth when I got here this morning.'

'Well enough, I should imagine—she and Margo are coming down for the week-end. She'll be glad to find you'll be with us as well, I think.'

'What makes you say that?'

'You've been kind to her, and she needed kindness after that young fool cut her up—for a little while she's been hating all of us; he said some pretty cruel things to her, so Georgina told me. It can't be much fun to have your dreams torn up so ruthlessly—and it must have been worse for a girl like her.'

'No looks, you mean?' It was Jason's voice, and Letitia closed her eyes. 'But she's not as plain as all that, you know, and she's a nice girl.'

'That's just what I mean,' observed Julius. 'There aren't many around like her any more.' They were strolling to the door now. 'Where are you dining?'

Letitia didn't hear Jason's reply because the door had swung to behind the men, but it would have made no difference. She had become deaf and blind and dumb for a while while her head buzzed with a variety of painful thoughts, which changed, within seconds, to sudden rage; he was as bad as Mike had been—worse, because he hadn't seemed like that at all. True, he had never been in the least interested in her, but why had he pretended to be friendly when all the while he hadn't meant it?

She began on the sink's contents, making such a clatter that the theatre staff nurse came out to see what was the matter, and when she got off duty at last, her cross face kept even the closest of her friends at bay, so she was left to brood over a book and peck silently at her supper, a circumstance so unusual that the young ladies around her looked at her with something like dismay; little Tishy was known for her sunny disposition and no one had ever seen her quite like this not even when Mike had thrown her over.

And the efforts she made to get out of going with Margo were useless; she didn't choose to tell her sister her real reason for not wishing to go to Dalmers Place, and the excuses she thought of wouldn't hold water with Margo. She got through Friday somehow, wishing Jason a good morning cold enough to freeze his bones when he arrived for the first case, and carrying out his instructions and giving him her reports of the patients' conditions in an austere manner which caused the faithful Mrs Mead to look at her as though she were out of her mind. It was at the end of the list, after everyone had gone and Letitia was setting the recovery room to rights in case an emergency should come in during the week-end, that Jason came back again. And this time she was in the middle of the room, rotating slowly, making sure that everything was just so before she left.

'Ready in half an hour, Letitia?' he asked her cheerfully. Obviously, she thought pettishly, her coolness of manner had escaped him, and what business was it of his when she left? Margo had told her that they were going down by train and would be met at the station.

'No. There's plenty of time before Margo and I leave, doctor.'

He raised faintly amused brows. 'I'm not sure what I've done, but it can't be so awful that you need to call me doctor. What's up, dear girl?'

She said levelly, her eyes on his face: 'Nothing—nothing at all. It was quite a list, wasn't it?'

Either he had never heard of red herrings or he wasn't easily led away from the matter in hand. 'Well, whatever the nothing is, you'd better get over it; it's George's birthday tomorrow.'

Letitia went a slow pink, a pale indication of the indignation burning inside her. 'I hadn't forgotten.'

'Good.' He glanced at the clock. 'Twenty minutes, then, at the front entrance—Margo already knows we're going down together.' He smiled quite kindly and went away, leaving her to rush round to the Home. Margo could have let her know; she would have something to say to her when they met. Letitia changed in an increasingly bad frame of mind and got to the entrance with one minute to spare, to find Jason and Margo, on the best of terms, already there, so that, naturally enough, she was ushered into the back of the car where she sat with her thoughts, answering politely when spoken to and trying not to look at the back of Jason's head, which, while not as interesting as his handsome face, had its own endearing qualities. The gay talk and laughter of the two in front of her did nothing to make the journey pleasanter, either.

And when they arrived the house seemed full of people. Georgina, of course, looking so glowingly happy that she was beautiful, and Julius, looking as he always did, completely content, and with them his cousins, Cor and Beatrix and Franz with an ecstatic Polly weaving amongst them on her short legs, and there were two people Letitia had never meet before too—Julius's eldest cousin Karel and a pretty girl of fifteen or sixteen, Katrina, Jason's youngest sister. They were swept indoors with everyone talking at once, and presently Letitia and Margo were taken up to their rooms, warned that dinner would be in half an hour or so and left to unpack while they talked to each other across the communicating bathroom.

'Don't change,' Georgina had told them, as she went. 'No one will tonight—we're going to dress up tomorrow evening, though.'

A remark which filled Letitia with disquiet because she wasn't sure if the green dress was grand enough after all.

She went downstairs with Margo in a little while and joined everyone in the drawing-room, and because she wanted to avoid Jason, she went to sit by Franz, and presently Karel joined them. He was a dear, she discovered, gay and amusing and with the happy knack of making her feel that she was the prettiest woman in the room, a feeling which she recognized as entirely false though it helped enormously, so that when Jason did come over with his sister she was able to laugh and talk in a perfectly natural manner—so much so, indeed that when they went in to dinner, he bent his head to whisper: 'So the nothing's gone, has it?'

Which brought it all back again even though she pushed it to the back of her mind and prepared to enjoy herself. It would have been difficult to have done otherwise; she had Cor, bubbling over with schoolboy high spirits, on one side of her, and on the other Karel; between them they kept her entertained throughout dinner, and afterwards, in the drawing room, she found herself with Katrina, who was so very like Paula in her ways that she felt they had known each other for a long time and readily agreed to go for an early morning walk with her before they parted, on excellent terms, to go to bed.

It was going to be a blazing hot day, Letitia could see that the moment she wakened the next morning, and a good thing too—now she could wear the British Home Stores dress. It really wasn't bad at all; the good suede belt lent it an air and her sandals, on bare feet, matched quite well. She tied her hair back and without bothering overmuch about her face, went silently through the rambling old house and down the stairs.

Katrina was already there in the hall, they found

their way to a side door and let themselves out into
the garden, and although it was barely seven
o'clock, it was already warm. They wandered along
out of the garden presently and into the lane with
Katrina, talking all the time, leading the way. They
had gone perhaps half a mile when she stopped and
exclaimed in a pleased voice: 'There is Jason!' and
there indeed he was, sitting in the hedge ahead of
them, chewing grass and contemplating the view. He
threw the grass away and got to his feet and came
to meet them. His good morning was bland. 'Now
this is a surprise,' he assured them, only he didn't
look surprised at all.

CHAPTER FIVE

JASON TOOK IT for granted that they would enjoy his company, and as a matter of fact, it would have been difficult to do otherwise; he could be very amusing when he wished and he and Katrina were on excellent terms with each other despite the difference in their ages. They strolled back to the house across the fields, and when Jason said: 'Run on ahead and tell Georgina we're on our way,' Katrina obeyed at once, flying away from them over the grass, turning to wave as she disappeared through the gates leading to Dalmers Place. Which left Letitia making uneasy conversation with Jason, something she found difficult enough to do, partly because she couldn't forget his cool voice in the recovery room, and when he said in his kind way: 'I like that dress, Letitia,' she felt sure that he was mocking her; it was a dress, that was all. To her mind it had bargain written all over it, she couldn't believe that her companion wasn't able to recognize a cheap garment when he saw one.

'It's from British Home Stores,' she snapped, and realized that he had no idea at all of such a place. Well, she thought fiercely, it was time he learnt. 'It's a chain store, like Woolworth's,' she informed him crossly, 'they have rows and rows of dresses, all exactly alike and all very cheap.'

Jason had stopped to look at her and twisted her round to face him. He said in a measured voice. 'It doesn't really matter if it's sack or something dreamed up by Christian Dior—the point is, it's pretty. In fact it has the edge on some of the ultra-fashionable clothes I'm expected to admire.'

'Whose?' she asked before she could stop herself.

He grinned down at her. 'Well, well—I was beginning to think you had no interest in my—er—leisure hours. I take girls out sometimes, you know—men do.' He put a finger under her chin so that she couldn't turn away from his blue gaze. 'And we aren't all men like Mike, my dear.'

He bent to kiss her cheek gently, tucked an arm under hers and went on walking towards the house, talking about a variety of small matters, for all the world as though they had never stopped. She mumbled answers and said yes and no and was glad when they went indoors and she could escape to her room and tidy herself for breakfast. She stared at her face in the charming winged mirror; his kindness had hurt. Which was perhaps why she devoted so much of her attention to Karel at breakfast and played tennis with him for the greater part of the morning. And after lunch on the terrace, when Georgina had re-

ceived her presents, she had spent the afternoon with
Katrina and Karel with occasional games of tennis
with Beatrix and Cor. It was evening when the cel-
ebrations really got under way; Letitia dressed in the
green silk, nervous that it wasn't quite up to the
occasion, and though when she got downstairs she
saw that it wasn't, it didn't matter overmuch, because its very simplicity made it look better than it
actually was and she was wearing the gold chain
and locket her parents had given her when she was
twenty-one—it was a large Victorian oval, heavy
and rather ornate, and showed up nicely against the
plainness of the dress and gave it an air of distinc-
tion.

Georgina, in guipure lace and the emerald earrings Julius had given her, was holding court in the
drawing-room, and as she and Margo went in there
was a burst of laughter which carried her well
through drinks and into dinner. She had Karel next
to her again and he stayed with her when they all
went back to the drawing-room, introducing her to
the guests who were beginning to arrive for the evening, and when someone put on the music, he
whisked her on to the floor before she had had a
chance to wonder if anyone would dance with her.
She didn't lack for partners after that, for she danced
well. Only when she found herself with Jason did
her feet become clumsy, but presently, charmed by

the music and the pleasure of dancing with him, she forgot her awkwardness and enjoyed herself.

'That was nice,' she told him as the music stopped last, and smiled up at him, almost pretty in the dim light of the wall sconces, but before he could answer her she had been danced away by Karel, to circle and sway and twirl in a very modern fashion which seemed a little surprising in the strictly brought up daughter of a country parson. But it didn't prevent her watching Jason revolving round the room in a rather more civilized way with a pretty girl whose hair was golden and whose dress must have cost the earth. They disappeared into the garden very soon, and Letitia dipped and swayed and smiled her way through the endless dance, longing to run after them and see what they were doing. There was a moon and the evening was warm—the garden was lovely; sweet-smelling and romantic, and the girl was the kind of girl men would kiss in the moonlight. She ground her nice white teeth at the very idea; if he asked her to dance again, she would refuse. Only he didn't ask her, and when the evening was over and they were all going to bed, his good night was so casual it sounded like an afterthought; rather as though he had forgotten to say good night to the dog, she decided bitterly.

Everyone went to church in the morning; a convoy of cars, headed by Julius's Rolls, followed by

the BMW, the Mini driven by the just seventeen-
year-old Franz and last, the rakish Porsche belong-
ing to Karel, in which Letitia had contrived to get
herself as passenger. They filled two pews in the
little church, and Letitia, squashed between Beatrix
and Karel, was very aware that Jason was sitting
beside her, so that instead of attending to the service
she was worrying about her hair being untidy at the
back and whether the collar of her jacket was just
so. Being in love, she mused silently while they sang
the last hymn, was an uncomfortable business.

They had a noisy lunch and then, because it was
such a glorious day, decided on a picnic tea. Letitia,
changing into the British Home Stores dress, medi-
tated on the advantages of being rich; no need to
worry about cutting sandwiches or hunting for paper
bags and rugs; Stephens, summoned by Georgina,
had listened attentively and with his usual fatherly
air, and had disappeared with his habitual quiet, and
when they gathered in the hall later, there, just as
she had guessed, were the two picnic baskets and
two rugs, folded neatly. The men shared them out
amongst themselves and the girls started off ahead
of them, Polly between Cor and Beatrix, Georgina
and Margo behind them and Letitia and Katrina
bringing up the rear. They were making for the
meadows, a quarter of a mile away, where they
sloped down to a small stream, a copse guarding the

hill behind them. It was pleasant there and cool, and the ladies of the party spread the picnic, while the men got the spirit kettle going and the children wandered off to look for fish in the stream. It was all very peaceful and Letitia, arranging slices of cake on a plate, wished it could go on for ever.

The picnic was a tremendous success, largely because it owed nothing to the modern aids of thermos flasks, cellophane-wrapped sandwiches and potato crisps. Georgina made the tea in a large brown teapot and Margo cut bread and butter with a bread knife on a bread board, just as though she was in a kitchen and not kneeling on the grass. And Letitia, having seen to the cake, unwrapped a jam sponge for the children and a pot of Gentlemen's Relish for the men, then started to dole out the strawberries into little glass dishes. The cloth, spread on the grass, looked very inviting, they clustered round it in great good spirits and ate everything there was before packing up in a leisurely fashion with a great deal of laughing and talking.

'I shall have a nap,' declared Julius, and stretched himself out and closed his eyes, while Georgina wandered off with Polly. Letitia, getting to her feet after strapping the picnic baskets, caught Jason's eye on her and spoke hastily. 'I thought I'd...' she began.

'Go for a walk?' he interrupted her. 'I'll come

with you.' He had her hand in his and was marching her away before she could think of anything to say. She was still cudgelling her brains for a safe topic—something impersonal—the weather, perhaps?—as he led her up the field towards the copse which crowned it. Unlike her, he showed no signs of unease at their lack of conversation; he said nothing at all, only wandered along, with her in tow, whistling under his breath. A rough track led left and right away from them when they gained the copse, circling the field on its outside, and facing them was a gate; still silent, Jason fetched up against it, and Letitia perforce stopped too.

From where they stood the view was charming; all the soft sweep of the country beyond. The gate gave access to a large, irregular field with a hump down its middle, so anyone walking along either of its edges would fail to see anyone or anything on their opposite side until they were almost at the top where the ground levelled out once more. They stood side by side, silently contemplating the scene until presently they saw Georgina and Polly climb the narrow little gate halfway down the field, and start rambling towards them, keeping close to the hedge.

They saw the bull seconds later, his great head raised, standing on the other side of the hump, sniffing the air. He began to move towards the centre of the field, unhurriedly but with purpose, aware that there were strangers in his field, although he wasn't able to see them because of the hump. As he began to amble up his side of the hump, Jason said quietly: 'George won't hear us if we shout, we're too far away. Go and fetch Julius, dear girl, tell him to run down the hedge on that side and get George and Polly through the gate. I'll stroll down the middle and hold the beast's attention.' He turned to grin at her. 'Possibly he's quite harmless, but we can't take risks, can we?'

Even at that distance, Letitia considered this description of the noble animal's disposition to be quite inaccurate; he was plodding slowly up his side of the hump still, looking anything but harmless, but she wasted no time in saying so, only turned and ran as Jason vaulted over the gate.

She ran well, and being country bred, found the stones and tree roots and unexpected bumps in her path no obstacle—besides, it was downhill. All the same, she was breathless when she reached the picnic party, rather scattered by now, but Julius was still there. He looked up in astonishment at her headlong flight and was on his feet before she got to him, tugging his arm with an urgent hand.

'Jason says come at once,' she said breathlessly. 'There's a bull—George and Polly...'

'Show the way,' Julius urged her, not stopping to

ask questions, but Letitia, needing no urging, was already starting back the way she had come. At the gate once more she paused. 'Jason said would you go down on that side—' she waved an arm, 'and get them through that little gate half-way down while he heads the bull off.'

Julius nodded, vaulted the gate in his turn and began to run towards his wife and little daughter, still pottering slowly along the hedge. Letitia could hear their laughter now, faint still, mixed in with the birds and the other summer sounds.

Jason was well down the other side of the hump now and the bull had stopped to look at him, and George and Polly had paused because they had seen Julius. Letitia, from her vantage point at the gate, thought Jason was getting dangerously close to the bull now and he had quite a long way to run back too, and it was uphill; he would never do it. She went cold inside as she turned to see how Julius was getting on. He had snatched up Polly and had Georgina by the hand and was racing back to the little gate; everything was going to be right after all, just so long as the bull stayed where he was.

But he didn't—he tossed his great head, then lowered it and advanced at a sharp trot; he didn't think much of Jason, who moved back up the hump to make sure that the others were safe, and they were; it remained only for him to get himself away. Letitia

knew then that he would never do it; the bull, with
nothing else to occupy his mind, was bent on reaching him as quickly as possible. She climbed the gate
neatly and began to run down the hump so that the
beast would see her too. He was still some distance
away, but she didn't like the way he stopped in his
tracks when he caught sight of her and changed
course in her direction. But the small distraction had
given Jason the chance he needed, he had gained the
crown of the hump and was racing towards her. She
turned and ran too, breathless with fright, quite sure
that she would be able to get over the gate before
the bull reached her. But she need not have worried;
Jason caught up with her within yards of it, picked
her up and tossed her over it as though she had been
thistledown instead of a healthy girl, and leapt after
her.

She had fallen softly enough into grass and rather
mushy weeds; he plucked her to her feet and
brushed her down, but the front of her dress was
stained and ruined; Letitia thanked heaven that it
had been so cheap and when he asked her if she was
all right, nodded, staring at him because, incredibly,
he was laughing. And he was only a little out of
breath too, whereas she had almost none at all, and
what she had she lost in a gasp of fright as the bull
fetched up within feet of them, only on the other
side of the gate. He glared at them for a moment,

then tossed his head and strolled away, and Letitia's gasp turned to a weak giggle.

Jason laughed again, a great shout of laughter, and turned her round to face him. 'Dear girl,' he said, 'dear brave girl,' and bent to kiss her.

Sudden tears filled her eyes. 'Oh, Jason,' she wailed, 'I thought...'

She managed to stop herself just in time as he put an avuncular arm round her shoulders and gave her a gentle hug, and presently, when she gave a resolute sniff, took out his handkerchief and mopped her face for her. And only just in time, for Julius came round the bend in the path to halt and say:

'You're all right, both of you? I can never thank you enough.' He smiled at them both, his face white and strained. 'Polly found it all quite fun.' His eyes slid over Letitia's blotchy face. 'Though I can't say I did. I left Georgina sitting in the hedge having a little weep, but I had to make sure you two were all right—we saw you running like hares.'

'A nasty moment,' agreed Jason, 'and if it hadn't been for our Tishy here I don't think I should have made it.' He took his handkerchief from her hand and gave her a little push. 'Run down the path to George,' he suggested, 'we'll follow,' and when she hesitated: 'Go along, Letitia, we'll explain to the others.'

She went then, grateful to him for realizing that

she wasn't in a fit state to answer a barrage of questions for the moment. The rest of the party had been on the other side of the stream when she had fetched Julius; she could hear them now, pounding up the path, eager to help. She heard Karel's: 'I say, what's up?' as she rounded the bend in the path and saw George with Polly on her lap. Polly was singing to herself and her mother had finished her little weep. 'And if only,' said Letitia to herself, 'I could look like that when I cry, instead of puffy and red.' She went and sat down in the hedge too, saying brightly: 'My goodness, what a scare! I'm still shaking—and I howled all over Jason, too.' She added: 'He was laughing!'

Georgina smiled a little. 'Men do the strangest things sometimes. You were so quick and brave, Tishy. Thank you, both of you,' she kissed Letitia's cheek. 'Weren't you afraid?'

'Terrified, and I should never have known what to do—it was Jason. I didn't know Julius could run like that.'

'Julius can do anything,' stated his wife simply. 'But you and Jason—I can never thank you enough...' She broke off at the precipitate arrival of Cor and Beatrix who flung themselves upon her with cries of: 'George, darling George, are you all right? Julius sent us to look after Polly so's you can rest a bit.'

The two girls watched the children go, this time with a delighted Polly between them. 'Dear Julius,' said Georgina, 'I expect he thinks I'm still crying.' They smiled at each other and Letitia said: 'You don't look a bit as though you had. I expect I'm still blotchy.'

'Only a little, and I don't think anyone will notice—sometimes men don't see things which we think matter frightfully.'

They got to their feet presently and followed the children, to join the group standing by the gate, and after the episode of the bull had been well and truly discussed they all wandered down to where they had had the picnic, and everyone sat down again and talked about it still more. Karel had attached himself to Letitia and his light, cheerful chatter made her laugh a good deal as well as serving to soothe her jumpy nerves, but even while she smiled at his jokes she was wondering why it was that Jason had wandered off with Cor and Franz, with no more than a smile for her.

Presently they began to wander back to the house in twos and threes, to change for the evening before meeting in the drawing room for drinks. Letitia and Margo were to be driven back to St Athel's later that evening, and although no one had actually said so, she had taken it for granted that it was to be Jason who would drive them, but when they came

down to the hall, it was Karel who was waiting for
them, and going the rounds, shaking hands and mur-
muring nothings. Letitia, offering a hand to Jason,
could see no sign of disappointment on his face.
Indeed, he wished her a good journey, assuring her
that Karel was just the companion to make the drive
a pleasant one. He made no mention of seeing her
again either, so that she said hesitantly: 'Well, I
hope you have a good journey too, you and Katrina—it was nice meeting her, I shall tell Paula all
about it when I go home.'

Letitia stared into his impassive face, longing to
say a great many things she knew she would never
utter. 'Good-bye,' she said at last, and when he replied: '*Tot ziens*', she turned away with a puzzled
face and promptly embarked on a gushing conversation with Franz, who looked taken aback but was
too polite to show it.

She sat in front with Karel this time and he kept
the conversation going at a rate which rivalled his
speed, and made her laugh a good deal as well. And
when they arrived at the hospital and he suggested
that she might like to spend an evening with him,
Letitia agreed, mainly, as she admitted to herself
later, because there was a chance that he might talk
about Jason. They parted on the friendliest of terms,
and as she went with Margo to the Nurses' Home,
her sister remarked: 'What a nice boy he is,' and

added innocently, 'You get on very well together, Tishy.'

Letitia pushed the door of the home open and they went in together. She said 'Yes,' suddenly beset with the appalling thought that perhaps Julius, or worse, Jason, had told him to be nice to her. They climbed the stairs to the first landing, where Margo had her room in the Sisters' wing, whereas Letitia was two floors higher. 'Tishy,' began her sister, 'Jason and I were talking—he has a plan; did he tell you about it?'

Letitia mumbled a no and managed a yawn. She didn't want to talk about him. She was still sore from his casual good-bye; she didn't like him at all even while she loved him so fiercely. 'I'm tired,' she declared, 'and I'm on early in the morning—won't another time do to tell me? I don't suppose it's important.'

'Not really,' Margo gave her a thoughtful look. 'Tishy, I was beginning to think you'd got over Mike; that you'd discovered that he was the bad apple in the barrel, but I'm not so sure.' She kissed her lightly. 'Poor little Tishy!'

'I'm perfectly all right and I've quite got over Mike,' declared Letitia peevishly, and at the same time wondered what Jason and Margo had been planning together. She wished Margo good night and went to bed, telling herself that the quicker she got him out of her system the better.

Impossible, because he was there the next morning, going unhurriedly across the recovery room to theatre, bidding her a cheerful good morning as he went. She gaped, muttered incoherently at him and then busied herself laying a tray which was already laid: she simply had to do something to cover the wave of delight which had engulfed her; not that it would have mattered if she had allowed her feelings to show, for he didn't pause for one second, but disappeared through the doors without a second glance. Letitia didn't see him again until he came out to inspect the first case an hour or more later; a gastrectomy that wasn't looking too good. They worked on the man together, silent save for Jason's brief directions, and when the patient was fit enough to go back to the ward, he went back into theatre with the smallest of nods.

And so the day wore on, with their dinner cut short because an emergency Caesarean was rushed in as the last case went down. The theatre filled rapidly; students, another doctor to see to the baby and a nurse to see to the doctor, the surgeon and his assistant. Sister and a handful of nurses—and Letitia, waiting quietly by the door, ready to take over the patient, her eyes on Jason, giving the anaesthetic. She had been with him when he had given the preliminary injection and started the anaesthetic, placidly reassuring towards his patient, talking in a quiet voice as he popped the needle in so that the anxious young woman smiled as she closed her eyes. Letitia remembered that now as she studied his bent head—but only for a moment, for the baby was there and everyone was smiling broadly, as they always did when there was a Caesar in theatre. When the small creature gave a peevish whimper, she sighed with relief in unison with everyone else there. There was something dramatic about a Caesar and satisfying as well.

Letitia took charge of her patient again, and when she had come round, stood back so that Mr Toms, the surgeon, could announce the news that she had a son before Letitia saw her back to the ward. After that there was the tidying up to do before she could rush down for some sort of a meal. She gobbled it as fast as she could and raced back; the afternoon list was due to start in five minutes and Staff Nurse Wills, who usually relieved her, had an afternoon off, leaving Mrs Mead and her to cope. The list wasn't a long one, thank heaven, so she got back, still chewing, with seconds to spare.

They were finished by half past four, and the last case had been obligingly quick in regaining consciousness once more, so that soon after five o'clock Mrs Mead was on the point of leaving, and Letitia, slapping instruments into their proper places with brisk efficiency, was trying to decide what she would do with her evening. Not much, she decided; she had very little money in the first place and what she had she must save so that she could go home on her next days off—she liked to go once a month, even though it meant going without puddings at dinner and the cinema. She would wash her hair, she decided, do her smalls, make a pot of tea and eat the rest of the biscuits she had, then have a leisurely bath before the others came off duty, and get into bed early with a book. She placed the last airway into its correct position and skipped along to the changing room. Jason was leaning against its door, looking like a man who had never done a day's work in his life. He picked a thread off the sleeve of his elegant suit and said: 'Hullo, I've been waiting for you, Letitia.'

'Me?' It sounded stupid, but she couldn't think of anything else to say.

'You.' He smiled and her heart turned over. 'Will you have dinner with me, dear girl?'

'No,' said Letitia.

He sighed. 'I'm not supposed to be here, you know,' he pointed out with patience, 'but something went wrong yesterday, didn't it?—before then, perhaps. You closed up like a clam—I was rather looking forward to the week-end at George's, but you had iced over...only when you came charging to my rescue at the picnic did you forget whatever it was. What was it, Letitia?'

He put out a hand and plucked her theatre cap from her head, so that her hair stood out in untidy wisps around her face. 'Remember I'm only an uncle type—you can tell me.'

'No,' repeated Letitia, fighting a desire to fling herself at him just as though he were an uncle—that was the last thing he was.

'Something someone said,' persisted Jason, just as though she hadn't spoken. He watched her face. 'Something I said—ah, now we have it! Tell me, dear girl. It will be quicker, you know, for I intend to stay here until you do.'

She took a quick look; he meant what he said. She took a deep breath and keeping her eyes on his face, began: 'I was here—last week, when you and Julius came through after the list. You were going out to dinner with someone called Wibecke. I was at the sink,' she jerked her head backwards, 'behind that door, and I was going to come out so that you would know that I was there, only before I could, you said...' She paused, not because she had forgotten a single word of it, but so that she might steady her voice.

'I remember exactly what we—what I said; that

you were a nice girl and not as plain as all that.' He spoke gently, his eyes very intent.

She looked away at last. 'That wasn't as bad as the bit before. You said "With Tishy?" as though the very idea appalled you, and now you've got the cheek to ask me out to dinner with you.' Her voice was bitter and regrettably wobbly. 'Are you doing penance or something?' She choked on her rage and when he put out a hand and turned her face to his, she tried to pull away.

'No, don't do that, Letitia,' he spoke firmly. 'I'm sorry you overheard what I said, but get this into your head—I wasn't appalled, only very surprised. You see, I had been warned that you were off men for the time being; it never occurred to me that you would agree to come out with me even if I had asked you, and I didn't know you very well then, did I? and I've known Wibecke for years. And as for the rest: you are a nice girl, and you aren't all that plain—you grow on one, you know, and one day you will grow on some man so much that he'll discover that you're the prettiest girl in the world for him.' He smiled down at her. 'You're a little goose, and I've been clumsy and I'm more sorry than I can say. I should like to take you out very much. The offer,' he added gravely, 'is being made entirely without pressure or suggestion from any one else.'

It was weak of her to give in—she knew that. He

thought of her as a nice, plain girl, he had just said so, quite safe to take out and unlikely to raise his pulse by a single beat. But she knew that he was a friend, when he added: 'Wear that pretty green dress, dear girl,' she said quite meekly: 'Very well, Jason.'

CHAPTER SIX

BECAUSE IT WAS still early in the evening, he took her to a restaurant which catered for theatregoers, Le Gaulois in Chancery Lane. She had read of it in the glossy magazines but she had never expected to see it from the inside. Jason ushered her in, explaining: 'We're not going to a theatre, but we can talk here in peace and eat early.'

It was a small place and very French, already more than half full as they were shown to their table. When they were seated, Letitia asked in a small voice: 'Were you so sure that I should come?'

His brows rose a fraction, but his voice was friendly. 'I booked a table while you were changing.' He smiled a little then and went on: 'I'm famished—we had a scratch meal at midday, didn't we? We'll have a drink and decide what to order, shall we?'

She sipped her Dubonnet and studied the menu. There was a great deal to choose from and to her at least it was wildly expensive. She remembered the canteen at the hospital, where they all counted their money before they decided what to eat, and uncannily he read her thoughts. 'The food's pretty basic at St Athel's, isn't it? What does it cost you to eat there?'

He asked the question with seeming idleness so that she was lulled into an unthinking answer. 'Well, I try to keep it down to three or four pounds a day, less if I can—we can't get pudding for that or any of the extras, but we all have tea and biscuits in our rooms, you know, and we share those round—and we buy chips.'

His expression didn't alter, only his eyes narrowed so that she was unable to read the expression in his face. She went on: 'Of course, we all eat too much starch, but it's nice and filling even though it's awfully bad for our figures.'

His voice was pleasantly detached. 'There doesn't seem much wrong with yours, dear girl,' and he twinkled at her so nicely that she chuckled.

'Well, I run round rather a lot, don't I?'

'You do—you work damned hard. I like your Mrs Mead, by the way. What a sensible woman she is—your right hand, I presume.'

The talk drifted to the shared interest of their work, and it was several minutes before he asked: 'Now, what shall we have? How about pâté for a start? We could follow it with salmon—they do it very nicely here with asparagus tips and quenelles of sole.'

Letitia wasn't at all sure what a quenelle was, but

it sounded nice. She agreed happily, disposed of the pâté when it came with real pleasure, and ate the salmon which followed it with an excellent appetite, and when she sipped the wine he had taken time in ordering, she said appropriately: 'Oh, claret, isn't it?'

He looked at her with some interest. 'How delightful to take out a girl who doesn't think only in terms of champagne and sherry. Where did you get your knowledge from? Do wines interest you?'

'I expect they would if I drank them more often,' she told him ingenuously. 'Father knows a lot about them and he says that everyone, women too, should have a knowledge of them, even if they never get a chance to drink anything else but the cooking sherry.'

'Your father is a most interesting man.'

She speared some salmon and popped it into her mouth. She had forgotten all about being awkward and disliking men; she felt, for the first time in weeks, composed and assured. It was a delightful sensation, and went, like the excellent claret, to her head just a little, so that she talked happily through the delicious trifle which arrived after the salmon, and well into the coffee, quietly encouraged by her companion, who, while not saying much himself, asked the right questions in the right places and looked interested. They sat a long time over their leisurely meal, and when at length he drove her back to St Athel's, she thanked him fervently for her evening.

Jason had got out of the BMW too, and they stood facing each other under the bright lights of the Accident Room entrance. She looked up at him, glowing with her love so that her cheeks were prettily pink and her eyes shone, and he stared back.

'Well, dear girl, that wasn't such an ordeal, was it?' he asked. 'For a nice girl who isn't so very plain, you made a great success of our evening.' His smile robbed the words of any unkindness. 'Looks don't count in the long run, you know, Letitia, but charm does, and you have plenty of that—and mind you remember it. I dare say Karel asked you to go out with him?' His voice had lost none of its calm, and when she nodded: 'He's a good chap—you'll enjoy yourself with him.'

The happy glow faded; this then was why he had taken her out—not so much for the pleasure of her company but to prove to her that she didn't need to worry about being dull or plain; that she could be an amusing companion for any young man who chose to ask her out—to break as it were the ice she had embeded herself in. A kindly act, but had he not, all along, begged her to consider him as an uncle? And now he had offered her avuncular advice!

She opened her eyes wide to hold back the tears,

and managed to smile. 'I'll take your advice, Jason. It was a lovely evening.' She offered a hand and had it gently engulfed. 'I hope you have a good trip to Holland, and please give my love to Katrina.'

He was still holding her hand. 'Oh, lord, I quite forgot that I was going to talk to you about her. Never mind, Margo has it more or less fixed up.'

She had no idea what he was talking about and when she asked all he said was: 'She'll tell you. Good night, dear girl,' and he didn't kiss her, though she had hoped that he would. She wished him good night too in a sober little voice, then went through the door he was holding open for her and ran across the bare, deserted expanse of the Accident Room and into the passage beyond without looking back. She made herself think of nothing at all while she got ready for bed, but the moment the light was out she was powerless to prevent her thoughts flooding back, and after a little while she allowed them to take over, lying with her eyes tight shut in the hope that sleep would come. It was a long while before it did, so that when she went on duty the next morning she looked washed out and her eyes felt like hot coals in her head.

It was on her way to the canteen that she met Margo, who stopped her with a sisterly: 'Tishy, whatever is the matter? You look absolutely grim!' And after a long look. 'Have you got a cold?'

Letitia shook her head, admitting vaguely to feeling tired.

'Well, it's a good thing you've got that holiday next week, isn't it? Katrina's bursting with excitement.' She paused and looked even more narrowly at Letitia. 'You do know she's going home to stay for a week or two?'

'No.' The surge of excitement made it impossible to say more.

'Jason was going to tell you—haven't you seen him since we were at Dalmers Place?'

Letitia nodded. 'Yes, last night.' She added: 'He said he'd forgotten to tell me something, but he'd leave it to you—I didn't think it was anything much.'

Margo looked a little amused. 'Katrina had never been anywhere else in England but London and Dalmers Place, so she wheedled Jason into asking me if I'd ask Mother to invite her to stay—you see, she rather took to you, Tishy, and she wants to meet Paula. So I telephoned Mother and of course she loved the idea—you know how lost she feels with only Paula at home. He's driving her down before he goes back to Holland. She'll be there when you go on holiday.'

'Yes.' Did that mean that she would see him again? she wondered. 'How long is she going to stay?'

Margo shrugged. 'I've no idea, but you'll be home for a week, won't you—and Paula will be there—they're just about the same age. If they get on well, I daresay Paula will be invited back. Nice for her.'

'Lovely. I think I'd better go to the canteen...'

Her elder sister looked her over with affection. 'Enough money for a good meal?' she wanted to know.

Letitia nodded; food would choke her, there was far too much on her mind. She would go over to the home and make tea. She had drunk one cup of this calming beverage when she was called to the telephone.

'A man!' shrieked a voice up the stairs, and Letitia, her head stuffed full with Jason still, tore down to the ground floor, her shoes and cap off, intent on getting there before he should become impatient and ring off. Only it wasn't Jason, it was Karel.

'Dinner?' asked his cheerful voice at the other end of the wire, 'and how about dancing afterwards?' And was she free that very evening?

She said yes without pausing much to think about it. Karel was fun to be with and perhaps an evening out with him would shake her out of this silly self-pitying state she had got into. On her way back to her room she wondered idly why he had asked her; certainly not because he fancied her, of that she was quite sure. They were very good friends, but that was all. Probably he wanted to tell her all about his blonde friend; even more likely, he had quarrelled with that young lady and was intent on making her jealous by taking Letitia out for the evening, something he could safely do since neither of them were emotionally involved. She drank her cooling tea and began to tidy her hair; she was adjusting her cap just so when a voice screamed up the stairs once more, begging her to go down to the telephone for a second time and adding a rider to the effect that it was a man again and would it be a good idea if Tishy had a telephone installed in her room so that the speaker might be saved the trouble of taking her calls.

She ran downstairs, making her excuses as she went, sure with childish faith that this time it would be Jason. It was. His voice, calm and friendly, sent a tingle of delight through her and took her breath, so that her hullo was gruff.

'Ah, dear girl, I'm at your home with Katrina—I expect you know about that by now.'

'Yes.'

'I intended driving back straight away, but your mother's offer of lunch has made me change my mind. I shall come up to London this evening and cross over tonight. Will you be free after tea?'

The tingle turned to a warm glow; he must like

her just a little, if he was going to ask her out; even
as she thought it she remembered she had just accepted Karel's invitation. She said in a small voice:
'I'm going out with Karel.'

'You'll enjoy that.' His voice, though she strained
her ear to catch any change in its tone, sounded as
placid as it always did; she wondered if he had put
Karel up to it in the first place, and the idea made
her add snappishly: 'Yes, I shall—he's such fun.'
And then, because her feelings were threatening to
overcome her: 'I really must go, I'm on duty in five
minutes.'

'Of course, dear girl. Any messages for your
mother?'

'Please give her my love. I hope you have a pleasant trip home.'

There was no tinge of regret in his good-bye, so
Letitia hung up and tore upstairs to her room to put
on her shoes and emerge a few seconds later, looking neat and tidy and unnaturally prim—a magnificent effort on her part when what she really wanted
to do was to fling herself on to her bed and howl
her eyes out.

There was no time to indulge in such weak feelings, however. She was kept hard at work until she
went off duty, and the serious business of making
the best of herself for Karel's benefit took all her
attention then—a waste of time and effort, it turned

out, for although he was pleased to see her and took her to one of the trendier restaurants for dinner, it was obvious that his pleasure in her company was largely due to the fact that she made a sympathetic audience while he alternately sang the praises of the blonde and then, sunk in the depths of despair because of their recent quarrel, begged Letitia for advice.

And when they danced presently, he kept up a monologue in her ear, recalling how he and his blonde had danced together, and how wonderful a dancer she was, so that Letitia felt she had two left feet and ought not to be on the floor at all. All the same, Karel was a dear, and once he was on good terms with his girlfriend once more, or had found himself another one altogether, he would be quite his old self. As it was, he had spared no expense on their evening and when he took her back to the hospital, told her that she was a jolly good sort and kissed her in a brotherly fashion, observing that she was a nice girl, and she, heartily sick of his tepid compliment, thanked him with charm, wished him luck with his blonde and took herself off to her room, where she got ready for bed and presently, lying in the dark, indulged at last her overwhelming wish to have a good cry.

The week before her holidays went surprisingly fast; for one thing, they were busy in theatre, so that much of her free time was taken up with getting her clothes ready, and for another, Georgina came up to do some shopping and invited her to join her and Margo for tea at Fortnum and Mason, luckily on an afternoon when she was free, for she liked the elegant tea room and hoped that someone, during the afternoon, would mention Jason. No one did, though there was plenty of talk about Katrina's visit. 'A nice child,' said Georgina. 'You would think that being the youngest of such a large family she would be spoilt, but she isn't—she's clever, of course— they all are. That family has everything although none of them ever mentions it.' She smiled at Letitia, listening avidly. 'Have another of these little cakes, Tishy, I'm going to; I shouldn't really, for I might get fat and Julius will tease me.'

Julius wouldn't do anything of the sort, thought Letitia; he would love Georgina whatever shape she was; probably he thought she was the most beautiful girl in the world. She sighed, wishing with all her heart that she might be loved like that. By Jason, of course.

She went home by train, with Margo to see her off at Paddington and the promise of her father to meet her at Exeter. The train was full and hot and she slept uneasily, waking finally just before they reached Exeter. It was nice to see her father waiting on the platform, she hugged him with delight and

got into the car beside him and they drove through
the busy city streets and out on to the Moretonhampstead road, and as they left the city behind
them she felt the breeze blowing coolly through the
car windows. 'This is glorious,' she told her father,
and he smiled understandingly. 'It's splendid to have
you home, Tishy,' he told her fondly, 'although a
week isn't long enough. That nice child Katrina
seems to be enjoying herself, she and Paula get on
very well together, but she's looking forward to seeing you again. Jason brought her down, of course—
a splendid man; knows about porcelain, too. He
much admired that Minton parian figure...'

'The dancer?'

Her father nodded. 'He's fortunate enough to have
a pair—children with dogs. I imagine he has quite
a collection of his own, I should dearly love to see
it.' He sounded wistful, so that she said robustly:
'Yes, I daresay, Father, but you have some nice
pieces yourself, you know—what about that Derby
biscuit figure?'

Her parent brightened. 'A splendid example,' he
agreed happily. 'Jason assured me that it was one of
the best examples he had ever seen.'

Jason, it seemed, had impressed her father. He
had impressed her too, though in a different way,
but there was no point in thinking about that now,
so she asked about her sisters and kept the conver-

sation strictly on the family for the rest of their journey.

It was wonderful to be home, to be hugged and kissed by her mother, embraced joyfully by Paula and Katrina, and then borne away to eat a huge tea with everyone talking at once, making plans sufficient to last a month, let alone a week.

'What happened to the gipsies?' asked Letitia.

Her father sighed. 'They made a splendid recovery and discharged themselves two days ago. They're back in their usual haunt and the boy came to fetch his dog only this morning.'

'But it's too soon.'

'Yes, Tishy, by our standards it is, but not from theirs. Probably they'll regain their strength twice as quickly as any of us soft-living people. They're children of Nature, you know.'

She registered a silent resolve to go and see them for herself; it would have to be when Katrina wasn't about though, she didn't think that Jason would want his young sister to go with her. Her mind made up on that score, she flung herself into the enthusiastic plans for the week ahead.

The good weather held. They were able to go somewhere everyday, walking on Dartmoor, driving down to Dartmouth and Salcombe, laden with the picnic basket and with Shep taking up much of the back seat. Letitia drove, with Katrina beside her and her parents wedged in the back, and once there, they bathed and lay about in the sun and ate hugely, coming home in time to get tea before Paula got back from school. It was delightful. Letitia, lulled by fresh air and the peace and leisure of the countryside, felt her touchy nerves soothed, and even though she wasn't happy, at least she was beginning to think sensibly. She could even listen to Katrina talking about Jason—something which she did very frequently—without her breath catching in her throat and her heart turning over. She assured herself that given time, she would be able to forget him; she had got over Mike, now she would get over Jason—sentiments which did her credit and held no water at all. Jason wasn't Mike; he wasn't just any man, she would never be able to forget him. All the same, she tried hard and by the Saturday morning, with only one day to go before she had to return to St Athel's, she considered that she was well on the way to relegate him into his proper place in her life—a casual acquaintance whom it had been pleasant to meet but who could just as casually be forgotten. She assured herself of this fact repeatedly, with absolutely no success, although she reminded herself that it was early days yet.

Paula and Katrina were going over to the doctor's house to play tennis after breakfast, which left Letitia free at last to visit the gipsies. She got up early, dressed without much thought as to her appearance in slacks and a denim shirt, and went downstairs to get breakfast. She had it ready by the time everyone else came down, and the moment the girls had gone she whisked through the chores, told her mother vaguely that she was going for a walk, and set off.

She was glad to reach the trees, for the sun was already hot on her shoulders, and once in their shelter she didn't hurry, but poked around her as she went there was plenty to see; wild flowers of all kinds, a multitude of birds and the wood's four-footed inhabitants. She whistled to the birds as she strolled along the path, then stood patiently waiting for them to reply, so that it took her some time to reach the path which would lead her to where the gipsies were camped in the clearing. She turned down it, still not hurrying; the girls wouldn't be home for lunch, her mother wouldn't mind if she got home late; it would be cold meat and a salad and she could help herself from the huge, old-fashioned larder. She paused to watch a blackbird, and when it flew away whistled to it. The answering whistle wasn't one that any ornithologist would mistake for a genuine bird call, and Letitia turned round to see who it was. Jason, coming towards her.

He came without haste and nor did he appear eager, just his usual calm self, and she wondered crossly if he ever allowed any deep emotion to disturb him. He certainly wasn't displaying his feelings now, if he had any. His: 'Hullo, dear girl,' was uttered in a voice which, while friendly, held nothing more.

She stayed quietly, waiting for him to catch up with her and said in her turn: 'Hullo. Have you come to see Katrina? She's playing tennis at Doctor Gibbs, didn't Mother tell you?'

He halted beside her. 'Yes, but time enough to see her presently. Are you on your way to visit the gipsies, by any chance? Your mother said you had gone for a walk.'

They were making their way down the path, close together because it was so narrow. 'Yes, they're back—did you know? They discharged themselves and I wanted to see how they were getting on. It was too soon.'

He said almost the same as her father had done. 'For us it might have been—they live nearer to Nature than we do.'

'Have you come to take Katrina home?' She had been longing to ask that, and now it had popped out.

'Yes, your mother has asked me to spend the night here and go back tomorrow. I'll give you a lift as far as the hospital, if you like.'

'Thank you. Are you going back to your home?'

'Yes—and staying there for quite some time, I hope. Katrina has visits to pay before she goes back to school and my mother will be back from visiting my sisters.'

She stopped to look at him. 'Oh—your mother? You've never mentioned her...' She went pink then because there had never been any reason why he should have done so, but he didn't appear to notice her discomfiture.

'She lives a few miles away from me,' he told her. 'We get on very well. My father died three years ago—he was a doctor too.'

'I'm sorry. Your mother must be glad that she has so many of you.'

'We like to think so. As a family we get on very well—just as your family does.'

They had come to the end of the path and there were the caravans once more, with the horses by the water and the lurcher lying in a patch of sunlight between the trees. He got to his feet the moment he saw them, his ferocious back changing to a pleased whine when he saw who it was. His welcome was boisterous, and Letitia, freed at last from his attentions, made a few ineffective attempts to brush down her slacks and was deeply vexed when Jason remarked: 'Oh, leave it, dear girl, they surely can't be worth all that attention.' His amused eye swept over her so that she frowned quite fiercely. 'Only a fool would come down here in anything else but jeans and a shirt,' and she was even more angry when he answered: 'I take it you keep an unending supply handy?'

He had laughed gently as he spoke. Letitia scowled at him and then had to change the scowl to a smile because the gipsy woman was coming towards them. She was followed by the rest of them, the old man and the boy and the young man, looking thinner and paler than they would normally be, but their eyes were bright and they seemed surprisingly fit. It didn't seem possible that they could be capable of taking up their old life so soon after being ill. 'Do you really feel all right?' she wanted to know of the woman. 'Shouldn't you have stayed a little longer in hospital?'

The woman shrugged. 'But why, missy? It is not our kind of life, closed up between walls, and Jerry here, he missed his dog. We shall do very well. You'll drink a cup of tea with us? We're beholden to you both for your help—you and the kind gentleman here, and it won't be forgotten.'

She made an inviting gesture towards one of the caravans and Letitia, with a glance at Jason, started to walk towards it. She didn't quite fancy tea, but she was too kindhearted to refuse hospitality when it was offered. They sat on an old bench outside the caravan, talking to the men—at least Jason did; Letitia got up after a minute or two and strolled across the grass with Jerry and the dog to give some sugar lumps to the horses, and when the tea came, she sat down on the caravan steps and drank it with the dog pressed close to her, hopeful that there might be more biscuits in her pocket, and the gipsy woman sat beside her.

She had, from time to time, stopped to talk to the gipsies when she had met them, but never for such a length of time as this. They were no fools, she quickly discovered, and it amused her to see Jason deep in conversation about trout fishing and obviously enjoying himself. It was when she refused a second cup of tea that the woman offered to tell her fortune for her. 'Turn the cup three times, dearie,' she advised Letitia, 'and hold it upside down with your left hand.'

'I don't think...' began Letitia, and caught Jason's eye; he was still talking about trout, but he was listening to her too. She did as she had been told and the gipsy took the cup from her and fell to studying it.

'A tall, fair man, dearie,' she began, and Letitia saw that the men were all listening now. 'Trouble and strife, but the life of a princess is waiting for you, for I see wealth and jewels and great happiness. Just as it should be for a kind young lady like you are.'

Her dark eyes flickered over Letitia's face. 'You don't believe me, but mark my words, missy, I'm one to tell the truth and that's what I see in the tea-leaves.' She cast the cup away from her and turned to Jason. 'And you, kind gentleman, shall I tell you your fortune?'

He answered her gravely: 'There is no need, I think,' and the woman nodded back at him.

'You're right, there is no need; I've told it all.' A remark of which Letitia took little notice; it had been easy enough for the gipsy to talk about a tall fair man when there was one standing beside her, and one was always told about the money and jewels and happiness waiting to brighten one's future. She didn't believe a word of it, although she thanked the woman nicely as they prepared to go.

They were half-way up the hill before she said: 'I'm glad they're all right.'

Her companion tucked a hand under her elbow and because there wasn't much room, pulled her closer. 'You're a nice girl,' he remarked, 'though I believe I've said that before.'

'Yes, you have!' she sounded quite savage. 'I'm sick and tired of being called nice—everyone says it!' She kicked at some nettles and when a briar tore her slacks she couldn't have cared less.

'Ah, yes—a bit monotonous, dear girl, but actually a compliment. A nice girl, from a man's point of view at least, means one who is pleasant to have around, with a soft voice and gentle ways and no ideas about contradicting him each time he opens his mouth, a girl who doesn't expect compliments with every second breath, or imagines that just because he is a man he's wildly in love with her.'

'She sounds like a hopeless prig,' said Letitia coldly. They had come out on to the main track through the wood once more and had turned towards the rectory. Jason took his hand from her arm and flung an arm round her shoulders instead. 'No, Letitia, never that, and just you remember that next time someone calls you a nice girl.'

Especially the bit about imagining he was in love with her, she supposed sourly. Had that been a veiled hint? she wondered uneasily. Surely she hadn't given herself away to him? She tried to think back to their previous meetings and became instantly confused; it was a relief when he continued in an ordinary voice: 'Katrina has had a splendid time here, I can never be sufficiently grateful. As she is so much younger than the rest of us I sometimes wonder if she has enough young company.'

'Well, we loved having her and I know Mother and Father will always welcome her if she likes to come again. Mother misses us all, I think. I don't know what she'll do when Paula leaves home.'

'It is the same for my mother, but of course there will be grandchildren enough to keep her fully occupied.'

'Your sisters have children?'

'Oh, a mere handful as yet, but I daresay that between us we shall produce enough progeny to satisfy Mama.'

She didn't mean to ask, but: 'You too—you're going to be married?'

He paused to look down at her, a little smile tugging at the corners of his mouth. 'But of course, dear girl—we all come to it, you know. Can't you see me in the role of father to a succession of children?'

Letitia could, only too clearly; he would be a wonderful father. She speculated as to the girl whom he had chosen—that Wibecke someone or other, perhaps; it didn't bear thinking of.

They had left the trees behind them now and as they crossed the rough grass he began to talk about other things, trivialities which kept them occupied until they reached the rectory, where he was instantly claimed by the Rector. Going to bed that night, Letitia reflected that she had seen very little of him during the day; certainly he had made no attempt to seek her out, only he had come looking for that morning, and had that been so that he might tell her, in a casual way, that he was going to be married? It seemed very likely. She closed her eyes on the unhappy thought, and hardly slept at all.

CHAPTER SEVEN

THEY LEFT after lunch the next day, with a decidedly
mopish Katrina sitting in the back, and Letitia, who
felt that way herself, took great pains to make conversation, plodding in an uninspired way through
such mundane topics as the weather, the charms of
the countryside at that time of year, the amount of
traffic on the road, and adding a few observations
as to the kind of crossing they might expect, the
prospects of fine weather in Holland and the pleasure of returning home. To all of which Katrina answered only briefly and Jason with a civility which
she found so dampening that after a little while she
too fell silent. It was, she felt, someone else's turn.
It was disconcerting when Jason, apparently reading
her thoughts, said: 'Katrina is silent because she is
unhappy at leaving your home, but presently she
will get over it, and I—I am silent because I find it
pleasant to drive with you beside me, knowing that
I don't need to talk; that you won't mind if you
aren't the centre of interest.'

A speech which Letitia found to be unanswerable;
he had made her sound like a chatty saint who
hadn't bothered much about her appearance; it also

had the effect of drying her up completely, so that they sat in silence for quite some distance.

'Perhaps I put that rather badly,' Jason said at length, 'but you see, I think of you as a friend and don't always bother to choose my words.' He made it worse by adding: 'Are you sulking?'

'No,' she said forcefully, 'I am not—I have no reason to sulk, have I, with compliments pouring down on me at such a fine rate!' She gave a small, indignant snort and stared ahead of her, aware that he had cast a lightning glance at her, but he didn't answer her, only after a minute or two suggested at his most placid that they might stop for tea.

'How about Shaftesbury?' he wanted to know. 'There must be a tea-room there.'

'Yes, there is,' said Letitia, mollified at the thought of tea. 'It's up by the walks…'

'Which walks?' asked Katrina. Apparently the idea of tea had cheered her up sufficiently for speech.

'Well, the town's on a hill, and there's a walk along the ramparts, there's a splendid view and sometimes local artists hang their paintings there, and you can look at them as you walk and buy one if you want to.'

Katrina rested her chin on the back of Letitia's seat, her voice wheedling. 'Jason, please may we go to these walks if we hurry a little over our tea, and if I see a picture I like, will you buy it for me, then I will keep it always for a remembrance.'

He agreed amiably to this suggestion, and now that Katrina was feeling more like her usual happy self, the conversation became quite lively, so that the time passed too quickly, at least from Letitia's point of view.

The tea-shop was of the olde-worlde persuasion and dispelled the last of Katrina's low spirits. They took their tea in one of its small, low-ceilinged rooms and then walked to the ramparts close by. Letitia hadn't exaggerated. The view was delightful and far-flung, the flowers bordering the walk were at their best, and sure enough, hung almost the whole length of the wall, were the paintings. Katrina skipped from one to the other, changing her mind every few seconds until Jason told her good-naturedly that there would be no time to buy any-thing at all if she didn't make up her mind then and there. Finally she picked on a small watercolour of the town and they went along to the end of the walk to where a woman was sitting at a table, knitting. Jason had paid her and Letitia was turning away when Katrina exclaimed: 'But Tishy must have a painting too—Jason, buy her one.'

It didn't sound right, put like that. Letitia was on the point of refusing on the grounds of not liking anything when Jason said blandly: 'But of course—

I've seen the very one, but it's to be a surprise. I'm going to get it now, but you're not to open it until you get back to the hospital.'

It would have been churlish to have refused. She thanked him nicely and strolled with Katrina to the end of the walk while he retraced his steps. He caught up with them as they reached the main street, the picture under his arm, and Letitia spent the rest of their journey consumed with curiosity as to what it might be. Only after they had reached St Athel's and they had wished each other good-bye, with almost tearful affection on Katrina's part and careless friendliness on her brother's, did Letitia climb the stairs to her room and once there, before unpacking or putting on the kettle for a cup of tea, open her package.

The picture was a watercolour; she had seen it as they had walked along the line of paintings that afternoon—a gentle painting of a small stream under the trees, with gipsies and a caravan beside it, not quite the same as the other, live gipsies, but sufficiently like to recall them vividly. For no reason at all she felt tears prick her eyes so that she had to sniff violently and blow her nose. She laid the picture down carefully on her bed and went to put on the kettle in the pantry at the end of the corridor. She met several of her friends on the way, which meant a pooling of tea, sugar and milk and much searching in cupboards for food, and when the ever-increasing number of young ladies had crowded into her room and one, inevitably, remarked on the picture, Letitia was able to say quite cheerfully that she had had it as a present, and no one had wanted to know who from; she had just been home and was presumably a gift from her family.

When everyone had gone, she walked over to the hospital, to the engineer's room in the basement, begged a nail from him and hammered it in with the heel of one of her winter boots. They weren't really supposed to hang pictures in their rooms, but it was a rule which, over the years, had lapsed. It looked exactly right on the wall opposite her bed and it would be the first thing she saw when she woke each day.

There was a heavy list in the morning and by the end of the first hour Letitia felt as though she hadn't been away at all. The patients were fetched, anaesthetized, operated upon and handed over to her care with a speed which was too good to last. It was almost time for her to go to dinner when an elderly man, admitted as a casualty with a stab wound in the chest, collapsed a few minutes after she had received him from the scrub nurse. She went to work on him at once, calling to Mrs Mead to warn the theatre, so that Julius came immediately, wasting no words, but dealing with the crisis with silent speed, while Letitia, well versed in such urgent work, handed him instruments, turned cylinder taps on and off when he told her to, erected a second drip and took the patient's blood pressure, it gave faint results presently and Julius said quietly: 'Good—I think we've got him,' and gave her a long list of instructions which she filed away neatly inside her sensible head.

It was another hour before the man was fit to be transferred to the ITU, and by then dinner time had come and gone, and what was more, the afternoon list was looming. Letitia retired to the changing room and gobbled the sandwiches Mrs Mead had fetched for her, drank some scalding coffee and without stopping to do anything to her face or hair, got into her theatre dress again and bundled on the mob cap, and even though the afternoon held no surprises, she was very tired by the time the list was finished, and hungry too. But it was only five o'clock, there would be no supper for another two hours and she had nothing to eat in her room. She finished tidying the recovery room, poked her head round Theatre door to wish Sister good night, and went over to her room.

She would have to go out to eat; there was a cheap little café just down the road where she could get a meal. She had a bath and changed into a cotton dress, then counted her money; she hadn't a great deal, but egg and chips would do nicely and if she had a pot of tea and some bread and butter she wouldn't need to go to supper. She did her face and hair in a hurry and went quickly down the stairs and through the hospital to the front entrance. The Head Porter, Nathaniel, was just taking over door duty and saluted her in the fatherly fashion he used towards the younger nurses.

'Got a date, Staff?' he wanted to know.

'Who—me? Heavens, no. I missed my dinner and I can't wait for supper, Nathaniel. I'm going down to the Cosy Café for a meal.'

She grinned at him and waved and went on her way, out into the busy street, packed with people going home from work, and grey and grimy despite the sunshine. The café wasn't very full, and Fred, who owned it, greeted her with a friendly nod; over the years the nurses at St Athel's had patronized him, and he knew most of them by sight. He came over to her table at once, wiped its plastic top and moved the pepper and salt an inch or two. 'What'll it be, luv?' he wanted to know.

'Egg and chips, please, Fred, and some bread and butter and a pot of tea. I missed my dinner.'

'And that's a damned shame, ducks—won't keep yer a mo'.'

It was stuffy in the little place, its air laden with the smells of warm vinegar and fried food and wash-

ing up, but it was nice to sit down and anticipate
her supper. When the tea came Letitia poured herself
a cup and then began on the egg and chips, eating
slowly to make them last, wondering if she would
be extravagant and have another lot. She decided
against it; she had to have new duty shoes before
the end of the month, and it was Margo's birthday
in a week's time, and she would need money for
those. She sighed and nibbled a chip, telling herself
that if she ate too much she might get fat; she became so engrossed in this possibility that she failed
to hear the doorbell pinging as it was opened. Only
when Jason sat down in the chair opposite hers did
she look up to stare at him, her mouth, luckily empty
of chips, half open. After a long moment she
achieved a 'Well...' and smiled a little uncertainly
because he was smiling his nice gentle smile even
though he hadn't spoken. When he did it was to ask:
'Is that your tea or an early supper?'

'Well, I missed dinner—we got held up, and the
canteen doesn't open until seven o'clock.'

He leaned forward to study her plate. 'Egg?' he
raised his eyebrows, 'and chips? I'll join you if I
may, dear girl.'

He didn't wait for her to answer but lifted a hand
to Fred, who advanced to their table. 'Friend of
yours, ducks?' he wanted to know.

Letitia smiled at him. 'Oh, yes, Fred. A doctor who works at St Athel's from time to time.'

Fred treated his new customer to a narrow scrutiny which the doctor bore with good-natured fortitude, before saying: 'OK, what'll it be, doc?'

'Egg—er—eggs and chips, I think, and tea.' He glanced over to Letitia's side of the table. 'That is tea?' His glance lingered on her empty plate. 'I can't eat alone. Letitia, could you manage another plateful and keep me company?'

'Yes, I could, thank you.' She answered promptly and with no beating around the bush.

'And fresh tea for us both, perhaps?' He sat back, quite at his ease, while Fred took away the used plates and probably as a concession to his customer's calling, wiped the table down with extra care. When he had gone, Letitia said: 'I thought you'd gone back to Holland—you said you were going last night.'

He looked at her with lazy blue eyes. 'So I did, but when we got to Dalmers Place, Georgina insisted on us staying the night, and I can't get a reservation until tomorrow.'

'Oh. How did you know I was here?'

'Nathaniel told me.' He smiled again and looked around him. The little place was filling rapidly with bus drivers and their mates, shabby down-at-heel men with the evening paper tucked under an arm, and the last of the shoppers stopping briefly for a cup of tea before going home to suburbia. 'You should have let Karel know you were free and asked him to take you out to dinner,' he observed mildly.

'Me?' she exclaimed. 'Heavens, no—supposing he had arranged to do something else with his evening.' She wasn't going to mention the blonde, after all, Karel had confided in her.

The tea came and she poured them each a cup and by the time she had done that, the eggs and chips had arrived, and since Jason began on his with every sign of enjoyment, she felt no need to conceal the fact that she was still hungry. She ate up her second helping with as much appetite as the first, polished off her share of the bread and butter and refilled their cups.

'Fred cooks very well,' she observed, not because she expected her companion to be interested in Fred's prowess in the kitchen, but because it was something to say. The doctor agreed with her readily, admirably concealing the fact that he had never in his life before been into a place like the Cosy Café, and that egg and chips, while a wholesome and sustaining dish, had little appeal for him, especially at six o'clock in the evening. He had, in fact, been looking forward to a quite different meal in a quite different place, with a bottle of wine and Letitia in her green dress sitting opposite him. As it was, he stirred his strong tea and smiled across the table at her, putting her completely at ease and allowing her to forget that the dress she was wearing was last year's and her appearance, while neat, was hardly breathtaking.

She offered him the sugar and asked: 'Did you want to see me about something?' and his answer was ready enough even if vague.

'Well, I needed to see someone and it seemed a good idea as I had this unexpected day. I shan't be coming over again for some time.'

Letitia digested this with a sinking heart, her eyes on her plate. So many times she had thought: 'This is the last time,' and now it really was. Even if Paula went to stay with Katrina, and she thought it very likely, there was little hope of her being included in the invitation.

'Mind if I smoke?' Jason's voice cut across her thoughts and when she said no, she didn't mind a bit, he lit his pipe and sat back, puffing gently at it while she finished her tea, then signalled to Fred, remarking: 'You're tired, aren't you, dear girl? I've got the car here, I'm going to take you for a gentle run—just for an hour or so—you can go to sleep if you want to.'

She choked back the yawn which threatened and said brightly: 'That's awfully nice of you to suggest it, but it's such a waste of your evening.'

'No, I like a quiet run now and then.' He added carelessly: 'I intended going anyway, if you like to come along...?'

Put like that it was apparent that he wasn't just making a polite suggestion. 'Well, if you're really going?' she said a little inanely, and got to her feet, praised her supper to Fred and wandered to the door, conscious that she felt nicely full and more than a little sleepy.

They walked back to the hospital, talking trivialities, and when he helped her into the BMW, Letitia allowed herself to sink back into its comfort as he turned the car into the evening traffic and presently, down to the river, to go at a leisurely pace along the Embankment to Chelsea and over Putney Bridge, and when she asked him where they were going, his answer was: 'Oh, follow our noses, don't you think, dear girl?' which naturally enough led them to Hampton and a pleasant side road alongside the river, but presently Jason left it and found his way to Cookham, and all the time he talked, a quiet flow of words which needed only the minimum of answers, indeed, thinking about it afterwards, she was quite unable to remember what he had talked about, only that it had been soothing and undemanding, and when he stopped outside a charming inn on the river bank and suggested that they had coffee, she agreed happily. After all, she wouldn't be seeing him again;

she might as well make the most of the evening. It was still warm and not late and they went through the inn and out on to the lawn beyond, where they had their coffee by the peace and quiet of the water.

'This isn't at all like Fred's,' observed Letitia. It struck her then that the doctor wasn't really an egg and chips man; perhaps he was still hungry, for he was very large. 'Did you have enough to eat?' she asked a little anxiously.

A muscle twitched faintly at the corner of the doctor's mouth. 'Indeed I did—I found it a very decent little café, too. I liked the way Fred made sure that I really was a friend and not just being a nuisance.'

'Oh, he's always been like that; we're allowed to go there in uniform, you know, and he's proud of that and it makes him feel responsible.'

Jason nodded. 'What happens to you when theatre closes down?'

'I'll be lent out to the wards, I expect—night duty, too. I shall't like that—you see, it will only be for a few weeks, so I shall have to stay in my own room, not move over to the night nurses' quarters, and that means I shan't sleep a wink. People try to be quiet, but someone always drops something or forgets and puts a radio on loud, and there you are, awake for the rest of the day.'

'No holidays left?'

'Yes, three weeks, but everyone wants holidays

now and I've just had a week and they're short on the wards. At least, that's what the Number Seven told me. If I had measles or something they'd manage very well without me.'

He laughed. 'So they would. Shall we go? You're on early in the morning, I expect?'

They went back a different way, through quiet stretches of road, their surroundings dim in the evening light. It was almost dark by the time they reached the hospital and the streets were quiet, too early for returning theatregoers, too late for anyone with a home to go to after their day's work. Jason drew up outside the main entrance of the hospital and got out to open her door.

'Did you enjoy your nap?' he asked on a laugh.

Letitia had tried so hard to stay awake; not to miss a moment of his company. She said, her voice stiff with annoyance at herself: 'I'm so very sorry, I tried to stay awake...' She stopped, aware that she hadn't put it very well, and he laughed again.

'Would you have gone to sleep if Karel had been driving?' he asked.

'No, for he would never have given me the chance—you should have given me a poke.'

She wondered why he sighed as he put his arms around her. 'This instead,' he told her, and kissed her.

She was surprised, for she hadn't expected that.

She stared up at him, her emotions churning around inside her so that she really had no sense at all. Then she stretched on tiptoe and kissed him back, and then, when he did nothing about it, said in a hopeless voice: 'Oh, Jason, good-bye,' and fled through the door and across the entrance hall.

She reached her room without meeting anyone and began to undress, appalled at her behaviour, appalled too at the strength of her feelings when he had kissed her, but then no one had ever kissed her like that before; he had wiped out Mike's milk-and-water efforts for good and all. And it hadn't been fair, it had made her forget her good sense and she had made a fool of herself in consequence—and what a good thing, she told herself savagely, that she would never see him again.

She was brushing her hair with terrible ferocity when Angela put her head round the door with the offer of a cup of tea. 'My goodness, Tishy,' she declared, 'you look as though you've been to your own funeral!' and she wasn't far wrong, decided Letitia gloomily.

Theatre worked flat out for the next week; as many cases as possible had to be dealt with before it was closed, otherwise when it re-opened the waiting list would be unmanageable. It meant that everyone on the theatre staff had to work longer hours and extra hard, but Letitia didn't mind; it suited her mood to be so busy that she had almost no time to herself and no time, either, to think. She made the extra work an excuse for going to bed early and joining, only for the briefest time, the sessions of tea-drinking which were usual in the home, and on duty she did her work just as well as she usually did, only with a quietness which discouraged the others from the customary chatting whenever there was a moment.

It was Julius who cornered her at last, strolling into the recovery room when the list was over for the day. 'Busy afternoon,' he observed laconically. 'Thank heaven there's another holiday just around the corner—which reminds me; I have something to ask you. Georgina is annoyed with me for forgetting...if I can arrange it, would you consider coming to Holland with us? Nanny's going to her home while we're away and Georgina thought at first that she could manage Polly and Ivo at Bergenstijn, but on second thoughts she isn't so sure. She wants someone there so that if we wanted to go away for a few hours, or even a day, the whole household won't be disrupted, and it has to be someone she knows and trusts. She thought of you. We must emphasise that you aren't expected to take Nanny's place, only be willing to take over if and when Georgina is away or caught up in the small amount of entertaining we do. Don't decide at once, think

about it for a day or two.' He had gone before she
had time to frame a single word.

She went along to see Margo after supper, perch-
ing on her sister's bed and drinking a mug of tea
while she repeated the doctor's astonishing request.
'And he didn't stop for an answer,' she ended. 'He
said think about it.'

Margo looked at her thoughtfully. 'Tishy, I think
I should go—after all, you'll only be put on night
duty until theatre opens again, and you know how
you hate that. Julius can arrange it, I'm sure, and
Georgina likes you, so you can be sure you won't
be overworked. I've been to Bergenstijn, remember,
it's well staffed and beautifully run.'

'Is it anywhere near…I mean, is it in the country?' Letitia longed to ask if Jason lived anywhere
nearby. If he did, she assured herself silently, she
wouldn't go, but Margo's answer made that unnecessary.

'Oh, it's on its own, nothing else close by, only
a village, and that's small. There's a swimming pool
and a tennis court and a gorgeous garden with a
pond—you'll love it. You've been looking a bit
peaked, Tishy—that week at home wasn't enough,
a change of scene might do you good. I daresay
Karel will be there for part of the time, as well as
Cor and Beatrix and Franz—I don't know about

Phena. You'll know everyone which will be nice, but do as you like, love.'

'I suppose I might as well.' It would be nice to see the country where Jason lived, even though his home was miles away from Bergenstijn, but at least it would be better than trying to imagine it, and Polly and baby Ivo would fill her days nicely; when she got back to St Athel's the theatre would be going harder than ever. She would have no time to brood, and a good thing too. 'I'll go,' she said, then drank the rest of her tea and went back to her own room. 'I hope I'm doing the right thing.'

A sentiment echoed by Julius, miles away at Dalmers Place, sitting opposite Georgina in their sitting room. 'If I weren't your devoted slave, my darling,' he pointed out, 'I should have flatly refused to have anything to do with it.'

Georgina looked suitably meek. 'Well, dear Julius, I hadn't meant to tell you yet, but I did mention to Jason that we were thinking of asking Tishy to come to Holland with us, and do you know what he said?' She beamed at her husband. 'He said: ''George, you're an angel, I've been racking my brains how to get the girl over to Holland.'' Don't you think that was nice?'

'I don't know about nice, my love. I think that whatever you did or do it will make no difference in the long run. If Jason is serious about Tishy, then nothing will alter his purpose in marrying her.'

'Now isn't that a comforting thought?' murmured Georgina.

Letitia didn't see Julius to speak to until just before the afternoon list on the following day, when he came into the recovery room.

'I've a letter for you from Georgina. I fancy she doesn't trust my powers of persuasion. I'll leave it in the duty room, shall I?'

Letitia laid the last of the airways neatly beside its fellows. 'Thank you, though I've made up my mind already. I'd like to come and help you with the babies, if you really think I can be of some use.'

'I'm sure of it, Tishy, and thank you. Georgina will be delighted. I'll let you know in a day or two what the arrangements will be.'

She nodded. 'What about Miss Phelps?' The Principal Nursing Officer and a bit of a dragon in a nice way.

'Leave her to me. As for clothes and so on, Georgina will telephone you.' A remark which set up a pleasant enough train of thought in Letitia's mind. Life would be quiet at Bergenstijn, but she would have to decide what to take of her rather meagre wardrobe; it kept her nicely occupied.

Georgina telephoned the next evening, just as Letitia was getting into the bath—indeed, she had ac-

tually got one foot in the water when there was a
terrific thump on the door and a voice shrieked at
her to go down to the telephone. She didn't wait to
dry the foot but flung her dressing gown about her
person and pattered down the stairs, leaving damp
marks as she went. It was only as she picked up the
receiver and heard Georgina's voice that she realized that she had been certain it would be Jason.
Disappointment closed her throat as she said
'Hullo', but Georgina didn't seem to notice anything
wrong; she plunged at once into plans: they were to
travel in three days' time on the Harwich night ferry
and would Tishy mind having Polly in her cabin?
And what about clothes? Three weeks, she cau-
tioned, it all depended on how long they would take
over the theatre, but a fortnight at least. 'So don't
bring too much,' she went on, 'just cotton dresses
and slacks and a pretty dress for the evening. That
lovely green thing you had on when you were
here—everyone said how sweet it was—oh, and a
mac. Julius said it was all right about your passport,
but I thought I'd mention it...'

'I already had a passport,' Letitia assured her, and
added diffidently: 'You really think I'll be useful if
I come?'

'Yes, Tishy, I do—Polly likes you, so she won't
mind not having Nanny and I won't mind leaving
both of them with you.'

'Well, I'll do my best—I'm looking forward to it. I didn't expect another holiday quite as soon as this.'

Georgina laughed. 'You wait until you've had Polly for a few hours before you say that, Tishy! Now, everything's clear, isn't it? Julius will come and fetch you, we can have dinner and then drive to Harwich, OK?'

'OK.'

It was surprising how easily everything went; Miss Phelps didn't seem to mind in the least that Letitia wouldn't be available for night duty; she spoke rather loftily about helping those who needed help in an emergency especially when the person concerned was one of the hospital consultants, and Letitia wondered what on earth Julius could have said to her. And her parents, when she telephoned, sounded very calm about it all; it was her mother who wanted to know if she would be seeing anything of Jason, to which she could only reply that no, she imagined not. It was funny, when she considered the matter, that she had no idea where he lived. He had never mentioned it and neither had Katrina. She promised to send a card when she arrived and a letter each week, and her father gave her a message to pass on to Jason about some porcelain, despite Letitia's certainty that she wouldn't be seeing him.

It was a decidedly pleasant sensation to be wafted

away from St Athel's in Julius's Rolls; she was tired, for she had worked until four o'clock that afternoon, but Julius, talking pleasantly about nothing in particular, revived her flagging spirits and they soared still further at Georgina's warm welcome when they arrived. They ate their dinner without loss of time and got into the car once more, with Polly, in her nightie and dressing gown and fast asleep, on Letitia's lap and Ivo in his Moses basket, sleeping too. At Harwich there was no delay. Julius drove on board and then with Polly in his arms, the two girls behind with the Moses basket and a porter with the luggage, led his small party to their cabins.

And very nice too, decided Letitia, looking round her. Small it might be, but it had everything she could need, even a shower, and the little brass beds looked very inviting. She tucked Polly into hers, refused the offer of a drink, wished her friends good night, and got ready for bed. She had never been out of England before and it was all rather exciting; if she had been on her own she would have gone on deck and had a look round. Instead she contented herself with several peeps from the small window before getting into bed and turning out the light.

It seemed no time at all before the steward was calling her with tea and toast, and Polly, waking up too, demanded to come into her bed and share it with her. They were making short work of it between them when Georgina came in, sat down on the end of the bed and picked up a finger of toast to nibble. 'It's only six o'clock,' she stated as Polly climbed into her lap. 'Julius has arranged to leave the ship last so we can have breakfast before we go. Could you be ready in half an hour, do you think? I've fed Ivo, he's asleep again, bless him. Did you sleep well?'

'Like a top.' Letitia drank the rest of her tea. 'I'll start on Polly now, shall I?'

Breakfast was a cheerful meal, with Polly perched beside her father and Ivo still asleep in his basket. The boat had been full and took some time to empty itself while they ate their way though bacon and eggs and toast and marmalade. By the time they had finished, almost everyone had gone; they went down to the car then and drove off the ship and through the Customs, on to the road leading away from the Hoek. Holland, thought Letitia excitedly. She stared out of the window and felt a thrill, even though the scenery was prosaic enough; and yet the houses that bordered the road were different, neat and square, the windows shrouded in blindingly white curtains.

Presently they joined the motorway to Rotterdam and there were no more houses, only flat green fields, very pleasant in the early morning. Rotterdam, when they reached it, she didn't much care for; it was large and bustling and in the distance were

the ugly outlines of the oil refineries. It was a relief
to leave the crowded streets behind, and tear on towards Utrecht. But before they reached that city,
Julius turned off the motorway into a quiet country
road, winding through water meadows and small
woods, with here and there a house or two. It was
charming, and Letitia said so.

'I'm glad,' said Julius over his shoulder. 'We live
half a mile further on, down a lane.'

Georgina turned to look at Letitia. 'Jason has a
house a mile from us,' she offered in her soft voice.
'He works mostly in Utrecht, you know, that's
where his consulting rooms are. I expect we'll see
something of him.'

She turned away again and Letitia was glad she
had. She wasn't sure what expression her face wore,
but inside her there had been a kind of explosion,
happiness and surprise and a kind of panic at the
idea of seeing Jason once more. She sat very still,
taking the deep breaths she had so often urged her
patients to take when they were agitated—it made
no difference at all, she felt as though she were
about to explode, perhaps if she were to shut her
eyes…but when she did, there was Jason beneath
the lids, so she opened them again, just in time to
see the iron gates which guarded Bergenstijn from
the outside world.

CHAPTER EIGHT

THE HOUSE stood at the end of a straight drive, square and solid, its large windows aligned precisely about its massive front door. Letitia, ushered inside amidst a little chorus of welcome, looked around her with curiosity and then remembered to mind her manners in time to shake hands with the elderly man who had opened the door to them.

'Hans,' Julius enlightened her, 'our friend and steward—and he speaks English.'

Letitia smiled widely and murmured suitably, then with Polly toddling beside her, went with Georgina into what was referred to as the little room, although it seemed remarkably large to her, but then as far as she could see, the house was large—Dalmers Place was large too, but in quite a different way, with a great deal of panelling and any number of small rooms, odd stairs and narrow passages. Here, she guessed, there would be plenty of space, and she was right, for presently, with Polly safely in Julius's keeping and Ivo sleeping in his basket, Georgina took her round the house, ending with the nurseries, two rooms at the end of the wide back landing on the first floor. Her own room was between them, with a bathroom of its own and every comfort which she had ever dreamed of. Being nanny in the Effert household must be rather super; Letitia was quite astonished when Georgina apologized for putting her in Nanny's bedroom.

'But it's beautiful!' she exclaimed. 'I've never seen such a pretty room, and it's got everything anyone could possibly want—besides, I shall be close to Polly and Ivo. I like it.'

'Oh, good. Let's go down and have coffee, shall we? Then we can take the children in the garden until lunchtime. Polly sleeps in the afternoon and Ivo wakes up to be fed.'

Letitia went to take another look at the nursery. 'Then may I sit up here and write some letters after lunch—I can keep an eye on them at the same time.'

'You don't mind? Everyone will be coming before dinner—Karel will bring the children with him—we haven't heard from Phena yet, perhaps she won't be coming just yet.' They started down the staircase. 'We'll work out some sort of timetable over coffee, shall we?'

It seemed to Letitia that she was being given too much free time, and she said so. 'I shan't know what to do with myself,' she protested, not much liking the idea of having too much time to think, knowing that her thoughts were bound to be of Jason.

It was Julius who said easily: 'Don't worry on

that score, Tishy—have you forgotten that my young cousins will be here? I doubt if you get a minute to yourself.'

They arrived late in the afternoon, laughing and talking and hugging first Georgina and then Letitia, talking Dutch and English as the mood took them, rushing to the kitchen to see Hans and Lenie, the housekeeper, tossing Polly into the air and going to admire baby Ivo. Even the dogs, Flip and little Schippershond and Andersen, the Great Dane, came in for their share of the excitement; the old house was alive with sound. Letitia, undressing and bathing Polly while Georgina saw to Ivo, was interrupted by the steady stream of visitors to the nursery—it was obvious that Julius's young relations loved Georgina dearly, while he could do no wrong in their eyes. A happy family; the sight of them together was heartwarming, although it made her feel lonely too.

They went to bed early, for they had all had a long journey of one sort or the other; it wasn't until Letitia was curled up in bed, the door open so that she would hear the slightest sound from the children in the next room, that she allowed herself to think about Jason, so close and yet so very far away. She was bound to meet him. She was still trying to decide how she would behave towards him when she fell asleep.

She still hadn't decided by the time she was getting Polly ready for bed the following day—it had been a busy one, but pleasant, for everyone had given a hand with the children so that Letitia had found ample time to talk to Karel, ask Beatrix and Cor about school and listen to the more serious Franz outlining his hopes of being a great surgeon later on. She had found time for a swim in the pool at the end of the garden, and taken Polly to admire the waterlilies in the lake. A lovely day, she decided as she obligingly turned herself into a horse so that Polly might ride her across the nursery floor. Halfway across it, they rolled over together, giggling and squirming, while Polly tugged the pins out of Letitia's hair the better to use it as reins.

'Ouch!' said Letitia, and rolled over to escape the small hands, narrowly missing a pair of large feet, expensively shod. Jason. She lifted a startled face to meet his amused eyes and felt Polly plucked from her shoulders, then with the moppet tucked under one arm, he swung her to her feet too, rather as though she had been a rag doll.

She was breathless, and not only because she had been romping with Polly. 'Bedtime games,' she managed. 'I'm a horse.'

He set Polly on a broad shoulder. 'You look like a girl to me. I asked where you were and was told that you were putting this moppet to bed—I imag-

ined you going about your duties with no thought
of horse riding, and what do I find? You, dear girl,
looking every bit as old as Polly.'

'Well, really!' She was struggling with her hair
and trying to look dignified. She hadn't imagined
meeting him again like this; vague ideas of seeing
him across a dinner table, with her in the green
dress, looking serene, or failing that, coming—
gracefully, of course—down the staircase with Jason
looking up at her from the hall below. She frowned;
things never turned out as she wished them to. 'Little children like a bedtime romp,' she pointed out
coldly. 'Polly is going to have her supper now, and
then I shall put her to bed.'

'No, Letitia, I shall give the brat her supper while
you go and tidy yourself. Georgina will come and
tuck her up as she always does, and the entire family
will watch over both your charges while you, I hope,
spend the evening with me.'

'Why?'

He chuckled. 'Shall we say that Georgina is concerned because you have had the children for most
of the day and she thinks you should have a little
time in which to enjoy yourself. You do enjoy yourself with me, dear girl?' His voice was blandly inquiring.

'Yes, thank you. But I came here to help with the
babies…'

'Listen, Letitia, you're hardly expected to sit and brood over them once they're asleep—and anyway, the house is full of people.' He smiled with such charm that she found herself smiling back. 'That's better. Fetch the hot mash or whatever revolting mess this infant eats, and I'll stuff it into her. I told Georgina we would be ten minutes, so leap to it, girl.'

Letitia, leapt, unheeding of her resolutions about being serene and cool.

Twenty minutes later, dressed in the green, her hair immaculate, her face nicely made up, Letitia presented herself once more in the nursery. Jason had fed his goddaughter the supper she had fetched, now he was lolling against the wall watching Julius tuck his small daughter in for the night. Georgina was there too, with Ivo over her shoulder, half asleep and hicupping after his feed. A domestic scene, and it had apparently struck Jason in the same light, for he greeted her with: 'Ah, here you are. I've done my stint, I'm merely filling in time watching the experts.'

'And very good practice it is for you too,' said Georgina firmly. 'Now away with you both!' She smiled at them in a motherly fashion and Julius said something in Dutch to Jason which made him laugh as he swept Letitia out of the door and down the stairs.

In the hall she hesitated. 'Where are we going?' she asked suspiciously. 'Do I look all right? It isn't anywhere grand?'

He turned her round slowly, his head on one side. 'You look charming, and where we're going isn't grand at all, at least I don't consider it so,' They called good night to the others as they went through the hall and out into the warm evening. There was an Iso Lele coupé parked on the sweep and Letitia paused so that she might have a good look. 'What a car!' she exclaimed. 'I'll feel like a million in it—is it yours?'

'Yes.' He stood half smiling, saying nothing more, and after a minute she said: 'Well, I like the BMW too.' And when he still didn't speak she got in when he invited her and settled herself in its comfort, although this was a waste of time as it turned out, for it was barely five minutes before he turned the car between two stone pillars, the gates between them wide open, and raced up the straight tree-lined drive. There was a wall at its end with a wide open archway in its centre. Without slackening speed, Jason drove through and pulled up with smooth exactness before a nail-studded door set in the side of what appeared to her to be a miniature castle. It was of red brick, with curved walls and a number of turrets, with a steep roof rising to gables at either end, and although the sweep before the door was large, Letitia glimpsed a high wall and water to one side of it.

'Whatever is this?' she wanted to know as Jason got out, opened her door and held out a hand.

'Niehof—my home.' He had tucked her hand under his arm and was walking her towards the door.

'Your home—it can't be!' She knew that sounded foolish as she spoke, and added even more foolishly: 'It's a castle.'

'Well, it began as a castle—I hope we've managed to give it a few mod cons since then.' He opened the door and propelled her, very gently, inside.

The hall was a little dim, but pleasantly so, with the black and white tiled floor which she had expected in such an old building. The walls were panelled in some dark wood, with brass sconces set between a great many paintings. There was a magnificent medallion cupboard against one wall and facing it, a painted chest, richly decorated. Letitia didn't know much about furniture, but her discerning eye could see that they were very old, beautifully cared for and probably very valuable. She would have lingered to study the strapwork on the ceiling and admire the gilt-bronze chandelier hanging from it, but she was urged towards a double door beyond the cupboard.

'Come and meet my mother,' Jason invited.

She tugged at the large hand holding her so firmly so that he stopped to look down at her. 'Now what dear girl?' he inquired blandly.

'You might have said...I had no idea...rushing me out like this without a word!' Her voice rose peevishly.

'I distinctly remember inviting you to spend the evening with me.'

'Yes, I know, but you didn't say where.'

'You don't wish to meet my mother?'

'Don't be ridiculous, of course I do.'

He bent suddenly and kissed her on her surprised mouth. 'Dear girl, correct me if I'm wrong, but is there any point in this conversation?'

He had the door open and was ushering her in through it before she could frame an answer which would have done justice to the occasion. The room was light and airy compared with the cool dimness of the hall, with a circular bay window at one side, and two french windows at one end. And here the ceiling was elaborately decorated with fruit and flowers and cherubs painted in delicate colours, and these same colours had been repeated in the furnishings—the curtains, carpet and chair covers—they all reflected the ceiling above them. The furniture was dark oak, polished with age and endless care, and everything seemed very large—and that, Letitia discovered, included the lady who had risen from a chair by the window and was advancing to meet them. An elderly lady, not far short of six feet tall and built to match, but so regal in her walk that her size seemed unimportant. She was flanked on either side by two hefty Alsatian dogs, who at Jason's low whistle trotted across the room to greet him.

'Ah, Mama,' exclaimed Jason pleasantly, 'may I introduce Miss Letitia Marsden to you—I don't need to say more than that, do I, for you already know a great deal about her.'

His mother smiled, softening her handsome features into motherliness as she extended a welcoming hand. 'Letitia,' she said in a surprisingly youthful voice, 'I have been looking forward to meeting you, for I have been told endless tales of you by Katrina. Come and sit down, my dear, and Jason shall get us all a drink.'

Letitia sat, aware of bitter disappointment because it was Katrina who had talked about her and not Jason, and her hostess went on: 'The child had such a delightful holiday with your parents. It was kind of them to invite her, and she has made a good friend in Paula, who I hope will visit us in a little while.' The charming voice ceased for a minute, and eyes as blue as her son's smiled into hers. 'Your mother and I have much in common,' she went on kindly, 'for we both have large families.' She accepted a glass from the doctor. 'I do not live here, you know, but with so many children to visit I stay with each of them for a week or two at a time and then go back to my own home. I lived here when my husband was alive, of course.'

'How could you bear to leave it?' asked Letitia, and wondered if she had sounded rude. Apparently not.

'When the children were quite small, I told Jason's father that if he were to die first, I wished to have a house of my own so that Jason, who inherited this place, would feel free to lead his own life, so I have a very pleasant house a mile or so away—far enough, in fact, for him to feel that he need not study my wishes about each and every small thing. It works very well.'

She smiled at her son, stretched out in an armchair facing them both, and turned back to Letitia. 'And you, my dear, you lead a busy life, I understand, and you are also a friend of Georgina?'

Letitia, recovered from her initial surprise and fortified by the excellent sherry, agreed to both remarks, adding the rider that Georgina was one of the nicest people she knew.

'Indeed, yes, and such a perfect wife for Julius; they are ideally suited.' The talk turned to the children and became general, with Jason saying very little, and once or twice when Letitia looked up and caught his eye she found herself forcefully reminded of his kiss in the hall; she went a little pink, remembering it, and saw him smile.

They dined in another splendid room, panelled just as the hall was, and with a similar ceiling, and here the furniture was of a later period; an oval table of walnut, with Chippendale chairs and a long, gracefully shaped sideboard. The meal was delicious and served by an elderly man who reminded her of Hans and was introduced as Jacobus; as old and trusted a friend and steward as Hans, that was obvious. Letitia, sitting between the doctor and his mother, wondered how many servants there were in the house, and if it was difficult to get them in such a rural area, and as though her hostess had read her mind, she offered the information that as well as Jacobus, Jason enjoyed the services of an excellent cook and two maids besides, as well as a full time gardener.

'Only because,' explained Jason, 'the people who worked for my father married and either lived in the house or settled close by, and now that their children are grown, they take it for granted that they should work here, taking over from their parents—a pleasant arrangement and an enviable one, I admit. Julius is in like case; you see, there isn't a great deal of work locally and few of them care to make the jour-

ney to Utrecht each day. Certainly they don't want
to live there.'

They began to talk of other things, and Letitia,
full of curiosity about the enchanting castle she was
in, had to bottle up the question she was longing to
ask. She might have asked them if she hadn't been
uneasily aware that Jason guessed at her curiosity
and was amused by it. She avoided his eye as much
as possible for the rest of dinner, and afterwards,
when they were having their coffee in the drawing
room, she concentrated upon her hostess, answering
him readily enough when he addressed her, but making no attempt to attract his attention.

Letitia had hoped that she might be taken on a
tour of the house, but no one suggested it. The two
rooms she had seen had whetted her appetite to see
the remainder, but she was, after all, only a guest
for an evening, and a not very intimate one at that.
She studied the ceiling with its enchanting paintings
whenever she had the opportunity, and tried to imagine what the rest of the house was like, and with a
careful eye on the clock, made her excuses at the
correct time, dogged by the memory of guests who
had come to dinner with her parents and stayed for
hours afterwards, while she and her mother fumed
silently, thinking of the washing up which would
have to be done before they could go to bed—not
that Jason and his mother would need to do that. All

the same, she made her farewells without lingering, thanked her hostess for a delightful evening, murmured suitably in reply to Mevrouw Mourik van Nie's hope that they would meet again, and walked to the door with Jason, who had shown a disappointing calm when she had suggested that she should leave, and over and above that, had made no effort to prolong her visit.

There was, of course, no reason why he should, her common sense told her, but common sense could be tiresome at times and held no comfort; nor did Jason's manner—detached and pleasant and nothing else. The unpleasant little doubt crept into Letitia's mind that perhaps he had asked her to his home as a kind of gesture; his share of entertaining her during her stay in Holland, a doubt which wasn't dispelled during the short journey back to Bergenstijn, for he talked about nothing in particular and never once hinted that they might meet again while she was there. As a consequence, she was unreasonably cross by the time they reached the house, although common sense again warned her that it was absurd to imagine, even for a moment, that just because he had kissed her—and very thoroughly too—and invited her to meet his mother and dine at his home, he was being anything more than commonly courteous.

She got out of the car with a falsely bright: 'Oh,

here we are already,' and flounced into the hall, just in time to come face to face with Karel, coming from the drawing room.

It suited her mood very well when he greeted her with a warm: 'Hi, darling Tish, what a desert of an evening without you,' which was the kind of nonsense she expected from him and which she quite rightly put down to youthful exuberance on his part. Normally she would have told him not to be so extravagant in his talk, but now she said in a voice as gay as his own: 'Then we'll have to make up for it some time, won't we?' She smiled at him with such overpowering pleasure as she spoke that he looked quite taken aback, for she didn't seem her usual sisterly self at all, but he liked her and not for the world would he have hurt her feelings—besides, he knew all about her and the Registrar, and Georgina had warned him to be kind.

'I'll take you up on that,' he declared, and caught her hands and whirled her round. 'We'll have an evening out.'

She declared 'Oh, lovely!' with rather more emphasis than was necessary, but that was only because Jason was still standing by the door, watching them. It annoyed her very much to see that he was smiling faintly, as though he were pleased. She let go of Karel's hand and went over to him.

'Thank you for my delightful evening, Jason.' She

smiled at him, though it was an effort. 'I loved your home,' she told him. 'It was so kind of you to let me see it, and I very much enjoyed meeting your mother.' She couldn't think of anything else to say after that; what she had said sounded a bit prosy, and Jason was being no help at all, standing there smiling as though he were amused at some joke of his own. She said a trifle sharply: 'Shall I let George or Julius know you're here?'

His brows rose gently and the smile widened so that she went red and said with a decided snap: 'How very silly of me—of course you have known Julius all you life, haven't you? I expect you use each other's homes as your own.'

'That's right.' His voice was silky. 'And we've known each other since we were in our prams, all of thirty-five years, and that is a long time before you were born, Letitia. No, don't worry about me, dear girl, I'll find Julius.'

He nodded affably at them both and strolled off across the hall and down the passage which led to Julius's study. Letitia waited until she heard the door shut behind him before speaking. 'I think I'll go to bed,' she declared, and stifled a quite convincing yawn. 'Such a lovely evening, but Polly will be awake early. Is George in the drawing room still?'

Karel nodded. 'I say, Tishy—remember that blonde I was telling you about?'

She paused on her way. 'Oh, yes, but I daresay you don't.'

He laughed, a cheerful bellow which surely penetrated the study door.

'You're right, I don't—what a wonderful sister you would have made for a chap, Tishy. There's a girl,' he paused and was suddenly serious, 'she's quiet and sweet and pretty, but not so's you'd notice—a bit like you, I suppose—prettier, of course. She doesn't care much for me—not yet. I wondered if you would meet her when you get back to London—I mean, if she sees you and you tell her you know me...'

Letitia forgot her own heartache and retraced her steps. 'Karel, of course I will. She sounds a dear and I'll do anything I can—I expect she heard tales about you from some of your more spectacular friends and it's made her uncertain. You want her to see your more serious side—isn't that it? And if a parson's daughter vouches for you...' She put her hands on his shoulders and reached up to kiss him in a sisterly fashion, unaware that Jason had come out of the study and was standing at the back of the hall, watching them. She didn't see him then, only after she had wished Karel good night and started for the drawing room once more, and as she could think of nothing to say, she remained silent, as did Jason, only he smiled again. 'Just as though he were glad,' she muttered to herself as she entered the drawing room, and Georgina, looking up from her magazine, exclaimed: 'Why, Tishy, is anything the matter? You look...'

'No, nothing at all. I've had a gorgeous evening. I had no idea that Jason had such a grand home—a castle, no less.'

Georgina studied her face. 'He's not a man to talk about himself or his possessions,' she said quietly. 'He's nice, though, don't you agree?'

'Yes,' said Letitia, and thought what an inadequate answer that was, and because there was so much she wanted to say and couldn't, she wandered off to look at the portrait of an overpowering gentleman in a bag wig, thus missing the look of satisfaction on her companion's face.

'I think I'll go to bed, if you don't mind,' she said presently, suddenly terrified that Georgina would start to talk about Jason.

'Of course I don't mind, Tishy, and thank you for being so sweet to Polly and Ivo. I thought we might all have a day out tomorrow if the weather's fine; we can take two cars and do some sightseeing. If I have Ivo in his basket with us, perhaps you'd have Polly with you in Karel's car. We could go down the River Vecht—some friends of ours live along there, but they're away—they won't mind a bit if we park in their grounds and sit by the water for our lunch. Would you like that?'

'It sounds lovely—you're sure you wouldn't rather I stayed here with the babies? I'd be quite happy, you know; the gardens are so pretty.'

Georgina spoke warmly. 'That's sweet of you, Tishy—I'll take you up on that in a day or two. We have to go to Wassenaar to see Julius's aunt and uncle. They're sweet but elderly and I think the children might worry them a bit, so I'll leave them at home with you. But Great-Uncle Ivo, he's quite another kettle of fish—in his eighties and an absolute darling and adores Polly. He's dying to see little Ivo, that's really why he's coming. You'll like him, though he's a bit outspoken.'

Georgina got up and cast her magazine on the table beside her. 'I think I'll go and sit with Julius until he's finished his writing—he likes that, and so do I.'

They went out of the room together and parted at the foot of the staircase. There was no sign of Jason.

But even with him constantly in her thoughts, Letitia found it impossible not to enjoy herself the following day. Karel might be head over heels in love with this girl of his, but he was still an amusing companion. She sat behind him in the Porsche, rather cooped up, with Polly on her lap and Beatrix beside her while Franz sat in front. Cor had gone in

the Rolls with the others after a fierce argument as
to who should go with whom, quickly decided by
Julius stating firmly that everyone would change
places on the way back. It was a blindingly hot day
and lunch was a protracted meal with everyone sitting at their ease by the river. After they had eaten
everything in the picnic hamper, Julius and Georgina stayed with Polly, who was sleepy anyway, and
the slumbering Ivo, while the others strolled off, and
it wasn't long before the younger members of the
party went ahead, leaving Karel and Letitia together.

'Now you can tell me all about this girl,' she
urged him. 'What's her name?'

He was only too ready to comply with her request.
'Mary. Her father's a solicitor, she works in the
Medical Secretary's office, a sort of filing clerk, I
suppose you'd call her. She wanted to be a nurse,
but she doesn't like to see people when they're ill,
although she's very sorry for them, of course.' He
shot Letitia a glance, defying her to comment upon
this, but she wisely remained silent, merely looking
sympathetic, which encouraged him to continue at
some length. He had been talking for quite a time
before she managed to suggest tactfully that they
should return. He agreed readily enough and catching her arm in his, began, for the second time, to
describe Mary's perfections. She was quite relieved
when the picnic party came into view once more;

they were all there, waiting for them, and it was
Julius who inquired: 'Had a nice walk?'

Letitia answered, aware that Karel was still up in
the clouds with his Mary. 'Very nice, thanks—we
got talking.' She smiled at Julius, who smiled back,
but although Georgina smiled too, she looked a bit
put out. Getting into the Porsche again, Letitia wondered why.

Everyone left the house after breakfast the next
morning to make the journey to Wassenaar, leaving
Letitia with the faithful Hans and the two babies.
The day passed quickly enough, and if from time to
time she entertained the hope that Jason might call,
she tried to ignore it. She put the little ones to bed
at their usual time, had a solitary dinner with Hans
at his most attentive, making sure that she ate the
delicious food he served her, and then went up to
her room. She had no idea what time the others
would be back and if she stayed downstairs she
would feel impelled to keep running up to the nursery to make sure that the babies were asleep, so she
sat in the day nursery, writing a letter home. She
had almost finished it when the door opened and
Jason walked in.

His 'Hullo,' was casual. 'No one home yet?' he
asked. 'Have you enjoyed your day playing
mother?'

Letitia closed her writing pad. 'Very much.

They're darling children, you know, and no trouble at all.'

He smiled then. 'You sound like Georgina. You had a good day out yesterday?'

He looked tired, she thought, and longed to ask him why; it was terrible to love someone so much and be unable to say the things you really wanted to say. 'Oh, lovely,' she answered brightly. 'It was so pretty by the river. We had a picnic on the bank in someone's grounds, a friend of Julius—I expect you know him too?' Jason nodded and she went on: 'It was gloriously hot too.'

'Too hot to explore the charming walk along the water?'

She answered without thinking. 'Oh, no—Karel took me, only we were so busy talking I didn't see nearly as much as I should have done.'

He was still smiling, but his face had grown very still; she thought for a long moment that he would never speak again; when he did it was in his usual placid voice. 'You can always go again—I'm sure Karel will be only too happy to take you.' He went to the door with an abruptness which surprised her. 'I must go home. Good night.'

Letitia stared at the closed door, puzzled, wondering why he had come and why he had left like that—the conversation had been harmless enough. She frowned and went back to her letter, mindful of the promise she had made herself that she would try not to think of him more than she could absolutely help.

She didn't see him for several days after that. It was Georgina who let fall the information that he was entertaining guests of Niehof, and later Julius told her that they had all been invited to an evening party there; all except herself, for someone had to keep an eye on Polly and Ivo—and after all, that was why she was there, wasn't it? Only Julius didn't put it like that.

'It's an opportunity for us all to go out together,' he explained. 'Usually that's difficult when Nanny's away, and it would have been out of the question now, only you are so luckily with us, Tishy. Jason thought it a splendid opportunity.'

So it was Jason who had suggested that she should stay home! In that case, even if she were asked, wild horses wouldn't drag her there. She agreed as to the excellence of the arrangement, her face and voice so wooden that Julius gave her a long, thoughtful look, frowning a little.

It was that same day that Great-Uncle Ivo arrived, driven in a motor-car—a Packard—which should have surely been a museum piece. Georgina whispered that the old gentleman went to great expense to keep it in running order and absolutely refused to exchange it for anything more modern. He was a determined old gentleman as well as being outspoken, she added, and Letitia could see that she was right.

Waiting on the fringe of the welcoming group she could see that here was a very old gentleman, bearing a marked resemblance to Julius, with a great deal of white hair and piercing blue eyes, greeting everyone in his own good time, and when he at length got to her, he looked her up and down before offering a hand for her to shake. 'Plain girl, aren't you?' he observed in a booming voice. 'Quite a taking face, though—a little like Georgina was before Julius married her—and look at her now, quite a beauty.' He chuckled. 'That's what comes of being happily married. You should try it, young woman.'

'Chance is a fine thing,' retorted Letitia with some asperity, and he burst out laughing.

'That's right, girl—you've plenty of spirit. I don't care for mealy-mouthed women myself. A dash of spirit lasts you all your life, and looks don't—remember that. And now I'll see my namesake.'

By the end of the day Letitia decided that she liked Great-Uncle Ivo; his tongue might be sharp and his manner somewhat dictatorial, but he loved his family and his manners were perfection despite his age. In the garden after tea, taking Polly to feed the ducks on the pond before bedtime, with Karel as escort, she ventured to ask about him.

'I can't remember him ever looking other than he does now,' Karel told her, 'and I simply can't imagine this family without him. I know Julius is the head of the family, but Great-Uncle Ivo is a kind of figurehead, if you see what I mean. I think we would all like him to go on living for ever, and unlike most people, we none of us need his money. There's none of that standing around waiting for him to die, if you see what I mean.'

'I suppose you're very rich,' Letitia observed idly.

'Yes, we are. Some ancestor made a pile in the West Indies and it's been taken care of ever since. Jason's a wealthy man too, though I believe the ancestor who started them on the road to riches was a bloodthirsty type who fought for William the Silent. Not that Jason's like that; as kind and generous as they come—can't think why he hasn't married; heaven knows there've been plenty of girls only too willing. No, he's the sort to marry some mouse of a girl because he's sorry for her.' He paused and then went on uncomfortably: 'I shouldn't have told you that, I suppose—about Jason being rich.'

'It doesn't matter, what difference could it possibly make? I'm not likely to meet him again once I'm back in England, and I don't gossip.'

'Lord, no,' he agreed warmly. 'I say, you haven't told anyone about Mary, have you?'

'Of course not. All the same, I think it's a pity

you don't tell Julius and Georgina.' She bent to pick
up Polly so that she could throw the bread they had
brought with them to the family of ducks paddling
towards them.

'Well, I can't—not yet. They'd not take me seriously—they'd think she was just another girl, and
she's not.'

Letitia felt a stab of envy for the absent Mary,
then had to stifle hysterical laughter when he went
on seriously: 'You see, Tishy, you wouldn't understand—you have to be in love to do that.'

She put Polly down. She was in love, but it hadn't
made things very clear to her, in fact she had never
been so muddled in all her life. She said quietly:
'Well, Karel, the thing is—I should imagine—to be
quite sure—both of you, and when you are you can
talk to Julius and he'll understand. After all, you're
old enough to marry and you've just told me you've
enough money to live on—besides, you're a good
surgeon, Jason told me so. You'll be a success even
if you didn't have a farthing of your own.'

'You are such a comforting kind of girl,' he assured her gratefully, and flung an arm round her
shoulders as they walked back to the house, and
Jason, standing at the open drawing room window
with Georgina and Julius, saw that.

Georgina made off with Polly when they arrived,
and Karel wandered off after a few words with Ja-

son, and Julius went with him, leaving Letitia, who fidgeted round the room, trying to think of some excuse for going too.

'I wanted you to know that I'm sorry that you can't come this evening,' said Jason presently, 'but I know you understand.'

Letitia rearranged the cushions on the enormous sofa before replying; of course she understood; what should Jason Mourik van Nie, a rich man who lived in a castle which took away one's breath with its miniature grandeur, want with a girl he had once described as quite nice? 'Of course I understand. Besides, Jason, I think you overlook the fact that I came here to look after Polly and Ivo—I'm being paid for it, you know. I hardly expected to be treated as a guest. They're all wonderful to me as it is, but there's no need to think that I mind. I don't.'

He was lounging against one of the chairs, staring at her. 'You've quite got over the Medical Registrar, haven't you?' he asked to surprise her.

All the same she kept her voice steady. 'Yes, quite, thank you.'

'Perhaps there's someone else.' It was a statement, not a question, so that she found it difficult to answer. When she remained silent, he said: 'I hope so, Letitia.'

She began on the cushions once more, for she couldn't stand still listening to him talking like that, and when he crossed the room towards her she held one of them in front of her as if to ward him off. He actually had his hands on her shoulders when she said in an unhappy little voice: 'Oh, Jason, please don't—not again, I couldn't bear it!'

He dropped his hands at once and she saw him wince. 'I didn't mean...' she began—it was no good, she would have to tell him that she loved him and that it wasn't fair to kiss her; heaven knew what she might have said if he had allowed her to go on, but he didn't. He said quietly: 'My dear girl, you don't have to explain anything,' and went out of the room.

When everyone had gone and Letitia had pretended to eat her dinner under Hans's worried eye, she went up to her room and sat by the window, staring out into the darkening garden. She had tried during the evening to think what she could say to Jason, but she had had no success, and now she was tired to death with only one thought in her head; that she loved him very much, despite the fact that he had never given her any encouragement to do so. A nice cry would have been the thing, but she seemed beyond tears.

CHAPTER NINE

THE PARTY had been splendid, everyone told her the next morning. Letitia listened to their cheerful talk about it, treasuring every mention of Jason, then suggested that as Georgina had had a late night she might take the babies into the garden until lunch time, an offer willingly accepted. Letitia went to sit by the lake, with baby Ivo in his pram and Polly busy picking daisies so that they might make a daisy chain together. It was quiet there; she would have been quite happy to have gone back there after lunch, but Georgina insisted that she should accept Karel's offer to drive her into Utrecht so that she might do any shopping she wanted, and indeed, she had presents to choose for her family. With his help she found something to please everyone before he took her to tea at the Esplanade Restaurant, a large cheerful place in the heart of the city. It was during tea that she managed to ask with a casual air where the hospital was.

'Oh, if you mean the one where Jason works—that's the largest, you know, we'll go that way presently, and you can see for yourself. It's pretty up to date.'

He was as good as his word, parking for a few minutes in the hospital forecourt and pointing out the various departments. Letitia looked at them all carefully, imprinting them on her mind, so that later on, when she was back in England, she would be able to think of Jason working there. It was cold comfort but better than nothing.

The days flew by; there was always something to fill them and whenever possible Letitia was included in the various outings, and when she stayed behind with Polly and Ivo there was the faithful Hans to look after her. She told herself that she was a very lucky girl, living in such comfort and with so little to do. She had struck up quite a friendship with Great-Uncle Ivo, too—it was impossible not to like the old gentleman, even though at times he was quite outrageous; besides, he often spoke of Jason.

'Knew him as a boy,' he told her one afternoon when they were sitting in the garden together. 'Young limb, he was—always at the top of a tree or away fishing or out with the dogs. He's grown into a decent chap, don't you agree, girl?' He had stared into her face so that she pinkened, furious at herself for doing so. 'Um,' said her companion thoughtfully, and then: 'God bless my soul!'

She was to go back a few days ahead of the others; partly because Karel intended to leave then and was giving her a lift, and partly because although the theatre would be opened again the day after she returned, Julius wouldn't be working until the end of the week. The last few days came and she had seen nothing of Jason; he might just as well have been at the South Pole for all the difference it made, but there was to be a party on her last evening and although Georgina hadn't said that he would be there, Letitia hoped that he would be. But as it turned out, it was the day before that when he came. Letitia was spooning Polly's supper into her small pink mouth when he walked in, so quietly that she didn't hear him until he slid into a chair beside her at the nursery table.

'Hullo.' He sounded as though they had seen each other only an hour or so ago instead of days. 'You're going home tomorrow, Julius tells me.'

'Yes.'

'With Karel?'

'Yes.'

'I've a free afternoon tomorrow, so I wondered if you would like to come over and see the gardens, they're rather nice just now.'

'Thank you, I'd like that,' and then, anxious not to seem too eager for his company: 'But I'm not sure about tomorrow, I must ask George.'

'I already have and she said go ahead. She'll be home all day, anyway, and had intended asking you if you wanted to go anywhere on your own.'

'Well, then—yes, I'll come.' It had been weak of her to say that; why not make some excuse and say goodbye now? That would have been the sensible thing to do, only she wasn't sensible any more. She stuffed rusks and milk, mashed together into a horrid pap, into Polly's willing mouth. 'Good girl,' she encouraged her, 'there's a banana for afters.'

'Revolting!' declared Jason. 'And she actually seems to like it. I've brought her some chocolate.'

'One small piece,' Letitia warned him, 'before I clean her teeth.'

He was unwrapping it while his goddaughter uttered cries of joy from a full mouth. 'You'll make a pretty fierce mum,' he observed, and added: 'A rather sweet one too.'

'I'll have to get married first.'

But he didn't answer her, only smiled and presently took a casual leave.

He called for her after lunch the following afternoon, relaxed and elegant, for all the world as though he hadn't come straight from a heavy morning's work at the hospital. Letitia had spent a good deal of thought on what to wear, rather in the mood of someone going to the block and wishing to put on a good show. She had decided at length on a blue and white striped cotton dress, last year's, so neither new nor as fashionable as she would have wished, but it was cool and pleasing to the eye, and she had tied her hair back with a matching ribbon and got out her best pair of sandals to put on her bare feet; she had bought them on a shopping trip with Georgina; they were blue too, canvas with a rope sole and really quite the latest thing.

Jason gave her an all-embracing glance, accorded her a cheerful hullo, then addressed himself to Georgina and Julius, lounging on the terrace, and standing there beside him, Letitia was conscious of doubt about the afternoon's outing. After all, he had no interest in her, not the kind she wanted, anyway. There was no need for him to put himself out. He had, after all, already done his share of entertaining her. She began, quite foolishly, to think of an excuse for not going. A sore throat? or a headache? No good, both he and Julius would at once examine her perfectly healthy tonsils and know it for an excuse, and a headache was too old a trick. And there was no more time to think of anything else, for he asked: 'Ready?' in a voice suggesting that she had kept him waiting, and urged her into the car. It was the BMW this time and she commented upon it.

'I quite thought you'd got rid of it,' she added.

'Lord no—I like a change, that's all.' He spoke laconically and after that they said very little on the short journey, but when they reached the archway again, she uttered an involuntary 'Oh, it's absolutely super!'

He agreed placidly and invited her to get out. 'My
mother isn't here,' he told her. 'My eldest sister's
children have taken the measles, and Mama has
gone, full sail, to render all aid.'

She turned to look at him. 'You sound as
though—as though you don't like children.'

She was conscious of his hand on her shoulder.
'On the contrary,' he assured her quietly. 'Come inside, it's far too nice a day to waste it indoors, but
there is one room, I believe you would like to see.'

Letitia would have disputed that point; there was
nothing she would have liked better than to stroll
from room to room of the lovely old place and examine its treasures at her leisure, but she could
hardly ask. She agreed politely and allowed herself
to be led down a short passage at the back of the
hall where he opened a panelled door.

'This is the oldest part of the house,' he explained. 'It was used as the solarium by the wife of
the man who built it. Mother used it as her sitting
room, just as all the ladies of the house did before
her. It has been empty for a year or two now.'

It was a small apartment, wainscoted to the plastered ceiling, with long windows leading into the
garden, an open fireplace with its log basket and
irons, and a high-backed brocaded chair drawn up
to its side, flanked by a lady's work-table, the blue
of its faded silken bag matching the curtains. It was

a delightful little room; Letitia ran a careful finger along the marquetry ornamenting the top of a small circular table in the centre of it and exclaimed on a little sigh: 'It's quite perfect. I can just imagine your mother, and all the other mothers before her, coming here for peace and quiet—she would have needed that now and again, I expect, with so many of you...' She was thinking aloud, forgetful of her companion for the moment. 'There would have been a great deal to do—children to see to and meals to plan and the house to run, and time to be with her husband—she would have wanted that too.'

She went to look out of the window and said dreamily: 'And such a lovely garden too.'

Jason opened one of the french windows, and without saying anything, gestured for her to pass through. 'There have always been roses here,' he told her, 'so that whoever was in the solarium would be able to see them and smell them too—there's a charming herb garden, too.'

They strolled down one path and up another, pausing to admire the lily pond and the formal Dutch garden with its neatly clipped box hedges, the flowers set so precisely that they might have been painted on canvas. Presently he suggested tea, and they went indoors, Letitia's head delightfully full of scents and flowers and a glimpse of a vast kitchen garden which in its way was just as beautiful as the flower beds. They used a small side door this time, which opened into a pleasant room with a wide balcony overlooking a lawn edged with trees, and here they had tea, with Letitia nervously pouring it from a Queen Anne silver teapot into Meissen cups so delicate she was afraid they would crack if she raised her voice.

She had worried about being alone with Jason; that she might feel awkward or shy, perhaps, but she was neither. He entertained her with a flow of talk which steadied her nerves nicely, so that when he suggested that she might like to go on to the balcony, she agreed readily. They stood side by side, leaning on its delicate wrought iron balustrade while he pointed out the distant summer house, the tiny stream which fed the pool at the end of the lawn, and Jaap the gardener, bending over the flower beds.

'He's been here for as long as I can remember,' Jason told her, 'he must be well into his eighties and works a full day still. It was suggested a little while ago that he should retire, but he was so upset that no one has dared mention it since.'

'I expect he loves his garden. Does he have any help?'

'Lord, yes, dear girl. He has a couple of lads whom he bullies unmercifully, though they take it like lambs.' He turned to look at her, and she noticed for the hundredth time how vividly blue his eyes were. 'Letitia, will you marry me?'

She was stunned into silence, goggling at him, her mouth agape, her eyes wide. 'Marry you?' she repeated, her voice high.

He nodded. 'That's right,' he agreed calmly, 'marry me.' He smiled a little and she waited, for surely he would tell her that he loved her, then it would be easy for her to tell him that she had loved him for weeks. But he said nothing at all, only looked at her, his eyes half closed against the sun, still smiling.

Not wanting to, she remembered what Karel had said—that Jason was the kind of man to marry some mouse of a girl out of pity. Somehow she kept her voice level and her face calm. 'It wouldn't do, Jason—I'm not the right person. You see, I'm not used to managing servants; we've only ever had old Mrs Barnes at home and she comes twice a week and does what she wants. I wouldn't know how to go about things, and they'd hate it, and after a little while you would too. And it's such a large house.'

'Just a house, dear girl, and my home—and everyone, down to the boy who does the odd jobs, likes you.' He bent down to fondle the two dogs sitting so quietly beside him. 'That's an excuse, isn't it, Letitia? You're not the girl to care one bit that I have rather a lot of money and everything that goes with it—you could manage an establishment twice the size of Niehof, and you know it. You're making excuses, dear girl.'

She had looked away because she wanted to cry and he mustn't see. She wondered what had decided him to ask her to marry him—probably an impulse born of his kindness, not love—he had been careful not to mention that.

'Yes,' she said in a small, well-controlled voice, 'I suppose I am.'

He stood up. 'Well, we'll forget the whole thing, shall we, dear girl?' And now his voice was as placid and cheerful as usual so that she had to take a quick look. He was watching her with eyes still half shut, so that she was unable to read their expression. 'We certainly mustn't let it spoil a beautiful friendship, must we?' He went on easily: 'Tell me, which way is Karel taking you home?'

'We're to go on the Ostend ferry, I believe. He'll drop me off at St Athel's.' Letitia heard her voice, sounding quite natural, answering him, and it was like listening to someone else speaking while her mind grappled with the fact that he had asked her to marry him—and she had refused when it was the dearest wish of her heart. Jason was speaking again.

'Ah, yes—quite easily done. He has only a couple more months to do, hasn't he? Has he any idea where he's going next? He's a good surgeon, Julius tells me, so presumably he'll specialize, and do well.'

She didn't want to talk about Karel, who didn't matter at all, but Jason seemed interested, and they had to talk about something, didn't they?

'Oh, yes—I think he will, and he's very keen to get on.'

'And young.' There was edge to Jason's voice which Letitia had never heard before. Probably he was irritated at their awkward little scene; she made haste to find a topic of conversation. The garden once more; she wore it threadbare, but Jason agreed pleasantly enough to her remarks, and presently the conversation was back again on safe ground; trees and shrubs and flower-beds, until he suggested that they should go.

'I hate to bring such a pleasant afternoon to an end,' he told her gently, 'but if you are to go to George's party, we should be going.'

He had become the genial host, thoughtful of his guest, and his impersonal good manners chilled her to the bone so that any wild ideas she had been turning over inside her unhappy head were most effectively damped. She accepted his suggestion in a colourless voice and sat silent beside him, composing a little speech to make to him later, when they would say good-bye.

Only it didn't turn out like that. True, he went

into the house with her and stayed for a drink, showing none of the signs which a man whose offer of marriage had just been refused might have been expected to exhibit. He was his usual good-humoured self, and when he got up to Letitia, who had been watching him, forgot every word of what she had planned to say. Not that it mattered; how could she have said it in a room full of people? How did you tell a man that you loved him to distraction and then ask him if he loved you with friends and relations milling round, listening to every word?

Letitia shook hands, and his hand was cool and firm and nothing more, and she thanked him for a pleasant afternoon and murmured suitably when he wished her a pleasant trip home. She watched him go, sickened by the very idea of going back to St Athel's and longing to rush after him and say so. But what would be the good of that? And perhaps it was fortunate that she hadn't had the chance to say the things she had wanted to say—she would have regretted it later, for he had never said that he loved her. Indeed, now that she came to think about it, he had changed the conversation so quickly that she would scarcely have had the opportunity to change her mind if she had wanted to. Perhaps he had regretted the words the moment they were out of his mouth and felt nothing but relief.

She saw the BMW shoot smoothly down the

drive, not listening to a word Great-Uncle Ivo was saying to her, so that she uttered replies at random, causing that old gentleman to look at her searchingly and bark:

'He'll be back, girl, he'll be back.' Which remark brought her to her senses more quickly than anything else could have done.

'No, he won't,' she told her companion in an empty voice. For a frightful moment she thought that she was going to disgrace herself by bursting into tears, but she choked them back. 'Do you suppose this glorious weather will last?' She asked the ridiculous question in a voice which didn't sound like hers at all.

'No,' said Great-Uncle Ivo, 'I don't.' He went on fiercely: 'You're a silly chit of a girl—Jason's a man in a thousand.'

'Oh, do you think I don't know that?' she almost wailed at him. 'Please don't let's talk about him!'

His old blue eyes surveyed her unhappy face. 'We were talking about the weather,' he said at once. 'We are having a glorious summer, though you probably don't agree with me, Letitia—and we each have our share of it. You have yours, my dear—a slice of summer.'

'A small slice of summer,' she corrected him, 'and it's finished. I'm going back tomorrow.'

'Ah, yes—with Karel. Such a dear boy.'

'It's kind of him to offer me a lift.'

As though he had heard his name, Karel crossed the room to them and a few minutes later Letitia was laughing and talking as though she hadn't a care in the world. It was difficult, especially when she remembered Jason's nonchalant wave of the hand as he went, but life had to go on, however awful she felt about it. She would have liked time to think, but Karel gave her none; he was demanding to know if she could be ready to leave by seven o'clock the next morning, and when Great-Uncle Ivo strolled away, he confided: 'I telephoned Mary, and she'll be in London—we'll get a few hours together. You don't mind?'

She summoned a smile. 'Of course I don't,' and she sighed without knowing it so that he asked her if she was tired. She shook her head, unable to tell him that the day had become endless now that Jason had gone.

It was pouring with rain in the morning; unexpected and suitable to her mood, but it was impossible to remain miserable in Karel's company; he was at his gayest and she did her best to match his mood, while a part of her mind thought of Jason.

It was, in a way, good to be back at work; Letitia flung herself into the well-known routine, telling herself that now she was away from Jason she would

find it easier to forget him; only she couldn't, she
went around with a sad little face, joining in the
lighthearted chatter of her friends, denying vigorously that anything was wrong when Margo chal-
lenged her in a big-sisterly fashion to tell her what
was upsetting her, and throwing herself wholeheart-
edly into the mild activities afforded by the thin
purses of herself and her friends.

She went out with Karel too. On the first occasion
she quickly discovered it was to receive a briefing
for the next invitation, when Mary would be there
too. She listened carefully while Karel regaled her
with dinner at the Snooty Fox. 'You see,' he told
her seriously, 'you're just the kind of girl to con-
vince Mary.'

Letitia spooned ice cream. 'What of?'

'Well, you know…you're so…so…' He paused,
and she supplied: 'Yes, I know—respectable,' and
he nodded.

'You mean that if she meets me and I say I'm a
friend of yours she'll be convinced that you're respectable too and not just fancying her?'

He closed his eyes and looked pained. 'Tishy,
what a vulgar expression!' and opened them again
to add: 'Yes, that's exactly it.'

'When's the great day?'

'Could you manage Wednesday evening? Do you
think this place will do?'

She looked around her. 'Yes, it's marvellous, and anyway, I don't know anything about these super places. Only would it be a good idea to take her—us—to the sort of place where she might meet an uncle or a father or mother—do you know what I mean?'

He picked up her hand lying idle on the table and kissed it. 'Genius!' he exclaimed. 'Of course! The Connaught—Julius takes George there. What a clever girl you are, Tishy.'

She grinned at him. 'Oh, I know—only don't go doing silly things like kissing my hand, will you? Mary might not like it.'

She would have liked a new dress for the occasion, but if she were to go home for her next days off, she wouldn't be able to afford one. She put on the green once more, quite sick and tired of it, and went downstairs to where the taxi Karel had sent for her was waiting.

As she got into it, she thought how right she had been to refuse his offer to come and fetch her, deeming it wise for him to concentrate on his Mary.

The evening began splendidly. Mary was a nice girl. She would, Letitia saw at a glance, be just right for Karel; she had a pleasant voice, a charming manner and was, moreover, quietly pretty, and as well as that, Letitia fancied that she had some rather old-fashioned ideas which Julius and George would approve of. They got on splendidly together, and Karel, a little over-anxious to start with, relaxed as dinner proceeded. When they had had their coffee Letitia, mindful of his suggestion, gave it as her opinion that she should go back to hospital.

'I'm on duty at half past seven tomorrow,' she explained, 'and I know you won't mind. It's been a lovely evening, and I hope we shall see more of each other, Mary—it's been so nice to meet an old friend again—' she waved a hand in Karel's direction. 'You're getting more and more like Julius, Karel, I expect you'll end up just as well known and liked. Let me know how the thesis goes, won't you?'

Mary, who had heard of Julius, looked happy, and Karel beamed. 'I'll take you to a taxi,' he offered as Letitia shook hands with Mary and started for the door. Half-way there she stopped so suddenly that Karel, right behind her, had to put out a hand to steady her. Jason was sitting at a table just ahead of them. There was an elderly gentleman with him, and they had been in deep conversation, but Jason had looked up and seen her. She walked on, her legs strangely wobbly, and nodded stiffly as she drew level with them, she was aware that Jason had stood up and that Karel had seen him too and expected to stop, but without looking back she crossed the foyer to get her coat, opened her purse to get its ticket and turned to hand it to Karel, struggling to think of some excuse for her strange behaviour.

Only it wasn't Karel, it was Jason. He didn't say a word but took the ticket from her nerveless hand, fetched her coat and held it for her. She wondered why he looked so pleased with himself as she thanked him in a die-away voice.

'Don't let me keep you,' she begged in a wooden voice, and was affronted when he said cheerfully:

'Unfortunately, you can't—I'm dining with someone who would hardly understand if I were to leave him between the soup and the fish.'

She walked away from him, although it needed all her will power to do so. 'I can't think where Karel has got to,' she said over her shoulder.

He caught up with her in a couple of strides. 'Gone back to his guest, I should imagine.' His voice was bland. 'I offered to see you to your taxi and he seemed only too pleased to get back to his table.'

She hurried to the entrance. 'How rude, how very rude!' she breathed furiously. 'I was his guest!'

They were on the pavement now and the doorman had gone to the kerb to get a cab. 'As chaperone, dear girl? I caught sight of you some time ago and I saw Karel's face when he was talking to the girl with you.' He grinned down at her. 'One of the best moments of my life,' he declared.

The taxi was waiting. Letitia said icily: 'How nice for you. I'll say good-bye.' She made to get into the taxi, but he put a large hand on its door. 'Say what you like, Letitia. We shall meet again very soon.'

'I don't want to see you, ever again.' She heard herself utter this whopping lie with utter dismay and wished at once to deny it, but she was in quite a nasty temper by now and no longer thinking very clearly.

Jason allowed her to enter and closed the door after her, and only when he had given her address and paid the driver did he say cheerfully: 'All the same, I'll be along, little Tishy.'

Letitia raged silently all the way to St Athel's, undressed in a tearing hurry and flung herself into bed, where she lay awake for hours, very unhappy because she had said all the wrong things, and also because he might take her at her word and never come near her again.

A needless worry, as it turned out; he was there the very next evening. Letitia had finished tidying the recovery room and was standing aimlessly in its centre when he came in, and although she had hoped, deep down inside her, that he would come, she hadn't expected him quite as soon as this, and certainly not at that hour when she was barely off duty. His hullo was friendly and her answering greeting was nothing better than a croak. He looked wonderful, she thought foolishly, standing there against the door, elegant and cool and remarkably satisfied with himself, and he shouldn't smile at her like that, it did something to her inside so that she couldn't think straight.

'I don't give in easily, dear girl,' he remarked mildly, 'even though it may appear so.'

She found her voice at that. 'Well, there has to be a first time for everything,' she told him shrilly, 'and now please go away, I'm busy.'

'You're off duty.' He was actually laughing at her. 'And why are you so cross, my darling girl?'

'I'm not, oh, Jason, I'm not!' She stamped a foot and said loudly, quite contradicting herself: 'I'm so furious—if only I knew how to gnash my teeth! I'm a mouse of a girl and you're sorry for me, just like Karel said, and I will not be pitied and patronized...'

He interrupted her quite ruthlessly: 'What utter rubbish!' He stared at her thoughtfully. 'Ah, I believe we have the crux of the matter—what did Karel say, my adorable Letitia?'

It all bubbled out in a breathless rush. 'That you had a robber baron for an ancestor but you weren't like him and that you could have married a dozen times, only you'd get c-caught by a mouse of a girl because you were sorry for her.' She paused for breath and opened her mouth to begin another tirade, only she burst into tears instead.

Jason's arms were very comforting—a little tight perhaps, but what was the pain of a few crushed ribs compared with the pleasure of being within their circle?

'Don't cry, my love,' he begged her. 'I have never considered you a mouse—indeed, you have reminded me of a very small dragon on various occasions. A mouse would never have coped with a bunch of spotty gipsies or an inquisitive bull.'

Letitia sniffed. There was something she had to know then and there. 'You asked me to marry you and then you seemed quite pleased because I said no.'

He let her go and put his hands in his pockets. 'Let us have a heart-to-heart talk,' he invited, 'and then I will ask you to marry me again.'

She took a step towards him. 'Oh…' She got no further; the door behind Jason had opened and Sister Hollins came in. The Theatre Superintendent was a youthful forty with a charming manner which concealed an efficient, slightly domineering nature, which was probably why she hadn't married. The younger, more flighty nurses had been heard to say that it wasn't for lack of trying. She gave Letitia a brisk smile and said in a voice to match: 'What, Staff, not gone yet? I'm sure everything is in perfect order. Run along now.'

Letitia didn't look at Jason. She said: 'Yes, Miss

Hollins,' in a meek voice which covered a multitude of feelings, and slid away to change. As she went she wondered how Jason would get away—he was a splendid prize for Hollins and she had looked as though she was expecting a nice cosy chat. She tore off her mob cap and theatre dress and in hospital uniform once more, started for the Nurses' Home. She would bath and change her clothes and wait for Jason. She laughed a little; he was going to ask her to marry him, wasn't he? Suddenly the world had become a wonderful place.

Letitia charged into the labyrinth of passages which would get her to the Home, and had almost reached the main corridor, half-way down which was the little door leading to a short cut, when she encountered Miss Page, and Office Sister and a martinet. Letitia skidded to a halt within inches of her, murmured an apology and made to slip past, but Miss Page had no intention of letting her go.

'Staff Nurse,' she observed awfully, 'why are you running? Is there a fire? Is there haemorrhage? And your hair is a disgrace—hanging in wisps, a most regrettable sight. I'm sure I don't know what girls are coming to!'

Letitia murmured again in a subdued way, almost dancing with impatience, and forced herself to listen meekly to a stern lecture. Only when Miss Page paused for breath did she mutter something soothing and tear off once more, uncaring of her superior's admonishing 'Staff Nurse!' as she turned into the short cut at last.

It was a sharp right-angled corner. She took it at speed, straight into Jason's arms. She felt them tighten round her with a strong sense of delight even as she said: 'However did you get here? What did you do with Sister Hollins?'

'Who is she?' asked Jason, and bent his head to kiss her.

'Jason—not here! Everyone goes this way—you can't...'

'Challenging me, my darling?' He kissed her again, in such a manner that she forgot where she was, and even if she had remembered, it wouldn't have mattered any more.

'And now we will have our little talk, darling Letitia.'

'Not here—Oh, Jason!' Two porters, wheeling an empty trolley briskly towards the corridor, went past, their eyes starting from their heads; a nurse, wrapped in the arms of a large, elegant gentleman was an unusual sight. They looked the other way when they encountered Jason's bland stare.

'Your room?' he suggested.

'You must be joking!'

'Then here. Now where were we, my darling dear?'

Letitia didn't care any more. She was possessed of a delicious sensation of not being responsible for her actions and not minding about it in the least. 'I met Sister Page,' she told him, slightly light-headed. 'Do I look very untidy?'

He was a man of monumental patience. 'No, my darling. Why do you ask?'

'Well, she said I did—she said my hair was a disgrace and I was a regrettable sight for a staff nurse.'

'Your hair is beautiful, so long and thick and straight; you are, in my opinion, quite the most charming sight in the whole world, and there is no need for her to fuss about you being a staff nurse any more. You will be my wife, fully occupied in running our home and bossing everyone around, and I daresay a bunch of tiresome brats as well.'

She was enchanted. 'They'll be the most wonderful children—only you haven't asked me to marry you yet; only that afternoon on the balcony, and you didn't say you loved me, so of course I couldn't say yes, could I?'

He said thoughtfully: 'I have tried so hard to decide when it was I first found that I loved you, dear girl. Perhaps when I saw you in that deplorable pair of slacks and old shirt, coming through the wood to meet me and not so much as a hullo, but a stream of words in which dogs and horses and gipsies were

all muddled together. But I don't think I was sure,
not then, and when I did know that you were the
only girl in the whole world for me, Karel was there
and I thought that it was he, and when you refused
me in such a businesslike fashion, I felt sure it was.
But I had to be quite sure, so I came over to see
you, and there you were, a kind of invisible third at
dinner with those two.' He grinned down at her.
'And your face when you saw me—oh, you contrived to make it severe, but you couldn't do anything about your eyes, my love.'

She stretched up and kissed him. 'Jason, I do love
you.'

His eyes, very bright, smiled down at her. 'Then
I shall propose...' he paused, 'but not, I think, for a
minute or two.'

The purposeful feet they had both heard rounded
the corner. Sister Page, primed for wrathful speech,
fetched up in front of them, momentarily taken
aback.

'Ah, Sister,' said Jason smoothly. 'Good evening,
and how delightful that you should be the first one
to hear our good news.'

She eyed him cautiously. 'Good evening, doctor.
I want a word with Staff Nurse.'

'I see that you don't quite understand,' observed
Jason, still smoothly. 'Staff Nurse and I are going
to be married.'

For a moment Sister Page looked like the cat who had caught a mouse and had it taken away. She cast a reproachful look at Jason and a frustrated one at Letitia and rallied sufficiently to say: 'Well, I'm sure I wish you both happy.' She looked at them rather uncertainly. 'Is it a secret?' she asked.

Jason answered: 'No, please tell anyone you wish.' He smiled at her and she smiled suddenly at them both before she rustled away, her back very straight.

The passage was empty. 'And now, dear heart, I am going to ask you to marry me, and if anyone interrupts me, I shall ignore them, and I hope you will do the same.'

Letitia was firmly tucked into his arms again. She looked at him, smiling.

'Yes, dear Jason, I'll do whatever you say.'

Romantic reads to
Need, Want

***...International affairs, seduction
and passion guaranteed***
10 brand-new books available
every month

Pure romance, pure emotion
6 brand-new books available
every month

***Pulse-raising romance
– heart-racing medical drama***
6 brand-new books available
every month

***From Regency England to
Ancient Rome, rich, vivid and
passionate romance...***
6 brand-new books available
every month

Scorching hot sexy reads...
4 brand-new books available
every month

LOOK OUT...

...for this month's special product offer.
It can be found in the envelope containing
your invoice.

**Special offers are exclusively for
Reader Service™ members.**

You will benefit from:

- Free books & discounts
- Free gifts
- Free delivery to your door
- No purchase obligation – 14 day trial
- Free prize draws

THE LIST IS ENDLESS!!

*So what are you waiting for —
take a look* **NOW!**

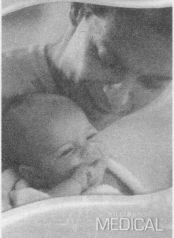